USA TODAY bestselling author **Naima Simone**'s love of romance was first stirred by Mills & Boon books pilfered from her grandmother. Now she spends her days writing sizzling romances with a touch of humour and snark.

She is wife to her own real-life superhero and mother to two awesome kids. They live in perfect, domestically challenged bliss in the southern United States.

USA TODAY bestselling author **Jules Bennett** has published over sixty books and never tires of writing happy endings. Writing strong heroines and alpha heroes is Jules's favourite way to spend her workdays. Jules hosts weekly contests on her Facebook fan page and loves chatting with readers on Twitter, Facebook and via email through her website. Stay up-to-date by signing up for her newsletter at julesbennett.com

RUTHLESS PRIDE

NAIMA SIMONE

SCANDALOUS REUNION

JULES BENNETT

MILLS & BOON

First Published in Great Britain 2020
by Mills & Boon, an imprint of HarperCollinsPublishers,
1 London Bridge Street, London, SE1 9GF

Ruthless Pride © 2020 Harlequin Books S.A.
Scandalous Reunion © 2020 Jules Bennett

Special thanks and acknowledgement are given to Naima Simone for her contribution to the *Dynasties: Seven Sins* series.

ISBN: 978-0-263-27923-8

0520

RUTHLESS PRIDE

NAIMA SIMONE

To Gary. 143.

One

"If your success was earned through hard work and honesty never apologize for it."

Joshua Lowell silently repeated the Frank Sonnenberg quote that had been a favorite of his father's. He pinched the bridge of his nose, a low, dark growl rumbling in the back of his throat. Too bad Vernon Lowell hadn't believed in the "practice what you preach" school of thought. According to that quote, his father had a ton of apologizing to do. Wherever he was—hell or a bungalow in some country without extradition policies.

Dropping his head, he refocused his attention to the spreadsheets displaying the previous month's profit-and-loss numbers for Black Crescent Hedge Fund's investment in stock of a telecommunication company. Compared with this time last year, the investment was doing very well. Their clients would earn more than a modest return, and Black Crescent would receive a substantial management and performance fee…

Unlike his father, Joshua had stuck to the more traditional investments such as stocks, bonds, commodities
and real estate. Vernon had been a daredevil in business,
which initially had made him one of the richest men in the
tristate area of New York, New Jersey and Connecticut.
That fearless and adventurous spirit had also increased the
millions his very select clients had invested with him into
high-yielding portfolios, and grew his boutique business
into one of most successful in the area.

It'd also cost those select clients millions. It'd devastated them.

So no, while some might call Joshua's business decisions rigid and even too conservative, he refused to do
anything different. Too many people's livelihoods and futures depended on him making those safe choices. He refused to be another Lowell who betrayed their trust. Who
destroyed them.

He'd been the last man standing when Vernon Lowell
disappeared—for both the company and his family. Because he'd left with not only his clients' money, but the
majority of his family's, as well. So even though the last
man sometimes wanted to yell and rage at the unfair-
ness of it all, at the grief and shame that often pounded
within him like a second heartbeat—at the death of his
own dreams—one thing the last man *couldn't* do was
slip up or falter.

He couldn't afford to. Literally.

"Josh, did you hear what I said? Of course you didn't."
Haley Shaw, his executive assistant, snorted, answering
her own question before he could respond. "Or you're just
ignoring me, which you should know by now doesn't work.
Whatever you're doing now can be put aside for just a few
moments. This is important," she insisted, an edge invad-
ing her tone.

"Haley. Not now," he said without glancing up from his spreadsheet.

"Well, I'm sorry to interrupt," a brisk, husky but very feminine voice that carried zero hint of apology interjected, "but I'm afraid it's going to have to be now."

Two small hands with slender, unadorned fingers flattened on either side of his computer monitor. Surprised, all he could do for several long seconds was stare at those delicate hands. At the short, unpolished nails, the thin map of light blue veins under sun-kissed skin. Why did he have the odd but strong urge to place his mouth right on the joint where hand met wrist—and sip?

Hell. They were fucking hands.

The mental but mocking admonishment didn't stop him from traveling up the lengths of her arms clad in white sleeves to slim shoulders partially hidden by light brown and gold-streaked hair, past a graceful neck and slightly pointed but stubborn chin with its slight indent to a face that—*goddamn*.

Deliberately, he eased back in his office chair, careful to control all the muscles in his face. He forced himself to maintain the cold, aloof expression that he'd adopted and mastered fifteen years ago as a defense. But inside… inside, lust slammed into him like a hurricane intent on leveling every structure in its path. And right now he was the only thing remaining, and *Christ*, he was shaking right down to his foundation.

Thickly lashed silver eyes that gleamed with barely suppressed anger. Striking cheekbones that lent a bold strength to otherwise ethereal features. A gently sloped nose and a mouth that had him gripping the arms of his chair like they were the last lifeboat that kept him from drowning. Thing was, he wanted to leap from the safety of the raft and dive into that wide, full-lipped mouth. Teach it what it was created for. Show it how it could give both of them the filthiest of pleasures…

His heartbeat echoed its thundering rhythm in his cock, pounding out a need that ricocheted through him.

Unsettled by his visceral reaction to this stranger—a stranger who had barged into his corporate office uninvited—he narrowed his eyes on her, allowing the corners of his mouth to curl in a derisive snarl.

Haley heaved a sigh. "Joshua, let me introduce you to Sophie Armstrong," she said, a thick coat of resignation painting her words.

"I don't know a Sophie Armstrong," he stated coldly to his assistant, although he didn't remove his gaze from the woman in front of him. Maybe some instinctual part of him recognized that she was the biggest threat in the room—a threat to his schedule, his carefully laid-out day… his control.

"The name would be familiar if you bothered to answer any one of my phone calls or emails." She snorted, cocking a dark eyebrow. "I've been trying to contact you, Mr. Lowell, and you've ducked and dodged every attempt."

He frowned. Yes, he'd been busier than usual lately, but he would've remembered if she'd reached out to him. "I've never ducked or dodged anyone." Not even when he'd desperately longed to. "Especially someone who doesn't have enough manners or sense to not force herself into a place of business where she wasn't invited or wanted without an appointment. Now that you're here, you have exactly thirty seconds—twenty-nine more seconds than I would give anyone else—to explain what the hell you're talking about."

Others would've—had—recoiled and backed down from the hard, ice-cold fury in his voice. But Sophie Armstrong didn't even flinch. Instead, she met his glare with one of her own. A quicksilver flash of surprise flickered within him. He wasn't arrogant, but he also acknowledged his appeal to the opposite sex. Understanding his money proved just as much of a lure as the appearance he'd inherited from his handsome father, he never lacked for female attention. Or sex.

But to this woman, he might as well be Quasimodo taking a break from his Notre Dame tower to hang out in the Black Crescent offices. Sophie Armstrong didn't bother to employ any advantage her beauty might press—not that it would. But she didn't know that.

No, unless antagonism passed for charm these days, she was confrontational and contemptuous.

And goddamn, if it wasn't hot.

She reached into the bag over her shoulder, withdrew a stack of papers and slapped the pile on his desk. "That's what I'm talking about. All the emails I've sent you. And I can pull out my phone and scroll through and play every voice mail—there are fifteen of them. All asking you to reply in a timely manner. Apparently, your idea of timely and mine don't coincide because I meant at least a couple of days and yours apparently runs along the line of seasons in Narnia."

The snort slipped from him before he could contain it. He shouldn't be amused. And he certainly shouldn't let her see it.

"You have five seconds left," he informed her, leaning forward and with a will that had been forged in the fires of desperation, humiliation and pride over a decade ago, he shifted his attention back to his screen. "I suggest you make the most of it."

A soft, feminine growl filled the air, and the reverberation of it rolled in his gut, clenching the muscles there so hard he nearly grunted in pain. With the wrenching came the dark but HD-clear image of her, head thrown back, all that hair sprawled across black sheets, beads of sweat dotting the slender column of her throat. And that same, rumbling growl vibrating from her. Only it sounded hungrier, needier...

Christ, he needed her out of his office.

"I'm assuming that king-of-the-manor-got-no-time-for-peasants thing intimidates other people, but I hate to break it to you. It does nothing for me." She crossed her arms over her chest, and if Jesus had come down at that moment and warned him against giving in to his baser needs, Joshua still wouldn't have been able to stop his gaze from dipping to the slightly less-than-a-handful but firm breasts that pushed against the plain white dress shirt. Guilt streaked through him, slick and dirty. He wasn't his father; he didn't ogle women or treat them like eye candy, there for his pleasure. Even women who made his dick hard but he didn't particularly like. "I'm telling you now—like I did in my last voice message and two emails—I'll be writing my story with or without you. But it would be a better one *with* you."

Story. What *story*?

A sense of foreboding wormed its way into his chest, hollowing it out. Making room for the churning unease.

"I repeat," he stated, the flat tone revealing none of the steadily encroaching panic that crept into his vision, that squeezed his rib cage like a steadily tightening vise. "What are you talking about?"

"The anniversary piece on the Black Crescent fiasco that I'm writing for the *Falling Brook Chronicle*. And unlike all of the articles written about that time period, I would like to include an interview with the company's current CEO."

Anger crystallized within him, hard and diamond

bright. And sharp enough to cut glass. The "get out" burned on his tongue, singeing him. But he extinguished the words before they could escape him, refusing to betray any emotion to this woman who sought to rip open the seams of the past, to expose old but unhealed wounds for public consumption. To relive the nightmare of his father emptying the family bank accounts as well as embezzling millions from his clients and disappearing, abandoning him, his mother and brothers to the wolves. The abrasive rub of judging eyes and not-so-hushed whispers. The smothering guilt that ten families were left devastated and destitute because of his father's actions. The agonizing pain from being deceived and abandoned by the man who'd raised him, who'd loved him and who he'd respected.

This woman had no clue about the pressure from the weight of that guilt, that responsibility. How they straddled his shoulders to the point of suffocation at times. How dealing had become second nature to him. There'd been no one to lean on when his father disappeared, when he'd taken on the responsibility of repaying the families so they wouldn't sue for the remaining money his father hadn't disappeared with. When his mother withdrew from the exclusive community of Falling Brook, New Jersey. When his twin brother, Jacob, fled to Europe to backpack his problems away, and his youngest brother, Oliver, dropped out of college and become the poster child for professional playboy, complete with a nasty cocaine habit.

Nothing in his Ivy League education—not even the economic courses he'd taken at his father's insistence—had prepared him for being alone, grieving and terrified with the fate of not just his family but ten others on his still-young shoulders. Of having to make the bitter decision of burying his own dreams so he could repair those of others.

He'd grown up fast. Too fast.

And damn if he needed an article written by an ambitious reporter—no matter if she possessed the face of a fairy queen and the body of a Victoria's Secret Angel—to drag him back to those desolate, black times when he'd breathed fear as much as he did air.

"No."

Joshua gave her credit—she didn't flinch at the flat, blunt answer.

Instead, she tilted her head to the side, that fall of thick caramel-and-sunlight hair sliding over her shoulder, and studied him as if he were a problem to solve. Or an opponent to wrestle and pin into submission.

"I can understand why you would initially be reluctant to speak with me—"

"Oh, you can?" he interrupted, trying but failing to keep the bite from his voice. Silently, he cursed himself for revealing even that much. The last fifteen years had taught him that he couldn't afford to betray the slightest weakness of character lest he be accused of being just like his father. Other people were allowed room for mistakes. He was not offered that courtesy. While others could trip up in private, his missteps were splashed across newspapers and online columns for fodder. Including *her* paper. "So you've had a—how did you so eloquently put it?—fiasco in your life and had every paper in the country report on it? Including the *Falling Brook Chronicle*? Which, if I remember correctly, was one of the harshest and most critical? Well, good," he continued, not granting her the opportunity to answer. "Since you have experienced it, you'll understand why I'm ending this conversation."

"I've read the past articles from the *Chronicle*, and you're right, they did cover it…punitively," she conceded. In the small pause that followed, the "can you blame them?" seemed to echo in the office. "But those reporters aren't me. You don't know me, but I graduated from Northwestern University with a BS and MS in journalism. While there, I worked with the Medill Justice Project that helped free an unjustly convicted man from a life sentence in prison. I've also won the Walter S. and Syrena M. Howell competition, was a recipient of the NJLA's journalism award and was a member of the journalistic team who won the Stuart and Beverly Awbrey Award last year, all well-respected awards. I don't intend to do a hatchet job on you or Black Crescent. As a matter of fact, I would like to write this article from a different angle—the artist submerged. From my research, I discovered you were once a very accomplished artist—"

"We're done," he ground out, rising to his feet, flattening his palms on the desk.

Hell, no. Pain, like crushed glass, scraped his throat and chest raw.

He hadn't been called an artist in fifteen long years. And hadn't picked up a camera or paintbrush in just as long. Once, his trademark had been oversize, mixed-media collages that provided cultural commentary on war and human rights. He'd poured his being into those pieces, falling into endless pockets of time where nothing had mattered but losing himself in photographs, oils and whatever elements captured what swirled inside him—metal, newspapers, books, even bits of clothing. But when his father had vanished, Joshua had put aside childish things. At least that was what Vernon had called Joshua's passion—a childish hobby.

It'd been like performing a lobotomy on his soul. But now, instead of channeling his anger, grief and pain into art, he suppressed it. And when that didn't work, he funneled it into making Black Crescent solvent and powerful again. Or took it out on a punching bag at the gym.

The whole shitfest with the hedge fund had left him with precious little—the death of his art career, the eradication of his relationships with his brothers, a ghost of a mother, an overabundance of shame and a ruined family company. But they'd been *his* choices.

All that had remained in the ashes after the firestorm were the ragged tatters of his pride because he'd had the strength, the character, to make those choices.

And now Sophie Armstrong sought to steal that dignity away from him, too.

No. She couldn't have it.

"Mr. Lowell," she began again with a short shake of her head.

But again, he cut her off. "I have a busy day, and you've had more than the thirty seconds I allotted. We're through talking. You need to go," he ordered, knowing his mother would cringe at the lack of the manners she'd drilled into him since birth. Not that he gave a damn. Not when this woman stood here prying into an area of his life that wasn't open for public consumption.

"Fine, I'll leave," she said, but nothing in the firm, almost combative tone said she'd conceded. She drew her shoulders back, hiking her chin in the air. Though she stood at least a foot shorter than him, she still managed to peer down at him with a glint of battle in her silver eyes. "You can try to erase the past, but certain things don't go away no matter how hard you try to bury them. The truth always finds a way of resurrecting itself."

"Especially if there are reporters always armed with a shovel, ready to dig up anything that will sell papers," he drawled.

The curves of her full mouth flattened, and her eyes went molten. He waited, his body stilling except for the heavy thud of his heart against his rib cage. And the rush of hot anticipation in his veins.

It'd been years since anyone had challenged him. Not since he'd proved he was his father's son in business and, at times, in ruthlessness. But Sophie Armstrong… She must not have received the memo, because she glared at him, slashes of red painting her high cheekbones, as if even now, she longed to go for his throat. Was it perverse that part of him hoped she did? That he wanted that tight, petite, almost fragile body pressed to his larger frame with those delicate but capable-looking hands wrapped around his neck…exerting pressure even as he took her mouth as she attempted to take his breath?

Yeah, that might make him a little sick. And a hell of a lot dirty.

Still… He could picture it easily. Could feel the phantom tightening of her grip now. And he wanted it. Craved it.

But not enough to rip open old, barely scarred-over wounds so she could have a byline.

"Thank you for your time, Mr. Lowell," she finally said, and disappointment at her retreat surged through him.

God, what was wrong with him? He wanted—no, needed—her to drop this "artist submerged" bullshit and get the hell out of his office.

She whirled around on her boring nude heels and stalked across the room to his office door. Without a backward glance, she exited. He half expected her to slam it shut, but somehow the quiet, definite snick of the lock engaging seemed much more ominous.

Like a booming warning shot across his bow.

Two

"The Black Crescent Scandal: Fifteen Years Later."

Joshua gripped the Monday issue of the *Falling Brook Chronicle* so tightly, it should've been torn down the middle. She'd done it. Sophie Armstrong had run with the story, placing his family's sordid and ugly history on the front page as fodder for an always scandal-hungry public.

He lifted his gaze to stare out the windshield of his Mercedes-Benz at the Black Crescent building. He knew every railing, every angle, every stone inch of the modern midcentury building built into a cliff. His father's aim had been for the headquarters of his hedge fund to stand out in the more traditional architecture of Falling Brook. And he'd succeeded. The building was as famous—or infamous—as its owner.

And his infamy had made page one of the local paper. Again.

Studying the imposing structure offered the briefest

of respites. Almost against his will, he returned his attention to the newspaper crinkling under his fists. He'd already read the article twice, but he scanned it again. It recounted his father's rise in the financial industry, his seemingly perfect life—marriage to Eve Evans-Janson, the pedigreed society daughter and darling whose connections further installed Vernon as a reigning king of Falling Brook; his three sons, who'd shown great promise with their Ivy League educations and fast-track career goals; the meteoric success of his business. And then his epic fall. Millions of dollars missing from the hedge fund's accounts. The death of Everett Reardon, his father's best friend and CFO of Black Crescent, who'd crashed his car while trying to elude capture. Vernon's disappearance.

The ten clients his father had stolen money from plunged into a nightmare of bankruptcy and destitution. The company's—Joshua's—agreement to pay back the families so they wouldn't file a lawsuit. How some of them still hadn't recovered from Vernon's selfish, unforgivable and criminal actions.

And then Joshua.

The artist turned CEO who had stepped into the vacant shoes of his father to save Black Crescent. Yes, it shared how he'd left his promising art career and turned the company around, saving it from ruin, but it also painted him as Vernon's puppet, coached and raised to take over for him since Joshua's birth. Which was bullshit. At one time, his path had been different. Had been his.

The article also cited that no one had heard from Vernon in a decade and a half, but despite rumors that he'd been killed in retribution for his crimes, there was also the long-held belief that his father was alive and well. And that his family was secretly in contact with him. That Vernon still pulled the strings, running Black Crescent from some remote location. Which was ridiculous. After his father initially vanished, his mother had hired a team of private detectives to locate him. Not to mention the FBI had searched for him, as well.

Fuck. He gritted his teeth against releasing the roar in his throat, but his head echoed with it. What did he have to do to redeem himself? What more did he have to sacrifice? He'd stayed, facing judgment, scorn and suspicion to rebuild the company, to restore even some of the money lost. He'd stayed, doing his best in the last fifteen years to repay those affected clients at least part of the fortune they'd lost to his father as promised. He'd stayed, enduring his brothers' ridicule and disdain for following in dear old Dad's footsteps. He'd stayed, caring for their mother, who'd become something of a recluse.

He'd stayed when all he'd wanted to do was quit and run away, too.

But he hadn't gallivanted off to Europe or found sweet oblivion in drugs and parties. Pride and loyalty had chained him there. Fatherless. Brotherless. Friendless.

And Sophie Armstrong dared insinuate he hadn't busted his ass all these years? That his father had done all the soul-destroying work.

His sharp bark of laughter rebounded against the interior of the vehicle. Its serrated edges scraped over his skin.

A part of him that could never utter the sacrilegious words aloud secretly hoped Vernon was dead. Just thinking it caused shame, thick and oily, to slide down his throat and smear his chest in a grimy coat. But it was true. He hoped his father no longer lived, because the alternative… God, the alternative—that he'd abandoned his family and emptied their bank accounts without the slightest shred of remorse and never looked back—sat in his gut, curdling it. If Vernon wasn't dead, then that would mean the man he'd loved and had once admired and respected had truly never existed. And with everything else Joshua had endured these past few years, that...that might be his breaking point.

His cell phone rang, and a swift glance at the screen revealed Oliver's number. On the heels of his past staring him in the face this morning, his chest tightened. He and his younger brother's relationship was...complicated. Oliver lived in Falling Brook, but he might as well be across the Hudson River or even farther away.

Once, they'd been close. But that had been before Joshua had stepped in to head Black Crescent in place of their father. He'd lost some respect in Jacob's and Oliver's eyes that day. And a part of Joshua mourned that loss. Mourned what had been.

Briefly closing his eyes, Joshua slid his thumb across the screen and lifted the phone to his ear.

"Hello."

"I'm assuming you've seen today's paper," his brother said in lieu of a greeting.

"Yes." Joshua stared across the parking lot, no longer seeing the building that had been the blessing and curse on his family. In front of him wavered an image of a perfect family. Of a lie. "I've seen it."

A sound between an angry growl and a heavy sigh reached him. "This shit again. Why can't people just let it die?" Oliver snapped.

"Because it makes for good copy apparently," Joshua drawled. "We'll ride this one out like we always do."

He uttered the assurance, and it tasted like bitter ashes on his tongue. He was tired of weathering storms. And more so of being the stalwart helm in it.

Oliver scoffed. "Right. Because that's what Lowells do." Joshua could easily picture his brother dragging his hand through his hair, a slight sneer twisting his mouth. "Do you know if Mom has seen the article?"

"I don't think so." Joshua shook his head as the stone of another burden settled on his shoulders. "I've sent Haley over to make sure the paper isn't delivered."

Thank God for Haley. She was more than his assistant. She was his taskmaster. Right-hand woman. And the bossy little sister he'd never had.

When the scandal around Black Crescent had broken fifteen years ago, and employees as well as friends had abandoned the company and the Lowell family, Haley—a college intern at the time—had remained. Even forgoing a salary to stay. Through the last decade and a half when Joshua had given up his own dreams and passion to step into the gaping, still-hemorrhaging hole his father had left, she'd been loyal. And invaluable. He couldn't have dragged Black Crescent from the brink of financial ruin and rebuilt it without her at his side.

The woman could be a pain in his ass, but she'd proved her loyalty hundreds of times over to his family. Because she was family.

"Since Mom doesn't leave the house too often, I'm not concerned with her mistakenly seeing it," Joshua continued.

Eve had become something of a hermit since her husband's crime and disappearance. Unfortunately, that option hadn't been available to Joshua.

"Good. I don't even want to imagine what this would do to her. Probably send her spiraling into a depression," Oliver said, and while Joshua and his brothers might not agree on much, this one thing they did—their mother's emotional health and protecting her. "I'll go by and see her this evening just to check in."

"That sounds good. Thanks," Joshua replied.

A snort echoed in Joshua's ear. "She's my mother, too. No need to thank me. Talk to you later."

The connection ended, and for a long second, Joshua continued to hold the phone to his ear before lowering it and picking up the newspaper again. He zeroed in on one line that had caught his attention before.

But is Joshua Lowell that different from his father? Appearances, as we know, are often deceiving. Who knows the secrets the Lowell family could still be hiding?

The sentences—no, not so thinly veiled accusations—leaped out at him. What the hell was that supposed to mean? Every skeleton in their closets had been bleached and hung out for everyone to view and tear apart. They didn't have secrets.

And where had she uncovered the photos included in the article? He scrutinized the black-and-white images. A few of his art pieces. His father as he remembered him with his mother on his arm. God, he hadn't seen her smile like that in years. Fifteen of them, to be exact. Him and Jake on their college graduation day, hugging Oliver between them. A family portrait taken at their annual Christmas party. The ones of him and Jake on campus. The snapshots of him painting in art class. The concentration and…joy darkening and lightening his face. He analyzed that image longer, hardly recognizing the young, *hopeful* man in the photo.

Well, Sophie had done her grave-robbing expedition well. He'd accused her of using her shovel to dig up old news. To acquire these photographs, she must've found a fucking backhoe.

Where had she gotten her information? She shouldn't have had access to those pictures, so who'd provided them to her?

There was only one way to find out.

Joshua tossed the paper to the passenger seat and pressed the ignition button to start the car.

He would go directly to the source.

"Great article, Sophie," Rob Jensen, the entertainment columnist, congratulated with a short rap on the wall of her cubicle.

"Thanks, Rob," she said, smiling. "I appreciate it."

"You did do an excellent job," Marie Coswell added when Rob strode away. She rolled in her desk chair to the edge of her cubicle, directly across from Sophie's. "But wow, woman," she tsk-tsked, shaking her head and sending the blunt edges of her red bob swinging against her jaw. "You didn't hold anything back. Aren't you even the least bit concerned the Lowells will retaliate? I mean, yes, their names were persona non grata around here for a while, but that was a long time ago. They have serious pull and power. Makes me real thankful that I'm over in fashion. No way in hell would I want to tangle with a Lowell, especially Joshua Lowell. Well, hold on. I take that back." She grinned, comically wriggling her perfectly arched eyebrows. "I'd love to tangle with that man—but nekkid."

Sophie laughed at her friend's outrageousness even as heat streamed up her chest and throat and poured into her face. Times like these, she cursed her father's Irish roots. Even her Italian heritage, inherited from her mother, couldn't combat the fair skin that emblazoned every emotion on her face. Good God. She was twenty-eight and blushing like a hormonal teenager.

"Holy shit. Are you blushing, Sophie? At what? The thought of Mr. Tall-Insanely-Rich-and-Hot-as-Hell?" Marie gave an exaggerated gasp. "Oh, you *so* are. All right, give. What happened when you stormed over to his office like it was the Alamo? Did you rip something else besides a strip off his hide? Like his clothes? What aren't you telling me?"

Sophie groaned, closing her eyes at her friend's exuberance and the *volume* of it. She loved the other woman, but she really should've been the gossip editor with her sheer adoration for it.

"Nothing happened. Clothes remained intact. The only thing stripped away was my pride." She winced, just remembering her ill-conceived decision to charge into Joshua Lowell's office and the ensuing confrontation.

That definitely hadn't been one of her finer moments. Thank goodness the front desk receptionist at the main level had been away from her desk. Otherwise security would've probably been called on her. Wouldn't Althea Granger, the editor in chief, have loved to receive that call about one of her investigative reporters needing to be bailed out for trespassing?

Why Joshua hadn't had her escorted out still nagged at her. Just as memories of the CEO did.

She shook her head, as if she could dislodge the question and the man from her mind with the gesture. As if it were that simple.

"Sophie." Althea Granger appeared next to her cubicle, as if her thoughts had conjured the older woman. With thick dark hair, smooth, unlined brown skin and beautiful features, she could've easily been mistaken for a retired model rather than the editor in chief of the exclusive bedroom community of Falling Brook's newspaper. But after stints in major papers across the country, she'd run the *Chronicle* with a steel hand, judicious eye and the political acumen of a seasoned senator for years. And she was Sophie's mentor and idol. "Could you join me in the conference room, please?"

"Absolutely." Sophie rose from her desk chair, ignoring Marie's concerned glance. Too bad she couldn't do the same for the kernel of trepidation that lodged between her ribs. Usually, if Althea wanted to speak with her, it was in her office. Not the more formal conference room.

Could this be about her article? No, it couldn't be. She instantly rejected the thought. Althea had personally read and approved the story before it'd run in this morning's paper. If she'd thought Sophie had gone too far, hadn't been professional or objective in her reporting, the other woman would've had no problem in calling her on it.

Then what could it...possibly...be... *Oh God.*

She almost jolted to a halt in the doorway of the room where most of their editorial meetings were held. Somehow, she managed not to grab on to the jamb to steady her suddenly precarious balance.

Joshua Lowell.

He stood at the head of the long, rectangular table, hands in the pockets of his perfectly tailored, probably ridiculously expensive navy blue suit, those unnervingly sharp and beautiful hazel eyes fixed on her.

How wrong that eyes so lovely—light brown with vivid brushes of emerald green—were wasted on such a hard, cold...gorgeous...face.

Okay. So, she hadn't fabricated how unjustly stunning the man was. It seemed unfair, really. Joshua Lowell, a millionaire, CEO, son of a powerful if notorious family, educated and sophisticated, and then God had deemed fit to top that sundae of privilege with a face and body that belonged pressed on an ancient coin or forever immortalized in marble for some art collector's pleasure.

She tried and failed not to stare at the angular face with its jut of cheekbones and stone-hewn jaw—the stark lines should've been severe, made him appear harsh. But the beauty of those eyes and the lushness of his too-sensual-for-her-comfort mouth with its fuller bottom lip softened the severity, making him a fascinating study of contrasts. Cruelty and tenderness. Coldness and warmth. Carnality and virtue.

Her gaze reluctantly drifted from his face to his broad shoulders, the wide chest that tapered to a narrow waist and hips. She couldn't see his thighs from her still-frozen position in the doorway, but her brain helpfully supplied how the muscular length of them had pressed against his slacks days ago. With his lean but powerful body, the man obviously worked out. Probably unleashed a lot of aggression there.

How else did he release emotion?

Stop it, she snapped at her wayward mind. *We don't care.*

Mentally rolling her eyes at herself, she forced her feet to move forward, carrying her farther into the room. Joshua Lowell might look like he flew down on winged feet from Mount Olympus, but he was still an arrogant ass. One who, most likely, was here either to try to get her fired or threaten a lawsuit. That ought to knock down his hot factor several notches.

Should.

"Sophie, please close the door behind you," Althea instructed. Once Sophie shut the door with a quiet click, the editor in chief nodded toward Joshua. "Mr. Lowell, I'd like to introduce you to Sophie Armstrong, the journalist of the article in today's edition."

Her pulse echoed in her ears as she waited, breath snagged in her throat, for Joshua to out her to her employer. But after a long moment, he only arched a dark blond eyebrow. His gaze didn't waver from her as he smoothly said, "Ms. Armstrong."

Relief flooded her, almost weakening her knees. Above

all things, Althea was a professional, and she wouldn't have appreciated finding out Sophie had met him before. No, correction. *How* she'd met him.

But suspicion immediately nipped at relief's heels. *Why* hadn't he told Althea the truth? What did he want? She didn't know him, but she doubted he did anything magnanimously without it benefiting him. And he owed nothing to her, the reporter who had just aired his family's dark past all over the front page.

"Ms. Granger, I would appreciate it if you gave Ms. Armstrong and me a moment alone, please." He'd added *please*, but it wasn't a request.

And Althea didn't take it as one, though she did turn to her and ask, "Sophie?"

No. The answer branded her tongue, but the last time she'd checked, she wasn't a coward. And since she'd crashed Black Crescent's proverbial gates, it would be the height of hypocrisy to claim fear of being alone with him now. Even if her heart thudded against her chest like a bass drum.

"It's fine," she said.

"Okay." She continued to peer at Sophie for several more seconds, and, apparently satisfied with Sophie's poker face, she nodded. "Fine, but, Mr. Lowell," she added, swinging her attention back to Joshua, "I'm going to trust the words *lawsuit* and *libel* won't be thrown around in my absence. If so, I fully advise and expect Sophie to end the conversation so I can introduce you to our legal department."

With a smile that belied she'd just threatened to sic lawyers on him, Althea exited the room, leaving her alone with Joshua. And a table that had provided adequate enough distance before seemed to shrink, leaving her no protection.

"I assume your editor doesn't know about your little excursion to my office," he stated, with that flat note she'd come to associate with him.

"No," she said. "But of course you already figured that out. Why didn't you tell her?"

"Because it doesn't serve me well to do so right now. And—" his voice deepened to a slightly ominous timbre that had trepidation and—*God*—whispers of excitement tripping down her spine "—if anyone is going to deliver trouble to your doorstep, Sophie Armstrong, it's going to be me."

That statement might not have contained *lawsuit* or *libel*, but it was still most definitely a threat.

"I assume you're here about the piece in the *Chronicle*." She switched the subject, not wanting to dwell on what kind of "trouble" he wanted to visit on her. "Why don't you just get to it?"

He studied her, his silence heavy but fairly vibrating with the tension that seemed to crackle beneath his stoic facade. And something—call it a reporter's instinct or a woman's sixth sense—assured her that it was indeed a facade. Which meant more lurked beneath the surface that he didn't want anyone to see, to know. Secrets. The journalist in her, definitely *not* the woman, wanted to ferret out those secrets. Hungered to expose them to the light.

"Yes, why don't we just 'get to it,'" he repeated, making her suggestion sound like something more wicked. "I want to know how you acquired the photographs in the article."

She crossed her arms over her chest and shook her head. "From my sources, and before you issue a demand wrapped up in a request, I can't reveal them."

"Can't," he pressed, "or won't?"

She shrugged a shoulder. "In this case, it's the same difference."

Another long beat where his unwavering, intense gaze

scrutinized her. "Do you know what you are, Ms. Armstrong?" he finally murmured.

"Let me guess. A bitch," she supplied, slipping a bored note into her voice. Wouldn't be the first time a man in his position had called her that name when she'd pressed too hard, questioned too much or just didn't go sit behind a desk or on a set and look pretty. Journalism, especially investigative journalism, wasn't for the weak of heart or the thin of skin. And that word seemed to be the go-to to describe a strong woman with an opinion, a spine and unwillingness to be silenced.

"No." A flash of disgust flickered across his face as if just hearing that word sickened him. Or maybe the thought of calling a woman that particular insult did… "Maybe you would prefer if I called you that. Because then you could justify my being here as sour grapes and damaged pride over a story. But I refuse to make it that easy for you. No, Ms. Armstrong, you are not a bitch," he continued, and the disdain that had appeared in his expression saturated his voice. "You are a vulture. A scavenger who picks at carrion until there's nothing left but the bleached, dry bones."

That shouldn't have hurt her. But, God, it did. It slashed across her chest to burrow deep beneath bone and marrow to the core of her that believed in fairness and truth. Never in her reporting had she gone out of the way to hurt someone. Which had been one reason why she'd gone to see Joshua in the first place. She'd wanted his side, to ensure the article hadn't been skewed.

Maybe it was a remnant from being the child of divorced parents. From that hyperawareness that ensured neither her mother nor her father feel like she loved one more than the other. That she didn't confide in, call or lavish attention on one without making sure she gave the other equal affection. That balance had been stressful as a child who'd felt torn between two warring parents. And now, as an adult, that careful balancing act had carried over into her job. She ensured she presented both sides of an issue. And for Joshua to attack that vulnerable center of her... It shook her. It *hurt* her.

"In your thirst for a juicy story and a byline, did you even once stop to consider the consequences? Did you pause to ask yourself how it would affect my family? My mother? She's had to deal with the fallout of someone else's actions for years. *Years*," he bit out, true anger melting the ice of his tone. Sunlight streamed through the windows behind him, hitting his dirty-blond hair and setting the gold strands aglow. Like an avenging angel. "She's suffered, and dredging up ancient history for the sake of salacious gossip will only inflict more harm. But, of course, you couldn't be bothered to take into account anyone or anything else but your own ambition."

"My own ambition?" she repeated, grinding the words out between clenched teeth. She lowered her arms and her fingers curled into fists at her thighs, as she almost trembled with the need to defend herself. To tell him that wasn't her at all. But screw that. She hadn't done a hatchet job; she'd simply done her job. Period. And she'd been fair. *Damn fair.* "You don't know the first thing about me, so don't shove your own biases on me. I understand that you might not be able to view the article objectively, but believe me, I showed admirable restraint. I could have included the complete, unvarnished truth about who and what you are. A truth I'm sure the 'hero'—" she sneered the word "—of Black Crescent wouldn't want to get out."

He didn't reply. Didn't react at all. His hazel gaze bored into her, and she refused to flinch under that poker face that reduced hers to an amateurish attempt.

"I have no idea what you're alluding to. I haven't done

anything wrong or that I need to be ashamed of. As much to the contrary as your story hinted at, I haven't been my father's puppet. I've done nothing but try to repair the damage he caused. That's all I've ever done."

Joshua probably wasn't aware of the strained note in his voice, the almost silent fervency that stretched from his words. Yes, she couldn't deny the truth of his statement. Even if the possibility existed that Vernon was pulling the strings all these years, it didn't negate the fact that Joshua had abandoned what had appeared to be a very promising art career to take over the family company. To head it and bear all the heat, enmity and distrust as well as the responsibility on his still-young shoulders. His twin, Jake, hadn't been seen in Falling Brook for fifteen years, and the younger brother, Oliver, had fallen into a destructive partying lifestyle. So everything had fallen to him, and Joshua had put aside his own dreams to take up the burden.

No matter how she felt about the man and his actions, she had to respect that sacrifice.

"Anything I've done, it was and is to protect and take care of my family. I have no shame in that," he said, and that air of arrogance, of utter lack of remorse just… Dammit, it just pissed her off.

"Now, that is rich coming from you," she drawled, propping a hip against the conference table.

His aloof expression remained, but he cocked his head to the side. "And what the hell do you mean by that?" he demanded, almost…pleasantly. But the glitter in his eyes belied the tone.

"Oh, I think you know… *Daddy*."

He blinked, continuing to stare at her. And his lack of response, of reaction, only stirred the anger kindling in her chest.

"Really?" she snapped. "You're going to continue to

pretend to not know what I'm talking about?" She chuckled, the sound brittle, jaded and lacking humor. "You only protect and care for the family you decide to acknowledge. But," she chided, tapping a fingertip to the corner of her mouth, "I suppose that a four-year-old daughter would be extremely inconvenient for someone who lives on that high horse you're so afraid to tumble off of."

Joshua slowly leaned forward and, with a deliberate motion, flattened his palms on the table. "I don't know why you seem to believe that I have a child, but I don't. That's crazy," he said, narrowing his eyes on her.

She snorted. "Just because you might claim you don't—and you definitely act like you don't have a daughter—doesn't make it so."

He didn't reply, but that piercing gaze didn't leave her face. His tall, rangy body remained motionless, coiled as if pulled taut by an invisible string—a string that was seconds from snapping.

She frowned, stepping back from her indignation and, okay, yes, battered pride and feelings, to analyze him more closely. Confusion, and, *oh God*, whispers of uncertainty darkened his eyes.

Could it… *Could he really not know?*

"I—I…" She stopped. Inhaled. And started again. "I'm not making this claim casually or lightly. I have very good reason to believe that you do have a daughter."

"I don't know what your reasons are, and I don't care," he said with the barest hint of a rasp. "And if you knew anything about me beyond your so-called research, you would realize how ridiculous your accusation is. Because that's what you telling me I have a child I've neglected is, Ms. Armstrong. An ugly, unfounded and *untrue* accusation."

She should've flinched at his menacing growl, at the

blistering curse. She *should not* be electrified by it. Should not be riveted and fascinated by the sign of heat and a loosening of his iron-clad control.

Should not be considering poking more at the bear, to see if he would roar instead of growl. To see if he would… pounce.

Ill-conceived and unwelcomed desire leaped and cavorted in her veins like a naughty, giggling child. One who didn't care one bit for the rules. She steeled her body against the dark urge to draw nearer to him. Against the almost irresistible need to discover if his body warmth seeped through his suit and see if it would touch her. To find out what scent his skin held. Something earthy and raw, or would it be cool and refined? Fire or ice?

She cleared her throat and inched back, her hip bumping one of the chairs flanking the table. *Jesus, woman. He's not the pied piper, and you aren't some glaze-eyed mouse.* And besides, if she decided to follow any man somewhere—which hell would have to fall into a deep freeze and sell snow cones for extra income for that to happen—it wouldn't be this icicle of a man who carried more baggage than a Boeing 747.

"Listen, I received this information from a source—one that I trust. And if you recall, I attempted to reach out numerous times to interview you for the article. If you had bothered replying to any of my calls, voice mails or emails, I would've addressed this with you. But the fact that you refused only lent credence to my suspicions that you had something to hide." She ignored the scoff he uttered and spread her hands wide, palms up. "I know you doubt my credibility, but I thoroughly researched your family to prepare for my article. And the truth is the rumor about an illegitimate child surfaced several times."

"This source you trust," he countered, "would it be the same one who provided those pictures?"

She hesitated but, after a second, nodded. "Yes."

Of the people she'd interviewed, Zane Patterson had proved to be the most helpful…and rich in information. Rich, hell. He'd been a gold strike. And none of what he'd had to share had been flattering. But considering his family had been one of those directly affected by the Black Crescent scandal, Sophie couldn't blame him for his animosity and bitterness. He'd lost everything—his family's financial security, his home and then his family. His parents had divorced a year later. And he blamed it all on the Lowells. The man still harbored a lot of anger toward that family.

Still, just because he hated them didn't mean he hadn't been able to give her plenty of material. Zane had been a year younger than Oliver Lowell, so they'd run in the same circles in high school. Therefore, he'd had the means to supply her with the kind of info that hadn't been available with a Google search as fifteen years ago social media hadn't been as prevalent as it was today. Not only had Zane given her the photos Joshua seemed so fixated on, but he'd also been the first person to mention Joshua having a love child that he refused to acknowledge. But, like she'd assured Joshua, Zane hadn't been the only person to assert the same.

"Fine. Keep your secrets," Joshua said. He turned away from her, studying the just-awakening main street of Falling Brook. The newspaper's offices were located in one of the older brick buildings lining the street, tucked between a women's clothing boutique and a bookstore. As he stared out the window, the sun's rays caressing his sharply hewn profile, he was like a king surveying his realm.

And maybe he was. The insular bedroom community

with its two-thousand-strong population of surgeons, CEOs, a few A-list actors and pro athletes had once looked at Vernon Lowell as a ruler, and Joshua's father had gorged on the admiration and reverence. By all appearances, Joshua seemed to be a more benevolent king, but no one could mistake the power, the air of authority and command that clung to him, as tailor-made to fit as his suits.

Part of her acknowledged she should be intimidated by that level of influence. In this community where money not just spoke, but screamed at the tops of its lungs, power of the press was a buzz phrase. If he wanted, he could have her fired. Blackballed, even.

So yes, she should be at least a little leery. But fear didn't skip and dance over her skin, leaving pebbled flesh in its wake. Exhilaration did. Being in this man's presence agitated and animated her in a way only burgeoning new stories did. And the why of it—she lurched away from digging deeper, scrabbling away from that particular crumbling, dangerous edge.

When he turned back and pinned her with that magnetic, intense gaze, she barely managed to trap her gasp. The force of it was nearly physical. The inane image of her holding her hands up, shielding herself from it, popped in her head.

"You're right," he announced.

She blinked, taken aback. Replaying their conversation through her mind, she shook her head, still confused. "About?"

"You offered me the opportunity to give my insight into the story, and I didn't take it. But now I'm offering you a chance no other reporter has been extended. Come spend a day with me at the Black Crescent offices. I'll grant you access to my world, and you can see and decide for yourself whether or not the rumors stated in your article are true. Or you might just discover that I'm just a business-man trying to repair the past while making a way for the future." He arched an eyebrow. "Either way, it will be an exclusive."

It's a trap. The warning blared through her head. And if she had the intelligence God gave a gnat, she would decline. But she was aware enough to recognize that the woman whispered that caution. The reporter's blood hummed with anticipation at this unprecedented oppor-tunity. She could pen a part two to her piece, and maybe it and the first one could possibly be picked up by the *Associated Press*.

Plus you get to spend more time with Joshua Lowell. The sly whisper ghosted across her mind. Spend more time with the enigmatic, sexy man who kindled a need inside her that she resented. A need that, if she wasn't careful, could compromise her objectivity and her job.

And that she absolutely couldn't allow. Nothing could get in the way of her goals, of her independence. Her mother had shelved her dream of becoming an architect to marry her father. And years later, when her marriage ended, she'd had to start from scratch, dependent on the scant alimony her father had grudgingly provided, having to work low-paying jobs to make ends meet while attend-ing college part-time. It'd taken years of dedication and exhausting, backbreaking work, but she'd finally attained her dream job. But Sophie had learned a valuable lesson while witnessing her mother's struggle. She would never become a casualty of a relationship. And never would she prioritize a man above her own needs, giving him every-thing while he left her with just scraps to remind her of what she could've had but had thrown away.

She had to take only one look at Joshua Lowell, spend one minute in his company, take one glance in those lovely but shuttered eyes to know he could strip her of everything. And not look back.

If she allowed him to. Which she wouldn't.

"I accept your offer," she said, resolve strengthening her voice.

He dipped his head in acknowledgment. "I'll have my assistant contact you to set up an appointment."

With one last, long stare, he strode toward her, heading toward the conference room door. As he brushed past her, she ordered herself not to inhale. Not to find out—

Sandalwood and dark earth after a fresh spring rain. Earthy and raw, it is.

Dammit.

"Ms. Armstrong." She jerked her head in his direction and met the gaze of the ruthless businessman who had dragged a failing company back from the edge of the financial abyss. "Don't mistake this for an olive branch or a truce. When you wrote and published that article, you threatened the peace and well-being of my family, and I don't take that lightly or forget. Use this as a chance for another smear campaign, and I'll ensure you regret it."

Long after he left, his warning—and his scent—remained.

No matter how hard she tried to eradicate both.

Three

Joshua pulled his car into the parking lot of his gym and stabbed the ignition button a little harder than necessary, shutting the engine off. Restless energy raced through him, and it jangled under his skin. He'd been this way since yesterday and his visit to the *Falling Brook Chronicle*'s offices. Since his confrontation with Sophie.

Tunneling his fingers through his hair, he gripped the short strands and ground his teeth together. Trapping the searing flood of curses that blistered his tongue. He'd gone there to question her about the photographs and her source for them. And he'd been slapped with a paternity accusation.

The *fuck*.

Even now icy fingers of shock continued to tickle his spine, chilling him. Trailing right behind it came the hot slam of helpless fury. He hated that sense of powerlessness, of—goddammit—self-doubt.

And he resented the hell out of Sophie for planting it there. For hauling him back to a time when he'd been drowning in fear, desperately swimming toward the surface to drag in a life-giving lungful of air. Despairing that he never would again.

Through the years, there'd been plenty of gossip about his family on top of the ugly truth about his father and his actions. It would be a lie to claim the whispers hadn't hurt him. That he didn't have scars from that tumultuous period. But he'd survived. He'd always had pride in the knowledge that he wasn't his father, that he didn't harm people out of selfishness and greed. He'd clung to that knowledge.

And in one conversation, Sophie had delivered a solid blow to that source of honor, causing zigzags to splinter through it like a cracked windshield.

Had he been a monk? Hell no. He enjoyed sex, but he still practiced caution. A man in his position and with his wealth had to. So he chose his partners carefully—women who understood he didn't want a relationship, just a temporary arrangement that provided pleasure for both of them—and ensured he used protection. Still, he understood that mistakes could happen. Nothing was infallible. But none of his ex-lovers had ever approached him about an unexpected pregnancy or a child. Because if they had, he would've never abandoned the woman or the baby. *Never.*

For Sophie to suggest—no, to accuse him of being able to neglect his own flesh and blood...

With a low growl, he shoved open his car door and stepped out, slamming it shut behind him. Seconds later, with his duffel bag in hand, he stalked toward the gym, ready to work off some of the anger and tension riding him like a relentless jockey on a punching bag.

An hour later, sweat poured from his face, shoulders and

chest in rivulets. Pleasurable weariness born of pushing his body to the limit sang in his muscles. Yanking off his boxing gloves, he picked up his bottle of water and gulped it while inhaling the scent of perspiration, bleach and the musk from bodies that had permanently seeped into the concrete floors and walls. This gym, located in the next town over from Falling Brook, wasn't one of those trendy establishments soccer moms and young CEOs patronized with stylish athletic wear and skin that glistened or, for God's sake, *dewed*.

Fighters grappled and trained in the boxing ring at the far side of the room. Huge tires leaned against a wall and a smattering of paint-flecked, scratched gym equipment hogged one corner while free weights claimed another. Grunts, the smack of rope hitting the concrete floor and rock music permeated the air. People didn't come to this to be seen, but to push their bodies, to beat them into submission or perfect working order.

So what the *fuck* was Sophie Armstrong doing here?

He scowled, studying the petite, frowning woman as she whipped the battle ropes up and down in a steady, furious pace. Even as the familiar anger and suspicion crowded into him at the sight of her in the gym he'd frequented for years—his sanctuary away from the office and home— he couldn't stop his gaze from following the slender but toned lines of her small frame that the purple sports bra and black leggings did nothing to hide. Without the conservative clothes that halted just shy of being plain, he had an unrestricted view of the high thrust of her smallish and utterly perfect breasts that slightly swelled over the rounded edge of her top. Though he ordered himself to look away, to stop visually devouring the enemy, he still lingered over the taut abdomen that gleamed with hard-fought-for sweat and the gently rounded hips and tight, sleekly muscled legs that seemed impossibly long for someone of her stature.

Like a sweaty elf princess who'd momentarily traded her gilded throne for a dusty battlefield. The silly, fanciful thought swept through his head before he could banish it. Thoughts like that belonged to the artist he used to be, not the sensible, pragmatic businessman he was now. Still… Watching her muscles flex, her abs tighten and those strong thighs brace her weight, he was impressed at the power in her tiny frame.

Impressed and hard as hell.

"Goddamn," he growled. Frolicking puppies. Spreadsheets with unbalanced columns.

His mother's shuttered face and devastated eyes when she read Sophie's article.

Yeah, that killed his erection fast.

And maybe it didn't snuff out the hot licks of lust in his gut, but it gave fury one hell of a foothold.

Clenching his jaw, he stalked across the gym toward the woman who had infiltrated his life and cracked open a door he'd hoped, fucking prayed, would remain locked, bolted and welded shut. Just as he reached Sophie, she gave the battle ropes one last flick, then dropped them to the floor with a thud.

"Stalking me, Ms. Armstrong?" he drawled, his fingers gripping his water bottle so tight, the plastic squeaked in protest.

He immediately loosened his hold. Damn, he'd learned long ago to never betray any weakness of emotion. People were like sharks scenting bloody chum in the water when they sensed a chink in his armor. But when in this woman's presence, his emotions seemed to leak through like a sieve. The impenetrable shield barricading him that had been forged in the fires of pain, loss and humiliation came away dented and scratched after an encounter with Sophie. And that presented as much of a threat, a danger to him as her insatiable need to prove that he was a dead-beat father and puppet to a master thief.

"Stalking you?" she scoffed, bending down to swipe her own bottle of water and a towel off the ground. With a strength that could be described only as Herculean, he didn't drop his gaze to the sweet, firm curve of her ass. He deserved a medal, an award, the key to the city for not giving in to the urge. "Need I remind you, it was you who showed up at my job yesterday, not the other way around. So I guess that makes us even in the showing-up-where-we're-not-wanted department."

"Oh, we're not even close to anything that resembles *even*, Sophie," he said, using her name for the first time aloud. And damn if it didn't taste good on his tongue. If he didn't sound as if he were stroking the two syllables like they were bare, damp flesh.

She didn't immediately reply, instead lifting the clear bottle to her mouth and sipping from it. His gaze dipped to that pursed, wicked mouth, and a primal throb set up in his blood, his dick. *Stand down*, he ordered his unruly flesh. His loose gray basketball shorts wouldn't conceal the effect she had on him. And no way in hell would he give her that to use against him.

"I hate to disappoint you and your dreams of narcissistic grandeur, but I've been a member of this gym for years." She swiped her towel over her throat and upper chest. "I've seen you here, but it's not my fault if you've never noticed me."

"That's bullshit," he snapped. "I would've noticed you."

The words echoed between them, the meaning in them pulsing like a thick, heavy heartbeat in the sudden silence that cocooned them. Her silver eyes flared wide before they flashed with…what? Surprise? Irritation? Desire. A liquid slide of lust prowled through him like a hungry— so goddamn hungry—beast.

The air simmered around them. How could no one else see it shimmer in waves from the concrete floor like steam from a sidewalk after a summer storm?

She was the first to break the visual connection, and when she ducked her head to pat her arms down, the loss of her eyes reverberated in his chest like a physical snapping of tautly strung wire. He fisted his fingers at his sides, refusing to rub the echo of soreness there.

"Do you want me to pull out my membership card to prove that I'm not some kind of stalker?" She tilted her head to the side. "I'm dedicated to my job, but I refuse to cross the line into creepy…or criminal."

He ground his teeth against the apology that shoved at his throat, but after a moment, he jerked his head down in an abrupt nod. "I'm sorry. I shouldn't have jumped to conclusions." And then because he couldn't resist, because it still gnawed at him when he shouldn't have cared what she—a reporter—thought of him or not, he added, "That predilection seems to be in the air."

She narrowed her eyes on him, and a tiny muscle ticked along her delicate but stubborn jaw. Why that sign of temper and forced control fascinated him, he opted not to dwell on. "And what is that supposed to mean?" she asked, the pleasant tone belied by the anger brewing in her eyes like gray storm clouds.

Moments earlier, he'd wondered if fury or desire had heated her gaze. Now he had his answer. Because he now faced her anger, now had confirmation that when she looked like she wanted to knee him in the balls the silver darkened to near black.

But when she looked like she just wanted to go to her knees for him, her eyes were molten, pure hot silver.

God help him, because, masochistic fool that he'd suddenly become, he craved them both.

He wanted her rage, her passion...wanted both to beat at him, heat his skin, touch him. Make him feel.

Mentally, he scrambled away from that, that *need*, like it'd reared up and flashed its fangs at him. The other man he'd been—the man who'd lost himself in passion, paint and life captured on film—had drowned in emotion. Willingly. Joyfully. And when it'd been snatched away—when that passion, that *life*—had been stolen from him by cold, brutal reality, he'd nearly crumbled under the loss, the darkness. Hunger, wanting something so desperately, led only to the pain of eventually losing it.

He'd survived that loss once. Even though it'd been like sawing off his own limbs. He might be an emotional amputee, but dammit, he'd endured. He'd saved his family, their reputation and their business. But he'd managed it by never allowing himself to need again.

And Sophie Armstrong, with her pixie face and warrior spirit, wouldn't undo all that he'd fought and silently screamed to build.

She must've interpreted his silence as an indictment, because her full mouth firmed into an aggravated line, and her shoulders slowly straightened, her posture militant and, yes, defensive. As she should be. "If it makes it easier to look at that pretty face in the mirror, then go ahead and throw verbal punches," she sneered. *Pretty face.* He didn't even pretend to take that for a compliment. Not that way her voice twisted around the words. "But I did the research, and the information I received was solid, and my sources were legitimate."

"Sources," he repeated, leaping on that clue. "So you had more than one?"

She didn't move, but she might as well as have slammed up an invisible door between them. "Yes," she replied after a long moment. "I didn't rely on gossip or groundless rumors."

"Your sources seem to believe they know a lot about not just my family, the inner workings of Black Crescent, but my personal life, as well," he said, drawing closer to her.

The seeds that their earlier conversation in the *Chronicle*'s conference room had planted started to sprout roots. Roots of suspicion and hated mistrust wound their way into his head, threading around his heart. He resented Sophie for planting those kernels of suspicion about the people who existed in his small inner circle. Small for a reason. Trial by fire had taught him he could trust a precious few, and only those precious few had access to his family, the details of his life. Could one of them be the "source" she referred to? As he'd done on the drive back to his office yesterday, he again ran through their faces: Haley, Jake, Oliver.

Haley, no. Never. She'd proved her loyalty hundreds of times over. But his brothers... Jesus, he wanted to dismiss any notion that they could've turned on him, but... He couldn't. They resented him, resented that he'd become their father, never appreciating the sacrifices he'd made so they could live free of the burden of Black Crescent and the dark shadow it cast. A shadow he constantly existed in but strove to, if not be free of, at least lighten.

"I want names, Sophie," he bit out, the dregs of fear, grief and anger at the possible identities of her sources swirling in his mind roughening his voice. He stepped closer until the scent of citrus, velvet, damp blooms and woman—*her*—filled his nostrils. Ignoring the lure of that sensual musk, he lowered his head, forcing her to meet his gaze. "If someone is digging into my life and giving information about me, then I deserve to know who they are." *Who I need to protect myself from.* "Every man has the right to confront their accusers."

She shook her head, her golden-brown ponytail brushing her bare shoulders. "No. The people who spoke to me did so on the assurance of confidentiality, and I won't betray that. And I absolutely refuse to expose them to the wrath of the Lowell family."

The wrath of the Lowell family? What kind of shit was that? "My wrath?" he murmured, edging closer. And closer still until one shift of his feet and their chests would press together. Their sweat-dampened skin would cling. His cock would find a home nestled against her taut stomach. "Do you still have your job? Have you found yourself and that paper you work for served with a defamation suit? If you went to any of the stores or restaurants around here, would you still be waited on or served? No, Sophie." He leaned down, so close his lips almost grazed her ear. So close, he caught the shiver that worked through her body as his breath hit her lobe. "If I wanted to wage war against someone who came after me, after mine, the first casualty would be you. And since you haven't been shunned or blackballed yet—because believe me, even with the stain on my last name, I have the power to do all I've mentioned—you haven't felt my wrath. Besides," he added, and this time he let his mouth brush the rim of her ear. Let himself get his first feel of her skin, her body even if it was just something as small as that. "I would never include others in the battle between us. This, sweetheart, is personal."

Air, quick and harsh, rushed from her lips, bathing his cheek, stirring the flames already stroking him from the inside out. God, he wanted to... Grinding his molars together so hard he should've tasted dust, he inched back, placing between them the space he'd so foolishly eliminated. As it was, he now fought the impulse to rub his thumb over the spot where his mouth had glanced her ear. Rub that sensation into his flesh as if it wasn't already branded there.

"Is that supposed to scare me? Should I file that under the threat category?" she shot back. And it would've been effective if it hadn't been uttered in a throaty whisper that rasped over his too-sensitive skin.

Damn her.

Damn him.

"No, Sophie. The last thing I want from you is fear." Let her translate that how she wanted. "But make no mistake, I intend to have those names from you. And that's not a threat, but a promise."

Not waiting for her response, he turned and strode away from her. But not for long. They had an appointment for a day together at his office. And he would see the vow he'd made come true.

Sophie would divulge the identities of her sources.

One way or another.

And as his blood hummed in his veins, still lit up like a torch from his interaction with her, it was the "another" that worried him.

Four

Back in the lion's den.

Sophie summoned a smile as she gave the first-floor receptionist of the Black Crescent building her name and waited while she called to verify her appointment. Turning, she stared at the large picture window, not really seeing the parking lot or the ring of towering trees beyond that shielded the property like an inner wall in a medieval fiefdom.

No, images of Joshua Lowell from when he'd cornered her at the gym yesterday flickered before her eyes. Flickered, hell. Paraded. Him, his lean but large and powerful body encased in a sweaty white T-shirt that clung to tendon and muscle, and loose gray knee-length basketball shorts. God, those shorts. If the shirt had her itching to climb those wide shoulders as if they were a scratching post and she was a cat in heat, then those shorts had her palm itching to slide beneath the damp waistband, skim over his ridged abdomen and farther down to grasp the long and thick length that she'd glimpsed the imprint of under the nylon.

Joshua freaking Lowell had been hard. *For her.*

And he'd called her sweetheart.

She still couldn't wrap her mind around that. He hated her. Okay, *hate* might be too strong a word, but he very strongly disliked her. Okay, *disliked* might be too soft a word.

Sighing, she shook her head, dispelling the mental picture, but could do nothing for the sensitive spot just under her navel. The spot where his cock had pressed against her as he'd whispered threats—forget *promises*, those had definitely been *threats*—in her ear. Idiot that she was, she should've been furious, or even a little intimidated, but no.

She'd just been turned the hell on.

And all she could think of was whether or not that sandalwood, earth and rain scent would transfer to her skin if his naked, big body covered hers. Would she wear him on her? Or would they create a new fragrance together—one made of him, her and sex?

Stop this. Now. The silent but strident admonishment rang inside her head, and she heeded it. She *had* to. In several very short minutes, she would once again face Joshua on his turf. Only this time she wouldn't have the benefit of surprise. He would have home-court advantage, so to speak, prepared for her, her questions, her preconceived perceptions of him. Joshua Lowell would be ready to battle. And as he'd warned her, he wouldn't lose.

She had to be focused and professional and, above all, could not think of how that beautiful body would feel moving over her...in her.

Dammit!

"Ms. Armstrong, they're expecting you upstairs. If

you'll take the elevator to the second floor, Mr. Lowell's executive assistant, Haley Shaw, will be waiting for you." The woman gave her a polite but friendly smile as she gestured toward the bank of elevators that Sophie was all too familiar with. She'd covertly stole into them to barge into the Black Crescent offices to interview Joshua Lowell.

"Thank you," she murmured, and followed the receptionist's directions.

Moments later, she stepped out onto the executive floor and approached Haley Shaw's large circular desk. The pretty blonde stood in front of it, smiling up at a tall, handsome man with light brown hair and a presence that screamed confidence and an intensity he couldn't mask. It was that intensity that had Sophie frowning slightly as she approached the couple.

Though both of their voices contained a light note of flirtation, and Haley didn't appear uncomfortable, the man seemed to invade the other woman's personal space, dwarfing Haley's not-inconsiderable height. As a woman who'd often encountered inappropriate advances in the workplace, maybe Sophie was extra sensitive, but it didn't stop her from nearing them and stopping at the executive assistant's side, facing the man, whose smile widened to include her.

Yeah, she didn't trust that smile at all.

In her experience, people who grinned that wide and tried hard to appear affable were usually hiding something. Using overt friendliness and charm as a deflection.

Something whispered to her that this guy was no different.

"Good morning, Ms. Armstrong," Haley greeted Sophie, surprising her a little with the warmth emanating from the welcome. The last time Sophie had been here, she hadn't made such a good first impression. "Can I introduce you to Chase Hargrove?"

"Mr. Hargrove." Sophie nodded, and he extended his hand toward her.

"Ms. Armstrong. It's a pleasure to meet you." Giving her another of those too-amicable smiles, he switched his attention back to Haley. "I have to go. I'll talk to you later, Haley. Hopefully see you then, too, beautiful." With a wink and crooked grin that even Sophie had to admit had her wanting to fan herself, he turned and strode toward the elevators.

"Wow," Sophie muttered as soon as the doors slid closed behind him. "He's definitely...not shy." She shook her head, huffing out a laugh. "Were you okay with how strong he seemed to be coming on? If not, you should tell—" *Joshua* hovered on her tongue, but after a brief hesitation, she said, "Mr. Lowell."

She scoffed, waving a hand toward the direction Chase had disappeared. "He's harmless. Believe me, I can handle him." Pushing off the desk, she swept a hand toward the double doors that led to Joshua's office. "He's waiting for you. Did you need anything? Coffee, tea, water?"

"I'm fine, thanks." Sophie would die on the hill of denial before admitting it aloud, but her stomach twisted with nerves and wouldn't be able to handle anything on it.

Haley nodded, and when they approached the door, she gave it a swift knock, then opened it. "Joshua, Ms. Armstrong is here."

Sweat dotted Sophie's palms, and her heart rapped against her sternum, but she managed a smile of thanks and shored up her mental shields as she moved into the office. After his visit to the *Chronicle* and their impromptu meeting at the gym, she didn't even try to delude herself into believing she could prepare herself for coming face-to-face with him again and not be slammed with the intense presence that was Joshua Lowell.

So when he rose from behind his desk, exposing that tall, rangy body to her, she just let herself soak him in. Took in the short, dark blond hair that emphasized the clean but sharp facial features. Met the green-and-light-brown gaze that seemed determined to strip her of all her defenses. Traced the wide, soft-looking mouth with its too-tempting, full bottom lip. Wandered over the muscular strength and animal magnetism that his steel-gray suit accentuated rather than hid in a cloak of civility.

Maybe not resisting the magnetic pull of his utter sexiness but rather immersing herself in it would strengthen her immunity.

Like a freaking flu shot.

"Sophie," he said, rounding the desk with a confident and commanding stride that shouldn't have set her pulse pounding. But God, did it. "I'm glad you could make it."

She arched an eyebrow. "You doubted I would?"

He halted several feet from her. And it reminded her of how close he'd been in the gym. How his scent had engulfed her. How his lips had brushed her ear even as he whispered threats into it. No. Not threats. Promises, he'd assured her.

And how sick did it make her that a part of her wanted him to follow through on them?

Very. Any therapist worth her or his degree would rub their hands in glee at the thought of getting their hands on her.

"Not for a second," he murmured, that gaze skimming over her emerald sheath and nude pumps before returning to her face.

Her skin hummed from the visual contact, and she fought not to rub her palms up and down her bare arms.

She wouldn't give him the satisfaction of knowing he affected her.

"Well, thank you again for the opportunity to tour the inner sanctum of Black Crescent Hedge Fund." See? She could be professional around him. "I'm looking forward to this."

He nodded. "If you'll follow me…"

For the next several hours, Joshua granted her an exclusive peek behind the curtain. Not only did he introduce her to his employees and explain what they did, but he also revealed how he'd implemented safeguards and a checks-and-balances system so what'd occurred with his father didn't happen again. In other words, he'd willingly policed himself.

She discovered a side of the company she hadn't known existed. Over the years, Joshua had donated a mind-boggling amount of money and time to local and statewide programs that assisted domestic abuse victims, literacy and the foster-care system, including his assistant Haley Shaw's own nonprofit organization. But not only did he help his community, he also invested in his own employees' futures by helping put the staff and their families through college with scholarships and almost-zero-interest loans.

And then there were the reparations he'd made to the families affected by his father's crimes. Joshua had made good on that agreement to repay the stolen funds.

By the time she followed him back to his office that afternoon, she was convinced Black Crescent wasn't the coldhearted, corrupt organization portrayed in the news and even by some of her sources.

By her.

"What you've done here is remarkable," she said as he closed the office door behind them. She shook her head. "Especially in the last few years. But I've only heard of maybe two of your philanthropic efforts. Why haven't you shared with the public what you've shown me today? I think most people would be amazed and as impressed as I am with all that you do for the community on a local and even national level."

"If someone brags about what should be their privilege and right to do, I question not just their motivations but their hearts. Besides—" he slipped his hands into the front pockets of his pants and a faint smile quirked the corners of his mouth "—I've found that most people, particularly the press, have never been interested in reporting anything positive about my family or the company."

She tried not to wince. And didn't quite manage it. "Touché. But to be fair, my article didn't attack you, personally."

"Fair?" he repeated, sarcasm hardening his voice. "Forgive me if I've never associated *fair* with the media. And attack? No. But for an article that was supposed to be about the so-called anniversary of the Black Crescent incident, you invaded my personal life in a way that seemed intrusive and unnecessary."

Her chin snapped up and her shoulders back, offended. "Am I supposed to apologize for being good at my job? I can't control what my sources tell me or where my investigation carries me. I *won't* apologize for the truth. Ever." She narrowed her eyes on him. "If anything you should be thanking me for not including the truth about your illegitimate daughter in the article. I can't say the same would've happened if—"

"Don't say it again," he barked. No, growled. And the ominous rumble of it snapped off her words like a branch cracking from a tree. Thunder rolled across his face, shadowing his eyes and pulling the skin taut across his cheekbones. He took a step forward but drew up short the next instant. "I am. Not. My. Father," he snarled. And somehow, that low, dark statement stunned her more than if he'd yelled it at her. "I would never, ever turn my back on my family the way that bas—"

He broke off, but the rest of his sentence might as well as have been shouted in the room, it echoed so loud, momentarily deafening her.

"The way your father did," she whispered, the words rasping her throat.

Joshua's face could've been carved from stone, but his eyes. God, his eyes damn near glowed with fury…and pain. Such deep, bright pain that the breath caught in her throat, and she ached with it. Ached for him.

She crossed her arms over her chest and turned away from him, eyes momentarily closing. Until this moment Vernon Lowell had been a story, a shadowy, almost urban legend–like figure who'd committed an infamous crime, then disappeared into thin air. But now, in his son's eyes, she saw him as a father—a father who had abandoned and hurt his son so deeply with his actions that even years later, that son suffered. Suffered in ways he hid so successfully that no one—least of all Sophie—had suspected.

That emotion—the intensity of it—couldn't be faked. So was Joshua telling the truth about the child? Did he really not know of her existence? Not only did she rely on her investigative skills in her job, but her instincts. And they were screaming like a pissed-off banshee that maybe, just maybe, he didn't.

Pinching the bridge of her nose, she bowed her head. *I can't believe I'm doing this.* But her heart had made the decision seconds before her brain caught on. And she moved toward the laptop bag she'd left on the couch in the sitting area of his office before leaving for the tour of the company.

Moments later, she had her computer removed and booting up on the coffee table. Glancing up at a still stoic and silent Joshua, she waved him over. "I have something to show you, Joshua," she murmured, using his name for the first time. Something had shifted inside her with that glimpse into his eyes. Standing on formality seemed silly now.

After a brief hesitation, he strode over and lowered onto the cushion next to her. Resolutely attempting to ignore the heat that seemed to emanate from his big body, she focused on pulling up a password-protected file. In several clicks, a report filled the screen.

A DNA report.

He stiffened next to her, and his gaze jerked to her. Silence throbbed in the office, as loud as a heartbeat, as he stared at her. She met his penetrating study evenly, not betraying the wild pounding of her pulse in her ears or the sudden case of dryness that had assaulted her mouth. She couldn't swallow, couldn't move. Common sense railed that she was making a huge mistake, maybe even violating her ethics. But her sense of decency—her soul—insisted that if she could somehow make this right, she should. If she could ease the pain that he would probably deny even existed, she needed to. Whether that was by confirming his daughter's existence or even having a hand in reuniting them... She didn't know. But she had to try.

He turned to her laptop and, leaning forward, scrutinized the report. Taking in his name at the top and the mother's name, which was blacked out. Scanning the results that ended in one determination: Joshua Lowell was a match for a baby girl born four years ago.

Slowly, he straightened. Shock dulled his eyes, flattened the lush curves of his mouth. Only his fists, clenched so tight the knuckles bleached white, betrayed the hint of a stronger current of emotion that could be coursing through him.

Finally, he shifted his gaze to her. "Where did you get this?" he asked, his deep voice like churned-up gravel. It scraped over her skin, abrading her. "Who sent it to you?"

"I can't tell you that."

"Goddammit, Sophie," he snapped. "How can you show me this and then deny me the resources to determine whether it's true or not. Real or not?" he demanded, fury sparking his eyes.

"I can't, Joshua," she insisted. Shaking her head, she spread her hands wide, palms up, on her thighs. "I wish I could, but I *can't*. I will tell you this, though. I believe the report is authentic. My source… I've held the actual report in my hand. If it's faked, it's a fabulous forgery."

"Dammit." He surged off the couch and stalked across the floor to the floor-to-ceiling window that made up one of the walls of his office. Thrusting the fingers of both hands through his short hair, he uttered a soft "dammit" again, then pressed a fist to the glass and cupped the back of his neck with the other. "How would they even be able to run a DNA test? I've never been asked or consented to giving a sample." He whirled around, his sharp features drawn, taut. "This doesn't make sense. Someone is playing games. They have an endgame that I don't know about and can't figure out."

Sophie stood and ventured a couple of steps in his direction. But didn't travel farther than those steps. Those pinpricks of caution that she'd felt in his presence before now stabbed at her. Warning her to. Back. Off. To retreat and regroup. Because at some point, she'd become too vulnerable to him. Too open.

And that should have her snatching up her belongings and running for the door like he'd just sprouted fur and fangs. Because in her position, vulnerability was a liability. For her and her job. God, she'd already revealed some of her research to him. What next? Ignore a lead? Refuse a story?

End her career?

She'd seen it with her mother.

She'd *been* her mother.

Shame, glittering bright and filthy at the same time, slicked through her like an oil stain. One would think she'd learned her lesson. Because it'd been brutal, but a good one. But those were the best. Or at least, they should be.

Bumping into Laurence Danvers at a local campaign rally four years ago had been an accident, so she'd believed for a long time. She hadn't known then that he'd planned the meeting that had seemed serendipitous. Fated. And she'd fallen so hard for his handsome features, his wide smile, his charm…his lies. She'd allowed her heart to blind her to his true nature. So when he'd first suggested a different perspective on an article she was writing about the city council election candidates, she saw it as his helping her see a different angle. When he'd convinced her that reporting an indiscretion from a candidate's past would be inflammatory and unfair—even though that candidate was running on a family platform—she'd conceded because he was only looking out for her career and reputation as a reputable reporter.

And when he'd demanded that she resign rather than reveal this same candidate had been accused of sexual misconduct by several women, she almost conceded. Almost. Too many times during her relationship with Laurence, she'd ignored her intuition. But that time, she'd listened, done some digging and uncovered that he was a longtime family friend to the candidate whose rally they'd met at.

Meeting her, seducing her, making her fall in love... It'd all been so calculated in an effort to use her.

In mere months, she'd almost thrown aside her career, her dreams, her integrity for a man. As Laurence had walked out her apartment door for the final time, she vowed never to be that vulnerable, that *foolish* again.

And as she stared at Joshua, she could feel herself already climbing that slippery slope. One misstep, and it would be a long, painful slide down. Hell, she'd already shown him part of her research. She shuffled back and away from him, both physically and mentally. She had to approach Joshua and this element of her story as a journalist, not a woman who wanted to cradle that strong jaw and massage away the deep crease between his eyebrows. Or soothe the confusion, anger and pain in his eyes.

"Someone is setting me up," Joshua continued, dropping his gaze to his clenched fist. As if disturbed by the outward display of emotion, he stretched his fingers out, splaying them wide and lowering them to the side of his thigh. "Nothing else makes sense. No one has contacted me about possible paternity or approached me for money. Not even threatened blackmail. Logic says that if there was a woman out there with a child I fathered, she would reach out to me for child support."

Sophie couldn't argue with his assumption. Joshua Lowell wasn't only a beautiful man; he was obscenely wealthy and very well connected, even in spite of the scandal. He could more than afford to provide for a child. And a particular kind of woman would use the situation to her advantage and try for more than money. Like forcing a relationship, marriage. Through her research for her article, she'd discovered that from the moment his father disappeared, Joshua had become a choirboy—well, if choirboys had the bodies and faces of Greek gods and exuded sex like a pheromone. But no hint of impropriety had ever been connected to his name in the media. A person didn't need to have a psychology degree to determine the reason behind that. And a woman looking to permanently bind herself to a powerful and rich family would realize that bit of information, as well.

She tapped a finger against her bottom lip. "That is… curious. Especially since the child is four years old now." This was her cue to walk away. To pack up her things, thank him for the opportunity to see the inside of Black Crescent and leave. "I can't give up my sources. But…if you need or want the help, I'll assist in finding out what's going on. Or try to."

Damn.

So much for walking away.

Joshua stared at her for so long, his eyes shuttered, his stony expression indecipherable, that the rescission of her offer hopped on the tip of her tongue. But as she parted her lips, he asked, "Will what you find out end up in the *Chronicle*?"

She extinguished the bright flash of irritation and offense that flared in her chest. Part of her understood his caution and suspicion. But the other half… "I'm not offering my help as part of some tell-all article," she ground out.

God, he really didn't think too much of her.

Which was fair because she didn't trust him, either. From her experience, most men—especially those with something to lose—did everything in their power to protect themselves.

Several more taut seconds passed, but Joshua finally dipped his head in a short, abrupt nod. "I appreciate your offer, then. If there's even the slightest chance that I could be a father, then I owe it to myself—and that little girl— to find out."

A rush of warmth flooded her.

Those aren't the words of a deadbeat father.

Her subconscious taunted like the know-it-all it was.

But her experience with Laurence had hammered home the truth that nothing—or no one—was as it appeared on the surface. Especially someone who had so much to lose like Joshua did—reputation, money and the added burden of a child. Though he managed to keep his private life more contained than others in his position, she'd still gathered images of him and gossip about him with socialites, some A-list actresses and businesswomen.

No middle-class, student-debt-ridden peasants. In other words, no one like you.

Oh, shut it.

Awesome. Now she was arguing with herself. She really needed to get the hell out of this office. This building. This side of town. The more space between her and Joshua right now, the better. If not, she might do something really inane and unforgivable. Like hug him.

Suddenly wary of herself, she turned, retracing the few steps back to the coffee table and couch. Clearing her throat, she sank to the cushion and, tucking a rebellious strand of hair behind her ear, closed her laptop. "I'll start looking into it on my end tonight." With hurried movements, she slid the computer into her bag and stood. Fixing a smile on her lips, she lifted her head and met his impenetrable gaze again. God, the man could give the Sphinx lessons in stoicism. "Thank you for the tour today. I really appreciate it, and I learned more about Black Crescent that I didn't know. That I'm sure many people aren't aware of. If I have your permission, I'd like to share the information in a follow-up article."

"Why?"

She frowned, stilling midprocess of slipping the strap

of her bag over her shoulder. "Because the public deserves to know about your philanthropic programs and generosity to the community. I get your reason for staying mum on the subject, but—"

"No." He cut her off with a hard shake of his head. "When I invited you here I knew it was for a follow-up article. I meant why are you volunteering to help me?"

Because you looked so lost, and I want to bring home what will make you whole.

The explanation lodged in her throat, stuck. And she didn't try to free it. One, he wouldn't appreciate her reason. Wouldn't believe her. Two, she was disgusted with herself for thinking it. For thinking she could give him anything, much less peace and comfort.

Yes, Joshua Lowell had the whole brooding, tortured millionaire thing down pat. His cold mask of reserve had slipped enough times that she glimpsed the dark mass of emotions he concealed. She shivered, unable to restrain the telltale reaction. What would it be like to be on the receiving end of all that unleashed passion? Because she sensed that when or if he finally let it all loose... It would be a thing of wild, raw beauty to witness. Like a roiling, ominous thunderstorm threaded with lightning. And when those bolts struck the earth? Electricity, heat, smoke.

Her pulse thundered in her ears, and she couldn't tear her gaze away from him. She couldn't deny it; she hungered to be that rich, open earth electrified by him. But he would assuredly leave her scorched beyond recognition afterward. And while her body might crave that burning, her scarred heart feared it.

Inhaling a trembling breath past the constriction blocking her throat, she shrugged a shoulder, grabbing for nonchalance and praying she accomplished it. "Because I'm an investigative reporter, and that's what I do. Investigate."

Hiking her purse strap up, she again curved her lips into a polite smile that she—please, God—hoped didn't look as fake as it felt. "I need to head out so I can get back in the office to take care of a few things." Dear Lord, she was babbling and couldn't stop. "Thanks again, and I'll be in touch."

Crossing the room, she extended her hand toward him even though her mind screamed, *What the hell are you doing? Don't touch him!*

But her body had a mind of its own. And as his strong, elegant fingers—an artist's fingers—closed around hers, she cursed the voltage that sizzled from their clasped palms up her arm, down her chest and belly to crackle between her legs. If he dipped his eyes, he would catch the hardened tips of her breasts that were probably saluting him from beneath her dress. No more lace bras around this man. Definitely not enough coverage.

Every primal, self-protective instinct within her had her muscles locking in preparation to jerk her hand free. But pride overrode the need, and she met his hazel stare with a steady one of her own. To prove how she refused to let her body's obviously questionable taste rule her, she even squeezed his hand.

But when his nostrils slightly flared and his eyes darkened to an emerald-flecked amber... Oh no, she'd miscalculated. Flames licked at her flesh, and in that instant, she had a vivid premonition of how he would look in the throes of passion. Hooded, but glittering eyes, skin pulled taut over razor-sharp cheekbones, mouth pressed to a flat, almost severe line, and that big, wide-shouldered, powerful frame held rigidly still as he let her adjust to the blazing, overwhelming invasion of him planted deep and firmly inside her.

Pride be damned.

She yanked her hand out of his grip and refused to rub her still-tingling palm against her thigh.

"Why do I think you're lying to me?" he murmured, and after a few seconds of bewilderment, she realized he referred to her weak explanation about her offer of assistance. "What are you hiding, Sophie?"

"I think you're trying to uncover conspiracy theories where there are none," she replied, flippant. "I'm the reporter. That's my job, to be suspicious."

"Where you're concerned, my fail-safe is suspicion." He cocked his head to the side, studying her so closely she sympathized with those butterflies pinned to a corkboard. He wouldn't make her fidget, though. Or make her reveal any of her closely held thoughts regarding him. They were hers, and not his to use to his advantage.

"Then why are you willing to accept my help?" she asked, bristling.

"Maybe for once I'd like to know how it feels to have the press working with me instead of against me. And—" his voice dropped, and an unmistakable growl roughened the tone, causing her flesh to pebble "—I believe in keeping my friends close and my enemies closer. And you, Sophie Armstrong, I plan to be stuck to."

Another threat he would probably call a promise.

A promise that shouldn't have sent waves of molten heat echoing through her.

But it did. They swamped her, and dammit, she wanted to be taken under.

"Like stink on shit, you mean?" she shot back, pouring a bravado she was far from feeling into her tone.

He shifted forward until only scant inches separated them. Like in the gym, his body filled her vision and his warmth reached out for her, surrounding her along with his sandalwood and rain-dampened earth scent. She held her ground, not in the least intimidated as he invaded her personal space. No, not intimidated. She was throbbing. Hungry.

"Closer," he whispered, his breath feathering over her lips in a heavy but light-as-air caress.

Just in time, she caught herself before she tilted her head back, chasing that ephemeral touch.

Okay, screw pride and standing her ground.

Any wise general recognized the wisdom of retreating to fight another day.

And as she pivoted and escaped Joshua's office, she convinced herself she was being wise not running scared.

She almost accomplished the task.

Almost, but not quite.

Five

Joshua pulled open the door to The Java Hut, Falling Brook's upscale coffeehouse on Main Street. The air from the air conditioner greeted him like a lover, wrapping around him with chilled arms of welcome. It might be only May, but the temperature already crept toward the midseventies. And he silently bemoaned the loss of the cooler spring weather. While many people worshipped summer because of days spent on the beaches, lounging by the pool and less clothing, he loved the dynamic and vivid colors and crisp breezes of fall and the rain-scented air and reawakening of life that spring brought.

But no matter which season reigned, coffee remained a constant. And a must.

The fresh, dark aroma of brewing coffee filled the shop, and he inhaled it with unadulterated pleasure. At nine o'clock on a Saturday morning, he needed caffeine like an addict itching for his next hit. It was his one vice. And yes, he got how pathetic and boring that made him.

But considering his father's roaming eye, Jake's wanderlust and Oliver's taste for drugs, he couldn't afford to indulge any. The Lowell men had a proclivity toward addiction, and compared with his father's and brothers', coffee was the least harmful and the only one Joshua could afford.

He glanced down at his watch: 9:11 a.m. Another forty-nine minutes before his mother's doctor's appointment ended, and he had to return to the office and pick her up. Tension tightened his shoulders, and an ache bloomed between them. Deliberately, he inhaled, held the breath and, after ten seconds, released it. The monthly…dammit, not chore. Eve Evans-Janson could never be a chore. Responsibility. As the oldest son, she was his responsibility. But the monthly task of escorting his mother to her doctor always weighed him down like an albatross slung around his neck. Not because he didn't want to be bothered. Never that. He loved Eve, and she'd suffered just as much—if not more—than him and his brothers.

But each visit reminded him of how far she'd deteriorated from the vibrant socialite who'd raised him, loved him and had been his biggest supporter and fan when it'd come to his art. While Vernon hadn't understood and viewed his passion as a passing fancy, his mother had been so proud and celebrated along with him when he'd scored his own gallery show. She'd been his loudest cheerleader.

That woman had disappeared, fifteen years ago, replaced by a quiet, withdrawn recluse who only rarely ventured past the gates of the family's Georgian-style mansion. Her numerous friends had been abandoned and now the butler, maid and chef were her friends. She left the house only for doctor's appointments, the rare appearance at a charity function or the occasions he practically forced her out of the house to go to lunch or dinner with him. Vernon's betrayal had humiliated her. Especially since she'd initially defended him with unshakable faith. When he'd disappeared, she'd believed he might've been kidnapped—or worse. The victim of foul play. But never would he have cheated his clients and friends or stolen from his family and abandoned them to be the recipients of controversy, scorn and pain. Yet, as the days turned into weeks and then months, and the FBI's evidence piled up, Eve had to face the truth—her husband and their father was a criminal who'd bilked millions from those who'd placed their trust in him, then thrown those who'd loved and depended on him the most to the wolves. She'd never recovered.

And now...now he did what he could to ensure she didn't fade away behind the walls that were less her sanctuary and more her prison.

He clenched his fingers into a fist, then purposely relaxed them, exhaling as he did. Dammit, if he had his father here right now, each finger would be wrapped around his neck. Disgust twisted in his chest. If only what he felt toward his father was as simple as anger.

Stepping to the counter, he shoved everything from his mind and focused on ordering. Moments later, with his Americano in hand, he turned toward the entrance, but slammed to a halt.

A petite woman stood next to a table near the huge window, her back toward him, the ends of her unbound hair grazing the tank top–bared skin below her shoulders. The black top molded to the slim line of her back. Dark blue jeans clung to the gentle flare of her hips, the gorgeous tight ass that could be an eighth wonder of the world and legs that could grace a runway and climb the rocky, tough face of a mountain.

An achingly familiar itch tingled in his palms and hands. Familiar and painful. The need to hold a paintbrush. To capture the beauty and strength before him. To immortalize it. His medium had been mixed-media collages, but he'd also loved to paint. And right now he would use bold, rich colors to portray the golden tones of her skin, the power in that tiny body, the larger-than-life vibrancy of her personality, the thick softness of her hair.

That hair.

The thick golden-brown strands reminded him of a mare his father had doted on when Joshua had been a boy. Like raw umber with lighter strands of deep, burnished sunlight. His father had babied that horse, brushing her coat himself until it shined.

A yearning for a return to those idyllic times yawned so wide and deep, Joshua barely managed to restrain his free hand at his side so he wouldn't rub the knot that had formed just below his rib cage.

He could hate her alone for dragging that memory out of the abyss even as he fought against the need to burrow his hands in the wavy mass up to his wrists, fist it, tug on it... Bury his face in it. He already had personal knowledge of how far he would have to bend to inhale her citrus-and-flowers scent. As small as she was, he could completely surround her. Until he met Sophie Armstrong, tall, statuesque women had been his type. But now...now he got the lure of a petite woman he could cover with his bigger body. She triggered a primal, almost animalistic desire in him to take down and conquer her even as he did everything in his power to drown her in pleasure. Not that Sophie would take anything easily. No, he imagined she gave as good as she got in bed as much as she did out...

Molten heat swarmed through him at the thought of holding those slender, strong arms above her head, pressing his chest to her small, firm breasts, having those toned thighs clasping his waist as he drove inside her. She would be so tight, so perfect, damn near strangling his dick.

As if sensing his scrutiny, Sophie glanced over her shoulder and met his gaze. Surprise flickered over her face, her gray eyes widening slightly. He wanted them to do that when he first pushed into her sex. Hungered to see them darken like they did now as she slid a long glance down his body, and he swore he could feel that perusal as if her fingertips brushed over his collarbone, chest, abs, thighs…cock. Blood rushed to his flesh, thickening it behind the zipper of his pants. Hell yes, he wanted that touch on his bare skin, light then hard. Gentle then bruising. Yeah, he wanted this fairy of a woman to mark him.

A frigid blast of ice skated over his skin, digging farther to muscle and bone so he was chilled from the inside out.

Of all the women he could get hard over, Sophie Armstrong, reporter for the *Falling Brook Chronicle*, was the absolute last. Just this morning hadn't he witnessed the evidence of her recent rehashing of the scandal with his father in the creases on his mother's face and in the slump of her stooped shoulders? Haley might have managed to nab the paper before it was delivered to his mother's home, but Eve had overheard the maid and butler talking about it in hushed tones. And she'd demanded to see the paper. Reading that article had taken a toll on her.

So even with Sophie's offer to help him determine if the paternity accusation was true or not, he could never trust her. Could never believe that he wasn't just the means to another juicy story. Who knew what her follow-up article would contain? Why the fuck did he agree to it?

No. Sophie was a threat to his business, his family… to his sanity.

But he'd never been led around by his dick, and he wouldn't start a new trend now.

Still, as her lush mouth curled into a smile, he had to remind his body of that.

He tossed his still-full cup in the trash and crossed the room toward her, because no way in hell would he run from her. Or the need that strung his body so tight. It was a wonder he didn't snap in two at the slightest movement.

"Sophie," he greeted, for the first time thankful for the avaricious media and eyes that forced him to perfect a mask of indifference. He swept a glance over the laptop bag that hung near her hip. "Working?"

"Yes, but from home today. I'm a creature of habit, though. Every morning I stop in here for a coffee and their cinnamon-and-brown-sugar scones. Have you had them yet? They're God's way of saying He loves us."

She released a throaty hum that had his gut clenching. Hard. He wanted to hear it again even as he longed to trap the sound inside her...with his mouth.

Goddammit, he needed to get control. And quick.

"No, I can't say I've had the pleasure," he replied. "I'll take your word for it."

She arched a brow. "Oh, really? That would be a first between us."

"Sheathe your sword, Sophie," he said.

"So you finally admit that you need every bit of help you can muster when going up against me?" she challenged, amusement lighting her eyes like glittering stars.

"I never said I didn't. Only a fool would encounter you and not be battle ready with everything in his arsenal available to him."

She heaved an exaggerated sigh and splayed her fingers wide over her chest. "I do believe that's the nicest thing you've ever said to me."

His wry chuckle caught him by surprise. The last thing he'd ever expected to do with Sophie was laugh. A warning for caution blared in his ears. He couldn't afford to let down his guard, become too comfortable around her.

"What are you doing on this side of town? The coffee here is great, but I've had what you keep at your office and it's pretty good, too."

"I'm not headed to work this morning. I'm waiting for my mother. She has a doctor's appointment right down the street."

She frowned and laid a hand on his lower arm. "I'm sorry. Is she okay?"

For a moment the flare of heat emanating from her touch seared his voice, rendering it useless. She might as well have settled her palm over his dick the way he throbbed and ached.

Gritting his teeth, he ignored the lust coursing through him like a swollen river and said, "Yes. It's just a regular checkup."

"Oh, okay." Her frown deepened for a moment, and it seemed as if she was going to probe further, but in the next instant she skated a quick survey up and down his frame. "So you're not going to the office, but *this* is what you wear on a Saturday morning?"

He didn't bother glancing down to take in the white long-sleeved shirt and black slacks. "Problem?"

She snorted, a smirk flirting with the corners of her lips. "Oh no. No problem at all. I'm just wondering what you wear to bed. An Armani suit? Or maybe a tuxedo."

The humor fled from him, chased away by the desire flaring inside him by the mention of "bed." Hell, she'd reduced him to a fourteen-year-old boy who got hard with the switch of the wind. That didn't stop him from cocking his head to the side and murmuring, "You're wondering what I wear to bed, Sophie? All you have to do is ask."

Slashes of red tinted her cheekbones and her eyes turned to liquid silver. Neither of them spoke as the air hummed with tension, pulsed with an unacknowledged lust volleyed between them. God, he wanted her. Why her—a reporter who sought to paint him as a puppet for his deadbeat father? Would she screw him, then riffle through his drawers to find dirt she could use for the follow-up piece on him and his family?

Something deep inside him objected to that, argued that she wasn't that kind of woman, but this time logic ruled. He'd known too many people who would sooner use him than blink. As a Lowell, men and women looked at him and saw money, connections, information and sometimes a good fuck. But never the man. Never the son struggling to make good and be honorable where his father had failed.

Sophie blinked, the desire clearing from her gaze, and at the same time he edged back a step.

"Pass," she rasped, then, clearing her throat, turned back to her table and gathered up her empty coffee cup, paper plate and plastic fork. "Seriously, though, Joshua," she continued in a stronger voice, that hint of humor returning. "Jeans. Ever heard of them?"

"Sounds familiar," he drawled, following her toward the exit. She dropped her trash in the receptacle and pushed through the coffeehouse door. "What is this sudden fascination with my clothes?"

She laughed as they moved out onto the sidewalk, stepping aside as more customers entered the café. He ignored the curious glances shot their way. After fifteen years, he should be immune to them. But he'd never managed it. They still got under his skin.

"Not your clothes. I'm just curious if you ever relax. If you're ever not Joshua Lowell of the Falling Brook Lowells, CEO of Black Crescent Hedge Fund and just Josh. Does anyone call you that?"

"My brothers did. But it's been a long time," he murmured. *Just Josh.*

There was no such person. Once upon a time there'd been. Josh had been an artist on the precipice of a promising career. He'd been the older brother to Jake and Oliver, who'd been friends as well as brothers. Back before they'd looked on him with scorn and resentment for following in their father's tainted footsteps. Josh had been carefree, laughed often and pursued his passion.

His family and the company wouldn't survive if he reverted to Just Josh.

If he tasted the joy, the life-giving fire of art again, *he* might not survive.

So no, Joshua Lowell, savior and CEO of Black Crescent, was much safer.

Sophie studied him with narrowed eyes, then, slipping the strap of her laptop bag over her head so it crossed her torso, she grabbed his hand in hers and tugged him forward. The shock of her skin touching his reverberated through his body and stunned him long enough that he didn't resist her leading him down the sidewalk. He should pull away from her, cauterize the connection that bled fire into his veins...

He flipped their hands so he enfolded hers, so soft and delicate, in his.

Minutes later, she paused in front of Henrietta's Creamery, the town's only ice-cream shop. He stared at her, confused and more than a little taken aback.

"Ice cream?" he asked, not bothering to eliminate the skepticism from his voice. "At nine thirty in the morning?"

She shook her head and mockingly patted his arm with the hand he wasn't clasping. "See? This right here is what I mean. When is there ever an inappropriate time for ice cream? Joshua, that stick in your ass. Was it surgically implanted, or did it just grow there naturally?"

The bark of laughter abraded his throat, shocking him

as much as her teasing. No one would ever dare to say that to him. Hell, no one would dare to tease him. But this slip of a woman knew no boundaries or fear. From the first, she hadn't been cowed or intimidated by him. And God, it felt good.

"Naturally. And it required effort and a lot of pruning and nurturing," he deadpanned, causing a grin to spread wide over her face. Jesus, she was gorgeous.

"Well, I volunteer as tribute to help you remove it. Starting with an ice-cream cone for breakfast. C'mon." She didn't brook any disagreement but jerked on the door to the shop and entered, pulling him behind her.

After a brief but spirited debate over the best flavors, they walked out with two waffle cones topped with a double scoop of ice cream—salted caramel for him and butter pecan for her.

Him.

Joshua Lowell.

Walking down the sidewalk lining Main Street. Eating an ice-cream cone.

Jesus, how did he get here?

But as Sophie tipped her head back and smiled at him, the light of it reflecting in her beautiful gray eyes, he embraced the moment. Embraced, hell. Hoarded it. In less than half an hour, he would be returning to pick up his mother, and the mantle of responsibility that he'd prematurely donned would fall back around his shoulders. Weighing them down with a pressure that was at times suffocating. Pressing them down with an anger-rimmed sadness that he'd never been able to completely banish no matter how many times he'd told himself that they didn't need his father. That they were better off without him.

Yeah, he was going to embrace this moment and grab on to it selfishly. Because as Joshua Lowell, Vernon's son, he didn't have many. The cost for that kind of greed was too high. As his father's actions had taught him.

"Now, I don't want to say I told you so…" she said, an impish smile curving her lips. "Oh hell, who am I kidding? I *so* do want to say it. I told you so."

"I think you might have held that in for two minutes and twenty-eight seconds," he drawled. "Congratulations."

She twirled her hand in front of her, dipping slightly at the waist. "Thank you. I'll have you know my restraint was hard fought."

He snorted, swiping his tongue through the cold cream and barely managing to contain a moan. When was the last time he'd indulged like this? Years. It'd been years.

"I don't want to alarm you, but people are staring," Sophie informed him in a stage whisper. As if he hadn't already noticed. "One woman just almost rear-ended the car in front of her at the stoplight." She gave a mocking gasp, splaying the fingers not holding the ice-cream cone wide across her chest. "Whatever do you think it could be that they find so interesting?"

Joshua didn't answer, but some of the peace and joy filtered from his chest, replaced by a slick, grimy stain that was a murky mixture of guilt, anger and helplessness. The sludge tracked its way across his chest, down to his gut, where it churned. He deliberately relaxed his grip on the cone but couldn't prevent the clenching of his jaw. A hint of neon-red pain flared along the edge.

"It must be so tiring," Sophie murmured, all notes of teasing evaporated from her tone. He glanced down at her, and those gray eyes looked back at him, warm and velvet with a sympathy he never believed he'd glimpse. At least not for him.

"What must be tiring?" he ground out.

"Feeling like an animal in a zoo. Always being on display," she replied softly.

Her observation struck too deep...too on point. He hated it that she saw it. Hated more that he'd allowed her to.

"Being fodder for any newspaper or online gossip column," he lashed out with a biting coldness that was meant to burn.

She bent her head over her treat and licked a melting trail of ice cream. In spite of the anger knotting his gut, lust slid through him in a thick glide, flowing straight for his already pulsing flesh. He wanted that delicate pink tongue on him. Trailing over him like he was the most delicious thing she'd ever tasted. He hungered to hear her moans of pleasure in his ears, have it vibrate over his skin.

His control was soaked tissue paper when it came to this woman.

"I left the door wide-open on that one," she said long moments later, voice quiet. "I won't apologize for my job—it's an important one, and I love it. But I will say I'm sorry that it's contributed to making you feel as if you were a fish in a bowl. I can't imagine that kind of scrutiny is easy."

"But deserved, some would say." They continued to walk down the sidewalk in a silence taut with tension. Or more specifically, the roil of emotions tumbling inside him. Shoving against his sternum, his throat, seeking an escape. A release. "There are days I believe I deserve it. Give people their due. They need to watch me and make sure I'm not exhibiting signs of becoming Vernon Lowell. They have the right to that transparency. Even years later. Even though—"

Even though there were times he wanted to yell that he wasn't his father. That it wasn't him that had wronged them. It wasn't his fault.

But he couldn't. Because in the end, the sins of the father were visited upon the sons.

In their eyes, as the head of Black Crescent, as the only one available to direct their anger and mistrust at, it was his fault.

And he couldn't argue with them. Because deep inside, in that place that creaked open only in the darkest part of night when he had no energy left to keep it closed, he agreed with them.

Beside him, Sophie sighed and tunneled her fingers through her hair, dragging the strands away from her face and offering him an even more unencumbered view of her clean, elegant profile. A small frown wrinkled the smooth skin between her eyebrows.

"Deserve?" she mused almost to herself. She shook her head. "I don't agree with that. While I do believe in the truth and that people have the right to be aware of events that affect their welfare and lives, they aren't owed pieces of a person's security, peace or soul. Each of us should have the right to privacy, and we don't need anyone's permission to covet it or request it. And this is from a reporter." She lightly snorted, again shaking her head. Pausing, she took another swipe of the ice cream, and her tone became more thoughtful than irritated. "My parents divorced when I was almost thirteen, and it was… Well, *unpleasant* would be an understatement. The nasty arguing and name-calling had been bad enough. But they saw me as an ally to be wooed, a prize to be won in a contest. And they attempted this by competing in who could tell me the foulest, most humiliating things about the other. How my father cheated or how my mother had sent them to the poorhouse with her spending. So many things a child shouldn't be privy to, especially about her parents.

"But they twisted the truth about each other in this acrimonious and desperate need to make the other appear as horrible as possible. Never realizing how they were slowly picking me apart ugly word by ugly word. Because all I heard was how it was my fault they were divorcing. My father cheated. That just meant he was so unhappy at home with me for not doing better in school or being a pest at home that he went somewhere else to find happiness. Or if my mother spent too much money, it was on me because I asked for too much."

She inhaled a breath, and he caught the slight tightening of her hold on the cone. After several seconds, she released a trembling but self-deprecating chuckle.

"Sophie…"

But she interrupted him with a wave of her hand. "No, I know none of that is true. Now, anyway. But back then…" Her voice trailed off, but seconds later, she lifted a slim shoulder in a half shrug. "They made my teenage years hell, but I should thank them. Because of all that, plus the shuffling back and forth to different homes, never feeling truly rooted or secure, I made sure that I would be able to stand on my own two feet as an adult. That no one would ever have the power or ability to ever rip the rug out from under me again. They also directed me on the path to my career. They fueled my desire to filter facts from half-truths or fiction. And, when it was called for, to shield the innocent from it."

He digested that in silence. "Which is why you didn't print the rumors about me having a daughter in the article," he added.

She nodded, not looking at him. "Yes. I know what you think of me, Joshua, but I wouldn't deliberately smear someone's name or hurt them. Not without all the facts that can be backed up and confirmed beyond doubt. Am I perfect? No. But I try to be."

He licked the melting ice cream in his hand, warring within himself about how much he could share with Sophie. Why he *shouldn't* share. But after her baring some of her chaotic childhood, he owed her. Still…

"Off the record?" he murmured.

She jerked her gaze to him, and in the dove-gray depths he easily caught the surprise. And the flicker of irritation. As if annoyed that he'd ask. But as lovely as she was, as honest as she'd been with him, he couldn't forget who she was. *What* she was.

"Of course," she said, none of the contrasting emotions in her eyes reflected in her voice.

"Of course," he repeated softly, staring down at her. *What the hell are you doing?* he silently questioned his sanity, but then said, "I deserve their censure because of my life before my father decided to screw us all six ways to Sunday. Mine was charmed. I won't say perfect, because in hindsight, it wasn't. Nothing is. But for me, it was close. My brothers and I—we didn't have to want for anything. Not material, financial or emotional. Dad was always busy building Black Crescent into one of the foremost hedge funds, but Mom? She'd been there, attentive, supportive, loving. We weren't raised by an army of servants, even though we did have them. But Mom—and even Dad to an extent—had been involved. We attended one of the most exclusive and premier prep schools in the country and, later, Ivy League universities. I knew who I was and what I wanted to be. I never had doubts back then. I held the world in my palm and harbored no insecurities or fears that I could have it all."

"I always wondered about that," Sophie said, that intuitive and insightful gaze roaming his face. "If you faced any backlash or disapproval from your father for choosing art over the family business."

Why the hell am I talking about this? He never discussed his art or his career ambitions. A pit gaped in his chest, stretching and threatening to swallow him whole with the grief, disillusionment and sense of failure that poured out. Those dreams were dead and buried with a headstone to mark the grave.

Forcing the memories and the words past his tightening throat, he barely paused next to a garbage can and pitched his cone into it. He couldn't talk about this and even consider eating. Not with his gut forming a rebellion at just the unlocking of the past.

"From my mother, no. Like I said, she supported me from the very first. When I was a child, she enrolled me in art classes, encouraged me to continue even when my father scoffed at it or dismissed my interest as a passing fancy. But art was...my passion. My true friend, in ways. Growing up in Falling Brook, we had to be careful about image, about never forgetting we were Vernon Lowell's sons and Eve Evans-Janson's sons. There was a trade-off for the life of privilege we led, and that was perfection. But with art? I never had to be perfect. Or careful. I just had to be me. I didn't have to curtail my opinions to make sure I didn't offend anyone or reflect on my father. I could be unfailingly and unapologetically honest. I could trust it more than anything or anyone else."

A vise squeezed his chest so hard, so tight, his ribs screamed for relief. Just talking about that part of him he'd willingly—but without choice—amputated brought ghostly echoes of the joy, the freedom he'd once experienced every time he took a picture, picked up a piece of metal, lifted a paintbrush...

He shook them off, shoving them in the vault of his past and locking the door. If he were going to discuss that part of him, of his life, he had to separate himself from the emotion behind it. Besides, that was who he'd been. That man had ceased to exist the moment his father had gone on the lam, leaving his family and ten others broke and broken.

"But to answer your question, there wasn't any strife. More so because I believe Dad thought I would indulge in art, get it out of my system and then come work for Black Crescent. Even when I scored my first gallery show the summer after I graduated from college, Dad was pleased for me, but he also told me I had a choice to make and he hoped I chose wisely. 'Wisely' being coming into the business with him."

Had his father known even then that he would be going on the run? Had he already planned his escape plan? Because only two months after that conversation, he'd disappeared.

"While researching the article, I always thought that was amazing. Do you know how many artists are capable of getting their own gallery shows so soon in their careers? But then again, I saw pictures of your work. God, you were phenomenal," she breathed.

The unadulterated awe in her voice snagged on something inside him, jerking and tugging as if trying to bring that ephemeral and elusive "thing" to the surface to be acknowledged and analyzed. He shrank from it. Not in the least bit ready to do that.

He never would be.

"Can I ask you something? And disclaimer—it's going to be intrusive," she said, dumping her cone into a nearby trash can before slipping a sidelong glance at him. When he dipped his chin in agreement, she murmured, "How could you step away from it? I'm just thinking of how I would feel if I suddenly lost my career. Or if I couldn't do it anymore. And not just reporting, but my purpose. Empty. And lost. How could you give it up so easily?"

"Easily?" His harsh burst of laughter scraped his throat raw. "There was nothing easy about it, Sophie. I had a choice to make. Family or a career in art." Leave, move to New York to escape the judgment and condemnation and pursue his passion, or stay and save his family and the business. Try to repair what his father had torn apart. Even when Jake had done just that, Josh had stayed. And there'd been nothing simple or easy about that decision. "In the end my father had been right. I would have to choose, and I did. Not that it'd been much of one. I couldn't abandon my family."

Not like him remained unspoken but deafening in the silence that followed his words.

"I'm sorry," she whispered.

He slipped his tightly curled fists into the pockets of his slacks. "For what?" he rasped.

"For assuming it'd been an easy decision. That you had to make it in the first place."

He drew to an abrupt halt, absently thankful they'd made it to the parking lot at the far end of Main where his car waited. Thankful no one loitered in the area, and that for once, they were away from prying eyes.

No one—no *fucking* one—had ever said that to him. Had ever thought to consider the cost of his sacrifice, the effect of it on him. And no one had ever thanked him or sympathized that he'd given up the best part of him to take care of family. A family in which two of its members resented him for making that choice.

Alone. Here, in this parking lot, partially insulated from the public that had judged him so harshly, the remnants of the past clinging to him like skeletal fingers, he could admit that for fifteen years, he'd been so damn alone.

That choice had cost him the closeness he'd once shared with his brothers. It'd stolen the plugged-in mother from his youth. The so-called friends he'd believed he had. Most of all, it'd left him bereft of his dreams and—how had she described it?—empty.

Yes. Empty.

But in this space, in this fleeting moment, he didn't. With this woman, with her silken skin, molten eyes and temptress mouth, he felt...seen. And it sent heat rushing through him like air caught in a wind tunnel—loud, powerful and threatening to rip him apart. He edged his feet apart, slightly widening his stance as if bracing himself against the overwhelming longing to touch, to hold, to *connect*.

He lifted his hand to brush his fingertips over her delicate jaw, waiting, no, expecting, her to wrench away from him to avoid his caress.

She didn't. Sophie stood still, her headed tilted back, gaze centered on him. She didn't flinch from him. Didn't question what the hell he was doing. No, those sweet lips parted on a soft gasp that went straight to his dick, grazing it.

Locking down a groan behind clenched teeth, he shifted closer, turning slightly to shield her from any curious spectators. A thick cocoon of desire might be enfolding them, but it didn't erase the fact that they stood off Main Street. But where minutes ago that would've prevented him from lowering his head over hers, moving nearer still until his chest pressed against hers and his thighs cradled the slim length of hers, more than ever, he was aware of the disparity in their heights and frames. His body nearly covered her, and the top of her head just barely skimmed his chin. The surge of lust sweeping through his veins, lighting them like an SOS flare, competed with the urge to protect. The impulse to conquer warred with the need to shelter. But instead of being torn in two by the opposing instincts, they melded, mating. Assuring him he could do both. That, by God, he *should* do both.

His fingers continued to explore her jaw, her cheek, the thinner skin over her temple, the slope of her nose in spite of the lust baying in his head like howling dogs. He followed the graceful arches of her eyebrows before traveling back down to trace the upper curve of her mouth, linger in the shallow dip in the middle. Then, he moved to that plumper bottom lip, savoring the soft give of it under his fingertips. He didn't offer just his thumb the treat of it. All his fingertips got in on the pleasure of the caress.

Her breath hitched, and again he fought back a moan at the gentle gust of air against his suddenly overly sensitive skin. Words crowded at the back of his throat.

Tell me I can have this temptation of a mouth that has woken me up, hard and hurting, for days now.

Will you let me fuck this mouth, Sophie? Will you let me defile it so you can taste the dirtiness of my kiss for days? Weeks?

But he didn't utter them. Instinct warned him that breaking this lust-drenched and pulsing silence with any sound would rip this opportunity away from him. Shatter the cords that held them here in this moment—cords that shimmered with heat but were as fragile as glass.

He'd hungered for this chance for too long. Battled himself over it too hard to abdicate it.

So, instead, he planted his thumb in the middle of the bottom curve, pressed until the tip of his finger grazed the edges of her teeth. When she didn't draw away from him but tilted her head forward to lean into the pressure, he shuddered.

And when she parted those beautiful lips and flicked her tongue over his flesh, he had his answer.

Not bothering to trap his groan in this time, he dipped

his head and took her. Releasing the greedy sound into her mouth, replacing his thumb with the slick glide of his tongue.

God, the taste of her.

Sweet like the butter-pecan ice cream she'd been eating. Sultry like air thick and perfumed after a spring rain. Heady like a shot of whiskey. Deliciously wicked. Like sex.

With hands going rough with greed, he burrowed one into her hair, fisting the strands and tugging. Tugging until her mouth was right where he wanted it...needed it. Her swallowed her small whimper, giving her a growl in return as she opened wider for him. Granting him entrance to her. To heaven.

He thrust between those beautiful lips, tangling his tongue with hers, dancing, dueling. Because Sophie wasn't a passive participant. Just as she challenged him in his office, in a newspaper conference room or a gym, she gave as good as she got here, as well. She sucked and licked, stroking into his mouth to demand and take.

His grip on her hair and hip tightened, dragging her closer, impossibly closer. His hips punched forward, grounding his erection against the softness of her belly. Fire ripped a scorching path up his spine, then back down to his dick. Jesus, she was about to set him off like a teenager copping his first feel behind the gym bleachers. Cocking his head, he delved deeper, a desperate hunger for more digging into him. One nip of her lips, one sample of her taste, and he was hooked, ravenous for more.

"Josh," she breathed against his damp lips. Hearing the abbreviated version of his name had his flesh hardening further, had him aching. And he couldn't not reward her—hell, thank her—with another drugging kiss and roll of his hips.

The ring of a phone shattered the thick haze of lust that enclosed them.

He lifted his head, the air in his lungs ragged and harsh. She stared up at him, those storm-gray eyes clouded with the same desire coursing through him like electrified currents. Her swollen mouth, wet from his tongue, glistened, and he'd lowered his head, submitting to the sensual beckoning of them when the peal of the phone jangled again.

Dammit.

Disentangling his hands from her hair and releasing the sweet curve of her hip, he stepped back, reaching in his pocket for his silent cell phone. At the same time, Sophie retrieved hers from the front pocket of her bag. Tapping the screen, she held the cell to her ear.

"Hi, Althea," she said, her gaze meeting his for a second before she turned away. Althea Granger, the editor in chief of the *Falling Brook Chronicle*. Her boss. "Yes, that's not a problem. Has anyone else picked up the story yet?"

A frigid deluge of water crashed over him in a wave.

For moments, he'd felt young again. Free again. He'd allowed himself to forget who Sophie was. Who he was. But reality had a way of slapping the hell out of a person and reminding him that life wasn't hand-holding and ice-cream cones or kissing a beautiful woman. It was hard, sometimes grueling work, disappointment and constantly brushing off scraped knees and bruised hands to get up and face it again.

He could still taste the unique and addictive flavor of her on his lips, his tongue. But he couldn't let Sophie Armstrong in. And her being a reporter was just one reason. A very good reason to keep his distance from her, but not the only one.

When Vernon had left, he'd broken his ability to trust. And his brothers had trampled on the pieces on their way out of Falling Brook. Even his mother had abandoned him. Not physically, but definitely emotionally. When he loved people, when he let them in, they left. They eventually abandoned him.

They eventually devastated him.

No, he couldn't trust Sophie. Leaving himself vulnerable again came at too high a price. And he had nothing left to pay it with.

"Okay, I'll head to the office now. See you in a few." Sophie ended the call and faced him again. "Sorry about that." She cleared her throat, twin flags of pink staining the slants of her cheekbones. Left over from their kiss—if that was what that clash of mouths, tongues and teeth could be labeled—or from the phone call. "I need to go into work for a few hours."

"I heard," he said, deliberately infusing a sheet of ice into his voice. As if just seconds ago it hadn't been razed to hell by lust. He glanced down at his watch. "That's fine. I have to leave, too." While he'd been taking her mouth, time had raced by, and he was due to pick up his mother in five minutes. But the errand was just a handy excuse to put distance between him and Sophie. Because in spite of his resolve and the reminder of why he couldn't become involved with her, he still had to threaten himself with self-harm to avoid staring at her mouth like a marauding beast. "Have a good weekend, Sophie."

Not waiting on her reply, he pivoted on his heel and strode back in the direction they'd come. And if that cloak of loneliness settled across his shoulders again, well, it was preferable to pain.

Preferable to betrayal.

And Sophie smacked of both.

Six

Sophie wove a path among the many businessmen, socialites, philanthropists and even a handful of celebrities crowded into the Ronald O. Perelman Rotunda of the Guggenheim Museum in Manhattan. The annual Tender Shoots Art Gala brought all the tristate area's glitterati out in support of the New York–based arts program.

Taking a sip of her cocktail, she dipped her head in a shallow nod at a woman whose diamond necklace and ruby-red strapless gown could probably pay off the entirety of Sophie's student loans. She held her head up, meeting the assessing gaze of every person she had eye contact with. Or maybe it just felt assessing to her. As if they were attempting to peer beneath the expertly applied makeup and strapless, glittery, floor-length dress that she'd needed a crowbar and a prayer to squeeze into in order to determine if she belonged.

Well, at an invite-only event that required fifteen thousand a plate fee plus a hefty donation for entrance, she didn't belong. She'd grown up in Falling Brook, one of the most exclusive, wealthiest communities along the Eastern Seaboard, but her family had been among the few middle-class residents who either owned businesses in town or worked for Falling Brook Prep, the independent K–twelve school. The kind of excess and luxury represented in the grand, open space surrounded by the spiral-ramped architecture capped by a gorgeous skylight exceeded her imagination and bank account. Thank God, Althea's partner was a stylist who had let Sophie borrow a designer gown for the night. And didn't that just increase the surreal feeling of Cinderella attending the ball before her carriage turned back into a pumkin that had filled her since stepping onto the curb outside the famous museum?

If not for Althea receiving an invitation because of the paper's piece about the event, the organization and the underprivileged youth it benefited, Sophie would be home, catching up on season two of *The Handmaid's Tale*. But since it'd been Sophie's article that had garnered the invite, Althea had convinced her to accept and attend. She should be grateful and flattered. But while she had no problem reporting on the country's wealthy elite, she drew a line at socializing with them. It reminded her too much of a time in her life when she'd been blinded by their world and the man she'd once loved who'd belonged to it.

Too bad she hadn't remembered not to cross that line that morning with Joshua Lowell.

A convoluted mixture of embarrassment, self-directed anger and a relentless, aching need jumbled and twisted deep inside her. Just thinking of how he'd cupped her jaw, gently caressed her face and then claimed her mouth had her shouting obscenity-laced reprimands at herself...even as she pressed her thighs together to fruitlessly attempt to stifle the throbbing ache in her sex. And all that led to her embarrassment. The man had sexed her mouth, then walked away from her without a backward glance. As if that devastation of a kiss hadn't affected him at all. If not for the insistent, commanding grind of his thick erection against her belly, she would've believed he hadn't been.

But no matter that he'd moaned into her mouth and had granted her a clear premonition of what it would be like to be controlled and branded by that big, wide-shouldered body, he *had* transformed from the approachable, almost vulnerable man who'd strolled down Main Street with her, licking ice cream in a way that had her sex ready to throw itself at his feet, to an iceberg who'd dismissed her as if their connection had been of no consequence. As if *she* were of no consequence. And hell, maybe to him, she wasn't.

Staring down into the glass, she didn't see the pale gold champagne but his shuttered expression and flat stare as she'd ended her phone call. A shiver ran through her, as if the ice that had entered that measured inspection skated over her exposed skin now. She didn't believe in deluding herself; she acknowledged that it'd been Althea's call that had changed him. He'd no doubt suddenly been reminded of what they were to one another. She was the woman who had dragged the darkest, most scandalous parts of his history back out, dusted them off and planted them on the front page of the newspaper for public consumption. Again.

Half of her was surprised he hadn't asked her if that kiss was off the record. Despite her best efforts, her lips twisted into a slight sneer. As if she'd treat him to an ice-cream cone just to butter him up for a scoop—no pun intended. Screw it. That pun was totally intended.

Smothering a sigh, she lifted her fluted glass to her lips

and sipped. At least this gala provided one purpose. Distract her from thoughts of—

Joshua.

Her gaze locked with a beautiful and all too familiar pair of hazel eyes. Lust gut-punched her like a prizefighter with a penchant for ear biting. If not for her locked knees and sheer grit not to humiliate herself in the four-inch stilettos, the blow would've knocked her on her ass. Beneath the bandage-style bodice of her dress, her nipples drew into taut, pebbled points begging for just a whisper of a caress from those long, blunt-tipped fingers. Pinpricks of electricity rippled up and down her exposed spine, sizzling in the base of her spine. And her feminine flesh... She stifled a needy and shameful moan. Her flesh swelled, damp and sensitive from just a hooded glance from those green-and-gold and way too perceptive eyes.

Good God, had she conjured him with her own wayward thoughts?

"Ms. Armstrong?" a low, cultured voice called her name, and Sophie yanked her scrutiny away from Joshua. A tall, powerfully built and handsome man stood next to her. Black hair waved back from a high forehead, emphasizing a face with strong facial features, a full, sensual mouth and intense blue eyes. He smiled, flashing perfect white teeth. "You are Sophie Armstrong, correct?" he asked, extending a large hand toward her.

"Yes," she replied, accepting the hand. He squeezed it lightly before releasing it. "I'm sorry, do we know one another?"

"No, we haven't officially met. But I've followed your career these past few years from Chicago to the *Falling Brook Chronicle*. I'm a fan of your journalistic style. Most recently, I enjoyed the pieces you wrote on the Tender Shoots Arts Council as well as the one on the Black Crescent scandal. Considering the topic and the many times it's been reported on, I thought you wrote an objective, well-researched article. Especially about Joshua Lowell and his former art career. I don't think many people remember the accomplished artist he was and the potential career he once had."

Accomplished artist he is.

The words burned on her tongue. No one with the kind of talent she'd seen in his work or whose voice contained the passion his had while describing what art had meant to him could turn off the God-given gift he'd been blessed with. Joshua might be the CEO of his father's company, but now more than ever after this morning's conversation with him, she was convinced the artist who'd created such awe-inspiring, magnificent pieces of art still existed beneath those expensive, perfectly tailored suits.

"Thank you. I appreciate the compliment, Mr...." She trailed off. The man still hadn't given her his name.

A half smile quirked one corner of his mouth. "Christopher Harrison. I'm one of the organizers of the gala and on the board of trustees for the Tender Shoots Arts Council."

"Mr. Harrison." She nodded. "It's a pleasure to meet you."

"Christopher, please. The pleasure is mine." He crooked an arm and held it out to her. "Can I escort you into dinner? I believe we're sitting at the same table."

A little bemused, she settled her hand in the bend of his elbow. "I'm sitting at your table?" she repeated, unable to keep out the edge of incredulity.

He chuckled. "I confess to using my position with the organization to finagle a favor and moving your seat." He shrugged, but nothing about him said *repentant*. "It's one of the perks of the job."

"Do I need to be worried about why you want my company at your table?" she mused, part of her amused, but the other part wary. Years ago, another sophisticated, handsome man had approached her at a function. And his motives had been anything but pure. Too bad that by the time she'd figured that out, he'd nearly devastated her heart and her integrity. Old suspicions died hard.

Speaking of suspicions...

The charged tingle dancing across the nape of her neck informed her where Joshua stood. And she directed her glance in that direction. Immediately, his hazel gaze snared hers. Burning into hers. For a second, it released her to flicker to the man guiding her through the throng of people. Even across the distance, she caught the firming of his full lips, the darkening of his eyes. And when he returned his narrowed scrutiny to her, the fire in them seared over her exposed skin.

She sucked in a breath, jerking her head forward. Because she needed to pay attention to where her feet and the man next to her were taking her.

Not because she could no longer stand meeting that slightly ominous stare that had heat spiking in her body like she'd transformed into a thermometer.

At least that was what she told herself. As she settled at one of the tables closest to the dais erected at the far end of the rotunda, she continued to remind herself of that. And even as the electrified crackle hummed under her skin, she refused to allow her attention to slip toward the table to her right. Joshua Lowell was just a man. Yes, a beautiful, imposing man who wore a tuxedo as if it'd been created with the sole purpose of adorning that tall, powerful body. A complicated man who was like a puzzle missing several pieces. Pieces she wanted to hunt down and fit into the empty spaces so she could determine who he really was. The arrogant, commanding CEO with the icy reserve? Or the passionate artist who revealed tantalizing glimpses of vulnerability and kissed like he could consume a woman whole and make her beg him to take more?

He's a man who wants revenge because of the story you wrote on him and his family. A man who denies the existence of his child and is using you to control if you reveal it or not.

Or maybe one who just desperately sought to discover if he truly had a daughter that he'd known nothing about?

Jesus, she was arguing with herself. It was official. Joshua—or this unwarranted and dangerous fascination with him—was driving her nuts.

That same fascination had her casting a glance to the neighboring table. She was a masochist. There was no other explanation. And yet, she found herself once more helplessly ensnared by a copper-and-emerald stare as she'd been in the reception area.

Flayed. That was what that intense, gorgeous and entirely too-perceptive scrutiny did to her. Leave her flayed, open and exposed. Did he see the dueling emotions he stirred in her—the desire for distance, to borrow some of that renowned aloofness, and the desire to feel the intimidating thick length of him again. Not against her stomach this time, but inside her. Stretching her. Marking her.

The woman next to Joshua, a stunning redhead in a black sequined dress that screamed couture, leaned into him, whispering in his ear. He turned to her, releasing Sophie from their visual showdown.

A shaft of…something hot and ugly pierced her chest. She couldn't identify it. *Wouldn't* identify it. Because it wasn't jealousy. The woman, with the onyx jewels dripping from her ears and encircling her neck, belonged to his world. They were perfect for each other.

"Do you know Joshua?" Christopher's question yanked

her from the rabbit hole that she'd been in the process of tumbling down. She met his curious gaze. Saw when it flickered toward the other table and Joshua and returned to her. "Are you two acquainted?"

"God, no," she denied with a small deprecating chuckle. Not a lie, exactly. She doubted anyone really *knew* Joshua Lowell. And something whispered that he preferred it that way. "I just wrote an article on one of the darkest periods in his and his family's lives. I'm sure he's not a fan of mine."

"Hmm." Christopher studied her, and she refused to fidget beneath that assessing regard. "I can understand that, I guess. Although, like I mentioned earlier, all things considered, it was a fair piece." He lifted a glass of wine and sipped from it, continuing to study her over the rim. "He's one of our major contributors to the nonprofit. Not surprising, really, with his own background in art."

Yes, she could see that. He might not create pieces anymore but imagining him pouring financial support into the lives of underprivileged youth so they might have the advantages of following the path he'd walked away from wasn't hard.

Still… She glanced over at one of the walls where numerous canvases, pen-and-ink drawings and framed photographs hung. The oversize, mixed-media collages that used to be Joshua's trademark would seamlessly fit in here. Did he ever wish they were? Did he ever dream of walking into this famed museum and seeing his pieces adorning these off-white walls?

Did it cause him pain to attend a gala celebrating art knowing he couldn't have this? Knowing others were doing what he'd been created to do?

She forced herself not to look at Joshua this time. Afraid she would see what she wanted to instead of who he really was. Maya Angelou had said, "When someone shows you who they are, believe them the first time." That day she'd barged into his office, he'd shown her the ruthless, dismissive and cold businessman. She needed to remember that, brand that image into her mind so when she started to visualize more—a sensitive, burdened man who grieved all that he'd lost—she'd shut that down.

And if that didn't work, remember Laurence Danvers. Remember how she'd spectacularly crashed and burned by almost choosing a man over her career, over her ethics. She'd paid for those errors in judgment, for her willing blindness.

Never again, though.

Returning her attention to Christopher, she finished dinner with a smile and surprisingly entertaining conversation. Charismatic and funny, he effortlessly charmed her, and when the dishes were cleared and the guests headed back toward the reception area for dancing and more cocktails, she accepted his invitation to join him out on the dance floor.

Tilting her head back, she smiled up at him. "Not that I doubt you could enjoy my company, but, call it a reporter's intuition, I just have the sense you didn't seek me out because of my smile. Or this dress. As gorgeous as it may be."

He grinned, his fingers tightening around her fingers. "It is that, but not as beautiful as the woman wearing it." When she arched an eyebrow, he tipped his head back, laughing. And drawing the attention of the couples swaying to the jazz music along with them. "Your reputation for a no-nonsense investigative journalist is well earned, Sophie Armstrong. I did have an ulterior motive when I approached you this evening."

"I'm waiting."

"Our nonprofit is always seeking out new ways to bring in donations and media coverage that will result in even more donations. Funding and philanthropic gifts are this organization's lifeblood," he said, the humor evaporating from his voice and the intensity that had radiated from him since their initial meeting intensified. "I read your article on the Lowell family and Black Crescent. But my particular interest in the piece was the attention placed on Joshua Lowell. The artist submerged, if I remember correctly. It started me thinking. What if the artist reemerged? Returned to the world where he once stood on the cusp of a promising career? Can you imagine the stir and the money that would bring to Tender Shoots?"

Against her will, excitement kindled in her chest. Yes, she could imagine this. All too easily. Maybe not if she hadn't walked along a sidewalk with him and caught the embers of a deliberately banked passion in his eyes, in his words. But Christopher was correct on all accounts. Joshua returning to the art world would be huge—for both the nonprofit and him.

"I agree it would benefit all involved," she replied vaguely. "But what does it have to do with me?"

"I have an admission to make, Sophie," he said, and unlike his playful confession earlier about the seating arrangements, this one caused an unsettling dip in her stomach. "After the article in the *Falling Brook Chronicle*, I researched you. I believe you, more than anyone, can appreciate the need to protect my sources, but despite telling me earlier that you didn't know him, I discovered you were spotted in Joshua Lowell's company several times."

She remained silent, not confirming or denying. But her heart thundered against her rib cage. Though there'd been nothing untoward or illicit about their meetings—*don't even* think *about the kiss!*—just the perception of conflict of interest could be detrimental to her reputation and career. Her original instinct to be wary around Christopher deepened, and she schooled her features into a polite but distant mask.

"I can guess what you're assuming, Sophie, and you're wrong," he murmured, voice gentling. "I don't intend to accuse you of anything or use my information against you or him."

"Then what are your intentions?" she demanded.

"I need your help in convincing him to consider a showing next year. Just because of who he is—the CEO of Black Crescent Hedge Fund—but also because of how he walked away from what critics had predicted to be an important art career."

Before he finished speaking, Sophie was already shaking her head. "I don't know why you'd think I possess the influence to convince Joshua Lowell to do anything, but—"

"Because I've seen how he hasn't been able to tear his gaze off you all evening. And how you've pretended not to notice—when you haven't been staring back at him," he interrupted. "Tell me I'm wrong."

Her pulse was a deafening beat in her ears, in her blood. "You're wrong," she rasped. And hated that her voice held the consistency of fresh-out-the-package sandpaper. "We barely know each other. And even if we were…more acquainted, Joshua Lowell has buried that side of himself. And it would take much more than a few words from me to resurrect it." *But what if there was a chance for him to discover his passion again?* She waved the hand that'd been resting on Christopher's shoulder. To dismiss his request or her own thoughts? Both applied. And anyway, it wasn't her business. Joshua wasn't her business. "I'm sorry, Christopher. I've enjoyed your company tonight, but your efforts on me were wasted. What you're looking for is a miracle, and unfortunately, I'm not in that market."

A sardonic smile curved a corner of his mouth, although his gaze on her remained sharp. Too sharp. "Okay, Sophie. But, if you please, just think about what I'm asking. And if one day you do find yourself in the position to carry influence with him, I and my organization would appreciate it if you would broach the possibility of a show with him. It would help so many students and could very well affect lives."

"Really?" she drawled. "The change-lives card? You're pulling out the big guns."

He chuckled, squeezing her fingers. "I'm nothing if not persistent and shameless."

Thankfully, he dropped the subject. But after their dance ended and she strolled off the crowded floor, a weariness crept over her. She was ready to call it an evening and moved across the room, removing her cell from her purse to place a call to the car service that had picked her up and dropped her off here hours ago. Accepting her thin wrap from the coat check minutes later, she stepped out into the warm May evening. Sounds and scents of the City That Never Sleeps echoed around her—honks, voices carried in the night, exhaust from the passing traffic and the frenetic energy that popped and crackled in the air. There'd been a time when she'd believed her future lay in New York or a busy city like it. But Falling Brook, with its slower pace and smaller population, was home, and she wouldn't want to live anywhere else.

"Leaving so early?"

She shivered as the deep, dark timbre of the voice that held a hint of gravel rolled over her. Vibrated within her. Tightening the wrap around her shoulders, she glanced at Joshua. Several inches separated them, but the distance meant nothing with that stare blazing down at her. Lighting her up. Pebbling her nipples. Wetting the insides of her thighs. Another tremble worked its way through her, and those narrowed eyes didn't miss her reaction.

"Are you cold?" he asked, already slipping out of his tuxedo jacket. The relief coursing through her that he'd misperceived the source of that shiver stripped her of her voice. But Joshua didn't need her answer. He shifted closer and draped the garment over her shoulders. Immediately, his delicious sandalwood-and-rain scent enveloped her, surrounded her as effectively as if it were his arms warming her instead of his jacket.

"Thank you," she finally said, mentally wincing at the hoarseness of her tone.

He nodded. A valet approached them, and Joshua handed him a slip of paper. After the young man strode away, Joshua returned his regard to her, sliding his hands into his pants pockets. "You're ending the evening before it's over?" he rumbled. "Did Christopher Harrison say or do something to make you uncomfortable enough to leave?"

"No," she said, adding a sharp head shake for emphasis. "He was fine. I'm just…tired. And I have a forty-five-minute ride ahead of me. So I'm getting a head start."

"You're driving?"

"Althea arranged a car service for me."

He didn't reply, but the full, sensual curves of his mouth tightened at the corners. He'd had a similar reaction to her editor in chief's name earlier today. As if he resented the sound of it.

"What are you doing out here?" she asked, glancing over her shoulder in the direction of the museum. "From what I saw, you seemed to be having a good time."

And by "good time" she meant the statuesque, gorgeous redhead he'd been seated next to at dinner. The ear whisperer. When she'd left the reception area for the coat check, Sophie had been unable to not take note of Joshua. And he'd stood on the rim of the dance floor, the other woman plastered to his side closer than ninety-nine was to a hundred. God, she sounded bitchy to her own self.

"Were you watching me, Sophie?" he murmured, that dark-as-sin voice dipping lower, stroking her skin in a smoky caress.

"Were you watching me, Joshua?" she volleyed back, just as quietly.

They stared at one another, the challenge they'd lobbied between them vibrating. The air thickened, taut with the tension emanating from their bodies.

"Come home with me."

The request edged with demand struck her in the chest. She locked her knees, but that only prevented her from falling onto her ass. It didn't prevent her mentally wheeling and sprawling in shock. She blinked up at him, felt her eyes widening, and her lips parted on a gasp she couldn't contain.

"What?" she breathed.

"Come home with me," he repeated in that slightly impatient tone that hummed with notes of frustration, anger and even surprise. But not directed at her. Through her rapidly ebbing surprise, she suspected all that emotion was aimed at himself. "I'll take you back to Falling Brook, but come home with me first. We need a place where we can talk openly…privately."

"About what?" she questioned, her heart racing for and nestling in her throat.

"About business that is just between us," he replied, purposefully vague, she suspected. Here, in front of the Guggenheim and anyone walking the Manhattan streets, he wouldn't be more specific than that.

She studied him, her grip tight on her sequined clutch.

Alone with Joshua. For possibly hours. Her mind—and common sense—balked. Absolutely not. The last time they'd been together, within feet of Main Street, he'd shown her the real purpose of her mouth. To mate with his. What would happen without the chance of prying eyes catching them? Without the constraints of being in public? He would probably be able to maintain his intimidating control, but her? She wouldn't advise any Vegas high rollers place bets on her. This man was proving to be her weakness, the chink in her professional and personal armor, and getting close enough to let him chip away more was lunacy.

Yet… She stared into his eyes. And almost glanced away from the coolness there. But at the last second, she looked deeper. And caught the shadows of need, of…loneliness. Both echoed within her, and something inside her reacted to them. Reached for them. For him.

Instinctively, she stepped back and away from him. To protect herself. But not from him. Herself. It'd been this same longing to soothe, to please, to be loved that had led her down the wrong path before. With Laurence, she'd been blind. But now, her eyes were wide-open to who and what Joshua was. And if she traveled this road, she would have only herself to blame for the catastrophic results to her career, her integrity, her heart. And God, she harbored zero doubts he would decimate her heart, leaving not even ashes behind.

"Come with me, Sophie," he murmured, holding out a hand to her as the valet pulled to the curb in a sleek black sports car that even her limited knowledge identified as an Aston Martin.

She stared at that palm with fascination, yearning and trepidation. Yes, she wanted him—what was the point in lying about the plain, bald-faced truth? But her body didn't rule her. Not anymore. If he intended to discuss her help on the paternity issue, they definitely couldn't do it out here on the sidewalk where anyone could overhear. And, her inner reporter chimed in, if he went off the record with her before, maybe he would agree to going back on and be willing to let her get that interview he'd denied her for the original story. Her deadline for the follow-up article was fast approaching.

And maybe she was just trying to justify her reasons for unwisely accepting his invite.

"Okay," she said quietly, slipping her hand over his and locking down the shiver that wanted to ripple through her as his fingers wrapped around hers. "But just for a couple of hours."

He nodded, his intense perusal scanning her face, then dipping down her body before returning to her eyes. Without a word, he escorted her to his waiting car. Within moments, she was tucked against the sinfully luxurious leather seat with Joshua behind the wheel. When he pulled away from the curb and merged with the moderate traffic, she couldn't help but admire the expert manner in how he handled the vehicle. A begrudging but warm throb settled just under her navel. If the man wielded such control over this four-thousand-pound rocket, how much would he exert in other places? Or... What would he look like if he loosened the reins on it?

Not my business, she informed herself with a mental sneer. Turning her attention to her phone, she called the car service back and canceled her ride. Then she settled back against the seat for the forty-five-minute ride back to Falling Brook. Other than asking her if the air was too cold and if she was comfortable, they barely uttered a word. But it didn't matter. The screaming tension crowded into the car with them did most of the speaking.

By the time he guided the car into the underground parking lot of a tall brick apartment building, she practically vibrated with the strain of fighting the desire coiled so tight within her and pretending as if he didn't affect her. Business. This was about the article. About their side investigation. She could keep it professional, because that was who she was.

Pep talk delivered, she didn't wait for him to round the car and open the door, but pushed it open herself and exited. He wouldn't open doors for his colleagues at Black Crescent, so he shouldn't for her, either.

Coward. You just don't want him any closer than necessary.

She flipped her inner know-it-all the finger.

And if she stiffened but didn't shift away from the broad hand he settled at the small of her back, well... She just didn't want to be rude.

Joshua led her to an elevator, and soon they were alighting from it into a huge apartment that could've fit her whole childhood home inside. She couldn't trap the gasp that escaped from her. Just as the charity event had exposed her to another level of wealth and luxury, so did his place.

Gleaming and pristine floor-to-ceiling windows that offered an unhindered and gorgeous view of Falling Brook and beyond. A king surveying his kingdom. The impression whispered through her head, and she had to agree. Shaking her head, she moved farther into the foyer, taking in the rest of his space. An open floor plan that allowed each room to flow seamlessly into the next. A sunken living room, freestanding fireplace, dining room with a table large enough to fit a large family with no trouble, a large kitchen with a floating island, beautiful oak cabinets and what appeared to be stainless steel, state-of-the-art appliances. Because why not? Although, something told her he most likely used the double-door refrigerator for takeout instead of cooking with the wide six-burner stove and oven.

Beyond her stretched a dim but deep hallway, and just off the living room stretched a railless staircase to an upper level. Expensive-looking but comfortable furniture filled the vast space, but there was something missing.

Art.

No paintings decorating the cream-colored, freestanding walls. No sculptures that people often staged on tables or in the wide foyer. Not even a knickknack on an end table. The absence glared at her, and she glanced sharply at Joshua, who remained standing next to her, watching her survey his private sanctuary.

"Let me take this for you." He settled his hands on her shoulders and his jacket that she still wore. Though it was undoubtedly made of the finest wool, it should've disintegrated under the heat from his palms. Grinding her teeth against the inappropriate response, she nodded. "Would you like a drink?" he asked, opening a door behind them and hanging up the jacket and her wrap.

"Sure." She headed toward the living room, where a large and fully stocked bar stood next to the dark fireplace.

"What would you—" His phone rang, cutting him off. He removed it from his pants pocket and glanced at the screen. "I need to take this. Help yourself, and I'll be right back." Pivoting, he headed toward the hallway, pressing the cell to his ear. "Joshua Lowell."

She stared after him for several moments as he disappeared into a room, shutting it quietly behind him. Only then did she move into the living room, releasing a heavy sigh.

A scotch sounded really good right about now.

Before long, she had a finger of the amber alcohol in a squat tumbler, and she raised it to her mouth for a slow, small sip. She hummed in appreciation at the full-bodied, smooth taste as it burned a path over her tongue and down her throat, settling a ball of warmth in her chest.

"Wow, that's good," she muttered, taking and savoring another mouthful.

Grasping the glass between her hands, she headed toward one of the windows and the magnificent and tranquil view. But there was a scattering of papers on the low chrome-and-glass table in front of the couch. How hadn't she noticed it before? The haphazard pile contrasted so sharply with the pristine order of everything else in the room. Hell, the apartment.

Unable to resist the lure it presented, she approached the table. Guilt crept inside her. Joshua hadn't invited her here to snoop. Yet, she still peered down at the papers.

A printout of names and notes written beside each in his heavy scrawl. Women's names. Now, even if God himself came down and admonished her for breaking the eleventh commandment—thou shall not poke thy nose into thy neighbor's business—she still wouldn't have been able not to look.

She recognized some of the names. A high-powered attorney who lived there in Falling Brook. A society darling known for her parties and benevolent efforts. A B-list actress one blockbuster away from catapulting onto the A-list. And about three other names she didn't recognize. But each one had dates typed next to them. Then a handwritten note about whether Joshua had called, made contact and the result.

No baby.
Child but two years old. Not the right age.
Has a little boy. Same age, wrong sex.

Her grip on the glass of scotch tightened until her fingers twinged in protest. Joshua hadn't been idle. This list bore that out. A list that apparently included the names of women he'd been intimate with in the last four years, if the earliest date was an indication. She wrestled down the hot flare of dark and unpleasant emotion that flashed to life in her chest and twisted her belly. Six women wasn't a lot, but damn, she resented each one because they'd experienced the passion he'd very briefly unleashed on her. With grim effort, she refocused on the paper in front of her. Joshua had clearly been working on finding the woman who was supposed to have birthed his child.

Shock and a softer, far more precarious emotion stirred behind her breastbone, melting into her veins like warm butter. Lifting her free hand, she rubbed the heel of her palm over her heart. Since her offer to Joshua on Wednesday to help research more about the DNA report, she'd done some digging. But she kept hitting dead ends.

She wouldn't stop investigating but... Could the DNA results have been mistaken? Either that or Joshua's outrage at her accusation of being an absentee father had been genuine, and he really didn't know he had a child out there. He hadn't left these papers out for her benefit, because he couldn't have predicted they would meet tonight. Briefly closing her eyes, she ran his past reactions in her head like a movie reel. The pain, anger and, yes, grief. Viewed in a different, more objective lens, she had only one conclusion.

She believed him.

"Snooping, Sophie?"

Body jerking in surprise, she tugged her scrutiny from the table to meet Joshua's hooded gaze. So absorbed in what she'd discovered, she hadn't heard him enter the room. But he stood several feet away, head cocked to the side, studying her with an impenetrable expression. Didn't matter, though. The anger emanated from him, sending the guilt in her belly into a tighter, faster tailspin.

"Yes," she admitted quietly. If her honesty startled him, he didn't reveal it. That shuttered mask didn't alter. "I'm sorry. I shouldn't have invaded your privacy."

He didn't reply, his eyes narrowing further. Finally, he closed the short distance between them. But he didn't approach her but headed to the bar and fixed a drink. Turning to face her moments later with a tumbler in hand, he continued to study her, slowly sipping.

"Go ahead and ask," he said, his tone as dark and smooth as the alcohol in his hand. "Don't hold back. Isn't that—" he waved the glass in the direction of the table and papers "—what you're here for?"

"Yes," she replied. It was the reason. At least the least complicated and safer reason. And the only one she wanted to admit to. "From your notes, I'm assuming you didn't find a woman with a child or if she did have one, not a child who was the correct age or gender."

He shook his head, tipping his drink up for another swallow. "No. None of them are behind the email you received or the DNA report. I'm not any closer to finding out the truth about whether or not I have a daughter."

"Is this list…complete?" She hated to ask—part of her didn't want to know the answer. No. More specifically, didn't want to know if there were more names. Not when a kernel of resentment and envy lodged just under her breastbone. But the question needed to be posed.

Joshua stared at her for several seconds before tipping his head back and loosing a hard and loud crack of laughter. But no hilarity laced the jagged edges of it.

"You're asking if I have more pages with a longer list of names hidden somewhere?" he drawled.

"Six women. Four years." She shrugged. And fought

back the hot blast of embarrassment from staining her cheeks. "It does seem a little on the thin side."

"When you're a man in my position, you can't afford to be reckless with women. Especially when your father was a whore." He chuckled. "Come now, Sophie," he mocked. "You didn't come across that bit of information in all of your research?" Oh yes, she had. But her poker face must've been woefully inadequate because he arched a dark brow and downed the rest of the alcohol in his glass in one gulp. Setting the glass on the bar behind him, he cocked his head to the side, a razor-sharp half smile tilting the corner of his mouth. "Of course you did," he murmured. "Well, don't leave me in suspense. Tell me what you dug up on Vernon Lowell's propensity for adultery."

"Joshua," she whispered, her mind, her traitorous heart rebelling at engaging in this.

Not for his father's sake? No, Vernon had been the whore his son had called him. She didn't want to go there for Joshua's sake. Because underneath that taunting, I-don't-give-a-damn tone, his pain echoed like a distant foghorn warning of upcoming danger.

"Don't stop now." The smile sharpened. "Do tell."

Inhaling a breath, she held it. Then slowly released it. He wasn't going to let this go. For some reason, he appeared in a masochistic mood, and was using her as his weapon of choice.

"Vernon was known to have a…" She hesitated, searching those gold-flecked hazel eyes. "Roving eye," she finished. Lamely.

"He fucked anything in a skirt." The bald, flat statement crashed between them like shattered glass. "That is what you were so diplomatically trying to say, correct? He was an unfaithful bastard who betrayed his marriage vows on a regular basis and didn't care if his wife found out. And she did find out. My mother always knew when he found a new mistress. And we—Jake, Oliver and I—all knew because they weren't quiet about arguing over it."

Surprise rippled through her. Vernon had married up when he'd wed his wife. Eve Evans-Janson had been a society daughter with a pedigree that dated past colonial times. Her connections had opened many doors for him. Most people would consider her rather plain in the beauty department, but Sophie had always thought her loveliness exceeded mere looks. From pictures and her own memories, she remembered the other woman carrying herself like a queen. Dignified. Proud. So why would a woman like her accept a husband who cheated so openly without care for her feelings?

"Why would she—"

"Put up with a man who not only couldn't, but wouldn't, keep it in his pants?" he finished in a derisive drawl. "Simple. Comfort. Money. Even though my father did whatever he wanted and refused to give her the one thing she desperately wanted—a daughter—she stayed with him because divorce was embarrassing. Reputation and the image of a perfect marriage and family were vital to her. So she looked the other way in public and cried and raged in private. And… Despite all his selfishness, she loved him. Desperately."

Sadness coiled around her heart and squeezed hard. She should be outraged on his mother's behalf—even angry with her for settling. For not demanding more for herself, for her children. But… Hadn't she been Eve at one time? Hadn't she loved a man so completely she'd been willing to ignore her instincts, look the other way, almost ignore her ethics? The only difference between her and Joshua's mother was she finally walked away and refused to lose her independence to another man again.

Another of those serrated barks of laughter echoed in the room, and Joshua raked a hand through his hair, disheveling the thick blond strands.

"God, why in the hell am I telling you this?" he snarled, turning away from her and stalking across the floor to the window.

The "of all people" didn't need to be said. It bounced off the glass walls, deafening in its silence.

She tried not to flinch. Tried not to allow the hurt to filter through. Tried...and failed.

"I'm not your enemy," she said to his wide back.

His shoulders tensed, but he didn't face her. "And I'm sorry if I implied that you were like your father. I didn't intend to." How to explain it'd just shocked her that such a virile, intense man who oozed power and sexuality had been intimate with only six women in four years? Hell, that didn't even average out to two a year. But given his history, the depths of which she hadn't known until this moment, she understood.

Sighing, she traced his steps and paused beside him, staring out over the beautiful view of Falling Brook at night. Houses, large and small, sprinkled among the trees and interconnecting map of streets, glittering like fairy lights. From this height, the town appeared almost magical. Serene. Made it seem as if they were hundreds of miles away instead of just several floors up.

"What do you see when you look out there?" she asked softly.

Tension and a cauldron of emotion continued to emanate from him, but when he replied, it was just as quietly. "A reminder."

"Of what?" It required everything in her not to glance at him, but to keep her gaze trained on the vista stretched out before them.

"Of why I do this." *Do what? What's* this? The questions bombarded her mind, but she forcibly held her tongue. And her patience was rewarded. "Why I continue to run a company I didn't ask for in the first place. Live this life that was my father's and not my own. For the last fifteen years, I've given it and Black Crescent everything—my dedication, my time, my loyalty, my goddamn soul. And in return? In return, I have a shade of a mother who I am powerless to help. My brothers don't speak to me because they hate who I've become a reflection of. My father is still MIA, and I have no idea whether he is dead or alive. And no matter how hard I work, how many hours I put in, how much money I bring in to repay those robbed and devastated by my father, it's never enough. I'll always be looked at with suspicion, judged for having the same blood in my veins as a criminal."

Her palms itched to touch him. To slide between him and the glass, smooth her hands up his hard chest and strong neck to cup his jaw between them. To, in some way, assume the pain that he wouldn't allow himself to show. But she caught herself, nonetheless. The sheer magnetism of this man dominated any room he stood in. Yet... How could anyone, after spending time with him, not see the emotions that roiled beneath that austere surface like water just under a boil?

"There's this gaping hole in my life," he continued in that gravel-and-midnight-silk voice. "And it doesn't matter what I do, I can't fill it. I don't know *how* to fill it." He shook his head, and he scoffed. "And the funniest, most pathetic part? When you first told me I might have a daughter, a part of me was thrilled. Because it meant that my life hadn't been a waste. That I had a purpose other than rebuilding the legacy my father nearly destroyed. That

I would be more than Vernon Lowell's son. I would be someone's father."

"You're not your father," she contradicted him, taken aback at her own vehemence. Even more so at the knell of truth that bloomed in her chest...deeper. Somewhere between the meeting where he agreed to take her help and finding that list of names, she came to believe him about not knowing he had a child out there. Or even if the child from the DNA report was his. She released a trembling breath, spreading her hand over her suddenly tumbling stomach. "You're not Vernon," she repeated, stronger, firmer.

And maybe he heard the belief in her voice. Because he finally looked at her, his green-and-gold eyes burning down into her. Straight through her.

"You're sure about that?" he ground out. But before she could answer, he turned fully toward her, his palm flattening on the glass above her head. "You were the one who accused me of denying my illegitimate child's existence. Of carrying on and not caring that I had fathered a baby and left it out there somewhere for her and her mother to cope on their own."

Yes, she had. Regret eddied inside her, and she briefly closed her eyes against the oily, slick slide of it. Her article had dragged the scandal out of the past, buffed it up and placed it out all shiny and new for people to feast on again. She had a direct hand in him standing here, surrounded by a darkness that seemed ravenous and ready to swallow him whole.

Her fault. So at least, she owed him the truth. Her truth. Even if he could give two shits about it.

"It's true," she murmured, tipping her head back and meeting his piercing gaze. "I did believe that. But that was before I knew you—"

"You don't know me," he growled.

"That's where you're wrong," she objected, shifting into his space. Surprise flared in his eyes, flecks of gold brightening. But then his lids lowered, gaze becoming hooded and hiding his thoughts. His reaction. But it didn't stop her from claiming another inch. If she took a deep breath, her breasts would brush the wide, solid wall of his chest. The tips of her shoes nudged his, and his scent, so earthy, so virile, so delicious, enveloped her, and she battled the pull of it. For now. "You might be several things—ruthless, proud, arrogant, rude and at times so cold I'm afraid you'll leave burn marks on my skin—but you aren't a deadbeat father. You would never force a child to suffer what you have. Much less one who belonged to you."

He didn't move; his chest didn't even rise and fall on ragged breaths. Like hers did.

"So you're wrong," she said, surrendering to her earlier need and reaching for him. His hand shot out, quick as a snake, and encircled her wrist, his grip firm but not bruising. The dominance of his hold throbbed low in her belly. Her heart thudded against her sternum, but not in fear. Excitement. Need. They both streamed through her, one a sizzling current, the other fierce and liquid hot.

Testing him—pushing him—she lifted her other hand, cupping his face and half expecting him to evade her. But he didn't. He remained still, rigid. Yet, he let her hand mold to the blade of his jaw and the hollow of his cheek. The bristle of his five o'clock shadow abraded her skin, and she logged it as another sensory memory to hoard and savor.

"I know you better than anyone else. More than the people who only see what you permit them to. More than the brothers who left you to fix what was so broken. More than the women you've allowed to touch your body." She traced the curve of his bottom lip with her fingertips. "Does that scare you, Josh?"

She deliberately used the shortened version of his name, increasing the charged intimacy snapping between them like a loose live wire.

With a low rumble, he cuffed her other hand, trapping it against his mouth. His teeth sank into the fleshy heel of her palm, and her groan rolled out of her, unbidden and un-restrained. The flick of his tongue against the same flesh, as if soothing it of the tiny sting, drew another moan from her, this one softer...hungrier.

"No, you don't scare me, Sophie," he said, nipping again at her. "Because that would mean you had the power to hurt me. And I don't trust you enough to give you that power." Tugging on her wrist, he eliminated the negligent amount of space separating them, and she shivered as her breasts crushed his chest, her thighs pressed against his. His erec-tion nestled against her belly. Whatever air remained in her lungs evaporated into vapor at the evidence of his arousal. For her. All for her. "But I want you. As much of a god-damn idiot it makes me, I want to fuck you until your voice is raw from screaming my name. Until you come around me, squeezing me so hard that my dick is bruised. Until my body aches from giving both of us what we need."

Oh. God. Each erotic word stuck her like tiny blows, her sex clenching over and over. Begging for the carnal image he drew. Pleading to be filled, taken, branded. She trembled, harder this time, thankful for the hard body and grips on her hands that held her up.

But doubts and threads of fear wound their way through the fiercely pounding desire. If she were smart, if she'd truly learned from the past, she would halt this...this thing with Joshua before it went any further. At the very least, she could be in danger of losing her job for a serious conflict of interest if anyone found out about this. But not even her career trumped the very real terror of being that woman she'd been with Laurence. Her love for him had turned her into someone she hadn't known, dependent on his approval, his affection, his attention. She'd almost lost everything over him—her career, her future, herself.

She wasn't in love with Joshua, though. The lust turning her into this clawing, biting sexual creature demanding to be satisfied was unprecedented, but that was physical. Chemical. Not emotional.

As long as she kept her fickle, hardheaded heart out of this, she could give her body what it craved and protect herself.

"One night," she said, almost wincing at the note of desperation in her voice. And how he, again, went still, that multihued stare boring into her. But neither made her rescind the condition. "One night," she repeated. "No strings. No expectations. Just two people beating back their demons together."

God, why had she said that last part? It revealed too much.

And Joshua didn't ignore it. Releasing her wrists, he cupped the nape of her neck with one hand and cradled her hip with the other. Holding her. Steadying her. And because it would be only for the night, she allowed herself to lean into his strength. To depend on it.

"You have demons, Sophie?" he murmured, his gaze roaming her face as if already searching out the answer for himself rather than trust her to give an honest answer to him.

Smart man.

"Don't we all?" she countered, and it would've been flippant if not for the rasp betraying the power of hers.

"I'll exorcise them," he growled, pulling her impossibly closer. "We'll exorcise them together."

His mouth crushed hers.

On a whimper, she willingly, eagerly parted her lips for the sweet and wild invasion of his tongue. Impatiently twisted hers around his, dueling, parrying, meeting him thrust for thrust, stroke for stroke. With her hands free, she fisted the lapels of his tuxedo jacket, not caring that she was wrinkling the clothes that no doubt had cost thousands. Nothing mattered except the taste of him, the power of him, the raw passion he whipped to a frenzy in her.

Greedy for more, she rose to her tiptoes, the stilettos she still wore aiding in the endeavor. She opened wider for him, silently demanding he take more, give her more. The hand on her nape shifted upward, tunneling through her hair, twisting, tugging. Tiny pinpricks danced across her scalp, and every one of them echoed in a path down her spine, settling in the small of her back. Restless, she slid her hands up his chest, over his shoulders and into his shorter hair. Clutching the strands, she held him to her, drowning in this kiss that should be either illegalized or memorialized.

Joshua tore his mouth from hers, trailing a scorching path over her chin and down her throat, licking and sucking. She slicked the tip of her tongue over her kiss-swollen lips, savoring the flavor of him on her. Teeth scraped over her collarbone, and she tipped her head to the side, granting him easier access. Her lashes fluttered, lowering, and she basked in each gloriously wicked sensation.

And yet, it wasn't enough.

An urgent need to touch bare skin—his bare skin—riding her, she released him to dive her hands beneath his tuxedo jacket and shove it over his shoulders and down his arms. He straightened, staring down at her from beneath a hooded gaze, letting her strip him. Unable to meet it, she dipped her head, focusing on loosening the buttons down the front of his dress shirt. And as she revealed inch after inch of taut golden skin, all traces of awkwardness vanished. She sighed, fingers slightly shaking, anticipation soaring through her. When she pushed the last button through its corresponding hole, she placed her palms on his corrugated abs, her sigh transforming into a dark, low moan at first contact of skin to skin.

Jesus, did the man harbor a furnace in his big body? Heat simmered underneath her hands, skating up her arms, over her chest and tightening her nipples beneath her dress before flowing farther south to culminate between her wet, trembling thighs. She squeezed them together and shuddered as it only increased the aching emptiness. The desperate need.

"You're so beautiful," she breathed, stroking up his chest and under the open sides of the shirt, slowly peeling it, too, from his body so it tumbled to the floor with his jacket. "Like a work of art."

She stiffened as soon as the words tumbled from her lips and jerked her gaze from his magnificent form to his face. But if her slip caused him any pain, he didn't show it. Or maybe, in this place where they were baring the bodies and just a little bit of themselves, the thought of his former passion didn't bother him.

Or maybe she was assigning more importance, more intimacy to this night of sex than it warranted.

Regardless, he deserved to be admired. To be worshipped. Smooth, tight skin stretched across wide shoulders and chest and down over a flat, ridged stomach. Brown hair dusted across his pecs and narrowed to a silken line that bisected the ladder of abs. Twin grooves lined both hips, disappearing beneath the waistband of his pants. Heeding the call and invitation of that delineated arrow, she followed the lines with her fingertips, dipping beneath the band…

"Slow down," Joshua ordered in a sharp voice that carried a bit of a snap. He emphasized the command by grabbing her wrists and, turning her with his body, pressed her back against the window. Transferring both of her wrists to one hand, he lifted her arms above her head, caging them against the cool glass, as well. It didn't stop her from twisting in his grip, arching toward him. Rolling her hips over the prominent thickness tenting the front of his slacks.

"Dammit, Sophie," he growled.

Then, with a jerk that left her breathless, he yanked down her dress, exposing her breasts to the air, his glittering gaze and, *oh God*, his mouth.

She cried out, her knees close to collapsing as he sucked so hard on her, the pull of it resonated high and deep in her sex. Could she orgasm just from this? Before Joshua, she would've scoffed at the idea of it, but with his tongue curling around her nipple, flicking it, drawing on it—she was a convert. Especially with her feminine flesh spasming, her hips bucking, seeking to grind that same flesh over him…

"Josh," she pleaded, tugging against his hold. "Please. Let me touch you." Yes, she was begging. And didn't care.

He loosened his grip, and she immediately took advantage, clutching his shoulders, digging her nails into the dense muscle. His grunt of pleasure fueled her on, and she raked a path down his back, then surrendered to the need to just…hold him.

Wrapping an arm around his shoulders and the other around his head, she embraced him, savoring the heat of him, the power of him even as he continued to sensually torment her flesh. Tipping her head back against the glass, she released another cry when he switched breasts, treating it to the same attention as its twin. Big, clever fingers plucked at and pinched the damp tip his lips didn't surround. He was driving her crazy. And damn if she wasn't enjoying the trip.

"No, don't stop." The plea escaped her along with a whimper when he dragged his mouth from her breasts down her stomach. She burrowed her fingers through his hair, cradling his head, attempting to pull him back.

"Not done, sweetheart," he murmured, straightening to swing her up in his arms. Once more rendering her lungs incapable of taking in air with both the show of strength and the softly spoken endearment.

They didn't go far. Just across the room to the dark freestanding fireplace. He lowered her back to the floor and, in seconds, had her side zipper down, the dress gone, and leaving her clothed in a skimpy black thong and silver heels. Her toes curled inside her shoes. For several long, charged moments, he stared down at her, his eyes more brown than green. Lust burned in them, throwing more kindling on the same fire razing her to the ground.

"Why do you hide this gorgeous body under those clothes," he ground out, his fingers flexing next to his thighs. "But if I'd known those conservative shirts covered these perfect breasts and lovely nipples… Or had a clue those knee-length skirts slid over these sweet little curves—" he slid a hand over her hip "—and legs created for squeezing a man's hips tight… Or how pretty and wet you would be—" he cupped her, and she swallowed a small scream at the possessive touch "—I would've had you up on my desk the first day you walked into my office, pretty much telling me to go screw myself. Did you know I wanted you then, Sophie? That I was picturing you laid out on top of my files and spreadsheets, your thighs wide, letting me pound inside you until everyone on the other side of that door knew that I was taking you, owning every scream and cry? Owning you?"

Shock rippled through her. At his explicit words and that he'd wanted her as far back as when she'd charged into his office. A tenderness that had no place between them tried to infiltrate the lust, but she battled it back. Self-preservation. She had to keep this about the sex.

Joshua didn't give her an opportunity to respond—if she'd been able to anyway—because he knelt between her legs. After whisking off her shoes, he stroked his hands up her calves, over her knees and palmed her inner thighs. Her breath, loud in her own ears, soughed in and out of her chest as she waited for him to graze the swollen, damp flesh covered by black lace. Air whispered over her but did nothing to cool the heat building inside her, stoked by his words and caresses.

His fingertips danced over her, and with a mewl that would probably embarrass her later, she rocked into the too-light but too-much touch. Sensitive and so deprived, her sex clenched hard, sending a spasm through her. She was ready to beg, to write a freaking formal entreaty, if he would only give her what her body literally wept for when he tugged aside the soaked panel of her panties and plunged a thick, long finger inside her.

She screamed.

And shattered. The release swept through her, over her, the pinched quality of it bordering on pain. It was good. So good. But still not enough. Even as the final waves of orgasm ebbed, the need returned, brewing underneath the blissed-out lethargy.

With a snarl curling his lips, Joshua yanked her panties down her useless legs and spread her wide for him. He dived into her, his mouth covering her still-quivering flesh, his tongue curling around the pulsing button of nerves cresting her mound. He growled against her, the sound vibrating against her, shoving her closer to sensory overload. He lapped at her, sucked, feasted on her in a way that should've been lewd, but instead was hot as hell.

"Josh." His name burst from her, a half shout, half whimper. Pleasure ratcheted from simmering to full-out conflagration. Her fingers drove into his hair, gripping his head, holding him to her. Pushing him away.

Too much.

Oh God, not enough.

He had to stop.

She'd kill him if he dared to stop.

If her mind was conflicted, her body knew what it wanted. What it craved. Her hips bucked and rolled under his mouth, urging him on. Demanding he give her everything he had. And as her lower back tightened and tingled in that telltale sign of impending orgasm, she gasped. Never, as in *never*, had she come more than once. She didn't think it possible for her. But the jerking of her hips, the shaking of her limbs, belied that belief, proving that she just needed the right partner to bring her to the brink of pleasure—and surpass it.

No. Not the right partner.

Joshua.

Another scream built in her throat, scratching its way up when he pulled away. Leaving her aching, throbbing, *hurting* on the edge of release.

"What?" she rasped. "Please." The two words were all she could manage, lust and an aborted orgasm confusing her.

Above her, Joshua surged to his feet. He snatched his wallet from his pants and tossed it on the floor next to her shoulder. In seconds, he wrenched his pants, shoes and socks from his big body, leaving him standing extraordinarily, unbearably beautiful before her. Joshua clothed in suits and tuxedos was gorgeous. Naked, stripped of all signs of civility, was…devastating.

As if drawn to him by an invisible thread, she sat up, rising to her knees, settling her palms on lean, powerfully muscled thighs that flexed under her palms. She sighed, sliding them up the defined columns…reaching for the thick, heavy, long length of him.

"No." His long fingers caught her hand before she could touch him. He knelt between her legs again, pressing her palm to his mouth and placing a searing openmouthed kiss there. "If I let you get your hand on me, this would be over quick. And, sweetheart, when I come, I plan to do it buried balls deep inside you, not on these pretty fingers."

He leaned over her, grabbing his wallet and removing a square foil packet. Quickly, he ripped it open and sheathed himself, then, *thank God*, he was over her, his erection nudging her entrance. Slowly pressing into her. Stretching her. Burning her.

Branding her.

Pain and pleasure mixed in a wicked, confusing blend that sent quakes rippling through her.

"Shh," Joshua crooned, brushing a kiss over her cheekbone, temple and, finally, lips. "Easy, sweetheart. You can take me. All of me." Until his reassurances, she hadn't been aware of the whimpers spilling from her or the restless shifting to get closer, to back away… She didn't know. The pressure of his possession… It filled her almost to overflowing. It overwhelmed her.

For a stark second, panic seized her. In this moment, she felt owned. Not just herself anymore. With him planted so deep inside her, she didn't belong to herself—she belonged to him. To them.

"Look at me, Sophie," he murmured, the soft tone carrying an underlying vein of steel. She couldn't help but obey and opened her eyes to meet his. Golden flames burned in a nearly dark brown field, scorching her. "Do you have any idea how you feel to me? So wet, tight like the most brutal fist but utterly fucking perfect surrounding me, squeezing me. Holding me. It's the sweetest hell. I might be covering you... I might be so goddamn deep I don't know if I can find my way out... But you have the control here. The power. So what are you going to do with me, Sophie? What are you going to do with us?"

His corded arms bracketed her head, and he held his large frame suspended above her, a very fine tremor running through him and belying the gentleness of his voice. And his words. God, they seeped into her, heating her, relaxing her tense muscles, dulling the edges of pain until only the pleasure of his dominance, his possession remained.

She released her grip on his upper arms and, sliding her hands up and over his shoulders, wound her arms around his neck, pulling him down for a slow, raw kiss.

"I'm going to take you. I'm going to wreck us," she whispered against his lips.

Hunger, dark and fierce, flashed in his gaze, but also delight flared bright and quick. Claiming control of the kiss, he pulled free from her body, then sank back inside, dragging a soft cry from her. Lifting her legs, she wrapped them around his waist, and he hissed, surging deeper. Filling her more. Thrust for thrust, she met him, taking him just as she promised. Wrecking them with each roll of her hips, each wet, voracious kiss, each scratch of her nails and whispered demand for "more, harder."

Carnal. Wild. Hot.

Joshua rode her hard, granting her no mercy. He buried himself inside her over and over, setting off sizzling currents with each drag of his cock through her channel. She cried out with the intensity of the pleasure, from the onslaught of it. Twisting and writhing beneath him, she chased the orgasm that loomed so close.

"Josh," she pleaded, desperate, greedy.

"Give it to me, Sophie," he ground out. "Come for me."

He palmed one of her thighs, spreading her wider, lifting her into his thrusting body. Sliding the other hand down between her breasts, he didn't stop until he circled the nerve-packed nub nestled between her folds. Thrust. Circle. Thrust. Circle.

The scream ripped from her throat as she exploded. For a moment, she fought against the release, afraid of the sheer ferocity and wildness of it. But it swelled stronger, swamping her, threatening to break her. Then reshape her into someone she was afraid she'd no longer recognize.

Closing her eyes, she surrendered.

Seven

Joshua stared at his computer monitor, but just like the previous hour, the report from his chief financial officer remained a blurred jumble of numbers.

"Dammit." Disgusted, he threw his pen down on his desk and shot to his feet. His chair rolled back, bumping against the bookcase behind it.

He scrubbed a hand down his face, then wrapped it around the back of his neck. Massaging the tense muscles there, he strode to the floor-to-ceiling window and stared out. Usually, the sight of the parking lot full of his employees' cars sent a surge of satisfaction spiraling through him. There'd been a time after he'd taken over Black Crescent when the lot had been almost empty. Only he, Haley and a few other loyal staff members had remained when the company fell apart. Those days had been…grim. Though he'd kept up a stalwart front for everyone, he'd been terrified. Of failing to rebuild the company and paying back the families his father had devastated. Of letting down those few who'd still believed in and trusted him when his father hadn't given them a reason to.

Of proving those who'd condemned him with "like father, like son" right.

His father. It always came back to him.

But it wasn't Vernon who had him distracted and unable to concentrate this Monday morning. How easy it would be to place the blame on him instead of *her*.

Sophie.

As if just the thought of her name jammed open a door he'd padlocked shut, images from Saturday night rushed through his head, a ceaseless stream of erotic snapshots.

Sophie, hips rolling and bucking to meet his devouring mouth as he held her thighs spread wide for him.

Sophie, twisting and undulating beneath him, voice cracking as she begged him to possess her harder.

Sophie, body arched tight, beautiful breasts pointed toward the ceiling, eyes glazed with pleasure as she came so hard it required every bit of his tattered control to prevent immediately following her.

Sophie, curled up against his side, her head resting on his shoulder, her soft, even breath caressing his damp skin. Her small, delicate hand splayed wide on his chest.

If the mental flashes of her uninhibited passion had his body hardening and arousal clenching his gut, then it was the memory of her cuddled into his body, sleeping so trustingly, that had a vise grip squeezing his heart.

And that grip unnerved him.

One night. No strings. That had been their agreement. The reasons for it—for him, at least—hadn't changed come the morning when they dressed in silence and he drove her home.

She was a reporter who had just done a story on him

and his family. How he'd let his guard down Saturday night and confessed his unhappiness about his life and the jacked-up state of his family even before the scandal still astonished him. That—his penchant to reveal things he'd never told another soul—was her superpower. And his downfall. He'd basically handed her information for her follow-up on him, and if she did write it, he had no one to blame but himself.

What was it about this woman that made him so vulnerable? That had him ignoring every self-protective instinct?

He couldn't do that again. Couldn't afford to. Couldn't afford to open Black Crescent up to any more controversy and couldn't afford to let her in. To open his heart.

Everyone he'd ever loved had abandoned him. His father with going on the lam. His mother by mentally leaving him. His brothers by withdrawing from him, then icing him out of their lives.

No, if she hadn't set the limits on their one night of the hottest sex he'd ever had or believed possible, then he would've.

"Joshua, I've been buzzing you," Haley announced from behind him. He pivoted sharply, bemused. He'd been so deep in thought he hadn't heard the phone intercom or his assistant enter his office. "Where were you just now?"

He shook his head, slicing a hand through the air to wave away her question. "Just going over my eleven o'clock appointment with Clark Reynolds from Venture Investments. What'd you need?"

Haley tilted her head, studying him through a narrowed gaze. She didn't outright accuse him of lying, but the speculation in her hazel eyes did. "Nice try. But deflection has never worked with me. Are you sure you weren't just mooning over Sophie Armstrong?"

He snorted, striding back toward his desk. "I've never mooned a day in my life."

"I know. And that's your problem."

"My problem?" He sank into his chair. "I wasn't aware I had one. Well, other than a bossy executive assistant who doesn't know when to let stuff go."

"Oh, you have one," she drawled, folding into the armchair across from his desk. Leaning forward, her dark blond eyebrows drew together in a frown. "When was the last time your life didn't revolve around this company, the employees or paying back the families affected by the scandal?"

"Haley," Joshua said, stiffening. "I don't—"

"I know you don't want to talk about it. You never do," she cut him off. "That's another problem. You might be the savior of Black Crescent, Josh, but that's not all you are. You deserve more. You deserve to have time to yourself, take a vacation. Leave this place at a decent hour. Have a private life. Yes, you've had relationships in the past, but when was the last time you just let yourself fall for someone? Let them interfere with your carefully regimented schedule and order? Let them make your life messy with laughter and love? I know the answer to all those questions. Never."

Joshua clenched his jaw, trapping the heated words that threatened to burst free. He didn't want to hurt her feelings. Haley might be his assistant, but she was also family. Like his younger sister. But this topic was off-limits. "Haley, I don't want to hurt your feelings. But this is—"

"None of my business, I know. But this—" she stood and set down the tablet she held on the desk, sliding it toward him "—makes it everyone's business."

He stared at her for several moments before dropping

his gaze to the screen. His irritation evaporated, dissolved by shock.

Pictures from Saturday night's art gala. Some depicted him and other partygoers, including the redhead he'd been seated next to at dinner, who'd propositioned him with a nightcap after the event. Those images didn't ensnare his attention or had his heart pounding like an anvil against his chest. Didn't have desire flaming bright and hot inside him.

The photograph of Sophie, so beautiful in the silver strapless gown that had molded to her slim figure and highlighted every curve, and him standing outside the museum had him battling back the surge of lust brewing low in his stomach.

Unlike with the redhead, he'd lost the polite but aloof mask he usually donned at those occasions. Though a small distance separated them, he stared down at her with an intensity—a hunger—that was anything but polite. And Sophie, head tipped back, exhibited a vulnerability that he immediately hated the photographer for capturing.

He tore his gaze away from the image and scanned the caption underneath.

Black Crescent Hedge Fund CEO Joshua Lowell and mystery guest...or date? Could it be the famous—or infamous—businessman is finally settling down?

Flicking a glance to the top of the page, he glimpsed the name of the site. And fisted his fingers next to the tablet. A notorious gossip website that focused on dishing dirty on high society. If he had a dollar for every time his or his family's names had been mentioned in this column, he'd have been able to compensate the bankrupted families years ago, and with interest.

Dammit. Had Sophie seen this? Possibly not. She might be a reporter, but she was also an investigative journalist. Not some gossipmonger.

"What's going on between you and Sophie Armstrong?" Haley asked softly.

He jerked his head up, having momentarily forgotten she stood across from him. "Nothing. She happened to attend the same gala as I did, and we were leaving at the same time. She wasn't my date."

"The columnist mentioned you two left together. That she got into your car," Haley persisted.

Dammit. Anger pulled hard and tight inside him. Fucking media. "I gave her a ride home since we were both headed back to Falling Brook. End of story." If the end of the story included his driving into Sophie's sweet body on a rug that he wouldn't ever be able to walk by again without seeing her coming apart on it.

Haley silently studied him again, her scrutiny too seeing, too knowing. "Neither of your faces say 'casual acquaintance' or 'friendly ride home.'" Before he could snarl a reply, she continued, voice soft, "And I'm glad."

He frowned, taken aback. "You're glad my privacy was invaded and I'm now a topic of speculation and gossip? Again."

Haley straightened, a flicker of emotion rippling across her face. But before he could decipher it, she arched an eyebrow, her eyes direct and unwavering. "No, I'm positively delighted that someone has managed to get through that thick layer of 'back the hell off' that you've wrapped yourself in these past fifteen years. I'm happy that you've found someone that you would let down your guard long enough to be captured by some random photographer. Because whether or not you want to admit it—or are ready to admit it—she *is* important to you. Now I'm just praying that you don't mess it up by pushing her away."

She turned away and strode across his office and left,

closing the door behind her with a quick snick. But her warning reverberated in the room like a report of a gunshot.

I'm just praying that you don't mess it up by pushing her away.

Mess it up? Push her away?

He'd have to let her in first.

And that wasn't happening. Ever.

Eight

What the hell am I doing here?

The question ricocheted off Joshua's skull as he sat in the back seat of his Lincoln town car outside Sophie's apartment building. Showing up here after the photo of them on the gossip site didn't rank among his smartest decisions. If anyone saw him here, it would only feed the fires of speculation. But he'd tried to call her to see if she'd seen it and give her a heads-up if she hadn't. Either she hadn't seen his phone call or she'd refused to answer, because he hadn't been able to reach her.

Logic argued that he leave it alone—leave her alone. But the thought of her being blindsided… Well, here he was sitting outside her home like some kind of goddamn stalker. Growling a curse, he shoved open the back door.

"John, I'll give you a call when I'm finished here," he instructed his driver.

The younger man behind the wheel nodded. "Yes, sir."

Closing the door shut, he stalked across the street and up to the two-story brick building with its neat side lawns and sidewalk bordered by honeysuckle. Just as he approached the door, a couple with a small child pushed through the entrance.

"Oops, sorry 'bout that," the man apologized with a grin. "This one's a little anxious to hit the park."

"No, no, it's fine," Joshua said, stepping out of the way and catching the door before it could close.

But his gaze remained ensnared by the little girl who couldn't have been older than four years old. The same age the child Sophie accused him of having was supposed to be. A sudden longing jerked hard in his chest, catching him by surprise. Years ago, when the world had been his to conquer, he'd wanted what this husband and father had—family.

Now? Now, a wife, a child... They just meant a person had more to lose.

Shaking his head, he moved into the large lobby, letting the door close behind him. An elevator ride later, he stood in front of Sophie's apartment. Before he could again question the wisdom of being here, he knocked. And waited. And knocked again.

Hell. He glanced down at his watch: 6:48 p.m. She should've been home by now, but then again, Sophie had the same work ethic as he did. It was one of the things he admired about her despite her choice of career. So she very well could still be at the office.

He had turned and taken a step away from her door when it opened.

"Sophie," he greeted, running his gaze from the brown-and-gold wavy strands that fell over the shoulders of a purple slouchy T-shirt that hung off one shoulder, down the black leggings to her bare feet with pink-painted toes.

Dragging his perusal back up, he couldn't look at her—not those slender, toned thighs, high, firm breasts or lovely dove-gray eyes—without thinking of how she'd looked, naked and damp from sweat, under him.

"Joshua, what are you doing here?" Joshua, not Josh, as she'd called him for most of those hot, dark hours they'd spent together.

Part of him wanted to demand she call him the shortened version again. And in that sex-drenched, husky voice. Instead, he slid his hands in his pants pockets and kept a careful distance between them.

"I needed to talk with you about something. I'm sorry for dropping by unannounced, but you weren't answering your phone today."

"Yes." She thrust a hand through her hair, drawing the strands away from her face. "I saw the missed calls. I intended to call you back but just got really busy."

He cocked his head. "You make a shitty liar, Sophie."

She dropped her arm, heaving a sigh. "What are you doing here, Joshua?" she repeated.

"I need to talk to you. And not out here in the hallway."

"I—" Indecision flicked in her eyes, her full lips flattening. Finally, after a brief hesitation, she nodded and stepped back. "Fine. Only for a minute, though. I'm working."

Suspicion flared quick and hot in his chest. Was she writing the follow-up article on him? On what he'd revealed to her? He hadn't stipulated that Saturday night had been off the record. Would she...?

He snuffed the thoughts out as he entered her apartment and closed the door behind him. But the embers of doubt... He couldn't extinguish them. How messed up was it that he harbored reservations about her trustworthiness, but he still wanted her with a hunger that gave him stomach pains?

"Can I get you something? I was about to fix a cup of coffee. But I have wine or a bottle of water," Sophie said.

The reluctance in her offer had a corner of his mouth quirking into a humorless half smile. Good manners probably had her extending the courtesy instead of truly wanting him to stick around and enjoy a drink.

So he accepted.

"Coffee is fine."

Again, her lips tightened, but she headed to the kitchen that was separated from the living room by a breakfast bar. Taking the opportunity, he surveyed the apartment. Though on the small side, the living room with its overstuffed couches, wood coffee and end tables and big arched windows appeared cozy rather than cramped. Lived in. Compared with his condo, her place was a home, not a place to just crash instead of the office sofa.

The room flowed into a space that could've been a dining area but Sophie had jammed with filled-to-overflowing bookcases, a tiny love seat and lamps. A reading nook. Easily he could imagine her curled up on those cushions, book in hand.

He tore his gaze away, returning it to her as she finished up the second coffee in the one-cup brewer. Though irritation practically vibrated off her petite frame, her movements were fluid, graceful.

"What are you working on?" he asked, needing to remind himself of who she was. What she did. What she was capable of.

"The follow-up article from my visit to Black Crescent. I need to have it in by the end of the week."

There it was. The reminder. Ice trickled through his veins. Yes, he'd invited her into the inner sanctum of his company and revealed the programs that were close to his heart, but now, tiny pinpricks of doubts stabbed at him over that decision.

"What?" Sophie propped a hip against the counter and crossed her arms over her chest. "Having second thoughts? *You* asked *me* to Black Crescent, remember? This time I didn't force my way in," she drawled.

"I don't need any help remembering…anything," he said, and yes, it made him an asshole to feel hot satisfaction well in him as slashes of red painted her high cheekbones. But he didn't care. Not when she couldn't hide the gleam of arousal in her eyes before abruptly turning back to the counter and the coffee cups.

"Do you take sugar or cream?" she rasped. And the sound of the slightly hoarse tone…

He barely stopped himself from stalking across the space separating them and pressing his chest to her ramrod-straight spine. From notching his hard dick just above the tempting curve of her perfect ass.

"Black," he ground out.

Seconds later, she handed him the mug with Shouldn't You Be Writing? emblazoned along the side along with a picture of a shirtless Thor and his hammer. He would've assumed the choice in cup was by accident if a smirk didn't ride the corner of her mouth.

"Cute," he drawled.

"It's one of my favorites. Nothing but the best for you," she purred, strolling past him with her own plain black mug back into the living room, where her laptop sat propped on the coffee table in front of the couch. "Not that I don't doubt my coffee is wonderful, but what are you really doing here, Joshua?"

The pointed question shoved away any vestiges of humor, and he took a sip of the steaming-hot, fragrant brew before replying. "Pictures of us together from the art gala were posted online in a society gossip column. I didn't know if you were aware. But in case you weren't, I wanted to give you a heads-up. Although you weren't named, the columnist included some speculation about our relationship to one another."

She huffed out a dry laugh. "Oh yes, I already know about it. Althea called me into her office today and asked if anything was going on between us. She's worried about the conflict of interest for the paper if the reporter of the story on Black Crescent is involved with the CEO."

"What did you tell her?"

"I told her no, of course."

"So you lied," Joshua drawled.

If he hadn't been watching her so closely, he might've missed the slight tremble in her hand as she set her mug on the coffee table. But he didn't. And he had to battle back the urge to cross the floor, take that hand, lift it and still the shivering with his mouth.

"It wasn't a lie. There isn't anything between us. Saturday was one night. One time. That was our deal."

"And if I want to renegotiate the deal?" he murmured.

The same shock that widened her eyes reverberated through him. Where had that come from? Asking for another night—another taste of her lips, another chance to drive into that sweet little body—hadn't been his intention when he'd pulled up outside her building. *Warn her, get out.* That had been the plan. But lust had overridden common sense and hijacked his mouth. But he couldn't exist within four feet of her and not crave her. Not want a repeat of the night that was branded into his memory with startling and unnerving clarity. Maybe he just needed to convince himself that his brain had exaggerated the pleasure he experienced. That nothing could be that good in reality.

And maybe he was just seeking an excuse to get her under him again.

He still didn't trust her. Didn't 100 percent believe that she wasn't using him for another story. But none of that stopped his dick from throbbing like a toothache—insistent, hurting and needing relief.

"Joshua…" She shook her head, ducking her head as she pinched the bridge of her nose. "I don't think—"

"Look at me, Sophie," he ordered, setting his cup on the breakfast bar behind him. He moved farther into the living room, not stopping until only inches separated them. She lifted her gaze to his, and her obedience in this when she refused to give it to him anywhere else had excitement and arousal plowing through him. "Look at me and tell me that you're not already feeling my hands on you. Tell me your nipples aren't already hardening, begging for my fingers, my tongue. Tell me you're not already hot and wet for me, desperate to have me stretching you again, filling you." He grasped her chin between his thumb and forefinger, tilting her head farther back. "You can tell me all of that, Sophie, and I'll walk out of here."

Her moist, warm breath broke on her parted lips, echoing in the room. For several long moments, she stared up at him with those molten silver eyes, her slender body swaying toward his, as if seeking his warmth, his possession.

A shudder worked through her, and, lowering her lashes, she stepped back, breaking his hold on her.

Rubbing her hands up and down her arms, she turned away from him. *Give me those eyes. Look at me,* battered his tongue, needing to get out. But he clenched his teeth, trapping the command. Pride imprisoned what sounded too damn close to a plea.

"Is it so easy for you?" she whispered.

He frowned, shifting forward, reclaiming a little of the

distance she'd inserted. It was an unconscious movement, as if his body couldn't stand not feeling her warmth or being wrapped in her scent.

"Is what easy for me?" he pressed.

"This." Pivoting to face him again, she waved a hand between them. "You don't trust me," she said flatly.

"No," he replied, just as blunt. "I don't."

Hurt spasmed across her face, but in the next instant her expression hardened into a cool mask that somehow appeared so wrong on her. Like an ill-fitting dress.

"Then why would you want to be with someone you believe would possibly sell you out for a story?" she scoffed, but a thin line of anger edged the question.

"A relationship with you and fucking are two different things," he said, voice hard, matter-of-fact. "And if that's what you're looking for from me, then we can end this now. I don't do long-term commitments. I'm not the man who can give you the happy home with a perfect, smiling family and well-behaved dog. But I am the man who can make you come so hard it hurts. Yes, Sophie. I'll make it hurt in the very best way," he murmured, lust gripping him so hard, so tight, he could barely draw in a breath. "I don't need to trust you for that."

Her thick fringe of lashes lowered, and her hooded silver gaze razed his skin. Red stained her cheeks and that lush mouth appeared even plumper, bitable. The aloof coldness had evaporated from her expression, leaving this one behind. And he recognized it. This face, stamped with arousal, had haunted his every waking and sleeping hour since Saturday night.

Yet, he couldn't deny glimpsing the flicker of pain beneath the lust.

Before his mind could check him, he took a step to-

ward her to…what? Ease it? Order her to tell him how to
make it disappear?

She shot a hand up, palm out, and he halted.

Thank God.

"I have my own stipulations. I don't have your trust,
fine. But I will have your fidelity. While we're doing…this
arrangement, you don't sleep with anyone else. Just me."

"Of course," he growled. "And the same with you. I'm
the only man inside you."

"Of course," she said, throwing his words back at him
with a snap. "And at any time either of us wants out, it's
over." He nodded, but she continued, "One last thing. This
stays here. No one else knows. Anyone finding out could
cost me my job. I might be losing some of my pride entering into this with you, but I refuse to lose my career."

She murmured the last part of that almost to herself,
and he scowled. What the hell did that mean? Before he
could demand an explanation, though, she stuck out her
hand toward him, the fingertips nudging his chest.

"Deal?" she asked.

He stared down at it, anger and wild, raw need crowding into him. Pride? Being with him stripped her of pride?
What else could he strip her of?

Grasping her wrist, he tugged her hand up to his mouth.
And licked the center of her palm, swirling his tongue over
the soft flesh. Her gasp reverberated around them, and she
tried to curl her fingers into her palm, but he stayed the
motion with his other hand, holding her spread wide for
him. He flicked a wet caress in between each finger before
sinking his teeth into the heel of her palm.

A shudder racked her body, followed by a throaty moan
that had his dick twitching.

"Joshua," she whimpered.

"Josh," he corrected, voice harsh, roughened by the hunger that gnawed at him like a voracious beast. "Say it." He trailed a finger down the elegant line of her throat, tracing the shallow dip in the middle of her collarbone.

"Josh," she whispered, and her swift capitulation was a stroke over his thick, pulsing flesh. And a caress to his pounding heart. She moved forward until her thighs bumped his and her breasts plumped against his chest. He fought to lock down the urge that howled at him to take her down to the floor and claim. Rising to the tips of her bare toes, she brought her mouth a breath away. He slid his tongue out, brushing that temptation of a full bottom lip. "Josh," she repeated, softer, huskier.

In answer, in reward, he took her mouth.

Releasing her hand, he cradled her jaw, pressing his thumb on her chin and tugging down to open her more to him. She tilted her head, complying. Breathing a snarl into her, he thrust his tongue past her lips, rubbing and twisting, coaxing her to play with him. Not that she needed any persuading. She met him, danced with him. Dared him. Nails digging into his shoulders through his suit jacket, she coiled her tongue with his, sucking hard, and the pull arrowed straight to his dick.

A savage, almost animalist burst of lust exploded within him, and he bent his knees to cup her ass in both hands and straightened, hauling her up his body. Her legs wound around his waist, her arms around his neck, settling her sex right over his erection. *Goddamn.* He clenched his molars together, reaching for his rapidly dwindling control. Still, nothing could stop him from punching his hips forward and stroking her up and down his dick. Her thin yoga pants and his slacks might as well as have been created of air. Her folds slipped over him, shooting electric pulses down his spine.

"Bedroom?" he ground out.

"Down the hall," she rasped. "Last door on the right."

In the small apartment, it didn't take long to find her room. With long, impatient strides, he entered and headed straight for the bed. Carefully, he lowered her to the floor, sliding his hands up over her hips, the indents of her waist, the sides of her breasts until he held her face in his hands. Tipping her head back, he stared into her eyes. And though desire rode him like a jockey hell-bent on leather, he paused, seeking any flicker of hesitation, of second thoughts.

"I need to hear you say it, Sophie," he said, his voice seeming to boom in the tense quiet of the bedroom. "Say you want this. You want me to touch you. You want me inside you."

He waited. And he would continue to wait. Because a part of him—the stubborn part that grief, pain and betrayal hadn't managed to amputate—*had* to hear her utter those words. Craved it like a drowning man seeking that life-giving gulp of air.

"I want this. I want you," she whispered, threading her fingers through his hair and pulling his head down until their noses bumped and her lips grazed his. "I want you to touch me. Want you so deep inside me I'll feel you tomorrow. Will you give it to me, Josh?"

He didn't answer her. At least not with words. But with his mouth, his tongue, his hands? God, yes. He dug his fingers into her hips, jerking her closer so she would have no doubts of her effect on him. Unable to help himself, he ground his cock into the softness of her belly, even as he devoured her mouth. And she held nothing back from him. Not her response, not her sexy little whimpers and cries. Had a woman ever fully let herself be so uninhibited, so vulnerable with him before?

No.

And he'd never been that way with another woman.

But with Sophie? Regardless of his claims of not trusting her, he couldn't throw up his protective shields with her. Not in this.

Here, they could be fully honest with each other. Naked in more than the baring of bodies.

Naked. As soon as the word entered his head, the longing, the greed in him intensified until it became a chant in his head.

Tearing his mouth from hers, he fisted the bottom of her T-shirt and yanked it over her head. And *oh God.* "All that time you were offering me coffee and arguing with me, you didn't have a bra on?" he snarled, palming her pretty, firm breasts and thumbing the pink nipples. Already tight, they pebbled further, and Jesus himself couldn't have stopped him from dipping his head and having a taste. And when she tugged on his hair, her groan accompanying the pricks across his scalp, he indulged himself and sucked her into his mouth, lashing the tip. Pulling free, he rubbed his lips across the beaded flesh. "If I'd known you were bare underneath that top, you would've been against the wall with my mouth on you as soon as I closed that door."

He grazed her with his teeth, wringing another cry from her. It became his mission to drag them from her, to earn a shudder from her slender frame. His mission and his pleasure.

While he switched from one breast to the other, Sophie removed his jacket, pushing it off his shoulders and arms, casting it to the floor. His shirt followed. Her nails raked down his bare back, trailing fire in their wake, and it was his turn to shiver.

Releasing her with a soft pop, he straightened, shifting forward and moving her backward until the backs of her knees hit the edge of the mattress. But at the last second, she twisted and, grabbing his upper arms, turned him. They switched positions, and she pressed her palms to his chest, her touch like live coals on his skin.

"My turn," she said, eyes so bright he swept a thumb underneath one. Then brushed his lips over the same spot. "Can't distract me," she breathed, and pushed.

He sank to the bed, his palms slapping down beside his thighs. She didn't hesitate, but knelt in front of him, and his thighs automatically spread, making room for her. His breath hitched in his lungs, and his body froze. Anticipation, lust and excitement hurtled through him, and he could only stare down at this beautiful, sensual creature as she fumbled with his thin leather belt and the closure to his pants.

The metallic grind of the zipper ricocheted through the room, deafening in his ears. She pushed the edges apart, exposing his black boxer briefs. Together, they studied the almost obscene bulge of his thick, long erection. Was she remembering the same thing as he? How he fit inside that too-tight and too-perfect sex? How he'd had to work his way inside her, claiming her bit by bit as she softened around him, strangling his dick even as she embraced it?

Because, God, he remembered. Remembered and wanted it so bad he'd become one huge walking ache.

Finally, when she snagged the waistband, his paralysis broke. He covered her hand with his, squeezing.

"You don't have to do this, sweetheart," he rumbled, offering her an out. Even though the thought of her tongue sliding down his column nearly had him coming without one touch.

"I know I don't *have* to," she said, lifting her gaze from his cloth-covered dick to meet his. "I *want* to."

Then she was gripping him. Stroking him.

Pleasure so sharp it danced on the edge of pain seized

him, and, head thrown back, palms flattened on the mattress, he strained against it.

Nothing, *fucking nothing*, had ever felt as good as this woman's hand on his cock.

Oh damn.

He stood corrected. Hot, wet warmth bathed the head, followed by gentle swipes of a tongue. His head jacked forward, *needing* to take in the sight of Sophie with her mouth full of his flesh.

Locking his muscles, he fought down the ball of fire coalescing and swirling at the base of his spine and lower. God, he was going to come. Right down her throat from just the swipe of her tongue. He closed his eyes but, seconds later, snapped them open, unable to not look. To stare. To behold this picture of knee-shaking carnality and brand it on his brain.

Lashes lowered, color painted her sharp cheekbones and one of those hungry whimpers escaped her as she swallowed him down, tongue rubbing, mouth sucking. Her fist pumped the bottom half of his pounding column, and her damp lips bumped her fingers each time she bobbed over him. Up and down, she tortured him, loving him, making him her slave.

Because right now he would do anything for her if she. Just. Didn't. Stop.

"Sweetheart," he growled, and the endearment was churned-up gravel in his throat. "You're trying to break me with your greedy little mouth. And I'm going to let you do it. I'm going to let you take me apart."

His words seemed to galvanize her, to fuel her passion. Tunneling both hands in her hair and tangling them in the thick strands, he didn't try to control her, just allowed himself to be swept along in the ride.

She took him deeper and deeper until the tip of him nudged the back of her throat.

She let him slip into that narrow passage, swallowed around him.

She elicited shudder after shudder, curse after curse from him.

And when the telltale sizzle snapped and popped down his spine, legs to the soles of his feet and then back up to the base of his dick, he didn't hold back. Didn't pull her off him.

He gave her everything. Every last bit of him.

Chest heaving, he waited for the dark edges crowding his vision to retreat. Only then did he loosen his grasp on Sophie's head and suck in a much-needed breath into his screaming lungs. That orgasm should've destroyed him, laid him out. Instead, it fed the desire that still flowed through him like an open pipe.

He clutched her shoulders and, surging to his feet, dragged her up with him. In seconds, he had her naked on the bed and under him. He attacked her mouth, voracious. The taste of him on her tongue only inflamed him more. Snarling against her lips, he nipped the full bottom one, then treated her chin and throat to the same erotic bites.

Once more he feasted on her breasts, licking, lapping and tweaking until she writhed beneath him, those kitten mewls spilling from her. God, he loved them. Hoarded them in his head so he could replay them later when he was alone in his bed.

He shook his head, dislodging the thoughts and the sharp stab of loneliness they lugged along with them. Skimming his lips down the center of her chest, he paused to flick his tongue in the bowl of her navel, then continued until he reached his goal.

Inhaling, he trapped the musky sweet-and-tart scent

of her. He jerked awake last night with this scent teasing him, tormenting him. Unable to resist the lure, he dipped his head and dived into her sex. One hand splayed wide on her lower belly to hold her down, he palmed her inner thigh with the other, granting him easy access to the flesh that he couldn't get enough of. Her scream danced around his ears as he slid his tongue through her swollen, soaked folds, circling the bud of nerves at the top of her mound. Over and over he returned to gorge on her like the delicious, addictive feast she was.

Her thighs clamped around his head, and her fingers dug into his hair, grasping tight, and he didn't let up. Not until he pushed her right to the edge of release—and over it.

And as she still shook and gasped on the waves of pleasure, he shoved from the bed and stripped. Removing his wallet and then a condom from the billfold, he tossed his pants to the floor and climbed back onto the mattress, crawling over her. Quickly, he sheathed his rock-hard flesh in the protection, then maneuvered her until she straddled his hips. His erection surged up between them, and he swore he could feel her labored gusts of breath on the tip.

"Ride me, sweetheart," he grated, cupping her hip and fisting his dick. "Take me."

Her eyes found his, and, without breaking their visual mating, she rose over him. Then sank down on him.

He was the first to break their locked gazes. Closing his, he released a hiss as she enveloped him, slowly accepting him. Both hands gripped her hips, steadying her. She fell forward, her palms slapping his pecs. Head bent, she pulsed up and down his flesh, taking more and more of him until, finally, she was seated on top of him. And he was so deep inside her, he had to, once more, battle back the rising of his orgasm.

"Sophie," he growled, bucking his hips as if he could screw just a little bit more of himself inside her, when there was nothing left of him to give. "So tight. So wet. So damn hot. I didn't—" He cut himself off before he could utter the rest of the too-revealing sentence. He hadn't imagined how perfect she took him. How she undid him. "You good, sweetheart?" he asked, flexing again, unable to help himself.

"Yes," she breathed, crushing a kiss to his lips. "God, *yes*."

"Take me, then," he ordered. "Take us both."

Lifting off him until only the head of his dick remained, she hovered for only a second before slamming back down on him.

Moments ago, he'd thought nothing had felt as good as Sophie's mouth on him. So wrong. Watching her rise and fall above him, face saturated with lust… Having her lush, muscular core sucking at him, fluttering around him—nothing could compare to this.

Jackknifing off the bed, he sat up, burrowed his fingers in her hair and captured her mouth, swallowing each sob, each whine. Wrapping her arms around his shoulders and head, she rode him, jerking on him, hips swiveling like the most carnal of dances. She wrenched her mouth from his, tipping her head back on her shoulders, lost in the pleasure she chased. The pleasure bearing down on him like a freight train with greased wheels.

Not without her, though. He wouldn't go without her.

Reaching between them, he slid his fingers down her quivering belly to the small, swollen bundle of nerves cresting her sex. One stroke. Two. Three, and he pressed down hard.

Her core clamped down hard on him like a vise grip, feminine muscles milking him. Grabbing her hips, he held her aloft as he thrust up into her, granting her every measure of the release that shook her like a leaf in a passion-whipped storm. Only after her screams ebbed to muted whimpers did he let go, hurtling into the dark, shattering abyss of release.

As he fell, slender arms encircled him.

And he held on.

Nine

Sophie rested her head on Joshua's chest, his steady heartbeat a reassuring thud under her ear. She should move. Should order him to leave since the sex was over, and her senses had winked back online. But her limbs, weighted down by postorgasmic lethargy and wrapped around his torso and thigh, wouldn't obey. Besides, when he'd left the bed to get rid of the condom, he'd returned with a warm, wet bath cloth to clean her. After that tender and thoughtful consideration, it would be rude of her to kick him out.

Okay, and that sounded weak even to her own ears.

She might as well just admit it; she wanted him here in her bed. His weight next to hers. His heartbeat echoing in her ear.

So dangerous. She was entering such treacherous, risky territory.

Saturday night, she'd been so certain that she would be able to contain the passion between them to one night. That she could walk away unscathed.

God, she'd been so arrogant.

He'd left her singed to her soul. And days later, she still felt the burn. So much that when he'd shown up on her doorstep, she'd tried to convince herself again that she could separate physical from emotional. That she didn't need his trust. Didn't need anything but another release that left her feeling like a postapocalyptic refugee.

Closing her eyes, she tried to block out the direction of her wayward thoughts, but that only caused a livestream of how she'd spent the last hour with Joshua. Of their own volition, her fingertips brushed her lips. And she shivered, experiencing again the fierceness of his possession.

He was the first man she'd gone down on. Had he been able to tell? No other had stirred the need to share that intimacy, to make herself so vulnerable. To give so much—her mouth, her throat…her control.

But Joshua wasn't just any man.

Somehow, he'd sneaked beneath her carefully constructed armor and touched more than her body. He'd infiltrated her heart.

Terror barreled through her as she admitted the truth to herself.

And this time, when she squeezed her eyes shut, it wasn't the erotic reel that played over the backs of her lids. It was her, alone, curled up on her couch, hurting. Her, staring at her computer screen staring at an image of Joshua with another woman on his arm. Her, crushed and lost, gazing at her apartment door, willing a knock to sound. For him to be standing on the other side.

Pain cascaded through her in a crimson shower. Pain and fear.

He'd warned her about not wanting a relationship. Straight up told her he didn't want to be in one with her or any woman. But especially not her. He might not have voiced that, but the words had been there, ringing in the room. Not a woman who might betray him or use him for a story. He would never be able to disassociate her from her job. So once more, she faced the decision—love or her career.

Well, she would be faced with that decision if he wanted her for more than sex.

Which he didn't.

But the fear went deeper than his rejection. It reached down to the core of her that dreaded becoming dependent on a man for her happiness, her security. Because when he left, where would she be?

A shell.

"That's the second sigh in as many minutes," Joshua said, his voice rumbling under her ear. He traced a meandering trail up and down her arm, and she savored his touch. Committed this relaxed version of him to memory. "What're you thinking about?"

Of how I'm foolishly falling for you even though I know you will shatter me.

"Actually, I was thinking about you." Not exactly a lie. But sharing the truth wasn't an option.

Tension invaded his body, and she hated it. "What about me?" he asked, the same stiffness coating his question.

Heaving a sigh—her third—she sat up, her hip pressed to his, drawing her knees to her chest and wrapping her arms around them. "While I was working on my follow-up article, it struck me again how much you do for those who are in your employ and this community. All without any expectation of credit or acknowledgment. It's so admirable, and if I could put all of that in bold, font size eighteen, I would. People should know that you're not just a CEO consumed with making money. You're not just another businessman with the 'rich getting richer' mentality. You actually care about people and their welfare and their success."

Joshua rose, resting his back against her headboard, the sheet he'd pulled over them pooling around his lean waist. "I don't do it for accolades or recognition, Sophie. None of that is important to me."

"Isn't it?" she whispered. His hazel gaze sharpened, narrowing on her. Though her heart lodged in the base of her throat, she pushed on. "You might not do it for public consumption, but I suspect personal acknowledgment drives you even more."

A frown creased his forehead, and anger, as well as another unidentifiable emotion, flashed in his eyes. "You have no idea what you're talking about," he snapped.

She should let it go. He obviously didn't appreciate her playing armchair therapist. Especially not from the woman he was just fucking. But she couldn't. Joshua might not want her outside this bedroom, but God, he deserved so much more than this half life he lived. He was too good a man, had sacrificed so much for family and those who had been devastated by the Black Crescent scandal. And if no one else cared enough to tell him so, to let him off the hook he'd leaped on himself, then she would.

"Maybe not. But I know what I've seen. And as I told you before, I know you." Lowering her legs, she curled them under her hips and fully faced him. "Every time you set up a new program assisting those less fortunate than you… Every time you donate to a worthy cause… Every time you make another payment in reparation to the families bankrupted by your father's actions, you attempt to erase a black mark you believe mars your name. A black mark that you didn't put there and isn't yours anyway."

"Sophie, stop," he growled, throwing the sheet back and swinging his legs over the side of the bed.

But she shot her hand out, grabbing his wrist. He could've easily shaken her grip free, but he didn't. Maybe he didn't want to hurt her, and she had no problem taking shameless advantage of that display of thoughtfulness.

She rose to her knees and crossed the small space of the bed until she knelt at his side. Tentatively, she reached for him, her hand hovering above his shoulder. Not willing to back down now, she gently touched him. He didn't jerk away, but he remained stiff, unyielding. A slash of pain lacerated her heart, but she refused to back down.

Not when his happiness could be the casualty.

"You've lived in your father's toxic shadow all these years. When do you come out of it?" she asked softly. "When do you get the chance to live in the sun in your own light?"

"That sounds like a pretty fairy tale, but there is no coming out of it for me. Not as long as my last name is Lowell."

"But what if there is? You have nothing left to prove—you've rebuilt what Vernon almost destroyed. You've repaired your family's reputation with your hard work, dedication and loyalty. You've reimbursed the families your father stole from. What more can you give? Your life...your soul?"

He scoffed, but she didn't let him accuse her of being dramatic, which she was certain had been his next comment. Before he could reply, she slid off the bed and scooped up her discarded shirt from the floor with a "Be right back. Don't move."

By the time she returned moments later with a black binder in her arms, she half expected him to be already dressed and ready to leave her apartment. He had pulled his pants on, but they remained unbuttoned, and he sat in the same place she'd left him.

Relief flooded her, even as fear trickled underneath. Would she be revealing too much when she handed him the binder? Would he see what she so desperately tried to keep hidden?

Inhaling a breath, she crossed the few feet separating them and perched on the mattress next to him. "Here," she whispered, handing him the thick folder.

He glanced at her, his gaze steady and unwavering on her face. Searching. Though everything in her demanded she protect herself from that too-knowing, too-perceptive stare, she met it.

"What is it?" he asked, voice low, intense.

"Look," she instructed instead of answering. "Please."

After another long second, he finally nodded and accepted the binder. Her heart slammed against her rib cage like a wild thing, reverberating in her head and deafening her to everything but the incessant pounding.

Slowly, he flipped the top open.

And froze.

Afraid to lift her gaze to his face—afraid of what she'd glimpse there—she, too, studied the image of one of his mixed-media collages. This one reflected the tragedies of war. With haunting photographs, pieces of metal that appeared to be machinery, newspaper and paint, he'd created a powerful work that, even though it was a black-and-white copy, thrust into her chest and seized every organ. She *felt* when she looked at his art. Anger, grief, fear but also hope and joy. Jesus, how could one man create such raw, wild beauty? How could he walk away from it? Had it been like cauterizing a part of himself? She couldn't imagine…

Silent, Joshua flipped to the next page. A black-and-white copy of a piece commentating on homelessness. Another page. A work celebrating women, their struggle, their suffering, their strength, their beauty. Page after page of his art that both criticized and celebrated the human condition.

When he reached the last copy, he sat there, unmoving, peering down at it, unblinking.

"Why?" he rasped, the first word he'd spoken in the last ten minutes as he perused his past and what had once been his future.

She didn't pretend to misunderstand his question. "When I was researching you and your family for the first article, I came across several stories about you as an artist. From your college and local newspapers as well as several art columns. They carried pictures of your art. And they were so... *Good* is such an inadequate choice. They were visceral. And to think you, Joshua Lowell, had created them..." She shrugged a shoulder. "I guess it became kind of an obsession. I hunted down any image of your work I could find. Finding out about this man who could drag this from his soul and share it with the world? I needed to talk to him, to discover how he'd become a CEO instead of an artist. And that's why I wanted the article to include that side of you. Because I was struggling with reconciling the two."

"That man doesn't exist anymore," Joshua stated flatly. "You're searching for a ghost. He was buried fifteen years ago."

"I don't believe that," she countered. He glanced sharply at her, but she didn't tone down her vehemence. "You might have tried, but he trickles through when you help others follow their own dreams about art. When you support them and give your time and money toward them. If you'd truly put that man aside, he wouldn't help others who need him. That passion to educate people about this world may not have been exhibited in artwork these past years, but you still reveal it in your actions."

He shook his head, and despite the grim line of his full mouth, a tenderness entered his gaze. "You see what and who you want to, Sophie."

"No, I see you. This." She smoothed a hand over the image of his artwork. "This is you. A visionary. An activist and change agent in your own way. An *artist*." She tilted her head, studied his face. "What if your life doesn't end with Black Crescent? What if, after all these years, it's your time to live your own life, the one you left behind for family? A family that you owe nothing to but love and loyalty. You once said you couldn't abandon your family. But then you abandoned yourself. What's the worst that could happen if you followed your own delayed dreams, your own passions? Your mother will be okay and taken care of. And your brothers? If they choose to cut you out of their lives, then that's their problem and issues, not yours. Now's your time. And you never know. Maybe if given no other chance but to step up and assume the mantle of responsibility that you've worn for so long, your brothers might surprise you and do it."

She hesitated. Did she tell him all of it? In for a penny and all that... Inhaling a deep breath, she held it, then exhaled. And leaped.

"I didn't tell you before now, but Christopher Harrison with the Tender Shoots nonprofit approached me about you at the gala. He read my article, saw the pictures of your art included in it. He wants to offer you your own show in Manhattan, at the Guggenheim. Not only to bring in money for the organization, but he would be excited about seeing you reemerge as the artist you were. Are."

For a moment—a quick, heart-stopping moment—a light glittered in his eyes. A light that could've been hope or joy. But then, in the very next, his hazel eyes dimmed. And disappointment squeezed her chest, her heart. He glanced away from her, staring at the far wall as if it revealed precious answers.

"That's not possible, and I'm not interested. You have no clue how it is to live under the weight of society's expectations," he murmured. His fingers curled into a fist atop the binder. But deliberately, he stretched them out, splaying them across the page—covering the image of his art. "You don't understand the burden of always knowing someone's waiting for you to misstep to prove that bad blood will out. It doesn't matter whether I continue to run Black Crescent or pick up a camera or paintbrush again. I can't escape, because I can't evade who I am. Joshua Lowell, Vernon Lowell's son."

She swallowed the silent sob of frustration, anger and grief. Grief for the man who believed he was forever tainted by the actions of his father. Who believed the only road available to him was the one he trod—even if it led to a future that wasn't his.

"Maybe not," she murmured, cupping his cheek and turning his face toward her. "But maybe I can help you bear the burden. Just a little."

Leaning forward, she brushed her lips across his, then covered his mouth with hers. His groan vibrated between them, before he turned, letting the binder fall to the floor, and hauled her up the bed. He took control of the kiss, crawling over her, finding his place between her thighs.

And as he consumed them both with his burning passion, she wept inside for him.

For the both of them.

Ten

"Josh, I'm heading home now," Haley announced from the doorway of his office. "Do you need anything before I leave?"

Joshua looked up from his computer. "No, I'm good."

Nodding, she stepped back, then paused, tilting her head to the side. "Everything okay with you?"

He leaned back in his chair, frowning. Other than a busy schedule and meetings all day, he was fine. He also had plans to meet Sophie at her apartment, so he was actually more than fine. But that, he kept to himself. "Yes, why do you ask?"

"You seem, I don't know—" her hazel eyes narrowed on him "—relaxed this past week. Something up I should know about?"

He snorted. "No, Haley. I'm good, like I said."

"Okay, if you say so."

"I say so."

"Well, not saying I don't believe you, but whatever—or

whoever—has turned you into the Zen version of Joshua Lowell, give them—or her—my thanks." With an impish smile and arched eyebrow, she stepped back and shut the door behind her before he could reply.

"Brat," he muttered, but after a moment, chuckled. Yes, she was definitely the annoying younger sister he never asked for. But he didn't know what he'd do without her, either.

Glancing at the clock at the bottom of his monitor, he nodded. Six ten. Finishing a review of the report his CFO had sent him would take only about fifteen more minutes, twenty tops. Then he could head out.

When was the last time he'd looked forward to leaving his office that had become his second—hell, first— home? Not until Sophie. A lot of things in his life could be separated into two eras. Before the Scandal and, now, After Sophie.

God, when had she become that significant in his life?

The answer blazed bright and sure. From the moment she barged into his office, demanding and so beautiful.

From the release of the article, to her revelation about his supposed child, to her ice-thawing passion and kindness... She'd changed his world.

She'd changed him.

A kernel of fear rooted inside him, and try as he might, he couldn't dislodge it. It'd been there since Monday night after she'd shocked him with the binder full of his previous artwork, and damn near taken him out with her body and the abandoned pleasure she'd offered him.

No one had ever taken the time to look further than the persona he presented. No one had bothered. Except for Sophie. She'd challenged him, as she'd been doing since their first meeting. Daring him to grab ahold of the dreams, the future he'd aborted when his father had disappeared. For a moment, he'd glimpsed what he could have, who he could be through her eyes. And the joy that had spread through him like the brightest and warmest of lights had been stunning. And terrifying.

Stunning because he hadn't felt such happiness in years—fifteen to be exact.

And terrified because he wanted it so badly. His old life back. The opportunity to work in his passion again. The possibility of his own show.

Sophie.

But he couldn't have any of them.

None of them were meant for him.

All he could do was be satisfied with the here and now, because it, too, would eventually end. Sophie would eventually leave him when she became discontented with what he could offer her. What he couldn't give her.

But he knew that going in. Everything ended. Everyone left.

Shaking his head, he frowned, refocusing on the work he had left to finish. But then a notification for an email popped up on the bottom of his screen.

The frown deepened, as did an unnerving sense of dread.

He hesitated, his cursor hovering over the notice. Dammit, what was he doing? It could be anyone. His clients and some of his employees worked longer hours than him. The message could be from any one of them.

Clenching his jaw, he resolutely clicked on the notification.

Anonymous.

Just like the name on the message that had arrived in his inbox yesterday.

Congratulations, Papa! Your daughter can't wait to meet you!

He'd passed it off as some kind of joke. Since no one had contacted him about a possible child, and Sophie hadn't found anything more concrete yet, he'd assumed the DNA test had been a mistake. Or a way to just mess with him by inserting his name at the top. Wouldn't he know, somehow *feel*, if he had a child out there? Though it'd thrown him, he'd ignored the email yesterday…and hadn't told Sophie about it.

But now, he stared at another email from the same person. Disquiet settled over him like a suffocating weight. Trepidation churned in his gut, and his grip on his mouse tightened until the casing squeaked a threatening crack.

He didn't want to open it.

So he did.

Don't know why you're denying it. I paid good money to make sure you'd get the proof.

The words blurred, jumbled together, then leaped into startling clarity. They glared up at him, almost blinding him. Tearing his gaze from the message, he pushed from his chair and stalked across the room, thrusting his fingers through his hair. But he couldn't escape the image branded into his head.

I paid good money to make sure you'd get the proof.

There was only one person who'd brought an illegitimate child to his attention.

One person who'd provided him with the so-called proof.

Sophie.

Anger rolled through him like an ominous storm cloud spiked with bolts of lightning. Hot, heavy, sizzling.

He'd been so stupid. So goddamn blind.

What had been her endgame? Send him on this wild-goose chase, pretend to help him just to get close and what? Write a story on the whole journey? Paint him as some deadbeat? Or a pathetic father on the search for a child who wasn't his? That maybe didn't even exist?

Pain tried to course through him, but he blocked it. Allowed the fury to capsize it.

Fury was better. It razed everything to the ground. Including the fact that he'd started to trust this woman, and he'd been betrayed.

Again.

Sophie stepped off the elevator onto the second floor of the Black Crescent building. Anticipation danced a quick step inside her, and she smiled. Joshua would be surprised to see her there, since they'd planned to meet at her apartment later. But she couldn't wait. She'd finished the follow-up article and wanted to give him the first look at it before Althea saw it Friday morning.

God, this trod so close to her experience with Laurence. She'd made the mistake of granting him the opportunity to read her articles first. But unlike her ex, Joshua wouldn't use this as a chance to sabotage the story or have her change it to fit his needs or agenda. One, Joshua didn't have an agenda. But two, and most important, he wasn't Laurence.

Nerves trotted in her belly, but they didn't trump the happiness spilling through her veins. This week had revealed even more of the man she'd fallen so hard for.

Yes, she could admit it to herself.

She loved Joshua Lowell.

And no, he hadn't rescinded his "no relationships" condition, but he felt more for her than someone to warm his—

or her—bed. She sensed it in his every small but genuine smile, the casual affection, the endearments, in the time he asked to spend with her.

God, did it make her pathetic that she was another woman believing she could change a man?

Probably.

But the knowledge didn't dim her smile as she knocked on his door, then pushed it open.

"Josh," she greeted, entering his inner sanctum. "I know we were supposed to meet at…" She trailed off, taking in the guarded, aloof expression she hadn't seen in a week. "What's wrong? Did something happen?"

She rushed forward to his desk, but drew to an abrupt halt when he rose, that glacial stare not melting or wavering from her face. No, it hardened, and dread curdled in her stomach. What the hell was going on here?

"Josh?" she whispered.

"Joshua," he corrected in an arctic voice that matched his gaze.

Only her hands flattened on his desk kept her from crumbling to the floor. But it couldn't prevent her heart from cracking down the middle and screams wailing from every jagged break.

"What's going on?" she rasped. "Why—"

Without shifting his contemptuous regard from her face, he slowly spun the monitor on his desk around to face her. She dragged her eyes from the stark lines and sharp angles that she'd just traced with her lips the night before and shifted them to the computer screen.

A thread of emails. From an address named Anonymous.

She skimmed them, her horror growing, the slick, grimy strands twisting around the happiness that had filled her only moments earlier, strangling it until only sickness remained. Bile surged up from her stomach, past her chest and raced for her throat. Convulsively, she swallowed it down.

Not because of what the emails stated; she had no idea who had sent them or what they were implying by paying to make sure Joshua had received the DNA test. Because she hadn't received any money. But obviously, just one glance at the anger and disdain in his green-and-gold eyes, and she knew—*she knew*—he believed she had.

The nausea swelled again with a vengeance.

"I don't know what this is supposed to mean," she said, reaching for a calm that had abandoned her the moment she'd stepped into this office. "No one gave me money to give you the DNA results. But you don't believe me," she added, voice curiously flat.

"What, Sophie? I'm supposed to believe you over my lying eyes?" he drawled, eyes snapping fire. "I wondered why you would show me the test when you were so adamant about protecting your research and sources." He loosed a harsh, serrated bark of ugly laughter. "Now I have my answer."

"You really think I would do this? Accept a bribe to trick you into believing you had a daughter?" she demanded, her own rage kindling, burning away the pain. For now. "For what? Why would I do that?"

"You're a reporter, Sophie. I don't know. An editorial piece that could grace the front of your paper might be a very good reason." A terrible half smile curved the corner of his mouth. "How would your editor in chief feel if she knew her star reporter resorted to underhanded tactics just to get a story?"

So much for the anger. Pain, red-hot and consuming, blazed a path through her. She could barely draw in a breath that didn't hurt. But she wouldn't allow him to see it. She'd given him everything—her trust, her faith…her love. And he'd shit over all of it.

No, he'd get nothing else. Most definitely not her tears or her pride. Fuck him.

"I don't know why I'm so surprised," she said, jerking her chin higher. "This is what you wanted. What you were waiting on. And that email is just the convenient excuse."

"Should I know what you're referring to?" he asked, the man who'd made her laugh, made her cry out in the most unimaginable pleasure, gone. And in his place stood the man of ice she'd originally met those weeks ago.

"You're so transparent, Joshua," she murmured, shaking her head. "You've just been waiting for me to screw up. To disappoint you. To leave you. Just like everyone else. But the sad part of it is I wouldn't have. I would've stayed by your side for as long as you asked. Longer. But you can't trust that. You can't possibly believe someone would put you first, would love you enough to never abandon or hurt you."

"Sophie," he growled, but she cut him off with a slash of her hand.

"No. You would rather self-sabotage and destroy what we had, what we could've had if you'd just let me love you and let yourself love. Instead, you would accuse me of something so horrible, so cruel that it's beneath me and definitely beneath you. You're nothing but a coward, Joshua Lowell." She shoved off the desk, silently promising her legs they could crumble later once she was in her car and away from this place, this man. But not now. "You've been running scared for so long that you can't even recognize when someone is running toward you and with you, not from you."

Pivoting, she focused on putting one foot in front of the other and not stumbling. Concentrated on just getting away. Even as part of her hoped, prayed he would call her name. Apologize. Take back the ugliness that had breathed in this office.

But he didn't. And another part of her broke.

As she reached the door, she paused.

Without looking back over her shoulder, she grabbed the doorjamb and stared straight ahead into the dim outer office.

"I love you, Joshua. When I didn't believe in it anymore, you showed me it could exist again for me. I don't regret that. But I do regret that you would rather hold on to the past than my heart. And for that, I pity you."

She pulled the door closed behind her.

Closing it on him…and who they could've been.

Eleven

"Well, if it isn't Joshua Lowell. Slumming it." Joshua glanced up from his whiskey to see a tall, lean but muscular man with dark brown hair and blue eyes sink down onto the stool next to his. "To what do we owe this honor?"

Ignoring the man and his irritating smirk, Joshua returned to his drink and stared blindly at the flat-screen television overhead, where a basketball game he couldn't care less about played. But anything was better than his empty, lonely apartment. Everywhere he looked, memories of Sophie bombarded him. In his living room. On his rug. In his kitchen. In his bed. It'd been only four hours since she'd left his office, her words ringing in the air long after she'd left.

I love you, Joshua... I do regret that you would rather hold on to the past than my heart. And for that, I pity you.

She loved him. How could she? He'd warned her he didn't do relationships. Didn't do happily-ever-afters. She'd called him a coward, but he had his reasons. And they were good reasons. They were…

Damn. He rubbed the bridge of his nose, pinching it, before lifting the tumbler to his mouth for another sip.

Yeah, even boring games, the din of conversation and subpar alcohol was better than the memories as his only company. Still, he thought while he glanced at the guy next to him as he called the bartender by name and ordered a beer, that didn't mean he wanted to be chatted up by a stranger with a chip on his shoulder. That smart-ass greeting had clued Joshua in that this man with his hard eyes and harder smile wasn't a fan of his.

Fuck. He'd come to this bar in the neighboring town for some peace, not more judgment from a drunken asshole.

"I heard the rumor you were here drinking, but I didn't believe it. Daryl, get another round for Mr. Lowell," he called to the bartender. "He looks like he could use it."

"No, thank you," Joshua told Daryl. "I'm good with what I have here."

"What? My money isn't good enough for a Lowell?" he drawled, a steel edge to his question. No, not a question. A gauntlet thrown down on the bar top between them.

Too bad for him, Joshua didn't feel like picking it up. That required too much effort, and he was just too tired.

"Do I know you?" Joshua turned, facing the other man, who seemed vaguely familiar, but his mind couldn't place him. "Because if not, then can you just tell me what your problem is with me so I can go back to my drink?"

A faint snarl curled the corner of his mouth. "Why am I not surprised that you don't recognize me? Why would you? From that lofty tower you rule from, it would be difficult to distinguish between the peasants. Even the ones you had a hand in destroying." Before Joshua could reply, the guy stuck his hand out. "Zane Patterson. Maybe you know the last name, if not me."

Patterson. The whiskey turned to swill in his stomach, roiling. God, yes, he knew that name. It'd been the name of one of the families that had been his father's clients.

"Oh, so I see you do remember." Zane nodded. "I guess that makes you somewhat better than your father, who screwed us over and never looked back."

"Yes, I do, and yes, he did," Joshua agreed, earning an eyebrow arch from Zane. Had the other man expected him to deny the accusation? To defend Vernon. He silently snorted. Not in this lifetime. Or the next, if his father was indeed there instead of lying around some beach surrounded by younger women and mai tais.

"What are you doing here, Lowell?" Zane asked, picking up the beer the bartender set in front of him. Sipping from the mug, he studied Joshua over the rim. "Drowning your woes, maybe?"

"Listen, I understand why you of all people can't stand the sight of me. But I'm here, just trying to have a drink. You can hate me from across the room."

"Still so high and mighty," Zane murmured. "Even after finding out you're no better than the rest of us. Worse, I'd say. You wouldn't catch me abandoning a kid of mine. But like father, like son, I guess."

Shock slammed into him, nearly toppling him from the stool. "What the hell did you just say to me?" he rasped.

A sardonic smile darkened Zane's face. "You heard me. Don't tell me the reporter didn't give you the DNA test results? I specifically chose Sophie Armstrong to share that with."

The shock continued to resonate through him like the drone of a thousand bees, but anger started to rush in like a tide, swallowing it. "You paid Sophie to make sure I received it?" he ground out.

"Paid her? Hell no. It was free of charge. And my pleasure." He again smiled, but it nowhere near reached his icy blue eyes. No, that wasn't correct. They weren't icy. Something volatile and…bleak darkened those eyes. Pain. If Joshua wasn't mired in it, he might not have been able to identify it. "Someone anonymously emailed the results to me," Zane continued, his level voice not reflecting the turmoil he would probably deny existed in his gaze. "And I just passed them along. The test spoke for itself, so I really didn't give a damn who sent them. But whoever it was must've known I wouldn't mind paying it forward. Your father and family destroyed my world, my family." Gravel roughened his tone, and Zane jerked his head away from Joshua. A muscle ticked along his jaw as he visibly battled some emotion he no doubt hated that Joshua glimpsed. After several seconds, the other man returned his regard to Joshua, his expression carefully composed. Too blank. "I was only too happy to return the favor. Everyone believes you're this perfect guy when you have a child out there that you won't even take care of. I can't wait for people to find out just who you really are."

Oh God.

He'd fucked up.

Numb, Joshua turned back to face the bar, Zane's hurt scraping Joshua's skin, his bitter words buzzing in his ears. He'd sent the DNA tests. Free of charge. Sophie had been telling the truth. No one had paid her to show him the results. She hadn't lied to him.

But… He'd known that, hadn't he?

Deep down, where that terrified, lonely and angry twenty-two-year-old still existed, he'd known she wouldn't have been capable of betraying him. She'd been right about him; he was a coward. So scared she would leave him like everyone else he'd loved, he'd jumped on the first obstacle that had presented itself to push her out the door. Save himself the pain of her rejecting him and walking away from him.

Even though he'd known she could never do what he'd accused her of. Not sweet, honorable, honest, strong Sophie. She said that she knew him better than anyone else, but he also knew her. Fear had kept him from acknowledging it in his office, but the truth couldn't be denied. He did know her.

And he loved her.

He *loved* her.

She'd seen beyond his tainted past and who his father was and had accepted him, believed in him, when he hadn't even been able to do the same for himself. She'd seen him as blameless, as a hero for so many people, as an artist with a passion and a dream. Sophie had never given up on him.

Now it was time he didn't. Time he believed in himself. In them.

Setting the drink on the bar, Josh reached into his jacket and removed his wallet. He threw down several bills that covered his drinks and a healthy tip before turning back to Zane.

"I'm sorry my father caused you and your family so much pain. He was greedy and selfish and had no thought whatsoever for who he would hurt. But I was every bit as much of a victim as you were. I lost my family, too. But I refuse to apologize or take on his guilt and shame anymore, though. I've tried to make amends for his sins. But I'm tired of it. I'm done."

Without pausing or waiting to hear what Zane Patterson had to say to that, he pivoted and strode out of the bar.

For the first time in a decade and a half, feeling...free.

* * *

"Dammit," Sophie muttered, jerking the strap of her laptop bag from the car door where it'd snagged. Huffing out a breath, she let it slip to the ground and reached in the back seat for the cardboard box that contained some of her personal items from her desk.

Tears stung her eyes as she scanned the framed photo of her and her mom on vacation at Myrtle Beach a couple of years ago, her favorite "only the strongest women become writers" coffee mug and several other knickknacks. She'd waited until almost everyone on her floor had left for the evening before she packed up most of the items and carried them to her car. Fewer questions that way. Especially since she hadn't yet informed her boss that she was leaving her job with the *Falling Brook Chronicle*.

It'd been her decision, and not one she made lightly.

And not because she feared Joshua would follow through with his subtle threat about informing Althea of being paid to pass on the DNA test. And also not because she was afraid her editor in chief would fire her after finding out she and Joshua had slept together.

No, she was leaving the paper and Falling Brook for herself.

Start over fresh.

Free of memories of Joshua and her own foolishness.

Maybe she'd return to Chicago. Or even go somewhere totally new, like Seattle. She'd visited once in college and had loved the eclectic and vibrant energy of the city...

"Sophie."

No. It couldn't be. Her stubborn, starved brain had conjured up his voice. She squeezed her eyes close, trying to banish it. The last thing she needed was to start imagining him when she was trying to let him go.

"Sophie, please. Can I have just a minute?"

Okay, this was no dream. Even her mind couldn't envision Joshua Lowell saying "please."

She carefully set her box back onto the seat, then pivoted.

And she really should've taken several more minutes to prepare herself for coming face-to-face with him after yesterday. God, it was so unfair. He'd stomped all over her heart. That should wear on a man. He should at least have new wrinkles. Bags under his eyes. Gray hair.

Horns.

But no, he was as beautiful as ever.

Damn him.

"What are you doing here, Joshua?"

"What is that?" he asked instead of answering, his gaze focused on the cardboard box before jumping to her face. "Are you planning on going somewhere, Sophie?"

"That isn't any of your business." Not anymore. Sighing, she shut the rear door and picked up her laptop bag. She'd just come back for the rest of her stuff later. "Now, please answer my question. What are you doing here?"

"I came to see you," he said.

She shrugged a shoulder, moving past him toward her apartment building. "Well, you've achieved that objective, so if you'll excuse me…"

A firm but gentle grip encircled her elbow, and she briefly closed her eyes, thankful her back was to him. He couldn't witness the pain and longing that streaked through her at his touch. She vacillated between ordering him to never put his hands on her again and throwing herself into his arms, begging him to hold her…to love her.

Why, yes. She was pathetic.

Deliberately, she stepped back, out of his hold. Then shifted back even farther so even his scent couldn't tease her.

Pride notched her chin up high as she forced herself to

meet his gaze. A gaze that wasn't cold like the last time they'd been together. No, it was softer, even...tender.

She hardened her heart, made herself remember how he'd accused her of lying to him, betraying him. Made herself remember that he'd cracked her heart in so many fragments, she still hadn't been able to find all the pieces.

"Sophie, one minute. That's all I'm asking, and then if you want me to, I'll walk away and never bother you again."

"Thirty seconds," she shot back. That was what he'd given her the first time she'd bulldozed her way into his office.

As if he, too, recalled the significance, a small smile curved his mouth. "I'll take it." He rubbed a hand across the nape of his neck and moved forward, but at the last second, halted. Respecting the distance she'd placed between them. "Sophie, I'm sorry. I'm so sorry for not believing in you. For accusing you of selling me out. For jumping to conclusions and painting you as the villain. For looking at you through the lens of my past instead of seeing who you really are. You were right about me. I was so scared you would leave me so I used whatever excuse I could to push you away first. I would rather be alone than risk the chance of someone hurting me again, betraying me again. And I punished you for my fears, my shortcomings. I'll never forgive myself for letting you walk out that door believing that I thought you capable of that. I know words are inadequate, but, sweetheart, I'm so fucking sorry."

Her lungs hurt from her suspended breath. His apology reached beneath skin and bone to her bruised and wounded heart, cupped it. Soothed it.

But the words were a little too late. The damage had been done. And she couldn't undo the hurt, the humiliation. The rejection of her love.

Her rejection of herself.

"Joshua, a few years ago, I met a man. Fell in love with him," she whispered. "I didn't know it at the time, but he was using me for his own ends. Not that you've ever done that," she hurriedly added, because of all he'd done to her, Joshua was incapable of that kind of perfidy. It just wasn't in him. "But I almost lost my career—I almost lost myself—because I loved the wrong man. A man who didn't love me in return. I did lose my way, though. And I promised myself I would never give up my job, my independence, my integrity, my soul for another man. The cost was too high, and I wasn't—I'm not—willing to pay it. But standing in your office last night, I found myself on the precipice of doing just that. I may not have betrayed you, but I almost betrayed myself. I won't put myself in that position again. I refuse to." She shook her head, a heavy grief of what could've been for them an albatross around her shoulders. "Thank you for coming here, but I don't need your apology. I know who I am. I know what I deserve. A man who loves and trusts me. Who won't ask me to be less so he can be secure. A life where I can have it all and not feel guilty because I compromised myself to get it."

"You do deserve all of that, Sophie," he rasped, the fierceness in his voice widening her eyes, leaving her shaken. "All of it and more. I—" He took that step toward her that he'd hesitated over moments ago. "I am that man who loves and trusts you. I'd never ask you to be less so I can be secure, because the greater you are, the happier you are, the more successful you are, the better I am as a man. The man who loves and supports you. Compromise? If you compromised who you are, I would never know the joy of having all of you, just as you are. Brilliant, strong, determined, driven, beautiful. Sweetheart—" he tunneled a hand through his hair, disheveling the short, dark blond strands "—you've shown me that I don't have to bear my father's burdens any longer. You've taught me that I'm not forgotten, that I am so much more than I ever believed possible. I thought what happened with my father fifteen years ago was the worst thing that could ever happen to me. But if it hadn't occurred, you wouldn't have written an article on it. You wouldn't have come crashing into my life. And, sweetheart, all the pain, all the fear, all the loss—I'd go through it all again in a heartbeat if it meant meeting you, touching you…loving you." He closed the distance between them and cradled her cheek. "If that box means you're leaving your job, please don't do it. That's a compromise you should never make."

Tears stung her eyes, and she choked on the hope that insisted on rising in her chest. She'd called him a coward yesterday, but now it was her who was terrified. Of being crushed again. Because unlike Laurence, he could destroy her, and though she would find a way to cobble herself together again, she wouldn't be whole.

No, she couldn't.

Not again.

As much as she loved him, she just…couldn't.

"Joshua, I'm sorry. I can't. I love you—I probably always will—but I'm not that strong. I…can't."

She couldn't contain her sob as she cupped his hand and turned her face into it. Kissed it.

Then fled into her apartment building.

Twelve

Joshua stood near the bank of elevators, the animated and excited hum of chatter from Black Crescent's lobby reaching him. Beyond the wall he stood behind congregated reporters and cameramen from the tristate area. All hungry and anticipating the announcement that Joshua had promised to deliver. Anything concerning Black Crescent Hedge Fund would've stirred their interest, but on a Saturday morning, coming from Joshua himself, who never did press conferences, they would've jumped on this tidbit. Just as he'd hoped.

The media expected a business-related statement. And they would receive that.

But so much more.

Joshua's future rode on this press conference.

"Ready, Josh?" Haley asked, laying a hand on his upper arm. Concern and just a bit of sadness darkened her hazel eyes. "Are you sure about this?"

He nodded. "I've never been more certain about anything in my life." He covered her hand with his and clasped it. "And just in case I've never said so before, thank you for everything you've been to this company and to me. Those first few years, I don't know if I would've been able to make it without you."

Tears glistened in her eyes, but, Haley being Haley, she tipped her chin up and cleared her throat. "You're right. You wouldn't have," she drawled.

He chuckled and, giving her hand one last squeeze, moved forward into the throng of media.

At his appearance, the noise reached a fever pitch as questions were lobbed at him from overeager journalists. But he ignored them as he stepped to the podium and microphone, scanning the crowded lobby for one person...

There.

Sophie stood in the middle, lovely and composed.

Relief barreled into him. He'd been afraid she wouldn't show up—had even placed a call to Althea to request Sophie's presence. But that hadn't guaranteed she would've agreed. Seeing her here, though, the anxiety that he'd fought off all morning kicked in the door of his calm. This was the most important moment of his life. Hell, he was fighting for his life—his future.

I love you—I probably always will—but I'm not that strong.

Her words, so final but so weary, echoed in his head. The resolve in her voice had set his heart pounding, terrified he'd lost her. But hope, his love for her and, yes, desperation refused to let him give up. He would go to war for her. He just had to hold on to her declaration of love. And his belief that she was stronger than both of them put together.

"Thank you for coming here today on such short notice," he said into the mic. Immediately, the voices hushed, but the excitement and tension crackled in the air. "I'm going to share my announcement and will take only a few questions at the end."

He inhaled, his eyes once more finding and locking onto Sophie. Her silver gaze met his, and he found the strength to continue there.

"Fifteen years ago, I took the helm of Black Crescent Hedge Fund after my father embezzled money from the company, nearly bankrupting it and devastating his clients and their families. Since that time, I've rebuilt the business and have tried to make reparations for his crimes. But today, I will be stepping down as CEO of Black Crescent."

A roar of disbelief filled the lobby and camera flashes nearly blinded him. Still, he kept his attention on Sophie, spying the shock and confusion that widened her eyes and parted her lips. Questions bombarded him, and he held up his hands, warding them off. Again, silence descended.

"Over the next few months there will be a search for my successor. He or she will be carefully handpicked to replace me as CEO. I'm sure you're all wondering why I'm resigning. I plan to go back to my first love, my art. I gave it up to run Black Crescent, but I've decided to return to it. And possibly—if the woman I'm in love with will agree to marry me—to plan a wedding."

Again, the room erupted. But he cared only about Sophie's reaction, and his heart seized at the shock and tears and…and love. *Please, God, let that be love glistening in her gray eyes.*

"I let my pride and fear blind me and hold me hostage for far too long. And I'm praying that it doesn't cost me her love. I've spent too many years in my father's shadow, worrying what other people thought. If I was worthy enough. But she brought me out of the dark and into the light with her love. And because she loves me, I am worthy. And I want to spend the rest of my life proving that she didn't make a mistake by taking a chance on me. If she'll have me."

He stared at her, silently willing her to let him tell the world her identity. But more, silently asking her again for her forgiveness and her love. Her hand in marriage.

It seemed like an eternity passed as he stood behind that podium, reporters yelling at him, cameras flashing again and again. But still, he caught her nod. Caught that beautiful smile that lit up her face, her eyes and his heart.

"Sophie, will you come up here with me?"

She didn't hesitate, but wound a path through the throng, and like Moses with the Red Sea, they parted, letting her pass. He didn't pay attention to anyone but her. His heart swelling larger than his chest as she neared. And when his hand finally enfolded hers, something inside him that had been hollow, filled. That lost puzzle piece slotted into its place, and he was whole. Complete.

He drew her close, and closer still until she walked into his arms. Bending his head over hers, he pressed a kiss to her hair. A shiver worked through him and he didn't care who saw it. She was in his embrace again. Her scent enveloped him. She warmed him. And God, he'd been cold for so long.

Leaning back, he cupped her face, tipping her head back. The tears he'd glimpsed seconds ago tracked down her face, and he wiped them away with his thumbs, brushing his lips across her cheekbones, the bridge of her nose, her lips.

"Sophie Armstrong, I'm who I was meant to be with you. I was created to love you, and I not only cannot imagine a future without you, I don't want one without you in it. Would you do me the honor of being my wife?"

"Yes, Josh," she said without hesitation and with a certainty and confidence that erased the hurt, shame and pain that had dogged him for fifteen years. "I love you, and there's nothing I want more than to live by your side."

With reporters exploding into chaos around them, he claimed her mouth.

And his future.

* * * * *

SCANDALOUS REUNION

JULES BENNETT

To Michael, Ryan and Christy.
Here's to all of our past distillery tours
and to the ones we've yet to take.
No such thing as too much research!

One

Sam sipped his black coffee and glanced at the stacks of mail on his desk. After being away for three weeks, the piles weren't too bad. His assistant had sorted them between junk and urgent. Sam opted to go with the junk first to get that out of the way.

As he reached for the piece on the top, his cell vibrated on his desk. He glanced to the screen, but didn't recognize the number. He set aside the piece of junk mail and answered his phone, already looking to the next piece.

"Sam Hawkins."

"Sam, hi. It's Maty Taylor."

Maty Taylor. No two words could thrust him faster or deeper into his past than the woman who'd left him brokenhearted...a woman he hadn't spoken to in sixteen years.

Refocusing on here and now, Sam struggled to catch back up to what she was saying.

"...the attorney representing Rusty Lockwood," she went on in her professional tone as if he were a total stranger...as if their intimate bond had been severed forever when she left. "I'm calling to set up a meeting."

Sam's hand froze on the letter addressed to him as he gripped his phone with his other hand.

"Maty."

Just saying her name seemed foreign, yet still so familiar, but he had to say it. He wanted her to nix the stiff tone and talk to him like she would if she ran into him on the street.

"I'm sorry, but did you say Rusty Lockwood? A meeting?" he repeated.

"Yes. I called last week and your assistant said you were out of town, so I wanted to catch you first thing this morning before your schedule got too busy."

Wait...what? Was she for real? Just calling out of the blue on behalf of his main rival and she wasn't even starting with a "Hi, how are you?" All of this was unbelievable, not to mention disappointing. How could she have any dealings with such a bastard?

"You work for Rusty Lockwood?" he double backed to ask, as he was still confused. It was too damn early for this bomb to blow up in his face. His past and present colliding to conspire against him? Oh, hell no.

When he and Maty had parted ways, he'd been in college and she was heading off to law school, set on changing the world. And where had she landed? At the door of the most crooked man Sam had ever known.

What the hell happened to the woman he knew?

"I'm his new personal attorney," Maty answered,

still using that professional, polished voice. "Which explains the nature of my call. I'd like to set up a meeting to discuss my client's generous offer to purchase your distillery."

Sam snorted and dismissed the ludicrous idea. He took a seat in his leather desk chair and opened the next piece of mail.

"Your *client* is well aware that I'm not selling now or ever, so your call and this meeting are irrelevant." He pulled open a handwritten letter and smoothed it out on his desk to read. "Is that all you needed to discuss?"

"Sam," she said, her tone going from poised to nearly pleading. "I'm only asking for five minutes."

Five minutes. He wasn't giving Lockwood five seconds. The man only wanted what he couldn't have, and Sam was tired of playing this game. Sam refused to sell his distillery, and Rusty refused to take no for an answer.

"What the hell, Maty?"

"Excuse me?" Maty gasped.

"How did you get messed up with a man like Rusty Lockwood?" he asked. "He's not a good guy."

Silence greeted him on the other end and Sam shoved the letter aside as he came to his feet, waiting to hear a defense from her side.

"My professional status or my reasoning behind my position are none of your concern," she informed him. "My main focus is getting this meeting set up."

There she went again with that tone. Sam gritted his teeth and clenched his fist at his side as he turned to stare out at the mountainside and the creek running directly behind the distillery. This place was his everything and he'd be damned if he let anyone get their hands on it…especially Lockwood, even if he wanted to do it by way of Sam's ex.

"What the hell kind of game are you playing?" he demanded.

"Game?" she repeated. "I'm not playing any game. I'm simply calling on behalf of my client. Can we meet on Wednesday at one? I'll come to you."

Sam shook his head and laughed. "I'm not meeting you, Maty, but I will give you a piece of advice. Find someone else to work for instead of that bastard."

Sam disconnected the call and slid his cell back into his pocket.

What the hell was going on and what was Maty Taylor doing back in town and working for the devil himself?

Sam wasn't the same love-struck eighteen-year-old he'd been, chasing after the sexy blonde four years his senior. He'd been naive enough to think they'd be together forever. What a joke. She chose law school over him, but looking back, her leaving was the biggest and best life lesson he'd ever had. He'd learned to guard his heart, focus on his career and build his brand.

Sam stared at the pile of mail he still needed to go through. The handwritten letter still sat there, but he didn't care about that. No, his mind was on the woman who'd contacted him out of the blue. He knew full well that wasn't the last time Maty would try. Rusty was a persistent bastard and Maty didn't give up on what she set her sights on, either.

Sam looked forward to seeing her again after all these years. He only hoped she'd prepared herself because he was stronger, more powerful and much more experienced than the last time she'd seen him.

* * *

"Damn it."

Maty muttered her curse, but frustration coupled with fear and anxiety pumped through her. Sam had the nerve to laugh at her and not even attempt to work with her on a meeting. Is that how he conducted all his business?

Even though he'd been a complete jerk, he still had that low, gravelly voice that made every nerve ending stand up. Damn him for still being sexy.

And she knew he was sexy because she had seen enough photos of him over the years, and time had most definitely been kind to him.

Sex appeal or not, he still didn't have to blow off her request like she meant nothing to him. They'd shared a past, yet he couldn't find time to meet with her?

Too damn bad. She had too much at stake to let Sam call the shots. Granted her situation wasn't his fault, but he was the only solution. If there were any other way to save her brother, Maty certainly wouldn't be contacting Sam again. But Rusty couldn't be dissuaded and his blackmail scheme was impossible to get out of so she *had* to get Sam to see her, and then she had to convince him to sell his distillery to Rusty Lockwood.

Giving up wasn't an option, so Maty would just have to go to Sam.

Rusty made it clear, in very certain terms, what her duties were as his new attorney. What she'd have to do to protect her brother.

No, she didn't like being blackmailed, but she had no choice but to do Rusty Lockwood's dirty work. Since coming to Green Valley to work for Lockwood Lightning, the world's largest moonshine distillery, she'd heard rumors of Rusty's bad reputation. He was allegedly skimming money off his employees' donations to a charity for children that he supposedly supported.

Thankfully that was not her area of law so he had other lawyers, likely crooked, handling that ordeal.

No, Rusty had other plans for her, and they were only marginally related to her law experience. He'd tracked her down specifically because of her past with Sam Hawkins.

They'd been in love once, planning a future together, until she'd decided to go to law school and he'd refused to leave Green Valley. They'd had to reevaluate everything and in the end, Maty left town without looking back.

Yet here she was again after a sixteen-year absence, and if she didn't get Sam to sell his distillery, Rusty would stop payments for the care and therapy of Maty's younger brother.

If that happened…well, it just couldn't happen. Maty had no other funds, nobody to help her, nothing to fall back on. She wasn't like Rusty or Sam, both of whom had more money than they knew what to do with. She was truly alone for the first time in her life and more vulnerable than ever.

Maty pulled in a deep breath and smoothed her hand down her black pencil dress. She didn't expect approaching Sam to be an easy task. If getting him to sell his precious distillery had been easy, Rusty wouldn't have needed to enlist her help.

She nearly laughed. He hadn't *enlisted* her help. He'd demanded it. He'd removed her from her other firm in Virginia, and he'd brought her here—going so far as to set her up in an old apartment that he knew held too many memories and making it clear her brother would have all the care he needed so long as she did his dirty work.

Rusty had to have dug deep into Sam's past to find her. She and Sam hadn't had a relationship since college—though she'd never forgotten him.

She'd been four years ahead of him, more eager to jump into the career world, while he'd still been finding his way and dealing with his mother's gambling addiction.

As serious as their relationship had been, as in love as they'd declared themselves to be, so many outside circumstances had wedged between them that eventually the last tie binding them finally snapped.

Maty swallowed the lump of emotions in her throat and forced away the memories. She wasn't that same woman anymore. There was a vast difference, a lifetime practically, between twenty-two and thirty-eight. She'd experienced heartache far beyond that of losing her first love.

Though she'd still wondered about Sam over the years. It would have been impossible to ignore the explosion he had made on the scene here in Tennessee and across the country. The youngest distiller to break one billion dollars in sales in one year and the youngest master distiller in history. She couldn't go to an upscale restaurant or even a pub back in Virginia without seeing his signature bottle behind the bar.

But here in Green Valley? Nothing. The only place you could purchase Hawkins gin, and soon to be bourbon, was at the distillery itself. Rusty Lockwood kept those hard liquor licenses tied up with his moonshine. There was no way to touch the iron-fisted mogul, or his hold on the locals, and Sam was in for one hell of a fight because Maty couldn't fail. She had everything to lose.

Blackmail was a crime, but Rusty was careful not to leave a trail. He was as crooked as they came and she was in the thick of his web now. Her only edge at this stage was the element of surprise. Clearly Sam had been stunned by her Monday morning phone call. She couldn't let the momentum stop. Not only did she need to keep Sam off his game, she had to move before her fears and her memories made her call off this whole thing.

Two

An hour after he hung up with Maty, Sam stood in his office staring at the letter that he'd started to open earlier that morning.

His eyes scanned over it, then read it once more because he was positive this was a joke. Even after dissecting each and every word, he was still just as shocked as he'd been the first time through.

He had questions—so many that he didn't even know where to start. One thing he did know, though, was that he needed to get his emotions the hell under control.

This cryptic letter couldn't have come at a worse time. He didn't believe in coincidences and he was going to get to the bottom of this.

Did Maty know about this letter? Did Rusty? Was Rusty going after him even harder now that the distillery was about to launch its first ten-year bourbon?

He still couldn't comprehend how Maty had gotten tangled up with such a shady businessman.

Hearing her voice earlier had catapulted Sam into the only time in his life where he'd thought everything seemed right. For those few years when they'd been together, he'd let himself believe in a future that he now knew didn't exist.

Granted he'd been naive and in love...but all of that was in the past. He'd certainly learned his lesson in letting people in. People had to earn his trust now and he didn't make it easy for them. But once they were in his inner circle, he did everything in his power to keep them there. Friends and trusted colleagues were invaluable.

Some people who knew his past might believe he had mommy issues, but he'd never trusted his mother, so that certainly wasn't the case.

No, his skepticism stemmed from one honey-blonde, doe-eyed beauty who looked like an innocent, but gutted his heart without any qualms or regrets.

As angry as he'd been at the time, looking back, Sam realized that had she stayed, neither of them would've been happy. They both had dreams and, unfortunately for that inexperienced, naive couple, the main component of those dreams had included successful careers before personal lives.

He'd wanted to hate her that day she left him, but even then, he'd loved her. Maybe he loved her for years afterward, but now... Well, he didn't know her. Did she look the same? Had she gotten even sexier with time? He hadn't looked her up on social media, hadn't wanted to go back in time when he'd worked so hard on moving forward.

His ex coming back into town after so long wouldn't

affect him. She could say or do anything she wanted and that still wouldn't change his answer on selling Hawkins. Sam pushed thoughts of Maty aside and focused on something he could actually control. He needed to figure out how to deal with this life-altering letter that had landed on his desk.

This letter, if what it said was true, changed absolutely everything he'd ever known as the truth.

All those years he'd asked his mother about who his father was and all she'd ever said was that the man was a bastard and they were all better off without him. But there were characteristics Sam had always wondered about. His mother's skin was much darker than his own, so he had always been curious what nationality or ethnicity his father was. Sam also had broad shoulders and a large frame, nothing like his mother's petite build. And the dimple he had beneath his scruffy beard. His mother didn't have dimples.

Little things that always had him wondering.

Was he holding the truth in his hands now? As much as he wanted that chapter of his past closed, he wasn't so sure this was the closure he wanted.

Sam swiped his phone up from his desk and shot off a text to his new acquaintance and friend Nick Campbell, telling him they needed to meet as soon as possible. Not only were Sam and Nick working to bring Rusty down, but Nick was also wrapped up in this untimely letter.

Sam had met the man only a month ago, but their lives were intertwined now.

Sam grabbed the envelope to check the stamped date. Nearly three weeks ago. This must've come just after he'd left for his trip, or maybe even the day he'd left.

Who knew, but clearly his assistant had put this in the junk pile by mistake.

His door flew open and Sam jerked his attention to the interruption. Joe, his loyal assistant, had wide eyes and was shaking his head.

"I'm sorry, Sam, she—"

"Good afternoon, Sam."

Maty Taylor busted through like the whirlwind he'd always remembered. The woman had always been bold, take-charge and confident. Looks like she hadn't changed.

But she had.

Her hair had gotten longer, the curls more prominent, her curves had filled out more, and that bright blue dress did nothing to hide the flare of her hips.

Get ahold of yourself. She's working for the enemy... which makes her an enemy.

Sam came around his desk and focused on Joe. "It's fine. Thank you."

Joe glanced to Maty once more before closing the double doors and leaving the two of them. Sam stood in front of his desk, crossing his arms and casually leaning against the edge. There was nothing casual about this impromptu reunion and Maty looked too damn sexy, too damn striking.

Maybe he should've researched her so he could've prepared himself for the reunion with this walking fantasy. He'd known that she'd show up. She wouldn't settle for another phone call and risk him hanging up. The Maty he'd known was hands-on and never afraid to tackle anything.

Damn, she looked too good and had him remembering too much, too fast.

Good thing his emotional walls had been erected years ago.

Hell, he'd been so naive when they'd first been together, he hadn't even realized he needed walls. He knew now.

Rusty had chosen his latest weapon well, but Sam didn't want Maty, or anyone else, in the middle of this battle. That old bastard was going to lose and he was going to make a damn fool of himself for trying all of these low-down tactics.

"I'm not selling." Sam kept his eyes locked on hers. "You can go back and tell your boss that my answer is the same as it was when his last attorney came to me and when you called me this morning."

Maty took a step forward in a pair of leopard print heels that had way too many fantasies popping into his head—like her on his desk wearing nothing but those shoes.

"Maybe we can find a solution where both parties are happy," she suggested, a soft smile forming over her pale pink lips.

She'd rarely worn makeup when they'd been together. Now she had her deep brown eyes outlined and something sultry was going on with those lashes.

Damn it. Glossy lips and doe eyes shouldn't have his body stirring, but they did…and those damn heels weren't helping.

If he didn't keep his focus, he would succumb to this physical attraction. How could she have such an impact on him in such a short time? He'd dated over the years; it wasn't like he was never around beautiful women.

But Maty was, well… Maty.

She'd always been different and a certain part of his life still belonged only to her.

"All parties involved?" he repeated. "This party is happy just the way things are," he informed her. "If Rusty isn't contented, that's not my problem."

Maty stared at him for another minute before her intense stare darted away, taking in his office. He watched as she made her way to the wall of black-and-white photos he had on display. He'd made somewhat of a timeline of his journey to get where he was today. He needed that reminder each and every day he entered this office, of how hard he'd worked, what all he'd accomplished, to keep him moving forward.

Of course she stopped right at the first photo of him in front of his first home-brewed beer. It had tasted like dirty bath water, but he was damn proud of that mistake. Every failure pushed him to be a better man…including the failure standing there looking like a lethal combination of brains and beauty.

"I remember this picture," she said, throwing him a glance over her shoulder.

Sam said nothing. What was there to say? She'd taken the damn picture, of course she would remember.

Maty had been there at the beginning, through his early experiments. She knew his goal of one day owning a distillery, but at seventeen, that had been so far out of the realm of possibility, he'd never dreamed it would actually happen.

When the silence stretched, Maty turned back around and Sam exhaled. Damn it. He hadn't even realized he'd been holding his breath, but when those eyes landed on him, he became paralyzed. If he didn't get his act together, she might just mesmerize him and take full advantage of his rekindled desire.

No matter what had happened in the past, there was no denying that she was even sexier than he remembered and his body didn't give a damn what had happened to his heart in the past. The ache seemed instant. He had to get her out of here.

When the quiet apparently became too much, Maty moved to the next photo. She crossed her arms and shifted her hips in a way that had his body stirring with unwanted arousal.

"You seem happy here," she murmured, tapping one perfectly polished nail against the glass.

"I graduated top of my class when I had everything stacked against me and my family to take care of."

She flashed him a glance over her shoulder. "Your mother."

Sam nodded. No need in denying the facts. Maty had been around long enough back then to know exactly the type of woman his mother was. All that had changed since Maty left, and now that Sam had money, was his mother always wanted him to bail her out of all her wrong turns.

"You didn't come here to do the whole memory lane thing," he accused, not wanting to delve into the past with her. "But you're wasting your time with anything else."

Now she turned fully, her arms dropping to her sides as she tipped her head. "Maybe I want to catch up," she countered. "Maybe I'm curious what you've been up to these last sixteen years."

"What I've been up to?" He laughed and opened his

arms wide. "Look all around you. What you and Lock-wood want to take from me is what I've been up to."

Taking his heart so long ago wasn't enough? Now she wanted his life?

Because this distillery, these employees, were absolutely everything. He'd worked too damn hard, countless hours, many sleepless nights to make Hawkins a reputable business. Even if Sam died, he wouldn't pass this legacy to Rusty. There was literally no way ol' Lockwood would get his talons on Sam's distillery.

"I'm not looking to steal anything," she volleyed back. "I'm merely here on behalf of my client who is willing to up his asking price. You haven't even heard the number and it may be worth considering."

Sam hated her professional tone. Hated that she was treating him like a regular client. Hated even more that she was tied up with that bastard. But…maybe she'd changed. Maybe she didn't have morals anymore. The girl he'd once loved had been loyal to her family, put her parents and her brother above everything.

Now, she'd drawn a line between them the moment she opted to take up with his rival. He couldn't help but wonder what events over the last sixteen years had led her to make this career decision.

"How's your family?" he asked, turning the tables on her.

Maty's face paled for a second before she tipped up her chin. "My parents were killed in a car accident two years ago. My brother is still in Virginia."

All of his anger and resentment washed away at her statement. He'd loved her family like his own, so the hurt that overcame him was partly selfish.

"Maty, I had no idea," he said, taking a step forward. "I'm sorry doesn't seem adequate, but I am."

Sam forced himself to stop before he did something stupid like reach out and touch her, in a vain attempt at consoling her. He was the one who was shocked. After all, she'd had time to process the loss. Sam had always admired Will and Monica Taylor. They were loving parents, the picture of happiness with their two children who were brilliant and destined for great things.

"So is Carter an attorney, too?"

Maty blinked and spun around to the pictures. "You've had some impressive celebrities stop through here."

When she tapped the photo of a popular country singer holding up a tumbler of gin, Sam took that as his cue to stop any talk of her brother…which made Sam want to find out even more. Maty and Carter had always been close, like best friends. The fact that she was so quick to move on with another topic raised some serious red flags. They would get back to this at a later time—Sam would make sure of it.

Maty finished her perusal of the black-and-white images and blew out a sigh as she made a slow circle of his office. "You've done really well for yourself."

"I don't need your approval."

Sam relaxed against the edge of his desk and crossed his arms as he met her stare across the room. Why did he let her affect him? He'd come a hell of a long way since they were together. He was proud of where he'd landed and where he was going.

"We seem to be getting off on the wrong foot," she stated. "Is it because of the past? Because—"

"My irritation has nothing to do with the past and everything to do with your arrogant client who thinks he can have anything he wants if he whines long enough, like a toddler. He might as well move on. There are other distilleries he could look into acquiring."

"True." Maty nodded in agreement. "But he wants yours."

Sam grunted. "And you just happen, conveniently, to be the attorney assigned to this mission."

Her eyes narrowed. Her lips pursed. What he wouldn't like to do to those lips under much different circumstances.

"Mr. Lockwood is aware of our past if that's what you're asking."

"And he hired you to do what?" Sam pushed off his desk, slowly closing the gap between them. "Did he think I'd meet with you? Maybe we'd start reminiscing like we are now?"

Maty's eyes widened as Sam reached up. With one fingertip, he slid a wayward golden strand of hair behind her ear. Just as silky as he remembered.

"Maybe I'd kiss you, plunge both of us back into the past." He leaned in closer, cursing himself for being a masochist, but he couldn't stop…or perhaps he just didn't want to. "Maybe I'd be so overwhelmed with lust that I'd agree to your terms."

A little closer, his lips hovered within a whisper of hers. She wasn't moving, he was positive she held her breath as her eyes dropped to his lips.

There it was. That same crackling tension they'd always shared. That same invisible string that pulled them together no matter how hard they fought it.

Sam touched her nowhere now, but damn if it didn't take every bit of his resolve to hold himself back. She had some floral scent that he didn't recognize, but it was driving him out of his mind.

"Sam," she whispered.

"Is that what you were hoping for, Maty? A little reunion sex and a closed deal?"

Sam grazed his lips across hers, his entire body tightened with arousal as she gasped.

Get a grip, Hawkins. You're being a jerk.

Gritting his teeth and clenching his fists at his sides, Sam took a step back. Those wide eyes still remained locked on his, but now they were a shade darker...just like they used to be when she was fully aroused.

There she was. That girl he remembered who always gave him every bit of her passion. She never could mask her desire.

Sam cursed beneath his breath and spun on his heel to circle his desk. He needed to put some space, or something substantial, between them. They'd been in the same room for ten minutes and already he wanted to slide that zipper down and see if she still liked lacy underwear.

"Go back to Rusty and tell him even you won't get me to sell," he ordered. "And maybe find yourself a client who isn't crooked, unless you are only in this for the money."

She'd never been about money before, but time changed people. Circumstances changed people. Maybe the death of her parents had done something to that moral compass of hers.

Regardless, these were not his problems and he had a company to run and a gala to prepare for in less than two weeks. He'd been gone for the past three weeks and this was only his first day back. Getting sexually distracted by his ex wasn't the best way to kick off his work week.

Maty smoothed her hair back and pasted on a smile that gave him another punch to the gut. He had a feeling she knew exactly how potent she was. Maty wasn't stupid or naive and he had to ignore her charms or any advances.

"I'll be in touch," she promised. "You might just be given a deal you can't refuse."

As she sashayed out with those swinging hips and honey hair bouncing, that's exactly what Sam was afraid of.

Sam needed a distraction, something to get his mind off the woman who'd just blown into his office and left her mark.

He stared down at his desk, at the letter he'd read earlier. It still sat on top of the envelope. It was rare for someone to write an actual letter these days, and he still couldn't believe that the words were true so he grabbed it, taking a seat as he read.

Sam,
You don't know me and by the time you receive this, I will be gone. My name is Lori Campbell. I'm Nick Campbell's mother. I do not mean to turn your life upside down, but I can't leave this world without giving my son the truth about his paternity, and I'm afraid I need to tell you as well.

Rusty Lockwood is Nick's biological father… something he just discovered. Rusty also fathered two other children and you are one of them.

I'm sorry to tell you this way, but I know my son will need family once I'm gone. He will have no one and I pray he finds someone he can lean on during this difficult time. If you would, I'd like you to reach out to him.

I hope Rusty doesn't cause trouble. I have sent a letter to the other brother as well. I wish you all well.
Lori

He still couldn't process it.

Rusty Lockwood was his biological father? How the hell did this woman know?

Sam was well connected with Nick Campbell now. They'd been acquaintances through the industry for a while, but just in the last month Nick had approached Sam about teaming up against Rusty Lockwood and putting an end to Rusty's local monopoly over hard liquor licensing.

Nick's mother had recently passed away, but Sam never knew her, never heard her name, actually.

Had Nick known Rusty was supposedly his own father? Is that why he wanted to tackle the mogul? Did he know that Rusty was Sam's father? Was that why he'd wanted to partner up?

Sam leaned forward, resting his palms on his desk. He blew out a breath and wondered what the hell he was supposed to do with all this information, all these questions.

Did he go to Nick? Did he stay quiet?

What about his mother? She'd kept this secret his entire life. Anytime he'd asked about his father, she would always say they were both better off without him. Sam had to agree, if Rusty was indeed his father. But how in the hell had his mother gotten involved with such a man to begin with?

Another realization hit him. Did Rusty know about his sons? If he did, had he shared that secret with Maty? Is that why she was back at this time to completely throw Sam off his game?

Between Maty dropping back into his life and working for the enemy, and this cryptic letter, Sam didn't know what to believe. But, one thing was for sure, he couldn't let his guard down.

He had to find out what the hell was going on.

Three

Rusty was blackmailing Maty. That could be the only explanation.

Even though she'd left him without looking back, Sam refused to believe that sweet girl from years ago had completely lost her common sense and turned so dark and unscrupulous that she'd take a job and a salary from Sam's enemy. What was her angle? Why come back to Green Valley and suddenly team up with Rusty after all this time?

Sam had had a full day of meetings and employee reviews that had occupied his time, but now that he'd gotten home and had more time to think, a blackmail scheme was all he could come up with. Not that he wanted Rusty to be holding something over her head, but Sam hated thinking the worst.

Maty had admitted that Rusty knew of her past with

Sam. No doubt he'd used that as the foundation for this game plan, but there had to be more than Maty and Sam's old connection bringing her here. What could Rusty have dangled in front of Maty?

Money? Maybe, but Sam hoped to hell she hadn't gotten that shallow.

As he stepped onto the second-story balcony off his master suite, the cell in his pocket vibrated. Sam shifted his bourbon into his left hand and pulled out his phone.

Nick's name lit up the screen and Sam hesitated for a second. He'd forgotten he'd texted Nick earlier. After that little meeting with Maty and then that damning letter, Sam was still struggling to get his head on straight.

Pulling in a deep breath, Sam swiped to answer the call.

"Hawkins."

"Sam, it's Nick. Sorry I'm just getting back to you. Silvia and I were at the site all day."

Nick Campbell and Silvia Lane had started a working relationship when Nick hired Silvia to be the lead architect on his late mother's mountainside resort. Sam didn't know the dynamics of their relationship, but he did know they were now married and expecting a baby. Everything seemed to be falling into place for Nick now, even after his world had crumbled when his mother passed. Sam had to assume she had written the letter close to her passing, knowing the end was near.

"Is something wrong?" Nick asked. "Your text seemed urgent."

Something wrong? If Rusty Lockwood was his father—*their* father—then yes, something was wrong.

"It is urgent, but I'd rather not discuss this over the

phone." Sam swirled his bourbon around his ice sphere. "Are you free in the morning?"

"This sounds serious."

"It is."

"Then I'm free in the morning," Nick declared. "Should I come to your office?"

"Eight o'clock," Sam confirmed. "My assistant won't be in until nine, so we'll have some privacy."

"Should I be worried?" Nick asked.

Sam had no clue how to answer that. "I just came across some information on Rusty and since we're working together on trying to get that license overturned, I wanted to share this sensitive material with you as soon as possible."

"You've piqued my interest. I'll be there."

Sam disconnected the call and tossed back his bourbon. Yes, the amber liquid should be savored and sipped. Sam wasn't in a savor and sip mood. He wanted hard and fast...liquor or a woman, he didn't care which.

Maty instantly came to mind.

Those curves had filled out even more since she'd been twenty-two. Her body wasn't the only thing that had changed. Her entire personality had shifted. What had once been fun and bubbly now seemed cold and closed off. She was hiding something and Sam should listen to his head and leave her be...but he couldn't. Something held her to Rusty and something, or someone, had her scared. Sam wouldn't want anyone to be in that position, let alone someone he used to care for.

Rusty was clearly using Maty because of Sam, so he couldn't just ignore the situation. Well, he could if he was a cold bastard like Lockwood, but Sam wasn't anything like that man.

The man who could possibly be his father.

Was that even true? He could go to his mother and find out, but she had always been so insistent that she never wanted to discuss his father, saying they never needed him. And she'd been too busy wasting her life at blackjack tables to really care anyway.

Sam was a big boy now—he could more than handle his own and with this letter surfacing, he couldn't just dismiss what could be hard facts.

Sam would confront his mother when he was ready. He was still trying to process everything himself and he had a feeling Nick might hold even more of the puzzle pieces Sam needed.

This alliance they'd already formed weeks ago to bring Rusty down had forged a friendship. But how would Nick react once Sam revealed the letter Lori had sent?

Maty had just taken off her boxing gloves when her phone chimed. She swiped the perspiration from her forehead with the back of her arm and reached for her cell on the window ledge.

The first thing she'd done when she'd moved into this tiny apartment was put up her heavy bag. Some people drank when they were stressed, some ate their feelings, but Maty preferred to punch and kick things. She also enjoyed art, but that was for when she had a calmer frame of mind. Her mood right now was far from calm.

She glanced at her screen and saw Rusty's name. A 7:00 a.m. call from the bane of her existence? Not how she wanted to start her day.

"This is Maty," she answered.

"Miss Taylor, I worried when I didn't hear from you

yesterday," Rusty started. "How did the meeting go with Sam?"

Maty pulled in a deep breath and reached for her water bottle. "We had a good talk."

"Good as in he agreed to the terms?"

Maty forced herself to remain calm. "I warned you going in that he wouldn't agree to anything at the first meeting. Sam loves that company that he's built and getting him to sell will take some time."

"That's something you don't have," he reminded her. "The month will be up before you know it."

As if she needed the recap of the ticking clock. Rusty not only blackmailed her into coming to Green Valley, but he'd given her a timetable that would be impossible to manage given even the best of circumstances…and these were far from great circumstances. Her stress level was at an all-time high; she worried about her mental state. But she worried more about failing her brother who needed the health care Rusty was paying for.

Maty had to jump through every hoop Rusty put in her path. She had to carry out his plans, no matter what she thought of the man or his schemes.

She had come back to Green Valley with every intention of succeeding and facing Sam Hawkins. The meeting with him actually went better than she thought. She managed to be in the room with him without apologizing for leaving so long ago, without throwing herself all over him because he was still the sexiest man she'd ever known, and he didn't claim to hate her. All in all, things could've been worse. Though she did leave with a whole host of brand new fantasies because he'd gotten broader, rougher, edgier. Everything about him exuded power—he was a man not to be messed with.

Yet here she was, doing exactly that.

Maty took a long pull of her cold water. She weighed her words to Rusty as she took a seat on the bench beneath the window.

"Yesterday was the first day," she explained. "You've had other attorneys attempt this bargain and even you yourself couldn't close the deal in several months, so don't expect a miracle on day one."

"I *expect* you to make this happen or you will not like the end result."

Intimidation seemed to be the key component Rusty used to wrap people in his plans. A man like Rusty would use any means necessary to get what he wanted. Likely that's how he'd landed where he was today.

Threats were how he'd gotten her to this point and as strong as she'd always prided herself on being, Rusty Lockwood had found her weak spot and used it to his full advantage. As if her life hadn't been degraded enough, now she had to work for the devil himself.

No doubt Sam thought she had turned into some kind of shark lawyer with only a paycheck in mind. As if she needed to give him more reasons to dislike her. Just the idea that Sam could hate her left a yawning pit in Maty's stomach. Out of all the people in the world, she truly cared what Sam thought of her.

She couldn't blame him for not wanting to sell his distillery, though. Why would he? He'd taken over a floundering company nearly a decade ago and turned it into a huge success. Within the next few years, his brand would be all over the world.

Sam had always had a very detailed dream and he

was living that vision every single day. He sure as hell didn't need the money.

That was the thing about Sam that Rusty would never comprehend. Sam wasn't in this industry for the money. He was here for the passion, the process. He'd always loved creating and studying and learning from his mistakes.

Rusty was about the almighty dollar and how padded his accounts could be, and that would ultimately be his downfall.

Unfortunately, his downfall didn't seem to be coming anytime soon. And Maty had gotten herself caught in Rusty's clenches. Until she could figure out a solution to all her problems—like winning the lottery— she was stuck.

"You were supposed to use your connection to charm him," Rusty added.

Maty clenched her teeth. She wanted nothing more than to have the power and the courage to tell Rusty exactly what she thought of him and this plan. She wished like hell she had the funding to care for her brother, and then she could go back to Virginia and actually live her life.

But she was stuck and she wasn't even sure the end result would turn to her favor. Rusty could end the payments for her brother's care, even if she did get this deal signed. All of this could be for nothing...but she still couldn't give up.

"Despite what you may think of me, or of any other woman you employ, I will not use sex to get what you want." The mere thought made her blood boil and her stomach tighten. "And I haven't seen Sam in sixteen years. Any bond we had is no longer relevant."

"Then make it relevant," he demanded, his voice booming.

Maty closed her eyes and gripped her water bottle, the plastic crackling beneath her fingers. She'd known going into this whole situation that luring Sam in would be an impossible task. But with her brother's care and her own reputation and career on the line, she'd had no choice.

At the end of this nightmare, she was going to have to find a respectable job and she needed to not have a giant black mark marring her name.

"I expect to be notified after each meeting," Rusty added a second before disconnecting the call.

Maty dropped her cell on the bench beside her and took another drink. She eyed her gloves and came to her feet. She might not have proper furniture, but she had a stress reliever and right at this minute, that was the most important thing.

She had to figure out how to keep her brother in the best possible care and convince Sam to give up everything he'd worked for, and she was down to twenty-nine days.

She'd never been more terrified in her life.

Sam opened the main door to the office building and let Nick pass through.

"Thanks for coming in so early," Sam stated, locking the door and motioning toward the hallway leading to his private office. "We can talk back here."

"You've been gone three weeks and you're back a whole day and find out something about Rusty that can't be discussed over the phone." Nick laughed. "That's pretty damn impressive."

Sam's gut tightened with guilt. He hadn't been to-tally up front and once he exposed the letter, he wor-ried how Nick would handle the news. Surely the death of his mother was still so fresh and raw, but Lori had stated she wanted family there for Nick once she was gone. Apparently, that family was Sam.

They stepped into Sam's office and he closed the door at his back.

"I'll get right to the point." Sam crossed to his desk and picked up the envelope. "I received a letter while I was gone. It sat here for three weeks, so I had no clue it even existed."

Nick's eyes landed on the paper, then focused back up onto Sam. "This is about Rusty?"

Sam nodded. "It's from your mother."

"My mother?" Nick's eyes widened, his brows rose. "She left me a letter, too. She said that…"

Silence stretched as Nick's attention remained on the envelope. Sam waited, giving Nick time to process or make the next move. Nick had to know now exactly what this meant for both of them.

After several yawning minutes, Nick took a step for-ward and reached for the sheet of paper.

"Do you care if I read it?" he asked.

Sam handed it over. He kept his eyes on Nick as he unfolded the letter and read. No expression, no sign of what he was thinking or feeling. Nick's eyes got to the bottom before he started over and read through it once more.

Nick dropped the letter to his side. "Do you believe this?" he asked.

"Should I?"

Nick raked a hand over the back of his neck and

stared down at the message once more. "Yeah. You should."

That's what Sam thought he would say. While Sam didn't know Lori Campbell, he doubted the woman had any reason to lie or upend her son's life once she was gone. Sam truly believed she wanted Nick to move on and find some family, and maybe she wanted to stick it to Rusty in the end, too. He couldn't say he blamed her.

Taking a step back, Sam leaned on the edge of his desk and crossed his arms over his chest. He honestly still didn't know how to wrap his mind around all of this.

"I don't know what I'm more shocked about," he stated. "That you're my half brother or that Rusty is our father."

Nick carefully folded the paper and slid it back into the envelope. "The Rusty revelation isn't new to me anymore, but I am surprised that I actually know one of my brothers."

Sam nodded. "It's all so surprising."

Nick nodded. "My mother left me a letter, too. She claimed there were two other boys that Rusty fathered. So now I know you, but there's still one missing. If he received the letter, he hasn't come forward."

"How long have you known?" Sam asked.

"I opened my letter at my mother's graveside."

Damn. That must've been a harsh blow at the worst possible time. But Nick's mom must have wanted these boys to know about Rusty for a reason. Maybe she just wanted to leave this earth with nothing on her conscience. Maybe she didn't want her son to be without family. Sam didn't know the answer, so he had to just move forward with the information he had.

And he was going to have to go to his mother and make her face her past and tell him the truth—as if their relationship through the years wasn't strained enough. He loved her, he truly did. He just didn't like her actions or the gambling habit she couldn't kick.

Sam refocused on the situation before him and vowed to talk to his mother later.

"Did you confront Rusty?"

Nick nodded and rested a hand on the back of the leather chair across from Sam's desk. "I did. You can imagine how that bastard reacted. He wasn't sorry my mother struggled as a single woman raising his child. He didn't even seem surprised that I was his son, actually."

"Are you certain about all of this, though?" Sam asked. "I'm not dismissing what your mother said, but shouldn't we have our DNA tested?"

Nick shrugged. "I don't want to confirm anything. My mother had no reason to lie and turn my life around, plus the lives of two strangers she didn't know. Taking a test won't change the way I feel about him or how he feels about me."

Sam agreed. Lori Campbell had written deathbed confessions and no matter what the truth truly was, that wouldn't change how Sam or Nick felt about Rusty. Besides, it wasn't like the old guy would welcome them into his life with open arms no matter what a test said.

"He's hired a new attorney to get me to sell Hawkins," Sam told Nick. "Maty Taylor. My ex-girlfriend from college."

Nick shifted and sighed. "Creepy that he dug that far back into your past. So how's that going?"

"I have to assume he's using her." The more Sam

thought about this whole charade, the angrier he got. "I'm nearly positive he's using her because she admitted he knew about our connection. We lost touch, but I can't imagine her turning into someone who condones anything Rusty does."

He planned on making an impromptu visit to her later today. Catching Maty off guard might be the only way to get to the bottom of this entire mess. Added to that, he wanted to see her. So what if they'd ended things long ago? Sam was human and she was damn attractive. Beneath that steely, sexy facade he'd noted a vulnerability he wanted to uncover and ultimately protect. She wouldn't like it, wouldn't want him interfering, but too damn bad. If Rusty was in fact doing anything to harm her emotionally, Sam wouldn't just interfere, he'd bust onto the scene and bring Rusty down single-handedly.

"I don't even know what to say." Nick's murmur cut into Sam's thoughts. "Mom mentioned two brothers, but I had no idea if anyone would actually seek me out or even believe what they'd read."

"If I didn't know you and know your current circumstance, I'm not sure I would've believed it," Sam admitted. "I don't doubt you trust all of this to be the truth, but I'm holding out. Not that having you for a brother wouldn't be damn cool, but I sure as hell hope that ass is not my father."

But Sam could tell by the look on Nick's face that he fully believed everything his mother had said.

Sam wanted to hold on to that sliver of hope that Lori was simply mistaken.

"So what now?" Nick asked. "Are you going to go to him?"

Sam had been thinking about that since reading the letter. "No. At least, not right now. I want to wait and see how he plays this game, and I want to know what the hell he's doing with Maty."

"You still care for her?" Nick asked, quirking a brow.

Sam went with straight honesty here. How could he not care? She was the first woman who had ever captured his heart, and maybe she'd kept a piece when she left. Going to her would open up those old wounds, but he wasn't the same man now. He could see her, still appreciate her beauty and tenacity and maintain his distance.

Right?

"I care for the girl I remember. I don't know the woman she is now, but I know that Rusty has no scruples and he'd take any advantage where he saw an opening."

Nick stepped forward and laid the envelope back on the desk next to Sam's hip.

"Do you want to keep that?" Sam asked.

Nick took a step back and shook his head. "No. She meant for you to have it and I have my own letter. I hope we can still work together to team up against Rusty."

"Now more than ever," Sam agreed.

"If you decide to confront him about the paternity issue, I'll go with you."

Sam appreciated that, but at this stage, he had no idea how to handle Rusty or this information. He'd like to have more solid proof than a letter from a deceased woman. But, on the other hand, he didn't want to know.

Above all else, he wanted Maty away from Rusty. Whatever was happening here was about to explode and he didn't want her in the cross fire.

"I should be going," Nick said with a sigh. "Are we meeting at the card game this Friday?"

About a month ago, the two of them had decided to crash the good ol' boys' poker game at the local pub, Rogue Wingman. Every Friday, Rusty and a bunch of his city council cronies meet for hours of gaming and Nick had asked Sam to join him to break into the game. The united front had startled Rusty and had gotten the attention of the council members. The moonshine king wasn't the only high roller in this area and younger, smarter crews were moving in.

Sam was sure there was some poetic justice here, seeing that it was Rusty's own sons, sons he'd supposedly abandoned, who would likely bring him down. If only they knew who the third party was and if he even knew the name Rusty Lockwood, then maybe Sam and Nick would have another ally.

"I'll be there," Sam told him. "But can we keep this letter and everything under wraps for now?"

"Ashamed of being my brother already?" Nick joked.

"That's the only part I'm ready to believe is true," Sam corrected. "I just want to figure out what move to make regarding Maty and Rusty. I have to keep the upper hand for as long as I can."

Nick nodded. "I understand. I did the same thing."

After Nick left, Sam went back to his desk and stared at the letter. His past and his future were colliding. He had to be very careful about what step he took next because he wasn't going to fall into some seduction trap and lose everything he'd worked for his entire life.

But he also wasn't stupid or naive. Seeing Maty again, even after all the time that had wedged between them, only dredged up each and every spark of desire he'd ever had for her. Only that desire was ten times stronger now. Her determination combined with those new curves drew him to her even more than he would've thought possible.

How could he keep his distance? How could he ignore the pull?

He had an enemy to fight and a business to protect and the woman he wanted more than anything might just disrupt all of his plans.

Four

Maty turned down the drive lined with evergreens, surprised there weren't armed guards or something just as over-the-top to keep out unwanted guests.

Thankfully she didn't have an obstacle to get through to get to Sam's house. It hadn't taken much effort to get his address, but she thought for sure there would be a gate at the very least.

Maty was also surprised to find he didn't have a mountaintop home. He lived down in the valley with a pond and decades-old trees all around, providing privacy…not to mention this forever-long driveway.

Finally, an opening in the trees gave way to a breathtaking three-story stone-and-log home. So very fitting for the Smoky Mountains and the surrounding areas. Not to mention very fitting for a man as powerful and strong as Sam. He would live in some place that was dominating and demanded attention.

Sturdy porch swings were suspended from each end and two rockers sat near the front double doors. The landscaping provided variations of greenery and a splash of color here and there. The entire place looked like something from a magazine and she could only imagine the inside. She already knew she'd be sketching this masterpiece later when she got back home.

Home. The run-down apartment that she hated staying in. She hated the memories from each room and if Sam ever found out where Rusty had put her…

Well, he couldn't find out.

Rusty had given her a lease in this apartment complex, in the exact same apartment where Sam had once lived. Everything Rusty did was methodical and deliberate.

Nerves curled through her. Coming to Sam's home was a bold, yet necessary move. She had to appeal to his personal side, not so much the business side. That's how Sam had always operated in the past, through feelings and emotions, so she had to assume he hadn't changed that much. If he wasn't even entertaining Rusty's very generous monetary offers, then Sam's distillery was very personal…a point she'd tried to make to Rusty, but her words had fallen on stubborn, deaf ears.

After she pulled her car around the circular drive, Maty parked in front of the steps leading up to the wide, welcoming porch and large mahogany doors. She'd known Sam would have a magnificent home, but she'd had no idea just how taking the risk of coming here would affect her.

She'd never been more nervous and keeping her brother safe was only part of those nerves. The other bundle belonged to Sam. After all this time, she hadn't expected to feel those stirrings of desire again. She hadn't thought it possible to still have such a strong pull to someone who had been out of her life for sixteen years.

But pulled to him she was.

What if he wasn't home? What if he slammed the door in her face? What if he hated her for the way she'd left him all those years ago? What if he hated her now for the reasons she'd come back to Green Valley?

So many questions swirled around, adding to her anxiety. There was no other option and there was no backup plan. She had to rely on herself and pull up every ounce of courage and strength she could muster because she was going to need it.

Maty grabbed her bag and her cell. Her lock screen showed a picture of her and her brother. Carter was her reason for every action lately and she had no choice but to get in between two powerhouses and pray she came out unscathed—and with the means to keep her brother in the care he needed.

No matter how scared or nervous she was about confronting Sam, she had to push through. Carter depended on her.

She stepped from the car and pulled in a deep breath of warm mountain air. Late spring was absolutely beautiful in Green Valley and coming home did help calm her nerves, somewhat. There was something peaceful about this place…so long as she ignored her reasons for returning.

Hoisting her bag on her shoulder, Maty rounded the car's hood and came to a dead stop. Sam stood at the top of the porch steps with his arms folded over his chest, staring down at her. There was no look of surprise, almost as if he'd been expecting her.

Maty gripped the strap on her bag and forced herself to take another step, and another. Fears and insecurities had no place here.

"I hope I'm not disturbing you," she said, holding his gaze.

"Depends on why you're here."

She offered what she hoped was a friendly smile as she reached the bottom of the steps. "To talk. Maybe catch up. We got started off all wrong."

"By wrong, you mean telling me that you work for a man I loathe or do you mean insulting me by believing I'll sell simply because you asked?"

Okay, so he wasn't going to make this easy. Well, neither was she. There was too much at stake and much more than she'd first thought. Now she also had to worry about what would happen to her emotions by spending so much time with Sam, digging deeper into the man's psyche to try to figure out how to get what Rusty wanted.

The more time she spent with Sam, the more her attraction grew. There was no fighting a passion that had once been so alive, so fierce. She hadn't taken that buried emotion into consideration before she'd come back to Green Valley.

Since Sam hadn't asked her to leave, Maty found another layer of courage and attempted to push aside that sexual pull. She mounted the steps and came to stand next to him. Sam shifted, allowing her more space.

"Your home is beautiful," she told him, ignoring his question. "You always did want something private and out in the middle of nowhere."

Because she couldn't stand his stare another minute, Maty glanced around the vast yard and focused on the chirping birds and the butterfly on the tip of a flower petal. The tall, majestic mountains surrounding them. More fodder for her doodles later.

"How long have you lived here?" she asked.

"I built this five years ago."

She turned her attention back to him. His broad shoulders filled out his tee a little too well and Maty was having a difficult time making small talk when she really wanted to reach out and glide her fingertips over that excellent muscle tone.

"It's a big house for one man," she told him, forcing her focus to his dark eyes.

"Is that your way of asking if I'm with someone?"

Maty laughed. "Not at all. You were just never the flashy type, so I'm curious."

Sam dropped his arms and pursed his lips. "Since you drove all the way out here, I assume you have some time."

Maty nodded. "I have nothing else to do this evening."

"Follow me."

Sam stepped past the front door and waited for her. The moment Maty crossed the threshold, her breath caught in her throat. If she'd thought the outside was impressive, that was nothing compared to the spacious living area open all the way to the back of the house.

The wall of windows across the room offered a spectacular view of another pond, half surrounded by more impressive evergreens. The living room was two stories with a balcony stretching across the top that connected one side of the house to the other. Three large iron chandeliers were suspended from the ceiling. The rich, dark flooring screamed rustic luxury.

The kitchen was back in the far right, but there were hardly any walls. A few sturdy wood beams gave support, but the structure was open and so absolutely perfect.

"I couldn't imagine living somewhere like this," she murmured, realizing her tiny apartment could fit in this entryway alone.

Maybe that's why he'd gone all out like this. Growing up in that apartment with his mother had to have been stifling and cramped. He'd always told her that when he attained his dream of owning a distillery, he would build a grand place for them to live.

For them.

They'd shared dreams at one time. Those days were long gone and that young, dewy-eyed girl now had to face the harsh reality that dreams didn't come true for everyone.

She'd had big plans of her own not so long ago. But then the crash happened, she lost her parents, she needed to provide round-the-clock care for her brother, her savings depleted…the future she'd planned was gone.

Maty would've given up all of her dreams and her career to have her family whole again. Instead, she was on the verge of losing that career and she'd have to start over with the care for Carter.

Unless she could win over Sam.

"I wanted an open space to come home to because I grew up in an apartment with just three rooms," he told her. "I knew I needed room to move."

Just what she'd figured. She was all too familiar with that three-room apartment. That's what Rusty had leased for her. Even living there alone, she felt the walls closing in on her.

Sam turned and started toward a wide staircase. "On the second floor I have three bedrooms all with their own bathrooms because when I have friends over, I want them to have privacy."

She had to walk fast to keep up as he pointed toward the wing of rooms. They weren't just bedrooms; they were literally their own suites. All breathtaking in their own way.

Sam crossed the balcony that suspended over the living room and headed up another set of steps.

"I put the master suite, the gym and the media room all up here because I wanted my own space away from where I was hosting guests."

She wondered who all stayed here. Friends? Girlfriends?

A stab of unexpected jealousy speared her. She had no reason to be jealous. She was the one who'd walked away to begin with and it had been sixteen years. It wasn't as if she'd not dated and she knew someone like Sam wouldn't have been alone, either.

Still, she didn't like the idea of him with someone else. She'd never thought of herself as a jealous person until now.

Until now, she hadn't thought she wanted Sam with such a fierce need, but here she was barely holding it together.

Sam opened a set of double doors and she was overwhelmed by the vast home gym setup. So much equipment, from machines to weights of all sizes and even a punching bag in the corner. After all this time, they still had some things in common. Strange, since neither of them had boxed when they were together.

She didn't get a chance to comment before he closed the doors and gestured to the next room. Maty made her way toward that opening and the moment he pushed the wide doors open and revealed the new room, she smiled. There were huge leather recliners and a black screen taking up an entire wall.

"I remember how much you love movies," she told him.

"And we couldn't ever afford to go," he replied. "Mom always gambled away any extra money. I have access to all new releases the moment they hit the theater."

Maty's heart ached for that boy she remembered. She'd known his mother had a serious addiction and that their apartment had been miniscule. But when they'd been dating, Maty hadn't paid much attention to how that had affected Sam. They rarely visited with his mother and Maty always assumed Sam was just embarrassed.

"I remember always wanting to take you to see the latest movies," he went on. "But we couldn't afford it and I was mortified. I always found some excuse rather than tell you the truth."

She'd known. Maty had been well aware Sam couldn't afford to take her. She hadn't cared about his financial status. Her parents would've given her the money to go, but she didn't want to embarrass him further or hurt his pride. Maty had been with Sam because she truly loved him and he made her laugh, made her feel alive. She hadn't been that happy since.

"This room is amazing," she told him, forcing her

thoughts to the here and now. "Is that a bar with a popcorn machine?"

"You think I wouldn't have a bar in my home?" he laughed. "I have five bars in total and the popcorn is a must for movie night."

"With extra butter," she replied.

He returned her smile. "No other way."

Something shifted, breaking that thick layer of ice he'd shoved between them. Nostalgia was the way to get to him. She hated using it, hated being vindictive and stooping to the level of Rusty's commands. For a minute, she'd forgotten about Rusty and had just enjoyed the tour of Sam's house and the memories that filled her mind. But that black cloud looming over her wouldn't go away and she couldn't lose sight of why she was truly here.

No matter how she felt about Sam, in the past or now, she had a job to do and it wasn't ending up back in his arms…or his bed.

Sam turned and went to the end of the hall where he opened another set of doors. This time he revealed his master suite. Everything in here demanded attention, from the king-sized bed on a platform in the middle of the floor to the two walls made up entirely of windows.

Even though his home was down in the valley, the views were spectacular. The mountains surrounded him, the pond looked even more vast and spectacular from here, and the sun had just started to set, casting an orange glow into the room.

"I wanted to feel like I was out in nature," he told her. "I wanted my room to feel like there are no barriers or walls around me."

Hence the windows and the bed in the center of the

room. His difficult childhood had altered him, making him into the successful man he was today. She was so damn proud of him, but she couldn't tell him. If she did, he'd break her down and demand to know why she was teaming up against him.

Sam turned to face her as she remained in the doorway. "So that's why I have this big house," he told her. "Because I can. Because I won't be confined by anything or anyone ever again. I always have to be in control of my surroundings, my life."

She completely understood everything he said, but this situation wasn't in his power to control. Rusty overshadowed both of them and there was not much she or Sam could do about it.

Maty wanted to reach for him, to console him in case the memories from the past caused him any pain. But she knew that was just a selfish move. She wanted to reach for him because he was even sexier than when they'd been together. Part of her wanted to feel those strong arms around her, and maybe she wanted to seek comfort from him. Why couldn't they console each other? At one time, they would've done just that.

Those broad shoulders threatened every single stitch in that dark gray tee. New ink poked out of his shirtsleeve and that dark hair was even more unruly than ever. There was something wildly erotic about the sight of Sam Hawkins. If people didn't know him, they'd never guess him to be a billionaire and the owner of the most up-and-coming bourbon distillery in the world. His gin had taken off years ago and the anticipation for the first bottle of ten-year bourbon was all the buzz.

It wasn't the money that made her want him. No. She wanted him because she remembered what they'd shared at one time and she couldn't help but visualize them that way again. She might have an easier time putting up resistance if she didn't know how perfect they were together, how magical his touch was, how he was the most unselfish lover she'd ever had.

Maty couldn't help but wonder if she'd made a mistake leaving all those years ago. She wondered if law school had been worth moving away from the man she loved. But she'd wanted to explore her dreams, just as he'd stayed behind to explore his.

"So, to answer the question you didn't come right out and ask, I'm single."

She shouldn't do a happy internal dance over that news, but she was a woman and he was sexy as hell. This bedroom alone begged for sex with that bed taking center stage. Maty easily saw them tangled in those gray sheets, never wanting to leave, and rolling toward each other in the morning hours to make love again.

"And you?"

His question pulled her gaze from the bed and onto the man. "Me? What about me?"

He took a step toward her and smirked. "I assume you're single."

"Why would you assume that?" she asked, wondering if he was going to keep walking toward her.

Yes. The answer was yes as he came to stand toe-to-toe with her.

"Because if you were mine, there's no way in hell I'd let Rusty anywhere near you." Sam leaned in just a whisper more. "And if you were mine, you sure as hell wouldn't be at the home of your ex-lover."

Maty leaned back as Sam loomed over her, looking at

her like he was about a breath away from kissing her…
or putting that staged bed to good use.

"But I'm not yours," she murmured.

Sam slid a fingertip across her forehead, smoothing her hair back and tucking it behind her ear. That simple touch continued down her jawline and stopped just beneath her chin. He raked his thumb across her lower lip and Maty couldn't stop herself from slipping her tongue over his rough skin. His eyes widened, his jaw clenched.

"No," he agreed. "You're not."

His hand dropped, but he didn't step back.

"So, is this part of your plan?" he asked with a smirk. "Come to my home, attempt to seduce me?"

Seduce him? Maybe he'd missed the part where he'd towered over her, making her want to touch, want to remember, want to *feel*. He'd shown her his bed and they'd lingered in this room for far longer than any other. Maybe that stroke over her face and mouth wasn't affecting him the way it was her.

But he was feeling something because he wouldn't be clenching his teeth with his nostrils flared and his lips thinned if her presence meant nothing.

"I don't have a plan," she answered honestly. "I'm here to talk to you. Nothing more."

He continued to study her as if he didn't believe a word she said. But she really had no plan. Maty had prayed something would just come to her once she arrived, and something had—a heavier dose of lust than what she'd experienced in his office.

Well, she'd wanted to connect with him on a personal level… She was getting her wish.

But lust wouldn't solve her problems. In fact, getting swept away by physical emotions and a flood of memories would cause only more issues and she already had enough.

And why wouldn't he step back and give her space?

"You wanted me to kiss you," he told her. "If I were to guess, you want more."

Maty tipped her chin and leveled his gaze. "You can guess all you want. And so what if I did think about a kiss? Maybe I—"

In a flash, Sam covered her mouth with his. Whatever she was about to say vanished with that powerful, potent kiss.

Yes, she was definitely relating to him on a personal level, but suddenly the sale of Hawkins was the last thing on her mind.

Five

Sam didn't know what the hell he was doing, but he knew he didn't want to stop.

Something in him snapped…something he'd brought all on himself. He'd taunted her, wanting her to admit why she'd come here. A big part of him didn't want her to say it, though. He didn't want to think that she would use her body to get what she wanted. That wasn't the Maty Taylor he had known. No matter what had happened since they parted ways, he'd never believe that's who she'd become.

She might have come here to talk, but she was also curious. That much was obvious from their first encounter when her eyes had raked over him.

Sam gripped her hips as he continued to devour her mouth. He nearly pulled back, until her fingers threaded through his hair and she let out one of those moans that always used to drive him out of his mind.

Damn it. Some things never changed. Even after all of this time, she still came alive in his arms. How could they pick up where they left off? How could this passion still be alive after all this time?

Sam cupped her backside and walked her a few steps to the door frame. As he lifted her against his body, she wrapped her legs around his waist and circled her arms around his neck.

"Sam," she murmured against his lips.

There was need in her tone, a need that matched his own.

But he couldn't do this. Damn it. As much as he wanted her, he couldn't take her to his bed…yet. He hadn't seen her for sixteen years and she was working for his enemy. He wasn't a young, horny eighteen-year-old who couldn't control his hormones.

Besides all of that, he had to focus on his business and trying to get his mother back on track. He didn't have time for distractions even if they came in the form of his sexy ex-lover.

Reluctantly, Sam released her to slide down his body and find her footing. Maty blinked and licked her lips.

"What are you doing?" she whispered.

"Saving both of us from a mistake."

And damn if it wasn't costing him his sanity right now. He thought he'd throw her plan back in her face, but all he did was get his body all revved up with nowhere to go.

"You kissed me."

As if he needed the reminder of who started this charade. He should've stayed on his porch and talked with her. Maybe he should've just asked her to turn around and head right back down his driveway.

But no. He'd had to show off and then get all cocky and bring her to his bedroom.

"Are you telling me that when you came to my house you didn't think that's what would happen? Because I'll call you a liar if you say yes."

Maty tucked her hair behind her ears and smoothed it all over one shoulder as she took a step toward him.

"Maybe I did think of kissing you," she replied. "I'm not sorry we kissed. I enjoyed it, actually, until you stopped."

Always so bold, so demanding. He'd loved that about her when he'd been younger, now…well, he would reserve his opinion for a later time, but an assertive woman was never a turnoff.

He was a masochist. He knew it as well as anything, but that knowledge didn't prevent him from curling his fingers around her hip and jerking her forward.

"So you're saying had I not stopped, you would've let things progress?" he asked.

Her eyes glossed over with another layer of arousal. "Why not? Clearly we're still attracted to each other."

His other hand went to the snap on her jeans.

Stop this madness before someone gets hurt.

But the devil on the other shoulder urged him on and Sam had always been a risk taker. He wouldn't be where he was today had he not stepped outside his comfort zone.

"We're different people than we used to be." The button slid through the opening and he eased her zipper down, watching her eyes for any indication he should stop. "I'm not naive like before."

"You weren't naive." Her breath came out on a sigh

when his knuckles scraped against her bare skin just above her panties. "We were in love."

Love? They hadn't even known what that term meant, though they'd tossed it around at the time.

All that was happening now was pure lust because he had a need for her, a need to see her come undone, to know that he was in charge and giving her exactly what she needed.

Perhaps that was a little of his past bruised ego coming to the surface, but he didn't care. Maty jerked her hips, silently urging him on as she continued to hold his gaze.

The damn woman was daring him and he never, ever turned down a dare.

Sam braced one hand beside her head and slid his other into her panties. Her gasp must've surprised her because she cut it off with a sexy bite to her bottom lip.

Gritting his teeth, he eased one finger into her. She groaned as her body arched. Sam continued to pleasure her, all the while taking in each and every facial expression and sweet little moan.

Her pale fingers curled around his dark wrist and that was just about the sexiest sight to see—her completely unashamed of taking what she wanted.

Sam worked her until she cried out and gripped his shoulders. He didn't want the moment to end, he wanted to draw out her pleasure so he could remember every aspect once she was gone and he was left in this big house all alone.

When her body ceased trembling, Sam eased his hand away and straightened her clothes. For the record, she did apparently still enjoy lace. Ironically, so did he.

Maty's head had dropped back against the door

frame and her eyes remained shut tight. The silence seemed to be deafening now and he had to take a step away, to put some distance between them before he continued what he'd started.

He shouldn't have done that, but he wasn't sorry he did. Maty had always been so passionate, so responsive, and right now he was a selfish bastard. They weren't the same lovers they had been…no, this grown up version of Maty was so much more in every way. She hadn't even tried to hold back; she'd let that pleasure roll over her and he only hoped she didn't have regrets.

"You still want to talk?" he finally said when the silence stretched too long.

Her lids fluttered until those expressive brown eyes met his. "Talk," she repeated, licking her lips.

She straightened from the wall and offered a soft smile. "You want to go from that to talking? You really have changed."

Sam crossed his arms, not because he didn't want to dive back into her, but because he did. Diving headfirst into a mistake might feel good for a while, but the end result wouldn't change this situation. She was still the enemy as far as he was concerned. A sexy, sultry enemy.

"I haven't changed," he countered. "I see something I want and I go after it."

She quirked a brow. "And you wanted to give me an orgasm with nothing in return?"

"Is that so hard to believe?"

Maty tipped her head, narrowed her eyes and studied him. "I've never met a man like you."

Sam weighed that statement, jealousy spearing him when he had no room for such nonsense. She'd been with other people, just as he had, but that didn't mean he wanted the visual thrown in his face when he still felt her coming undone around him.

"You'll never meet a man like me," he countered.

"So now what?" she asked, smoothing her shirt down over her pants. "Do we go back to the tour? Christen another room?"

Sam couldn't help but laugh at her bold questions and he figured she was only half joking. Shoving his hands in his pockets, he shrugged.

"You came to me," he told her. "What do you want? The truth this time."

Maty sighed and pursed her lips. "Honestly, I want to know what you've been up to since we split. I mean, I know you're clearly a megamogul now and pretty much a celebrity, but I don't know about the personal side."

So she wanted to know more, most likely to use against him later or to take back to Rusty. Fine, Sam would play along, but he was also keeping his guard up. Something was going on with her and he had a sickening feeling Rusty was up to no good where Maty was concerned. Sam was more worried about her than he was himself. He could handle Rusty, but Maty…she had a vulnerability about her, one he didn't recall from the woman he used to know.

Besides that, Maty didn't know what an evil man Rusty was and Sam didn't want her to find out. He wanted her as far away from Rusty as possible, but she didn't seem in any hurry to remove herself from this mess.

"Follow me," he told her. "We'll take a walk around the pond. It's a nice night."

"Afraid to talk near the bed?" she joked.

Sam took a step toward her until she backed against the door frame again. He braced his hands on either side of her head and leaned in.

"Maty, when I decide to have you, I won't give a damn if there's a bed or not."

Her eyes widened with arousal and Sam pushed away, heading back downstairs before he completely lost his mind and showed her just how much he wanted her.

How long should a body keep tingling after a fierce orgasm? Because Maty wasn't sure when she'd settle, and having Sam right next to her wasn't helping matters. Neither was the veiled promise he'd made.

When I decide to have you...

Oh, he'd delivered those words with such conviction and confidence. She knew the more time she spent with Sam the more she'd feel that underlying attraction, but she'd had no clue he'd be so damn infuriating. She'd been ready to rip his clothes off and he'd brought her outside for a leisurely stroll around one of his ponds.

"I take it Virginia didn't work out for you?"

As if that's what she wanted to talk about?

"I'd rather talk about you."

The sun was still hanging on, but within the next half hour, the orange glow would be gone, replaced by a beautiful starry sky. The peaceful night surrounded by such beauty should be calming... Maty was anything but calm.

She didn't know what to say, what to feel or how to act, between the intense moment in his room, the tour where he'd basically justified why he lived in such a vast home, and the sole purpose for her being back in

Green Valley to begin with. How the hell could she ever be calm again?

Maty kept in step with Sam, but he came to a stop and jerked his cell from his pocket. He cursed and shoved the phone back in, but not before Maty saw the name on the screen.

Carla Hawkins.

"You can take that," Maty told him.

"I'll call her back." The words came out through gritted teeth. "You wanted to catch up."

He started walking again and blew out a sigh. Maty didn't know the dynamics of his relationship with his mother, but she didn't want to come between them. She knew how protective Sam was toward Carla and how he'd always wanted to get help for her, but she'd refused over and over.

"How is your mom?" she asked.

"She's addicted to gambling, same as before." His tone left no room for comment. "So why are you back? All to work for Lockwood?"

Maty slid her hands into her pockets and watched her pointed flats crush the blades of grass. "I'm back to start a new life here."

"And that new life includes working for a cold-hearted bastard?"

"I can work with any client I choose without justifying it to you or anyone else."

Sam stopped and gripped her elbow. "For someone so confident, you seem rather defensive."

She stared back at him, trying to ignore that strong, warm grip and the tingles it produced. "Fine. You want to know all about Rusty. It's simple. He wants your business."

Sam nodded. "I'm aware."

"And I'm not going to stop until I seal this deal."

Sam stared at her. His lips quirked in what seemed to be a smile, but then it vanished. "Then this should be interesting, because I would literally die protecting my company from the clutches of Lockwood."

Maty knew he meant every single word, but so did she. There had to be a way. She just had to find it.

"I know you're working overtime trying to find a way to get into my world now," he told her, dropping his hand. He took a step closer. "I'll let you in, Maty. But I won't give you a thing that belongs to me. Not my business and sure as hell not my heart."

Six

The next morning Sam still cursed himself for exposing his thoughts. He'd wanted to let Maty know, again, she was wasting her time, but somehow that young gullible man he'd once been crept up and took over all his actions.

Unfortunately, he didn't have the headspace to worry about his own issues at the moment—he had to deal with his mother's…yet again. She'd called this morning in a panic over her bills and Sam couldn't deal with hysteria over the phone, so he made the quick ten-minute drive from his home to the small mountainside cottage he'd purchased for her several years ago. He might have bought the house, but he wasn't paying her bills. He wasn't.

Sometimes he had to get tough with her because she relied on him way too much. Not that he didn't want to help, but he wanted her to help herself. That was the only way she'd get a grip on reality and stop throwing her money away.

He loved his mother, but she had a problem, and he wasn't going to be her enabler. Tough love was difficult at times because he never wanted her to think he didn't care. If he didn't care, he would leave her alone and not help at all.

And since she'd called, now was the perfect opportunity to confront her about the letter and the truth that had been revealed to him. He wanted to hear her side, to give her a chance to explain how in the hell she'd gotten tangled up with a man like Rusty to begin with.

Sam pulled into the drive behind her little red car. He grabbed his cell and stepped from his truck. His mother was on the porch swing smoking a cigarette and holding a cup of coffee in her other hand.

"Honey, you didn't have to come out here," she called to him as he started up the drive. "I'll get this figured out."

"That's what you always say." He mounted the steps and shoved his cell in his pocket. If she hadn't wanted him to come, she wouldn't have called. "How much do you owe?"

"Which person?" she asked, tears forming in her deep brown eyes. Even with her dark skin, circles beneath her eyes showed just how stressed she was.

She always got upset over her debts, but they weren't a surprise to her, so why did she continue this vicious cycle?

"The electric company, your loan shark. Take your pick."

Her wrinkled lips thinned and she narrowed her eyes. "You're always so judgmental. Is that why you came out here? To put me down again and remind me that you have no problems?"

He had no problems? She had no clue…but she was about to get one once he sorted out this mess. His mother was usually loving and kind and compassionate, but when she got in a bind, she turned angry and mean. She was on a path of destruction that seemed to be getting worse.

"How much, Mom?"

"Including the bills that are overdue, I need twelve thousand dollars."

Twelve thousand was nothing to him, but it was a lot when discussing a damn utility payment. And it was a hell of a lot when he'd just bailed her out of another debt last week.

He wanted nothing more than for her to be trustworthy and competent. He wanted his own mother to come work for him at a dynasty he'd created, but…that wasn't reality. That fact niggled at him every single day. He wanted her by his side, he wanted them to have a trustworthy relationship, but he had to trust her first. And, for that to happen, she had to want to get better.

"That's a hell of a late fee," he replied.

"I might owe my friend Sally a few thousand," she murmured around her cigarette. "And the rest is for some bills that I didn't mention last week because I thought I could handle it."

Story of their lives. She always thought she could "handle it" and never once had that been the case.

"If Sally was your friend, she'd quit loaning you money to gamble away. And bills always come first. Always."

His mother blew out a puff of smoke and stared out

at the mountains. "It's hard," she cried, the tears spilling now. "I try, Sam, you know I do. I had such a good run the other day."

Just like every day for years before that. Sam knew her routine. Wake up, fire up the coffee pot, get online to start her day of losing money. He saw the image in his mind that made up nearly every single moment of his childhood. But lately she'd seriously gotten much worse than she had been and it was time to make this madness stop.

What would it take for her to stop? What would it take for her to realize she would never recoup what she'd lost and that she needed money to live on? Where would she be if he didn't have the funds to bail her out?

She'd told him the money he received when he'd turned eighteen was from her winnings, but now he knew the truth…or what was likely the truth. Receiving money from Rusty Lockwood to keep him out of any parenting responsibilities was no doubt how Sam had received his funds.

Funds he'd used to start up Hawkins. He still didn't know how he felt about that. There was some irony in the fact that the very man who wanted to buy Sam's distillery was the one who'd funded the start-up.

"Give me the name of the woman you owe. I need more to go on than Sally, and give me your utility statements. I'll take care of them and you're not getting a penny more."

"I'm your mother." She jerked that teary gaze back to him. "I don't bring in as much money as you."

"If you took the money from your job and didn't gamble it away, you would have a nice nest egg."

She likely didn't even know what a nest egg *was*,

considering she gambled away more than she made at her position as an office assistant. The simple idea of saving probably had never even crossed her mind.

This all had to stop. He'd discuss taking over her banking account, but first there were more pressing matters to dig into.

Sam crossed to the rocker and took a seat as he watched his mother volley between her coffee and her cigarette.

He wasn't sure how to approach this subject. Sam had no clue how she'd react or if she'd even admit who his biological father was. But he'd never been one to dodge difficult subjects and this one was the biggest bomb that had ever dropped into his life. He deserved to know the truth. He also believed his mother deserved to tell her side of the story.

"I received an interesting letter in the mail," he began.

Carla tipped back her coffee mug and set the empty glass on the porch railing. She leaned back in the swing and turned her attention his way.

"Do you know Lori Campbell?" he asked.

Her brows drew in and she shook her head. "Never heard of her," she replied.

"She passed away a month ago, but she left behind a letter." He kept his eyes on his mother. "For me." Sam didn't see any recognition in her eyes.

"Why are you telling me a dead woman left a letter for you?" she asked, then her eyes narrowed. "Did you get someone pregnant?"

"No, Mom. Lori was the mother of an associate of mine." *A brother.* "Her son is Nick Campbell. He's renovating the old building on Elkin Mountain and turning it into a resort in honor of his mother. She claims that Rusty Lockwood is my biological father."

The cigarette slipped from her hand, landing on the concrete porch. His mother's eyes were wide, as was her mouth.

"Judging by your response, I'll take her letter to be accurate."

Pain sliced through him. She'd known this truth for over thirty years and chose to keep it from him. He'd never even been given the chance to decide what to do about his father, whether or not to seek out a relationship.

On one hand he understood her fear. His mother never would've been able to battle Rusty. But Sam could. He was.

"That man is a bastard," she ground out. "We were better off without him."

"We were, but there came a time when you could've told me the truth. I can handle it, mentally and financially," he added. "How much money did he give you to keep out of our lives?"

"Fifty thousand." She shifted in the swing and pushed her long black hair behind her ears. "I wasn't gambling so much back then and I was at least smart enough to invest half for your future. The other half I used to buy a reliable car and get a different apartment."

At least she'd thought to invest that money for him or who knows where he'd be. Sam was confident he'd still be a master distiller since that had been his goal, but would he have been able to put a down payment on the distillery he had now? Maybe not.

"I don't fault you for doing what you thought was

best," he told her. "But there came a time when you needed to tell me the truth."

"And then what?" she demanded. "You would've gone to him and expected some grand reunion? You're in the industry. You know what an evil man he is."

Sam nodded. "I'm well aware."

Blowing out a sigh, Sam came to his feet and crossed to the railing. He curled his palms on the wood plank and stared out at the fog burning off the tips of the mountains.

"I don't know what the correct answer is," he finally stated. "But I know that I don't like finding out the truth and being blindsided by a stranger. And to find out he's my enemy. You know how much I hate that man."

The swing creaked and his mom's footsteps shifted across the porch as she came to stand beside him. She patted his hand and Sam knew this wasn't easy for her, either. Him coming here and confronting her was just as shocking as the truth was to him. She'd carried this secret for over thirty years.

"I worked for Rusty," she began. "I cleaned his house for about two months before our affair started. I was only eighteen and had no idea what I was going to do with my life, but then I fell for his charms and ended up pregnant."

Sam couldn't help but sympathize, knowing how difficult that time must have been for her. A scared teen, legally an adult but with no direction—that had to have been terrifying.

"I was so naive," she mumbled. "I guess I thought he'd move me into that big mansion and we'd raise the baby together. I mean, to my knowledge he wasn't seeing anyone else. Of course I found out later he slept with everyone coming and going. The man had no scruples in business or in his personal life."

"So he offered you money and tossed you aside?" Sam guessed.

"Pretty much," she replied. "So I took that money and invested so you'd have enough to start a good life. Not like me. I wanted better for you."

Her voice broke on that last word and guilt had Sam turning and pulling her into his arms. She'd lost weight. His mother had always been a petite woman, but now she seemed almost frail. He'd have to keep a better eye on that because if she wasn't taking care of herself, then this addiction was even more out of control than he thought.

"I'm sorry I'm a disappointment," she murmured into his chest.

Sam eased back and wiped away her tears. "You've never been a disappointment. If I didn't love and care for you, I wouldn't be here. But you have to let me help you and you have to want help. It doesn't matter what I think of you. You have to love yourself enough."

She nodded and sniffed as she stared up at him with red-rimmed eyes. "I'm trying, Sam. I promise."

He knew this wasn't her life's goal; he knew she had aspirations. Nobody set out to become addicted to something. But he had to deal with the woman she was now. And he refused to let her continue down this rabbit hole of despair.

"I'm going to get your bills squared away and we're going to get you help," he told her.

"And Rusty? What are you going to do about him? He's such a powerful man."

Sam laughed. "He's an arrogant bastard who thinks

he can bully his way around. I'm not worried about him and you shouldn't be, either."

She patted the side of his face, just like she'd done when he was young. "Be careful."

Be careful. Sure, no problem. Rusty was a nonissue. The man was on a downward spiral and wouldn't even be able to touch what Sam held dear.

Speaking of… Maty.

Being careful around Russ wasn't difficult, but watching his back where Maty was concerned was harder. Because they were far from over.

He'd barely gotten started with her.

Enemy or no, he'd gotten a sample of the woman she'd become and he wanted more.

Seven

After visiting his mother and putting in a full day of work, Sam was more than ready to unwind. Unfortunately, that was impossible with the thought of Maty on his mind.

The other night when she'd been in his home, her passion had been even more potent than he remembered. The way she didn't give a damn, the way she let him pleasure her…and the way she was more than ready to keep the intimacy going. Her raw honesty about what she wanted had humbled him and damn her, he hadn't been able to focus on much else since.

So here he was, heading toward the address he'd been surprised to find associated with her name…an address he knew all too well. She hadn't said a word about her accommodations.

More secrets.

The area had once been thriving, but now this part

of the valley had certainly seen better days. The apartment complex had gotten even more run-down than when he'd lived here as a teen.

Between his emotions from Maty's return and their very personal reunion, and this shocking revelation about where she was living, Sam had a sinking feeling that coming here was a mistake.

Wouldn't be the first one he'd made.

Sam turned into a parking lot with two sets of apartment complexes on each side. He glanced at each door for the familiar number and spotted Maty's car at the end, right in front of the place he'd called home for his entire childhood.

So she did live here. This wasn't just some error his assistant had made while digging around for the address.

Anger flooded through him. This had Rusty's slimy hands all over it and Maty was clearly the pawn. Sam had been furious with Rusty for hiring Maty, but now Sam was flat-out pissed. Whatever game Rusty was playing would be coming to an end because Sam would be putting a stop to it.

Taking advantage of his mother all those years ago and toying with Maty now was enough to make Sam want to head straight to Lockwood Lightning and punch that man in the face.

He'd have to settle for getting even by keeping Rusty away from the distillery and everything else Sam held dear.

Sam parked next to Maty and stared at the door he'd walked through thousands of times as a child. He wasn't scarred by his childhood. His mother loved him unconditionally and poured herself into this tiny apartment.

But that was a lifetime ago and being back seemed surreal.

He wondered how Maty felt when she came back to this town and lived in a run-down apartment building. What had happened to her job in Virginia? What had happened to her family's money?

Sam had no idea, but Rusty did and likely that's what he'd used as leverage to get her here. In order for Sam to properly help her, he needed the full story.

After Sam locked his truck, he made his way up the cracked sidewalk to the chipped black door. Nothing about this place was welcoming, but Maty had put a bright yellow wreath on the door to make her apartment stand out.

Sam tapped his knuckles on the frame and stepped back to wait. He heard muttering and bustling on the other side, and he kept his focus on talking to her and not exploding over why she let Rusty manipulate her into moving here…to this exact residence.

The chain rattled and a moment later the door swung open. Maty's eyes widened. She held the phone to her ear and blinked away her shock before turning and walking back inside, leaving the door open for him. Sam took this as a silent invitation to enter.

"Just tell him I'll be there as soon as I can manage," she stated. "And make sure to tell him I love him."

Sam closed the door behind him as Maty disconnected her call. He examined the place, not knowing what to expect.

The old carpet had at least been replaced with some cheap vinyl faux wood flooring. There was one sofa, one chair, one lamp. No pictures on the wall, but there was a little throw pillow with flowers. A small glass jar sat on the two-person kitchen table. The jar held a bouquet of wildflowers that looked liked she'd plucked them from the side of the road.

The place was oddly familiar, yet different from the life he'd had here. A punch of nostalgia hit him, but he pushed it aside. Whatever mind game Rusty was playing, Sam wasn't going to get caught up in it.

"Why are you here?"

Sam turned his attention from his examination of the room to the woman who looked like she'd rather the grim reaper had shown up than Sam. Too bad. He wanted answers—he *deserved* answers.

"I thought I'd swing by on my way home and see if you wanted to get something to eat."

That lie rolled right off his tongue. He'd looked her up initially to see if they could pick up where they'd left off in his bedroom, but the moment he saw that address, he'd wanted answers.

She propped one hand on her hip and clutched her cell in the other. He also wanted to ask who she'd professed her love to, but that was none of his business.

Maty had clearly gotten home not long ago because she still wore one of those tight business dresses that reminded him of some naughty librarian fantasy with the way she had her hair pulled back.

But she'd kicked off her heels somewhere. Her bare feet shouldn't turn him on, but they did. Everything about her, from her appearance to her smart mouth to her vulnerability, seemed to be pulling him in...and that was before she'd come apart in his arms. Since then? Well, he was a mess of emotions he couldn't get a grasp on. He wanted her more now than ever.

"You stopped by unannounced to ask me to dinner?" She quirked a brow. "You're lying."

"Fine. I'm lying," he admitted. "I'm still hungry, so do you want to go get something?"

She quirked a brow. "You're not going to say anything about where I'm living?"

Sam ground his teeth and weighed his words. As much as he wanted to unleash his questions and anger, he also had to stop and think. Rusty was attempting to pull the strings and Sam was damn well going to be the one to cut them.

If Rusty had dug back into Sam's past to find this place, then likely Rusty knew Sam's mother's name, too. Did he remember her at all? Or was she just another woman in his past that he'd paid off and discarded?

"What do you want me to say?" Sam countered. He took a step toward her, noting her eyes as they raked over him. "All of this is part of Rusty's warped plan. He wants to get me thinking of our time together, remind me where I came from. Hell, I don't know what his angle is, but I know the end result he wants and he's clearly using you to get it. Do you want to tell me what he has over you?"

Her lips thinned. "I've already told you what I have going on with my client isn't something I can discuss."

"Considering I'm the common denominator, I'd think you could fill me in."

Maty blew out a sigh and reached up to her hair. She pulled out one pin, then another, until the mass of blond strands tumbled around her shoulders. She shook her hand through the waves and Sam's entire body tightened. He wanted to feel that silkiness over his body, through his fingers.

There was no doubt she just wanted to get more comfortable, but her actions seemed to border on seduction. The power she held over him now was different from that in their past. Sam was walking a fine line here, but he couldn't pull himself away from the little minx.

"Listen, I'm tired and cranky," she told him. "I just want to put on my leggings, take off my bra and do nothing."

Sam smiled. "Don't let me stop you from taking off your bra."

Maty rolled her eyes and turned toward the hallway leading to the bedroom. "That's such a man thing to say," she muttered as she disappeared.

Sam wanted nothing more than to follow her, but he didn't get the vibe she was in the mood for his shenanigans. He certainly could use something to take the edge off his mood. This bizarro world he'd found himself in with Maty and Rusty and his mother was taking its toll.

Keeping all the proverbial balls in the air was more of a full-time job than running a billion-dollar company.

When Maty came back moments later in black leggings and an off-the-shoulder tee, he gritted his teeth and clenched his fists at his sides. How could she look even sexier completely dressed down, with her face washed free of all makeup?

Because this was the Maty he remembered. Simply beautiful, casually elegant. She embodied everything he loved about women…curves and natural beauty.

"Are you going to just stand by the door or are you coming on in?" she asked.

"I haven't decided."

She crossed her arms over her chest, bringing attention to the fact she had indeed forgone the bra. Torturing him must be her hobby.

"Why did you decide to come see me to begin with?" she asked.

"I wanted to see you."

"You wanted to pick up from the other night," she corrected with a smile.

Sam shrugged. No need in denying the truth. He wasn't sorry he wanted her and he knew the feeling on her end was quite mutual.

"But now I want to know why you're here, in this apartment, and why you're letting Lockwood jerk you around."

She said nothing and Sam knew they would stand here and butt heads until one of them conceded…but neither was a quitter. She was just as strong willed as he was, which only added to the attraction that had nothing to do with their past and everything to do with the woman she was today.

He wanted to get to know that woman. He shouldn't, but he did. The last thing he had time for was getting tangled up in…hell, he didn't even know what to call all of this. There was no relationship—they hadn't even started a fling, though he didn't want to ignore that possibility.

After those sexy few minutes in his bedroom, he'd fantasized about her since. He'd bet his entire distillery on the fact that she'd been replaying those moments, too.

But it was that distillery that was at stake here.

At the end of the day, she still worked for his enemy, the one trying to take everything he'd dreamed of and worked for.

That didn't mean he couldn't enjoy her physically,

though. It just meant he couldn't let anything develop beyond sex.

"Let me worry about my personal life," she told him.

Closing the distance between them, Sam reached up, sliding the pad of his thumb across the darkness beneath her eyes.

"You're exhausted and living in an environment that is much less than you deserve. Let me help you."

Her eyes never wavered. "Because you want in my bed."

"Wanting you in *my* bed has nothing to do with this," he countered, dropping his hand to her bare shoulder. "I don't like seeing you so worn down and being taken advantage of."

Before she could respond or argue, Sam took a step back. "Go get some shoes. I'm taking you to get something to eat."

She glanced down. "In case you missed it, I'm not dressed for going out."

Oh, he hadn't missed a thing about her...hence the state of his constant arousal, and it wasn't taking her out in public that he wanted.

"Nobody will see you but me," he assured her.

Maty cocked her head. "Why does that sound dirty?"

He couldn't help but laugh. "If you're offering..."

She rolled her eyes and headed back toward her room. "Let me get my shoes."

A small victory, but he had a feeling the more time that passed without him knowing what was going on between Maty and Rusty, the deeper he'd be pulled into her world.

Was he playing right into Rusty's scheme? Was Maty in on this plan? He didn't think so, but at the same time, he hadn't seen her for sixteen years and here she was playing on his every emotion.

That was fine. There was no reason they couldn't pick up where they left off the other night. No reason they couldn't enter into a brief affair. They'd danced around this attraction for the past few days…the attraction that was only growing each time they were together.

Sam was taking back control of this entire ordeal and he would come out on top, unscathed and heart intact.

Maty shouldn't have been surprised when Sam turned into his driveway.

"Are you making dinner?" she snorted.

"Actually, my chef made up a variety of things earlier today, so you have your choice."

He pulled into his attached garage and the door closed behind them. Something about that closure had her pulling in a deep breath and wondering what would happen now. Sam was right that she was vulnerable and scared and being jerked around by Rusty, but telling Sam wouldn't fix the problem. If anything, it would only add to her issues because Sam would likely try to ride to her rescue.

She had to stand on her own, to find her footing in this new chapter of life. Falling back onto the man she'd once loved and left wouldn't be looking forward or helping her rebuild her life.

Maty would find a way to get all of this worked out so nobody got hurt. Well, she might get a few emotional scratches, but that was better than her brother not receiving the care he needed. She would do anything for him…he was the only family she had left.

Tears pricked her eyes. She hated being emotional, especially in front of Sam. Crying didn't solve anything and she didn't have time for the breakdown she desperately deserved.

Once upon a time, she'd had everything. Her family, a lucrative career, and she'd been only one rung away from making partner at the most prestigious firm in Arlington, Virginia.

All of that changed in the span of a year when her parents died, her brother was injured and Rusty blackmailed her.

Here she was at rock bottom, back in her hometown, and the one man she didn't want to see her at her absolute worst was now the one man she wanted to lean on the most.

When he stepped out of the truck, Maty patted her eyes and opened her door. Sam was already there, reaching for her hand.

"You want to talk about the tears?" he asked, his broad frame blocking her from exiting.

Nothing ever got past the man. He'd always been so in tune with her feelings and emotions when they'd been together before. Perhaps that was just a by-product of being raised by a single woman.

"Not particularly," she replied. "Do you want to talk about your bad day?"

Sam's lips twitched. "Let's go see what my chef prepared."

Clearly they were at a standstill. Fine by her. The less personal involvement they had, the better in the long run. Orgasms didn't count.

Maty followed him into the house. The kitchen had the largest concrete island she'd ever seen. She could appreciate this space more now than when she'd been here for the five-minute tour of the main floor and the hour up in the bedroom.

She took a seat at one of the sturdy wooden bar stools at the island and set her bag next to her. She watched as Sam bustled around in the fridge, pulling out various dishes.

"We're having a buffet," he told her as he continued searching. "Why don't you get into the wine fridge and grab something that interests you."

"You like wine?" she asked, going to the far wall that held an impressive-sized wine cooler.

He tossed a glance over his shoulder, his gaze raking over her. "I'm a connoisseur of all the fine things."

Yeah, they weren't just talking drinks anymore. As if she weren't on edge enough, adding in the impossible-to-ignore attraction certainly wasn't helping.

Maty chose a chilled Pinot and set it on the island. "Where's your opener?"

Sam grabbed some napkins and forks and nodded to the corner of the minibar. Maty spotted the electric opener and had the cork off in no time.

The view out the back patio doors was absolutely breathtaking. With the sun setting behind the mountains in the distance and the calm of the evening, Maty relaxed somewhat. Sam wasn't pushing for her to tell him things she couldn't and he wasn't trying to get her out of her clothes.

With her current state of anxiety, she wasn't sure she could turn him down for either request too much longer. She desperately wanted someone to lean on, someone to offer her much needed advice. There was no one. Not anymore.

The people she spoke with the most were Carter's nurse and Rusty Lockwood. Neither of them were people she could confide in.

"If you keep looking like that, I'm going to think you hate my company."

Maty glanced over to Sam who stood with his hands resting on the edge of the island. She stared at the ridiculous display of food and couldn't stop the laugh.

"How hungry are you?" she asked.

"Starving—and you probably only had some granola bar or microwave noodles for dinner."

Actually, she hadn't even made it to her microwave yet before he came, so he didn't know everything.

"Sit," he ordered, pulling out a leather chair that should have looked ridiculous at a dining table, but seemed masculine and fitting. "I'll make you a plate and pour you a glass of wine."

At this point she didn't care if he had ulterior motives. The fact that someone was feeding her and supplying wine was all she needed to relax…even if just for a minute and even if she ended up in his bed.

Because she knew without a doubt that's where they were headed. Maybe not tonight, maybe not tomorrow. But Maty was certain that she wouldn't get out of Green Valley without landing in Sam Hawkins's bed again.

Eight

Sam had put away all of the leftovers, poured Maty another glass of wine and sent her into the library. She'd always been a bookish, artistic type. She'd been quite the artist when it came to pencil sketches and she'd always loved to read. His library had quite the variety of books and even an art desk in the corner. The room was tailor-made for her, though he'd never admit to any such thing if she asked him about it.

Right now, he wanted her to feel safe and calm. Something had bothered her today and he wanted her relaxed.

His own day had been a blow to the face, but at least he knew the truth. Now he could move forward with the facts and use this knowledge as just another leg up over Rusty.

There was just so damn much to do. He needed to get his mother help, he needed to confront Rusty, and he needed to figure out how he and Nick were ultimately going to fight Rusty and win.

Then there was Maty.

Dealing with Maty sounded like a simple thing, when in reality she assaulted all of his emotions about every aspect of his life. She comprised a good piece of his past and was now settling all around his future. Having her back in Green Valley had thrown him off, but he couldn't say he was sorry.

And now she was back in his house because he couldn't just leave her be. Damn it, why did he have to care if Rusty was taking advantage of her?

He cared because he was nothing like his bastard father.

What would Maty say when she found out the truth?

Sam certainly admired her strong will, but at this point that hard head of hers was going to get her hurt and possibly damage her career. Rusty was still being investigated for illegal dealings and Sam didn't want Maty anywhere near that.

If the truth came out that Rusty was indeed stealing from the funds his employees set aside specifically for Milestones, a children's charity, Rusty Lockwood would be finished...and so would anyone associated with him. Sam truly wanted Maty to have that career she'd left so long ago to achieve.

What happened to her family money? That question kept niggling at the back of his mind. Had she gotten involved in some scandal or made really poor financial choices? Something had happened to rip away the wealthy lifestyle Maty had grown up with.

Sam raked a hand over the back of his neck and headed from the kitchen toward the library. He stopped short at the open double doors. Maty had climbed up on the mobile ladder and was raking her fingertips along the spines of a series he'd never had a chance to read.

He couldn't help but admire her curves in those damn leggings and the way she reached had her T-shirt coming up and allowing him a nice glimpse of pale skin just above her waistband.

Gritting his teeth, Sam stepped in, making sure to slide his feet across the hardwoods to announce his presence and not frighten her.

"You've got quite a collection," she told him, still surveying her options. "I'm pretty sure I'd have to move my office to this room and never leave if I lived here."

If she lived here. That image hit him hard.

What seemed like a lifetime ago, they'd planned on living together. He'd had no money to offer, no home, but he would've done anything to give her whatever she wanted. He would've moved every obstacle, slain every demon to make her happy.

Yet she'd had other goals...goals that didn't include him.

Now, though, it seemed their roles had reversed.

Pulling a book from the slot, Maty glanced at the cover and carefully climbed back down. Sam crossed to see what she'd chosen.

"Historical," he muttered, looking at the title. "That always was your favorite subject."

She met his gaze. "History is so fascinating. That's how we got to where we are today. The culture, the laws."

Her intelligence had always impressed him, attracted him, and now was no different. There was so much similar about her, yet so many things had changed. How could he *not* want to get to know her more? To unveil each and every layer she'd added since leaving town?

"Do you always bring your ladies into your library?" she joked with a teasing smile. "Because I have to tell you, this room is a panty dropper."

Her face instantly shifted to a deep pink.

"Forget I said that," she quickly added. "I don't want to know what you do with women in here and I'm sure as hell not dropping my panties."

Sam tipped his head. "No? Well, that ruins all of my plans for the evening."

"You brought me here for sex? So predictable."

Sam shrugged. "I brought you here because I wanted some semblance of happy at the end of this terrible day. After I saw where you lived, I figured you'd want to explain how that happened. I'm trying to help you out of a situation I have no clue how you got into, and you're driving me out of my mind."

In so many ways. He wanted her physically, but he had to know what the hell she was hiding. Until he had all the ammunition on Rusty, moving forward was going to be the equivalent of walking through a minefield.

Maty let out a shaky sigh and turned. She crossed to the oversized desk beneath the long row of glass windows giving an impressive view of the mountains in the distance. She set her book down and shifted to lean against the edge of the desk.

Whatever war she was waging with herself, she clearly didn't want Sam as a witness. Too damn bad. He couldn't help her if he let her keep hiding...he'd been through that enough with his mother.

"Rusty offered me a job and a place to live if I came here," she told him as she crossed her arms over her chest. "I had no idea the place he had chosen was your old apartment until I arrived in town. I had nowhere else to go."

"Why didn't you just rent something else?" Sam asked. "I know a great Realtor who could hook you up with something in a better area, probably with some great views."

Her smile didn't quite reach her eyes. "Thanks, but I've got it covered."

Clearly she didn't have "it" covered or she wouldn't be in an apartment that was run-down and held memories for both of them. None of this made any sense.

Sam slid his hands into his pockets and kept his attention on her. The confidence and light he'd always associated with Maty didn't exist anymore. Even when she'd first called him, when he first saw her, she'd exuded that strength. But now…something, or someone, was pulling her down and he intended to find out what or who it was.

"What's Lockwood holding over you?" he asked.

She spun around to face him, that determined expression staring back at him, but there was still an underlying layer of fear. He could see it and he needed to penetrate that barrier she'd erected.

"Nothing I can't handle," she assured him with a smile that she clearly had to work for.

Sam took a step toward her. "You keep saying that, but you look exhausted."

"Well, if you'd sell your distillery to Rusty, then my stressful job would be over." She shrugged. "Do you want to discuss that?"

"Never."

"Then we're at a standstill."

Like hell they were. This interchange wasn't that simple or tidy. Frustration rolled through him and he knew there would be a good amount of time spent in his gym with the punching bag later.

"If you won't let me put you in touch with my Realtor to find you something you deserve, then get your things and move in here."

Maty stared at him, her eyes wide with shock. Hell, he'd surprised himself because the words had come out before he could fully think them through. But he wasn't sorry and had he given the idea more thought, he still would've said the same thing.

"I can't move in here, Sam. I work for Rusty and you and I are…we're…"

Sam slowly closed the distance between them, placing his hands on the desk on either side of her hips. "What are we, Maty?"

Her hands came up to his chest and she pressed against him. "Ease up there, pal. You're trying to make me say something that I'm not ready to admit."

Sam laughed and nipped at her lips. "Careful, babe. That lawyer side is starting to show."

"Because that's what I am before anything else," she replied. "My career is the one thing I have. It's my own and I have little else right now."

She'd lost so much, that was clear. But how?

Sam eased back, but not much. "So you've put your career before everything since you left? No relationships, no marriage?"

Her eyes darted away. "Nothing like that."

Interesting. That was a long time she'd been gone and she'd never pursued a relationship? Not that he had gotten into anything serious, either.

"I mean, I dated," she amended. "I've had lovers."

He shouldn't be jealous, that was absurd. He hadn't been celibate for sixteen years so he knew she hadn't been, either.

And yet, he didn't want either of their past lovers to be dropped between them.

"Listen, don't make a decision right now," he told her…though he wanted her to say yes and just move in. "Think about it. You'll see staying here with me is for the best. You've seen how much room I have. You don't even have to see me if you don't want. If I'm the one helping you, then Rusty won't have a leg to stand on and can't hold anything over you."

And that was the gist of this entire situation. Sam wanted to be the one Maty needed.

A sad smile spread across her face. "You make it sound so easy, but that's not how reality works."

"Look—"

She held up a hand and eased away. "Why don't you tell me about how you came to be the youngest billionaire and master distiller in Tennessee."

She wanted a distraction from Rusty? Discussing Hawkins wasn't exactly the distraction he'd been thinking of, but it was his second favorite option.

"Fair enough," he agreed. "You know I always liked to experiment with beers when I was younger, but that wasn't where my passion was. I wanted more. When I was eighteen, my mother informed me that she'd invested a large sum of money when she found out she was pregnant with me."

Maty's eyes widened in surprise. "Wow. She did that? Um…sorry. I just never took her for someone to save."

Sam nodded. "No, it's okay. It's not like her gambling habit is a secret. She invested the money before her addiction really took hold."

"I didn't know you had that money when we were together," she told him. "Not that it matters."

"I didn't say anything because I didn't think of it as money I could use." Sam took a step and rested his hip on the back of a chair. "I'd been with her long enough to know one of us needed to be responsible and I didn't know when that money would be needed in an emergency."

Maty offered a smile as she tipped her head. "You always were mature for your age."

He had been, but he still hadn't been enough for Maty to stay. Now, though, he controlled his destiny, his relationships. Everything. He'd never let his defenses down again. Remaining in power over all aspects of his life was the only way to secure his heart.

"I tried bourbon at a tasting I went to and fell in love," he went on. "I knew that was what I wanted to do. Of course, there was much more that went into my start-up, but that's the dream I had and when I found out the old bourbon distillery in town was going to be sold, I knew that was my chance. The place hadn't been bringing in the profit it should've to keep running. I was literally in the right place at the right time to restart and all of the working equipment was there. I just had to use the funds that Mom invested. It was a risk because if I failed, we had nothing to fall back on. I poured my entire life into Hawkins from day one."

An idea sparked and he came to his feet and reached for her hand before he could talk himself out of this craziness. Why was he trying so hard for a woman who had shoved him aside years ago and wasn't letting him in now to help when she so desperately needed it?

"Do you trust me?" he asked.

Maty's brows rose as she laughed. "Should I not trust you? I'm the one keeping secrets."

"We all have secrets, Maty." And he wasn't ready to divulge his. He raked his thumb over the back of her knuckles. "Do you trust me?"

Her face instantly sobered and she nodded. "You keep asking me that. I trust you."

Those three simple words, said with such conviction, hit him hard. A sliver of hope speared him. Maybe, just maybe, he was getting through to her.

Here she was, stuck in the middle of a fight that had absolutely nothing to do with her. She deserved to know the truth, but at the same time, she wasn't exactly forthcoming with her own issues. So how the hell could he open up to her?

Sam squeezed her hand and smiled. "It's time for a field trip."

Maty had no clue what Sam had in mind when he'd mentioned a field trip, but sneaking in the back door of Hawkins Distillery certainly wasn't on the top of her list.

Well, she wasn't exactly sneaking since she was with the CEO, but it was dark and they hadn't used the main entrance.

"Isn't there a front door?" she asked as she stepped inside and Sam typed in a security code before flipping on the lights. "This feels very illegal."

Sam laughed. "I assure you, this is all very legal."

Maty glanced to the high ceilings, the large vats.

Hoses seemed to run in all directions. The exposed brick walls added charm to the old building. All of the rustic areas mixed with modern day machinery seemed so Sam...a little rough around the edges, but polished.

"This building is amazing," she told him as she continued to survey the open space and the production area of the distillery.

"I figured you'd think so. It was built in the late 1800s." Sam moved around her and went to the far wall in the corner. "If you look here, they've marked when the flood came through in 1903."

Maty glanced up to where he pointed and noted the old plaque that had bronzed with age. She'd actually done a report in high school about that flood.

"This building was originally built as a hospital," she told him.

Sam nodded. "It was completely empty when William Wallace bought it to turn it into a distillery. When I purchased the place from him, we had to upgrade quite a bit for what I wanted, but the bones were here for me to work with."

Maty listened as he spoke with passion about not only his work, but also this building. He'd done so much, moving slowly to make sure he got things right before he opened the place up to the public for tours and tastings. He claimed he led several of the tours for years, without telling anyone he was the new owner. Maty loved that side of him, the side that was just an everyday guy who was doing what he loved.

Sam might be a billionaire, but he wasn't one who sat in an office all day. He truly loved every aspect of his work and it showed.

She followed him as he explained the process from

the making of the mash to adding the yeast for fermentation. He explained how many hours or days everything had to wait between each step. The timing of a batch was crucial, even before it ever made it into a charred barrel.

"And you're about to unveil your first ten-year bourbon in a few months, right?" she asked.

Sam nodded. "That's one of the first things I did when I took over. I wanted to produce bourbon. That's been my ultimate goal. Our gin is the number-one seller in the country, third in the world. I'm hoping the bourbon takes off just the same."

Maty smiled. "I'm sure it will. You're Sam Hawkins. There's nothing you can't do."

His eyes ran over her. "There are some things that prove more difficult than others."

She held his gaze for a few silent, intense moments. Maty's attraction, and clearly Sam's, was only growing with each passing moment they spent together. Plus, seeing him here in his element, doing something he'd always wanted to do, really put things into perspective. He was even more attractive than she'd remembered. There was this new layer to him she hadn't fully gotten to know, but now that she saw yet another passionate side to him, she couldn't deny her growing feelings.

Sam had set out to do exactly what he wanted and he'd let nothing stand in his way.

Maty had always wanted to be an attorney, and she was. But now that Rusty Lockwood had entered the picture, he was stealing the joy from Maty's and Sam's dream careers.

How could the monster be stopped? Because Maty truly didn't see any way around him, and if she confided in Sam, no doubt Sam would go straight to Rusty and demand he release Maty from her contract. Then where would her brother end up? Maty sure as hell didn't have the funds to help him, not anymore.

Her brother hadn't had insurance, so after the funeral expenses were paid for, the remainder of their inheritance had gone to medical bills. Maty had sold the family home and used that money as well. Her job had kept her going for only so long before more medical bills started coming in.

Little by little, she'd lost her grip on the life she'd built for herself. She'd sacrificed her relationship with Sam to make her career dreams come true—now look at her. She was on the brink of losing everything and that initial sacrifice had all been in vain.

"Show me more," she stated after a while, wanting to focus on something positive and because she was actually so proud of Sam. "Do you have the bottles ready to go for the new bourbon?"

Sam's lips quirked. "We do, but those aren't being unveiled yet."

"Not even to me?"

He crossed to her and slid his hand over the small of her back, guiding her through the maze of equipment. "Especially not to you."

Because she worked for Rusty.

She had to understand where Sam was coming from, but that didn't mean his words hurt any less. She'd told him she trusted him, but he still didn't trust her. As long as she worked for the enemy, Sam would always have his guard up.

Maybe he'd have his guard up even without Rusty.

After all, she was the one who had walked out. But… he hadn't even fought for her.

She'd always wondered if she would've given up everything for him, if he'd asked. But he'd been supportive of her dream and encouraging. How could she hate him for letting her go?

Damn those passive-aggressive thoughts. Nothing could change the past and she had enough of a mess with her present and future. There was no need to be looking backward.

"I can show you the warehouse where everything is stored," he countered. "But no pictures."

"I didn't even bring my purse or phone in," she replied.

Did he really think she'd take photos of everything here and send them back to Rusty? She wasn't that dedicated to the mogul. Her only loyalty came from ensuring her brother's health care, nothing more.

With Sam's hand on the small of her back, Maty was having a difficult time remembering why intimacy with him was a bad idea. Her body still zinged from that orgasm he'd given her days ago. Now here they were, in the evening, with not a soul around and all she wanted to do was strip out of these clothes and tell him to do whatever he wanted so long as it ended in pleasure for the both of them.

As they crossed the stone path that led to another building, Maty wanted more than anything to reveal the entire truth. She hadn't lied when she said she trusted him. She just didn't want him to think he had to save her. That was definitely not the attention she wanted from Sam. She didn't want his pity or his white knight rescue.

There had to be a way to make Rusty happy, allow Sam to keep his company, and keep her brother in the right care.

"You ever have bourbon?" he asked as they reached the old stone building with a modern metal door.

"I tried brandy once." She turned to face him and smiled. "I honestly thought it tasted like lighter fluid."

Sam laughed. "I'll ignore the fact that you've never had lighter fluid and just say that not all bourbons are the same and they definitely are quite different from brandy."

"I promise to try Hawkins when it releases."

Sam's hands came up to rest on her shoulders. "Maybe we can work out a deal where you get your very own complimentary bottle."

Maty couldn't help herself. She was going to play along.

The shadows across Sam's face seemed to make him menacing, mysterious. But she knew him. Even after all this time, she knew him.

"What did you have in mind?" she asked, knowing she had ventured into the "playing with fire" category.

There was this pull to Sam, stronger than the pull when they'd been younger. She found him even more fascinating, more powerful, more everything than sixteen years ago. He'd set his sights on a goal and nothing had stood in his way—not even losing her.

Confidence and integrity were serious turn-ons for her and Sam had all the qualities she loved in a man. Too bad she couldn't have this man back in her life.

Maty was so damn proud of him, especially considering his background. While she'd had all the makings for a successful future, her world had still crumbled.

The instant her parents and brother were in that accident, Maty had found herself spiraling down a black hole.

No matter what, she intended to claw her way out and land back on her feet again without begging anyone for help.

"I'm sure we can think of some way for you to get an exclusive bottle," he promised with a wink.

"Sexual?" she asked.

Sam shrugged. "If that's what you want."

"I'd rather buy a bottle than be gifted one after sex."

"Then why did you bring it up?"

Maty glanced away, afraid her emotions would show. "I assumed that's where you were headed with your thoughts."

He smoothed her hair back and framed her face, forcing her focus back to him. "I respect you a hell of a lot more than to exchange booze for sex, Maty. And any man who would treat you in such a demeaning manner should have his balls kicked up to his throat."

"Ouch," she cringed.

"I'm serious."

Those dark eyes held hers and she knew he took her welfare very seriously…that was part of the issue and the entire war she waged with herself. She'd love nothing more than to dump her problems on someone else and tell them to fix them. But that's not how she was raised and she was much stronger than that.

Sam leaned in and nipped the sensitive spot just below her ear, then stepped back, but he settled his hands on the dip in her waist. Shivers spread all through her as she stared back at him.

"What was that for?" she asked.

"Because I know you like that spot…or you always did, and I want you to know that I'm here. No matter what's going on with you and Rusty or whatever it is you're afraid to tell me, I'm here if you decide you need someone."

Maty's throat burned with emotion and she willed herself not to cry at his genuine words. How easy would it be to fall back into that comfort zone with Sam? Even though they had changed over the years, he still understood her.

But there was still so much standing in the way of her and Sam. The possibility of a relationship was so far-fetched, it seemed virtually impossible. She'd walked out on him once and was now working for his enemy.

But, one thing stood out above all else. She wanted Sam with a fierceness she was done denying. There was no reason she couldn't push those conflicts aside just for one night.

Tonight, she was taking what she wanted.

Nine

Sam had no clue what had come over Maty.

She had wrapped herself around him, plastering her body against his, kissing him like she'd been waiting the entire sixteen years to do so.

Sam gripped her backside and pulled her pelvis against his as he returned the passionate kiss. They'd been working up to this since that first moment she'd strolled into his office. She was too damn smart, too damn sexy, too damn…emotionally out of his reach.

Except now. And wasn't that what he wanted? The physical?

Sam sure as hell didn't have time to nurture a relationship. Hell, he was taking care of his company, his mother, getting started with a new brother, and maybe another… Then there was Rusty.

Not someone Sam wanted to filter through his mind while he had a handful of Maty.

Sam released her mouth, but nothing else.

"Why now?" he asked, trying to catch his breath.

She licked her lips and Sam's entire body tightened in response. He started walking her backward while she spoke.

"Because I want this," she told him as she nipped his chin. "And because, for tonight, I want to forget all the secrets and all the fears and every outside source that's telling me this is a mistake."

Fears. He knew she had them and he wanted more than anything for her to lay them all on him so he could protect her. But once again she was putting her career ahead of him. He expected nothing less, but that didn't mean he had to like it.

Why wouldn't she let him help? Yet another topic he didn't want to settle between them…

He wanted nothing more than to erase everything and everyone except this moment right here.

As he urged her into the warehouse, he quickly glanced away from her and punched the code before turning on a minimal amount of lighting and locking the door behind them. The hour grew later, they were alone, but he wasn't taking any chances.

Sam lifted her until her legs locked around his waist. He carried her to the side where an old bench sat next to the door.

"Is this part of the tour?" she asked with a smile.

"You're getting the exclusive VIP."

He sat her down and before he could reach for her clothes, she had her hands on his jeans. He wasn't about to stop a woman who clearly knew what she wanted. To know she was still so passionate, so ready for this, only turned him on even more.

The moment she jerked his pants and boxer briefs down, Sam reached behind his neck and grabbed a fistful of T-shirt and yanked it over his head.

Sam turned them and sat on the bench. Then he looked up and his eyes locked with hers. He'd never seen a more beautiful sight. Her lids were heavy with desire, her lips swollen from his. There was no hesitation, nothing that made him think she'd have regrets later. She had the slightest smile, a strand of hair had fallen over her forehead and down onto her cheek. She kept her attention on him as she peeled out of her clothes. One garment at a time, she performed the simplest, sexiest striptease until she stood before him completely bare.

"Get my wallet, back of my pants, and get out protection," he demanded.

When she bent over to retrieve the condom, Sam took every single second to admire her curves, her creamy skin. When she stood back up and shook her hair away from her face, Sam couldn't stop himself from reaching for her.

He gripped her hips and tugged her forward. "Put it on me," he growled, anticipation consuming him.

Maty tore open the package and rolled the protection into place. Sam gritted his teeth at her intimate touch. He'd never thought he'd be with her again. The possibility had never entered his mind. But now that she was here, he was going to take in every single moment... because this time might be the last.

They were using each other tonight. He wasn't naive anymore. She didn't want to be with him beyond sex, and he couldn't be with her after this, either. There was no happily-ever-after for them, like he'd assumed their first time around.

But he sure as hell wasn't going to turn away this sultry vixen as she started to straddle his lap. Maty's fingers curled around his shoulders as she stared down at him. He always liked to think he was in control, but at this moment, he was utterly powerless. Maty could do whatever she wanted and he would be more than willing to sacrifice his body to be her playground.

"Touch me," she demanded.

Sam filled his hands with her breasts—he replaced one hand with his mouth. The moment he covered her, she sank down and joined their bodies. Maty cried out and jerked her hips, urging Sam on even more. He was so consumed by this woman, watching her come undone all around him had to be the most erotic moment of his life.

True, they'd been together before, but nothing had prepared him for this very captivating version of his Maty.

Before those last two words could freak him out or cause him to worry, Sam curled his fingers around her hips and let himself go. She smoothed his hair back, rested her forehead against his, and pumped her hips in a way that made him go out of his ever-loving mind. She murmured something he couldn't quite make out, but he wasn't trying, either.

His body trembled for quite some time, and he was in no hurry to come out of this euphoric state. Having Maty enveloping him, having his every sexual fantasy come to life right here in his warehouse…this was much more than he'd ever expected.

"Is the tour over?" she finally asked.

Sam wasn't near ready to take her back. He palmed her backside and gave an arousing squeeze.

"We're just getting started," he promised.

* * *

Sam shoved his hands in his pockets and walked through the alley to meet Nick at the back door to the bar where Rusty and his cronies were inside for their weekly card game.

The sun hadn't quite set, but the taller building cast a shadow onto the narrow space. Nick waited outside the door and nodded as Sam approached.

"Does this all seem different now?" Sam gestured between them. "This truth is still processing."

Nick shrugged. "We're still the same people and thankfully neither of us are like that asshole in there."

Sam laughed. "True."

"Nothing is stopping me from bringing him down," Nick stated. "Knowing that you're my brother and in my corner only makes me more determined. You can get moonshine anywhere around here, but I want gin, bourbon, scotch… I want it all. My patrons deserve options and not to be limited… Never mind. I know you understand, I just get so pissed going around and around with this damn game Rusty is playing."

Sam listened and completely got where Nick was coming from. Rusty was the epitome of a bully and the man didn't give a damn who he hurt or stepped on, so long as at the end of the day, he continued to rake in the millions he believed he deserved.

"Listen, now that we both have more ammunition on him, we can really put the screws to Rusty," Sam stated. "You know his time is limited and he's not going to be able to keep up his monopoly on this area. Younger, smarter, much more powerful people are coming up and not backing down at his demands. He doesn't know how to handle that."

Nick nodded. "No, he doesn't. He called me the other day and asked me to reconsider exclusively serving his moonshine at the resort. He said he'd even work on a special batch just for my place."

Sam grunted. "I'm sure he would offer anything to a new resort that has so much buzz around it."

Which was why Rusty wanted his hand in all the distilleries, namely Hawkins—because of all the buzz.

"Well," Nick stated. "My assistant sent some informative stats to the city council members regarding the amount of revenue that would come into each restaurant and hotel should the liquor licenses open up."

Sam crossed his arms and rocked back on his heels. "Smart. Lockwood can't hold on to this stranglehold forever. His time is limited."

"I agree and we're just pushing this right along," Nick added with a smirk.

"I'm about finished with being subtle and nice," Sam stated as he nodded toward the closed door. "Let's go play some poker."

Before Sam could take a step, Nick held up his hand. "Everything okay?" he asked.

Sam sighed and wondered how Nick knew something else was on his mind. He'd taken Maty back to her place last night after she'd completely blown his mind in the warehouse. He hadn't mentioned her moving in with him again, but he hoped the seed had been planted and she'd seriously consider it.

What irked him now was that the idea had taken root in his own mind. He actually wanted her in his house.

In the beginning, he'd wanted her there to take the control away from Rusty, because if Maty was under

Sam's roof, then he had more leverage to help her and find out what the hell she was hiding.

But now…

Damn it, now he wanted her there for all those reasons and so much more. He wanted to protect her, he wanted her to feel safe and to stop this battle she would never win, and he wanted her in his bed.

"Woman troubles?"

"I don't have a woman, but I have problems," Sam stated honestly. "Let's deal with this problem first. Rusty has been a pain in my ass for years."

"Then let's see if we can't push this along," Nick said as he reached for the door handle. "When all this is wrapped up, maybe you'll want to let me in on the woman you claim you don't have."

Maybe he would. Maybe having a brother would reveal a whole new set of emotional doors, ones that would open up opportunities for Sam to move forward and trust others again.

All of that, including Maty, would have to be dealt with later. Right now, he had a poker game to attend.

Ten

"But that's not possible," Maty cried into her phone as she slammed her car door. "Carter's care is paid up for another month."

"I'm showing an email that states his stay and medical assistance will be terminated at the end of next week, but I wasn't given any indication on where he will be moved," the director of the facility stated. "I'm sorry to call so late, but I was working on some reports and was surprised to see this change since Carter has only been here a short time. I was hoping you could let me know where he's headed so we can contact the new facility and get the paperwork started."

Maty gripped her phone in one hand and fished her keys from her bag with the other. She had no idea what was going on, but she knew exactly who was holding the purse strings.

"Can I call you back?" Maty asked as she shoved open her door...or tried to because the damn thing kept getting stuck. "There's just been a misunderstanding and I'll get this squared away."

"Yes, of course. Thank you."

Maty disconnected the call and shoved her shoulder against the door to get the damn thing to open. Once she was in, her mind was racing. She didn't give a damn that it was late on a Friday night, she wanted some answers.

She dropped her purse on the table inside the door and immediately dialed Rusty. Of course the call went to voice mail. He could never be bothered to answer his cell, not even for her. He always called her back after he'd seen the missed call.

Maty shot off a text that she needed to speak with him and it was an emergency. Why in the hell had he messed with the payments? Why had he informed them that Carter wouldn't need a room after next week? There was nowhere else for her brother to go and without insurance or money up front, nobody would take him.

Part of her wanted to cry for being put in this position, but the practical side of her knew that nothing would be solved if she cried. Time was not on her side and she had to find some answers, then she had to find a solution.

She stared at her phone, willing it to ring. Frustrated, infuriated and beyond exhausted, Maty grabbed her bag and headed back out the door. She didn't even think about her next move, she simply got in her car and drove to Sam's house.

She hadn't seen him since he'd dropped her off at her apartment last night after her VIP tour of the distillery.

At this point, she wasn't sure what to say to him, at least not about their intimacy. What could be said? They clearly didn't have an issue with sex—granted that had never been a problem, but they weren't young and in love anymore. She had a serious problem and there was no way to get help unless she laid out her cards.

Which was how she found herself pulling into Sam's drive a few minutes later. These rash decisions weren't typical for her, but desperate times and all that.

Tears pricked her eyes, and she blinked them away as she pulled up to the steps of Sam's home. The moment she put the car in Park, the skies opened up and rain poured down. Groaning, Maty reached into her door pocket for her mini umbrella. She shoved open her door and attempted to gather her purse while opening the umbrella.

The damn thing wouldn't budge. She jerked at it one more time, but her hip bumped the side of the car and she closed the door on her purse.

Rain pelted against her as she jerked open the door and tugged her purse free to bang against her side. Once the door was closed, she finally got the umbrella up as she started toward the stone steps leading to the porch. A gust of wind caught her off balance and the umbrella jerked inside out.

Cursing, she tossed the damn thing into the landscaping and raced up the steps. Sam was probably inside laughing at her this entire time, nursing some tumbler of bourbon, while she stood out here soaking wet and shaking off the excess moisture like a dog.

It was then she realized the dampness on her face was rain mixed with tears. Angry tears, fearful tears, worried tears—she had them all and they weren't stopping anytime soon. There was only so long she could hold it together and she'd reached her breaking point.

She pressed the doorbell and waited, swiping the moisture from her face. After a moment, she used the door knocker and waited. And waited.

Damn it. She should've called or texted instead of assuming he was home. Where was he? Not like he had to check in with her or anything, but she needed him to be here. She needed to get this process moving. After the phone call she'd just had, there was no time to waste.

Furious, Maty pulled out her cell from her purse and dialed Rusty again. She left yet another message and then tossed the phone back into her bag and glanced around the porch. Rain continued to beat down and she eyed the broken umbrella in the landscaping. She was positive there was some resemblance between that damn thing and the shambles her life had become.

No matter, her first priority was to make sure her brother's care continued and he remained exactly where he was.

A rumble of thunder rolled through and Maty crossed to the porch swing. She wasn't going anywhere until she talked to Sam. A call from Rusty would be better, but she had to be more proactive than ever before.

Maty pointed her toe onto the porch floor and pushed off to send the swing swaying. Her mind traveled back to when she and Sam would lie in the back of his truck bed on a sleeping bag and stare up at the stars. They'd discuss the future, one they'd assumed they'd spend together. He'd always said he'd have a porch swing. He'd always told her he'd make a name for himself, to be someone she'd be proud to call hers.

But her goals had ultimately pulled her away from

him and no matter how much she'd tried to make everything work, having a long-distance boyfriend while attending law school hadn't been ideal. She couldn't give up her life's goal to study law for young love any more than Sam could give up his goals to follow her to law school. If she'd stayed and ignored what she'd truly wanted, she would've ultimately resented Sam. Maybe she should've tried to find her way back, but she'd been away so long fulfilling her obligations that she hadn't been sure how to try again.

She'd never wanted to hurt him and yet here she was, ready to hurt him all over again, but this time she had no choice.

Rusty wasn't backing down and he was forcing her hand by stopping the funding for Carter's care.

No matter what her feelings were for Sam, in the past or now, she had to promise him anything to get him to sell Hawkins. Her brother's well-being depended on it and her heart would just have to break again.

The poker game could've been worse. Sam was out only a few hundred bucks, but Rusty hadn't been in attendance. Perhaps he had something else to do, but Sam figured the old bastard was just avoiding him.

Even with Rusty's absence, Sam and Nick came away with a victory. A little chatter amongst the city council about the new resort and the new bourbon launch this fall was more than enough to pique their interest in revisiting how they approached liquor licenses.

Sam adjusted his wipers to a faster speed as he pulled into his drive. The lights slashed across the concrete and the trees flanking either side of the drive. His mind rolled from one thought to another, from one issue to the next.

Maybe he could have everything he wanted. The licensing opened up to where he could supply his own hometown with his own creations, ruining Rusty Lockwood…*and* he could have Maty.

He hadn't spoken to Maty yet today and he knew she had to be thinking of last night just the same as he was. Every touch, every kiss. Each moment kept playing through his mind. He wanted her to move in with him now more than ever.

As he approached his house, he spotted her red car in front of his porch. Sam pulled into his garage and, instead of going into the house and out the front door, ran up the stony path through the rain toward the porch. He did a quick glance toward her car to see if she was sitting inside, but he didn't see her. He did, however, spot a broken umbrella lying in the middle of his buttonbush.

The second he raced up the steps, he spotted her… asleep on his porch swing. The rain continued coming down in sheets and thunder rolled in the distance.

Sam swiped the rain from his eyes and raked a hand over his hair to get rid of the moisture. He didn't dare move closer. She looked so damn peaceful, even with those dark circles beneath her eyes. He wanted to erase any sign of stress or fear from her life. He wanted to give her everything she'd been robbed of…for reasons he still didn't understand.

Strands of honey hair had fallen over her shoulder and rested against her cheek. She still had on her shoes, her cell was clutched in one hand, but her purse was on the porch floor.

Had she been waiting on a call?

Sam pulled his cell from his pants and glanced to the screen. She hadn't called or texted him.

Did this mean she wanted to discuss moving in or had she just shown up for a repeat of last night?

He wouldn't mind both, actually.

Sam went to the front door, typed in the code to unlock it and reached inside to disarm the security system before turning his focus back to Maty. He took her purse and set it inside the entryway on the table, then he came back out. There was no way to avoid disturbing her sleep, but maybe he could make this as easy as possible for her.

He slid one arm around her shoulders and the other beneath her knees and scooped her up against his chest. Her phone fumbled a little in her hand, but ultimately landed where their bodies joined. Maty stirred, but her eyes remained closed as her head lolled toward him.

She was dead tired and working herself like a damn racehorse for a jackass who was using her. Sam still wasn't sure what was going on, but he knew Maty would literally break before admitting weakness.

As he carried her into the house, he knew full well that she wasn't weak. She never had been. This woman was one of the strongest he'd ever known and her coming back here, attempting to take on Sam as an opponent, just proved how strong willed she was. When faced with a losing battle, she still pressed on, determined to win.

How could he not admire her? How could he not find her strength so damn sexy?

The cell buzzed between them and Sam stopped before he could mount the steps. Maty's eyes flew open and she started moving to the point where he was afraid he'd drop her.

Carefully, he set her down and held her phone out to her, but not before he saw Lockwood's name on the screen.

Son of a bitch. The man had the absolute worst timing—not that there was ever a good time for Rusty to cause an interruption, but it was like he knew when to be the biggest pain and he reveled in the moment.

Maty grabbed the cell and swiped her hair from her face. She glanced around like she wasn't sure how she'd gotten into his house, but then she answered the call and turned her back to Sam.

Considering this was his house, he wasn't going anywhere and he'd be damned if he'd give her privacy right now. He reset the alarm and waited, knowing this call could be key in helping him figure out what was going on.

"What the hell are you doing to me?"

Sam was shocked at the way she answered the phone, but those words only confirmed exactly what he'd thought, what he'd been afraid of. That gut feeling grew deeper, the ache of realizing whatever Rusty held over her must be pretty bad for her to have such a reaction.

"You're playing a game with his life," she cried as she started for the steps.

Sam thought she was going to go up, but she reached up with a shaky hand and held on to the banister. Slowly, she turned to sit on the second stair. Her fingers curled around the wrought iron and she rested her head against her hand. Weariness and frustration radiated from her and Sam wanted to slay every damn dragon she faced—especially if they shared the same dragon.

But at this point he still didn't know what exactly he was up against.

"You ask the impossible," she murmured.

When her voice cracked on that final word, Sam had heard enough. He crossed to her, grabbed the phone from her hand and disconnected the call.

"Sam," Maty cried as she sprang to her feet. "You can't do that."

"I just did," he countered. "I'm not going to let that bastard continue to beat you down. What the hell is going on?"

Of all the reactions he expected, tears welling up in her eyes was not one of them. Her face crumbled as she turned away on an audible sob. He honestly expected her to fight him, to argue or grab her cell and call Rusty right back. He expected her to ignore his demand, but he'd not expected her to emotionally break down.

All the more reason to end this cycle of fighting and get her to talk to him. Everyone had a breaking point and Maty had obviously just reached hers.

Sam shoved her cell into his pocket and closed the narrow distance between them. Gripping her shoulders, he pulled her back against his chest and waited for her to say something. As much as he wanted answers, he didn't want to see her hurting. Nothing was worth her pain, not even him gaining more leverage over Rusty.

Maty's body shook and the racking sobs absolutely broke him.

Turning her, Sam lifted her in his arms once again and carried her up the stairs.

"I'm not staying," she sniffed. "Sex isn't why I came."

He said nothing as he continued up to his master suite. He'd have to be a completely heartless jerk to assume she was ready for anything other than shelter. That's all she needed at this point. Shelter from Rusty, from herself, even from Sam. She needed to feel safe and damn it if he wasn't going to be the one to give her the haven she needed.

"I can't stay here," she muttered, the fight literally draining from her voice. "I have to fix this. You have to... I'm sorry. You have to sell the distillery. I know how hard you've worked and it's your passion. But please."

Like hell. He wasn't selling. He wasn't letting Rusty trample all over her, and he sure as hell wasn't letting any of this continue another day.

Sam stepped into his room just as a flash of lightning lit up the glass of the balcony doors. He laid her on his bed and smoothed her hair from her face. Reaching over, he clicked on the small accent lamp on the nightstand and sank down on the edge beside her hip.

Her watery eyes stared up at him. "I don't have time for this," she told him. "I have to make sure Carter stays where he is."

Carter? What did her brother have to do with this entire ordeal?

"You're not making sense, sweetheart."

She closed her eyes and pressed her fingertips to her forehead. "My brother needs medical care. I can't afford it anymore."

"Medical care for what?" Sam asked, leaning down closer to hear her mumbles.

"The wreck that claimed my parents." She opened her eyes and focused on him once again. "That wreck left my brother paralyzed, and he needs twenty-four-hour care. Governmental aid isn't enough to cover the high-quality care he needs. He's at River Bend in Arlington right now."

Paralyzed. Damn. Why hadn't she told him that before? Why hadn't he searched deeper into her past to figure out what was going on? He knew she'd battled something, but he'd been too consumed with his own issues, too distracted by his reaction to having her back in his life that he hadn't gone that extra step.

Because he'd been consumed with seeing her again and he'd been rendered useless by his hormones.

Now here she was, clearly being manipulated by Rusty in a way Sam had never imagined and in a more infuriating way than he'd expected.

"Rest," he told her, hoping he could make her realize he wasn't the enemy. "I'll take care of it."

Her eyes widened with fear. "No. You can't."

"I will," he assured. "You said the other night that you trusted me. Now is the time to put that trust to the test."

She started to sit up, but Sam placed his hands on her shoulders and eased her back down. She wasn't going anywhere tonight...or for a long time if he had his way about it. She needed to find a place where she could rest and recover. Self-care was something he insisted his employees take time for and Maty was a hell of a lot more important in his life than they were...more important than he wanted to admit even to himself.

"Trust me," he murmured, staring straight into her worried eyes.

"Don't take on Rusty," she pleaded. "He's awful, Sam. You can't get mixed up with him."

Too late.

"I'm taking over," he told her, placing a kiss on her forehead. "Don't worry about your brother, Lockwood or even yourself. It's all on me now and I swear to you, this will all be taken care of."

Every single bit. He hadn't been able to fix their relationship in the past, but he sure as hell could fix her situation now. There was no money, no powerful man, absolutely nothing that would prevent him from making all of this right for her.

He would take on Rusty and it would be a damn pleasure to ruin the bastard. Father or not, Rusty Lockwood's reign of bullying and controlling was officially over.

Eleven

Hands roamed over her hip and down to the dip in her waist. Maty arched, relishing in the promising, arousing touch.

That talented hand moved around to the front, teasing the edge of her panties at that most sensitive spot high on her inner thigh. Her hips jerked just as the fresh aroma of coffee overcame her.

Coffee? Who the hell was making coffee at a time like this?

Maty blinked, focusing on the foreign room.

Oh, no. No, no, no.

She was in Sam's bedroom and Sam's hand wasn't on her at all.

"Don't let me stop you."

Her own hand had been teasing the edge of her lacy panties, but she'd clearly been dreaming that touch belonged to Sam…and she'd been caught.

Maty jerked around to see him standing at the end of the bed, mug in hand, naughty grin on his face.

Why did she have to be dreaming about the man while in his bed without him? Couldn't she just have a fantasy in private?

Maty grabbed the sheet and yanked it up over her waist.

"Where are my clothes?" she asked.

He moved around to her side of the bed and extended the mug. "I removed your shoes and pants after you fell asleep. I figured you should be comfortable. I assure you, you're the only one who did any touching of that body."

Maty rolled her eyes and sipped the coffee.

"I assume you still take vanilla creamer and sugar."

She eyed him over the rim. "You keep vanilla creamer?"

Sam shrugged. "I bought it yesterday since I asked you to move in the night before."

"Should I be impressed that you remembered my coffee order?" she asked, ignoring the topic of her moving in.

"I impressed myself," he told her with a wide grin. "You hungry?"

Damn it. He was being all cute when she just wanted to be angry. But she wasn't angry with him. She was angry at herself for being caught in this trap to begin with and for showing so much vulnerability by coming here in the first place.

"Do you want to get down to business or do you want to get breakfast first?" he asked.

She clutched the sheet and narrowed her eyes.

"I appreciate the invitation, sweetheart, but by business I meant discussing your brother and Rusty."

That got Maty's attention. She glanced around for her phone.

"I need to—"

"You need to do nothing," he told her. "Your brother's care is paid for through the next five years."

Maty gasped as she stared back at Sam. "What?"

"I called first thing this morning and spoke to a wonderful lady named Pearl and she was all too helpful and delighted that Carter would continue his care at River Bend." Sam sat down next to her, took the mug from her hands and placed it on the nightstand. "So, that's taken care of for a while. Is that all that Lockwood held over you? I'm assuming you had to get me to sell or he was cutting off funds for your brother? I am still trying to figure out what happened to your money, though I'm assuming funerals and medical bills wiped you out."

Maty couldn't believe what she was hearing. The cost of Carter's care for one year alone was staggering and he'd paid for *five* all before she'd even had her first cup of coffee.

He'd also figured out each and every one of her puzzle pieces and put them together like an expert. He wouldn't have gone to all that trouble if he didn't care... would he?

Still, as grateful as she was, she was also embarrassed that she couldn't take care of her own family... her *only* family.

"I—I don't know when I can repay you," she admitted, humiliated that she couldn't even stand on her own two feet right now.

"You're not repaying me anything, ever." Sam laid his hand over hers. "Now would be a good time to say thank you and then tell me you're moving in so Rusty doesn't hold anything else over your head."

"What?"

He shook his head. "That came out wrong. I didn't help your brother as leverage to get you to live here. I helped because he needs the best care and I don't want Rusty to have any more power over you. He might be an asshole but the facility he paid for is one of the best, which I'm assuming is how he kept blackmailing you."

"How do you know it's so good?" she asked.

He leveled his gaze on her and Maty knew he'd obviously done some research while she'd been sleeping.

She didn't say a word. Sam was right and now that he knew the truth, there was really no need for her to stay here. Maybe she should go back to Virginia to be with her brother, try to rebuild her life. She needed to find a job before Rusty made good on his promise and ruined her completely. At this stage in the game, she didn't have the means or the energy to fight him.

Maty pushed away from Sam and sat up. "I have to go," she told him, but he didn't budge. "Move, please."

"You don't have to go anywhere."

"I do. I can't—"

"Stay," he commanded. "Move your stuff in here and we can work this out."

Confused, Maty jerked. "Work what out?"

"You want to get back at Rusty for using you? Stay and help me take him down."

Maty studied his face. He was serious. Sam's jaw clenched as his stare held hers. She had never seen him this determined, this…almost angry.

"All because he wants to buy your distillery?" she asked. "That's what has you so upset?"

"My issues with Rusty go well beyond that," he replied. "I intend to see him pay no matter if you stay or not, but…stay, Maty. Just stay."

She'd never heard him sound so sincere. No, that wasn't right. He'd been extremely sincere when he'd asked her to stay the first time, when they'd been young. She hadn't been able to let herself even think about the possibility of staying the first time, but now…

Could she stay?

Could all of this be that simple? Or would Sam try to take over everything the way he'd handled these issues with Rusty? She'd prided herself on being independent for so long, but maybe it was time to admit she needed help. There was nothing shameful about being human and needing a hand.

And she couldn't deny Sam, not when her needs were too great, her heart becoming too involved.

Wanting a physical relationship with him was so naive, so not the place she was in her life right now, but here she was.

"Quit analyzing everything and just go with your gut," he told her. "When I asked you to stay, what was your first reaction?"

"Yes." She gripped the sheet in her hands. "My first thought was to ignore everything and say yes."

"Then say it now," he implored.

Maty closed her eyes and pulled in a deep breath. Why couldn't she? If her brother was safe, for a good amount of time now thanks to Sam, then Rusty had no hold over her. Sam would help her make sure Rusty didn't ruin her reputation to the point she couldn't get another job. She was free to do what she wanted…with whomever she wanted.

She'd meant it when she'd told Sam she trusted him. But did that trust extend to her heart?

Focusing on Sam's intense gaze once again, Maty swallowed. "And if I stay, then what?"

"We work to show Rusty that he can't manipulate people to get what he wants whenever he wants."

Sam seemed so intent on this plan…which made her realize that he held some animosity toward Rusty that had nothing to do with her. Whether she stayed or not, she had a feeling Sam would seek revenge and succeed in achieving it.

For messing with her life and her brother's, Maty was on board. Plus, how could she deny herself the one man she'd always wanted? Maybe she was a fool, but at this point, she really had nothing to lose. She had to make a fresh start sometime. Maybe it wouldn't work here, maybe it would. She'd never know if she didn't try.

"I'll stay," she told him. "For now."

The smile that spread across his face curled her toes and left nerves dancing in her belly.

What had she just agreed to?

A wave of relief washed over Sam. She was his…for now anyway. He hadn't thought much beyond getting her to agree, but he wasn't going to question anything.

Did he want her in his bed? Hell, yes. Did he want her to be where he could be reassured she was safe? No doubt.

Did he want something beyond all of that? Honestly, he was afraid to even let his mind travel down that path.

Right now, he had more on his plate than at any other

time in his life. Moving his mother into a treatment program for her gambling addiction, playing games with Rusty, having a half brother, reuniting with the woman he'd fallen in and out of love with...

Just going down the list boggled his mind. Because on top of all of that, he had a distillery to run and a milestone bourbon launch to prepare for.

Which reminded him...

"Are you free next Friday?"

Maty blinked and leaned back against the pillows. "Friday? I don't think I'm busy. I mean, I need to figure out employment before Rusty has a chance to tarnish my name. He's too sneaky, so nailing him for slander might prove to be difficult and—"

"Rusty won't touch your reputation. Trust me." Sam would make damn sure of that. "So you're free Friday?"

She reached for her coffee and curled her fingers around the mug. If she had half the amount of confidence as she used to, she'd soon feel better about taking these next unknown steps.

"I'm visiting my brother sometime, but that's flexible. I can be free on Friday," she told him. "What's going on?"

"There's a private showing at Hawkins. Strictly for my high-end buyers and a few others I've invited to sample the bourbon that we will roll out in a couple months. It will be the first time anyone outside my elite group of employees has seen or tasted any of the ten-year bourbon."

He was both nervous and excited. He'd waited a decade for this moment...longer if he added in all the years he'd dreamed of becoming a master distiller.

"I want you there with me," he added, sliding a hand over her thigh.

She sipped her coffee and set it back down and stared at him a moment before letting out a snort of laughter.

"You want me to attend some open house, gala, VIP event when I was the one hell-bent on getting you to sell the entire company?"

He squeezed her leg through the sheet. "You were acting out of desperation because a man was blackmailing you."

"What do you think he's going to do when he finds out what all you've done?" she asked. "When he knows there's no more leverage over me and he's not going to get what he wants?"

"I can't wait until he finds out," Sam replied honestly. "I want him to realize he can't manipulate people, and he sure as hell can't have my distillery. He can make all the moonshine he wants, but I have a feeling his empire may be collapsing soon."

Lockwood Lightning had been under investigation for a month now regarding some embezzling when it came to the charity Rusty claimed to support financially. That was just another reason Sam wanted Maty away from that toxic man.

"I had nothing to do with his dealings with the charity," Maty told him. "When Rusty brought me on, he made sure to keep all other legal aspects private. My only job was to reconnect with you and find a way to get you to sell. He was willing to volley back and forth if you didn't agree to the amount he originally set."

"That's what someone like Rusty will never understand," Sam replied. "I'm not in this for the money, so no offer would've made me give up what I love."

Maty smoothed her hair back and pulled it over one shoulder. "I hate being used as a pawn," she complained. "I want to help you take him down for what he did to my brother and to me."

A plan formed faster than Sam could comprehend, but once the idea took root, he knew it was damn brilliant.

"Keep working for Lockwood," Sam suggested.

Maty nearly jumped. "What?"

"Let him think you have me considering an offer. I don't even care if you tell him you're staying here. Do what you think is best, but just make him believe things are going his way."

Maty's brows drew in as she tipped her head to the side. "Are you using me?"

Sam shifted on the bed until he had both hands resting on either side of her head and he was within a breath of her face.

"Never," he promised. "If you don't want to be part of this or if you want no more dealings with him, I'll make sure you never have to worry about him again. Just say the word."

Her wide eyes studied him. "No. I'm all in with you."

And because he was this close and she looked too damn sexy rumpled in his bed, he slid his lips over hers for the briefest of moments.

"I'll never use you, Maty, and I won't let anyone else use you, either."

He kissed her again, this time coaxing her lips apart because he wanted more…he needed more.

Her fingertips feathered over his arms and onto his shoulders as she pulled him in deeper. Sam eased up further onto the bed until he lay mostly on top of her.

He was careful to keep his weight shifted so he didn't crush her.

"Do you still trust me?" he murmured against her lips.

She nodded as she closed her eyes and tipped her head, silently seeking more. But he needed to hear the words.

"Say it," he demanded.

Her eyes met his as her lids fluttered open. "I trust you, Sam. I always have."

"I will make this right for you," he assured her. "And for your brother."

"I know you will. You already have."

"I haven't done enough," he countered. "Not yet."

She started to say something else, but Sam eased back and gripped the hem of her shirt. He hesitated, waiting for any indication that she wasn't ready, but since she'd just agreed to move in with him, he had to assume she was on the same page.

"Do it," she told him.

Being demanding in the bedroom was the sexiest damn thing. Maty had always been bold, assertive. It was one of the main things that had attracted him so long ago and his response now was absolutely no different.

She might have gotten knocked down, but he knew Maty. She would rise from the ashes and be stronger than ever. Sam intended to be right there beside her.

That instant thought scared the hell out of him.

He had no clue where it had come from so he jerked the shirt up and over her head. Sex he understood, but all of the other deeper emotions that kept resurfacing he had no clue what to do with.

Once she was down to only her lacy panties, Sam stood and stripped down. When her eyes raked over him, he pulled in a deep breath. How could his ego not swell when she looked at him as if he were absolutely everything?

"Are you going to stand there all day or are you going to do something about this ache?" she asked.

Sam weighed his options and reached down to jerk the sheet away. Then he hooked his thumbs in the lace on her hips and pulled her panties down her legs and tossed the garment over his shoulder.

"I believe you already had a head start earlier," he told her. "Were you dreaming about anyone in particular?"

Maty's face flushed and he couldn't resist the mix of adorable and sultry. Lying bare in his rumpled bed was a fantasy he hadn't even realized he'd left lingering in his mind. Having her back was both perfect and terrifying. No matter how much he allowed himself to enjoy her body, he couldn't forget that she had left him before. This time, though, he had no preconceived notions about any happily-ever-afters or promises. There was only here and now.

"You expect me to go solo?" she asked, quirking a brow. "I can do that at my apartment."

Sam climbed onto the bed and straddled her, bracing his hands on either side of her head. "You're not going back there," he told her. "The place was a dump when I lived there and it's even worse now."

Maty stared up at him. Her fingertips trailed up his arms and over his shoulders until she threaded her fingers through his hair. He didn't want to control her, but he did want her safe. If he had to be stubborn about it, he would.

"I'm sorry about all of this," she told him.

Rage bubbled within him that Rusty had put her in a position of impossible circumstances and yet she still felt the need to apologize.

"None of this is your fault," he insisted. "But I don't want anything outside of this room to come in here. Right now, there's only us. Problems don't exist."

A smile spread across her face as she eased her legs wider, allowing him to settle even more between her thighs.

"Your world isn't as realistic as mine," she told him. "Money can solve your problems."

"Then we'll use all of my money to solve yours. We can discuss that later."

She started to open her mouth, no doubt to argue, which was clearly an occupational hazard as a lawyer, but he covered her lips with his. Sam didn't want to bicker. He didn't want her to worry about a single thing except feeling each other.

Maty arched against him as her knees came up on either side of his hips. The warmth of her body welcomed him in and he didn't recall another woman who'd ever made him feel this content, this wanted. She'd always been special, always been his.

His?

No.

She wasn't his. He had too much going on. She could be his physically, but emotionally…never again.

"Protection," she murmured against his mouth. "I'm on birth control, but I don't have anything else."

Oh, he had it, but he didn't want to use it with her if he didn't have to.

"I don't want a barrier," he told her, kissing his way along her jaw and down her neck. "I'm clean and I've always used protection."

He eased back slightly to see her face, to try to gauge what she was feeling, thinking.

"I trust you," he told her.

She framed his face, raking her thumb over his bottom lip. "I haven't been with a man in nearly two years. I'm clean."

Maybe he shouldn't be so thrilled at the fact she'd been alone, but he couldn't deny that he was happy to know she hadn't been with someone in a long time. He wanted all of her to be all of his...but he couldn't keep allowing his thoughts to get too wrapped up in feelings. If he continued to do that, then he would become too emotionally involved.

Sam reached down and gripped her inner thighs, spreading her farther apart. Maty's hips slowly tilted toward him, her eyes never leaving his.

Easing one finger over her heat, Sam continued to watch her. Nothing was sexier than Maty when she was aroused, so he slid into her and worked her with his hand. He shifted on the bed, making sure she knew exactly who was in charge here...though it wouldn't take much for the roles to be reversed.

With his free hand, Sam reached up and slid his palm over her abdomen and up to her breast. Her nipple pebbled beneath his touch and his body responded. Gritting his teeth, he willed himself to take his time. As much as he wanted to join their bodies, he also knew she deserved everything he could give.

Sex wasn't the answer to everything, but it sure as hell would take their minds off things for a while and it felt damn good.

"Sam, please."

Her plea was like gasoline on the fire. His body responded and he wasn't sure how much longer he could deny them both and draw this out.

"Tell me what you want," he demanded.

She reached her hands toward him. "You. Please."

That was all he needed to hear.

Sam came up onto his knees and gripped the back of her thighs. Her hands fell back beside her head, giving her a completely submissive look as she lay ready and willing for him.

The second he joined their bodies, Maty cried out and gripped the pillow in her hands. Sam kept hold of her legs as he started to move. Watching her back arch, her eyes close, her mouth open in ecstasy nearly drove him over the edge.

Maty locked her legs behind his back as she jerked her hips faster against his. Her cries and pants filled the room until her entire body convulsed around him, her knees tightening against his hips as her pleasure overcame her.

Sam wanted to watch her, he wanted to make this last, but he couldn't hold on another second. He followed her release and let the climax consume him.

Maty eased up onto her elbows and watched him, her eyes locking with his. There was something he couldn't identify in her expression, something that he hadn't seen before.

As his trembling slowed, Sam leaned down and covered her mouth with his. He released her legs and slid his hands over hers on the pillow, lacing their fingers together.

He didn't want this moment to end, didn't want her to ever leave his bed…and maybe his life.

That was something he'd have to work out on his own because he wasn't professing anything to her, not when both of their lives were so unstable. He'd been hurt by her once before, and while he planned on keeping her safe and secure, he also wasn't letting his guard down again.

Twelve

Maty stood in the library and pulled in a deep breath as she stared out at the pond. With her cell in one hand, she clutched a glass of wine in the other. She didn't necessarily believe in liquid courage, but having something else to focus on other than this phone call was imperative.

Sam had left for the distillery, to finalize plans for the gala. She honestly had no clue what she was going to wear, but that was another worry for another time.

She gripped the phone and waited. Rusty rarely answered her calls on the first try. She always had to keep calling or she had to leave a message and wait. For someone so hell-bent on buying out his rival, one would think he would answer every single time she called.

Everything with that infuriating man was a mind game.

As usual, Maty got his voice mail and yet again she

left a message. Frustrated, she ended the call and took a sip of her Pinot. She couldn't just sit around Sam's house all day and drink wine and play on her phone. She had to be proactive and search for another job.

But where?

The pressure wasn't as strong now that her brother's care was paid for. She had time to figure out if she should go back to Virginia or stay in Tennessee.

Her brother was in Virginia and she didn't want to be too far from him. Sam was in Green Valley.

She couldn't just restructure her life because last night had blown her mind. She couldn't send out résumés in this area simply because sex with Sam was even more powerful and intense than ever before. Good grief, how ridiculous could she be?

Anything deeper than sex that they'd had was in the past. All of this happening between them now was just… Well, she didn't know what label to use.

She knew she wanted to be here, she knew she wanted more of what they'd shared yesterday, but she had so many fears. What if Sam completely took over— as he was so good at doing—and she lost control of her life? She wanted to stand on her own, even though right now, she valued his help. She just didn't want him thinking he could dictate everything for her from now on.

And what if Sam was using her only as a way to pass the time? What if he was using her as more leverage against Rusty?

She had said she didn't like being a pawn in Rusty's game, but she didn't want to be a pawn for anyone. As much as she loved being with Sam again, she wouldn't be some intricate piece in his ploy, either.

Her cell vibrated in her hand and she glanced down to the text on the screen.

Marly and Natalie are coming at one for options for the gala. They work for me. Don't ask prices. Pick out anything you want.

He was sending people here? Like her own personal shoppers? Who did that? She was more than capable of going out to shop on her own. Granted her funds were extremely limited until she found a new job, but she didn't want Sam to completely take over her life now that she'd moved in. That's not why she'd agreed and she had to make sure he understood that. She couldn't have him hovering over her or making all of her decisions.

Maty hit Reply.

We need to talk about all of this taking over you're doing.

She hit Send and reread the message. Did that sound ungrateful? She just didn't know what to do or how to react to this. She certainly wasn't used to someone else caring for her and making decisions. She knew he cared…he had to, right? He wasn't going through all of this with her just for sex.

Maty shook her head and turned from the calming view—which wasn't calming her at all—and glanced at the wall of books. A book didn't interest her right now, so she glanced to the desk and spotted a notepad. Yes, that's what she needed to relax her because her paranoia was taking over. She'd doodle and draw a bit.

As she settled into the oversize leather desk chair, her

cell vibrated again, but not with a text. Rusty's name lit up the screen.

She took another sip of her wine, settled her glass beside the notepad and answered.

"Rusty," she greeted with a smile hoping the fake gesture came through in her tone. "Thanks for returning my call."

"I assume you have news for me."

She hated his smug tone; it always made her feel like he was on some other level and she was far beneath him.

It would be a pleasure to help Sam bring him down. Men like Rusty Lockwood had no respect for other people.

"I think I have Sam almost ready to commit."

"I knew I just had to tighten the reins," he scoffed.

Maty had to grit her teeth and take a reassuring breath to not verbally explode all over the bastard. Playing with her brother's health was not a way to get on her good side and now that she could fight back, she was coming up with both fists swinging.

All of this gave her renewed hope that she was finally positioned toward the right direction in this new chapter of her life. Not that she purposefully wanted to be deceitful, but these were circumstances she'd never expected and she had to make the best of an impossible situation. At least with Sam knowing the truth, Maty had more control over her life than she'd had just yesterday.

"It will require more money," she told him, immediately thinking up the lie on the fly. "An extra ten million on top of the offer you already extended."

"Ten million? That's ridiculous."

Maty smiled and swirled the contents of her glass.

"That's the price he said, so if you want this as bad as you say you do, I would agree."

Or maybe he had to use his extra funds to pay off his other attorneys for the cheating he had been doing with the Milestones charity. Oh, the tangled web he was weaving…

"See if you can get him to come down," Rusty finally replied.

"So when you said any amount, you didn't really mean it," she retorted. "If money is a problem—"

"I don't have financial problems," he growled. "I'm Rusty Lockwood, damn it."

Oh, that sounded like he had a multitude of problems *because* he was Rusty Lockwood. Perhaps this dynasty he'd started illegally forty years ago was starting to crumble. Maybe he knew he was about to lose what he'd worked for. A scandal the magnitude of one around stealing from a children's charity would certainly be damning to a company that prided itself on donations and with a reputation of encouraging its employees to contribute as well.

Maty had no sympathy for this monster. He'd sought her out during her most vulnerable time and forced her to face her past. Granted she didn't mind being reunited with Sam, but the stakes were too great. Her heart was on the line now and all she had left was her reputation… something she wouldn't let Rusty Lockwood tarnish.

"Then agree to this arrangement and I'll get the legal forms started," she told him, pouring out all the confidence and BS she could muster. "We can wrap this up in a couple of weeks and Hawkins Distillery will be all yours."

Silence again. She hated the quiet almost as much as

she hated his smugness. All of that dead air made her twitchy because she knew he was thinking…calculating. There was nothing more dangerous than a maniac who had time to plot.

Maty had faith in Sam, though. He wouldn't be swindled or deceived and he was always working ahead, formulating the perfect approach.

"Fine. Ten million on top of the original offer and I want this done by the end of next week."

What a jerk. Little did he know…

"Fine," she agreed. "But next time I call, you'll need to answer. I don't have time for phone tag."

Rusty chuckled. "I'm a busy man, Ms. Taylor. I'll answer when I'm ready."

With that, he hung up and it took everything in her not to throw her phone across the room. Instead, she tossed back the remaining wine and cursed under her breath.

"Arrogant bastard."

"I couldn't agree more."

Startled, Maty jerked her head up to see Sam leaning against the door frame. His width consumed nearly the entire opening and that dark gaze held her in place. Her heart beat a heavy rhythm and she wasn't sure if it was from being startled because she'd thought she was alone or from the sexy man only a few feet away.

"I thought you were at the distillery."

Maty tried to be calm as she set her empty glass on the desk and pocketed her phone. After last night, she hadn't seen much of him. He'd gotten up, kissed her forehead and told her he'd see her later. He'd suggested she make his home like hers. Easier said than done when she was a nervous wreck.

Sex changed everything. Great sex changed every thought and was slowly working on her heart. So she hadn't been able to relax in his home. Couple that with the call to Rusty and she needed that wineglass refilled.

"I'm quick when it comes to decision making," he told her with a half grin. "And my assistant had already chosen most things considering he knows me better than nearly anyone."

At one time that honor had belonged to her, but she'd thrown away their bond for her future. Look how well those dreams had turned out. She'd wanted something of her own, something she could be proud of. What would she have done had she stayed behind?

That was all in the past and she couldn't change the decisions she'd made years ago.

She could, however, decide what type of future she was going to have. Regaining control was a step in the right direction. She just had to watch that next step so she didn't end up with a heartache.

"I take it from the drained glass of wine and your muttering a moment ago that the call didn't go well?"

Maty shrugged. "I talked him into ten million more than the original number."

Sam stared at her for a moment before he busted out laughing and crossed the room. "We didn't discuss that."

"No, we didn't. I sort of made it up as I went along."

He came to stand directly in front of the desk and her heart quickened once again. That seemed to be the norm lately whenever Sam got near. Even with the past they shared, this was simply an entirely new dynamic. They had both been young before and had assumed love could carry them through anything.

Now, well, they were older and more experienced—and more cautious.

He glanced down to the empty wineglass and the notebook. "Trying to relax?" he asked.

Maty shrugged. "Nothing's working."

Sam circled the desk and came to stand before her. When he reached his hands out, she took hold and came to her feet.

Trailing those rough fingertips up her arms, Sam and his simple, innocent touch caused a curl of arousal to spiral through her. She continued to stare up into those dark, heavy-lidded eyes.

"Remind me not to get on your bad side," he told her, gripping her shoulders and offering a sultry smile. "You're quite impressive. I might be looking for an attorney to add to my team."

Maty stilled. "Excuse me?"

"Would you want to work for me? No blackmailing," he quickly added. "I'm not saying this because I'm sleeping with you, either. I expect the best from my employees and they have to be honest and loyal."

She wanted to reach up, to rake over that stubble along his jaw and feel it on her palm. She wanted to feel that connection, the way they had last night.

But she also had to remain strong and keep her common sense in front of her heart for protection. Just because he was intrigued by her professional skills and they were more than compatible in the sheets, didn't mean everything would be shiny and perfect in a working atmosphere. A job with his company would be longterm and a leap she wasn't ready to take.

"I can't jump right into working for you," she explained.

His brows drew in. "Why not?"

"Because... Well... I just can't."

He smirked. "Not a very good defense. Try again."

Maty pulled away and turned toward the windows. She took a few steps, just to put a bit more distance between them so she could gather her thoughts. Her gaze landed in the distance at the pond and the mountains surrounding the property. She wondered what this would look like in the fall, imagining all the vibrant colors, and if she'd be around to see the beauty.

"I may be in Virginia," she murmured, still staring out the window. "I'm not sure I'll stay here."

Silence crackled in the air and she glanced over her shoulder to gauge his reaction.

"I guess I shouldn't have assumed you'd stay."

There was a tone in his voice she couldn't quite name. Part of her wondered if he'd be hurt if she left, but neither had promised each other anything.

Maty turned fully to face him. "I don't know what I'm doing," she admitted. "I want to be near my brother. He's all the family I have left. At the same time, what if I'm meant to be somewhere else? I mean, I know you graciously paid for Carter's care, but at some point I need to take over. I need my own insurance and I need to make my own life and start over."

"Who says you can't start over in Green Valley?" he asked.

Maty studied his expression, not sure if she actually saw more than lust, more than revenge. There were so many emotions that made up this Sam as opposed to the Sam of sixteen years ago. She and Sam had both been through quite a few changes, yet here they were right back together, still unable to deny their attraction.

"I can't make a life-altering decision right now," she told him honestly. "Can I just…can I stay here with you until…"

Sam took a step, then another, until he closed the distance between them. He framed her face and tipped her head back as he towered over her.

"You can stay here as long as you want," he murmured, leaning down to graze his lips across hers. "I won't be the one to make you leave."

That statement held so much power, and put the decision solely on her…just like the first time. So much had changed, yet so much had remained the same.

Maty would stay until everything with Rusty was resolved and after that…

Yeah, it was the *after that* that terrified her because she wanted so much, but she dared not hope and risk a broken heart again.

Thirteen

Sam stared at the glass decanter that he'd designed himself. Well, he hadn't exactly come up with the design, but only one other person would know that.

He couldn't believe the day of his first official bourbon release was actually approaching. First, the gala to really hype up his high-end clientele and then in just a few short months, the first distribution would take place around the world. In five more years, he'd unveil his fifteen-year bourbon, five more would be his twenty. There was a cycle he was starting and he couldn't wait to see what the future held.

The warehouses were stocked with barrels that were rolled on a very strict schedule. Sometimes he'd walk through those pathways between the stacks to take in the aroma of charred wood and bourbon. There was really nothing like that scent. Sam couldn't believe this was his life now and he never took for granted a single day or all the possibilities of things to come.

His professional life—he had a strong, firm handle on. It was the personal aspect that had gotten so far out of control, he had no idea which part to fix first.

His mother was going to finally get the help she needed, the clock was ticking on Rusty's little game monopolizing the hard liquor industry, and Maty...

Hell, he had no clue.

If he were being honest with himself, he wanted more. Maybe that was the past talking, maybe that was this new phase they'd entered. Who knew?

He did know that now that he and Maty had stripped each other and had fast, frantic sex in the main warehouse, he'd never be able to walk through there again without getting somewhat aroused.

He couldn't wait to take her to the gala. He wondered if she'd know the significance behind the shape of the bottle. Would she even remember? Was he a complete fool for using the design she'd drawn for him so long ago?

Maybe, but this was his company and he'd damn well do what he wanted. Besides, this design had been his favorite option and the only one he'd actually considered.

Sam placed the glass bottle back in his office safe and secured the door with the code. The familiar ring from his cell chimed from his desk.

He crossed his office and grabbed the phone from a pile of brochures from potential distributors he'd been researching. Nick's name flashed on the screen and Sam welcomed the distraction from his thoughts.

"Hey, man. What's up?" he answered.

"I don't have much time because Silvia is making

me choose different lighting for the bathrooms at the resort. Don't ask. That's a whole ordeal I don't want to get into."

Sam laughed. "Okay. So why did you call if you're swamped?"

"Because I just heard that the city council called a special meeting for Friday afternoon."

Sam stilled. "I assume this is about the liquor license or you wouldn't be postponing your lighting date with your wife."

"Such a smart-ass," Nick muttered. "We have to be related."

Sam couldn't help but smile. He had a half brother. This was beyond anything he ever could've imagined. Sam wanted to know all the details of their pasts and how they now intertwined. He also wanted to know who their other brother was.

So many other factors were taking precedence right now, though.

"Yes, to answer your question," Nick went on. "It is about the licensing. Nobody knows this meeting is taking place, but I have an inside guy."

"And you don't think Lockwood knows what's going on? Isn't he the one with all these guys in his pockets?"

Sam had to play the devil's advocate. He had to cover all his bases in order to stay a step ahead of the game. But his point was quite valid. All of this was an utter mess because decades ago, when Rusty started illegally making and selling moonshine discreetly, he became part of the good ol' boys' club where council members overlooked some of Rusty's dealings in exchange for white lightning.

So when moonshine became legal not too long ago,

Rusty already had an in and secured his hard liquor license, and the council wrote the laws for the county that made moonshine the only hard liquor to be sold in restaurants.

"I trust this person completely and I truly believe Rusty will have no clue," Nick replied. "Apparently you and I have intrigued some of Rusty's cronies, and the facts we've presented coupled with the resort and your new bourbon reveal is enough to get them thinking on the right path. Listen, I know you have the gala that night, but I wanted to give you a heads-up in case something happens and Rusty decides to cause a problem."

Sam gripped his cell and sneered. "I dare him to try to cross me. He won't like the outcome."

"Oh, he won't like the outcome of this meeting, I'm sure," Nick stated with a chuckle. "Hopefully with both of us at the gala, he won't be dumb enough to make a move in front of so many heavy hitters in the industry."

Everyone from politicians to restaurateurs to billion-dollar CEOs was invited and expected to attend. Who didn't want to be part of this new endeavor? The hype around a new bourbon was huge, but add in Sam being the youngest master distiller in the country and the media was having a feeding frenzy. Sam sure as hell didn't want Rusty or any other scandal to tarnish what promised to be a perfect night.

"I need to go," Nick told him. "Apparently she's found the lights she wants. I'll see you Friday."

Sam disconnected the call and was about to shove the cell in his pocket when it chimed again with a text from his mother.

Can you come by later?

He shot back a quick text.

Sure thing.

Glancing at the time, he knew he could go ahead and leave. All of the reports were done, he'd done a couple of employee reviews and he'd managed to confirm all parties involved in going to his house on Friday to help Maty get ready for the gala for her hair and makeup. Not that it mattered what she wore or what she did with her hair. The woman was shockingly stunning and stole his breath every time they were together.

But he couldn't wait to have her by his side. Maybe it was all egotistical, but Sam wanted her to be proud of all he'd accomplished. When they'd been together before, that's all he'd wanted. Impressing her had been paramount because at the time he'd felt so unworthy. She was a rich girl from a prominent family. They'd welcomed him from the start, but he'd always felt like he didn't belong in their big fancy house with matching silverware and dinner parties.

Now, though, he realized that her family had been good people. They truly hadn't cared about his background or his financial status. They were supportive of his wild ideas to one day own his own distillery. They could've laughed or blown it off, considering he had no money, but they'd entertained his thoughts. Sam still couldn't believe they were gone. He hated that Maty had lost them, that she was dealing with her brother's paralysis and this mess with Rusty. She'd been handling too much on her own and Sam wasn't going to let her carry the load alone any longer.

He would do everything he could to get her back on

her feet, to make her feel better about this new chapter she had to start without her parents. Sam wanted the best for her, but he didn't know what that was…only she could decide that.

Part of him wanted her to decide to stay in Green Valley for good, but the other part was terrified she'd do just that. If she stayed in Green Valley, then what? Would they try for a real relationship again? Was life really that easy?

Maybe, maybe not.

He was a fool for even allowing his thoughts to wander down the path that led to some silly happily-ever-after. Maty had admitted that she wasn't sure Green Valley was for her, so he might as well just enjoy the hell out of her while she's here and keep his heart and emotions out of the equation. Hadn't he learned his lesson the first time around?

Sam took the back way out of the office and headed to his truck. He didn't typically have anxiety, but between this reunion with Maty and the Rusty situation possibly coming to a close soon, how could he not be on edge?

He cranked up the music and took the windy back roads to his mom's house. He needed those extra few minutes to clear his head. He knew he needed to maintain some sort of emotional distance from Maty, but that was proving to be more and more difficult. He couldn't just shut off his emotions. No matter how much he'd dodged relationships for all these years, that didn't mean he was cold or unfeeling.

He wasn't going to try to pretend he wouldn't hurt if she left. Maty had always had a hold over him that he'd never been able to explain.

Sam couldn't help but wonder what, if any, hold he had over her.

When he pulled into his mother's drive, she stepped out onto the cottage porch and smiled. She looked more tired than ever, but she was still a beautiful woman. She'd worked herself hard her entire life, sometimes making poor decisions, but she loved him with her entire being.

She'd put aside that money from Rusty when he'd paid her off. If she hadn't cared about Sam, if she'd been that selfish, she never would have thought of her unborn baby's future.

Sam loved her just as much. He wanted to see her well. He wanted her to get the help she needed, the help she had finally agreed to get. He wanted her to come out on the other side with a renewed hope for her future and a fresh start.

Just like Maty was doing.

Damn it. Every thought lately circled back to her. He wouldn't mind if he could pinpoint what the hell they had going on. Sex would take them only so far and it was a hell of a ride while it lasted, but then what?

Ignoring the impending thoughts of an end he didn't want to experience again, Sam stepped from his truck and headed up the stone sidewalk.

"You didn't have to leave work early," his mother told him as he mounted the steps.

Sam bent down to kiss her cheek and smiled. "I'm the CEO. I have nobody to answer to except my mother."

She rolled her eyes and swatted him, but her playful mood quickly sobered.

"I just wanted you to know the facility called and they can take me in on Friday morning instead of Monday."

Friday morning. Which meant she wouldn't be there to see his gala, to see the unveiling of the bourbon and to share that monumental moment with him.

Her health came first, though. Above all else, he wanted her to get to the sanctuary that would heal her.

"That's great news," he told her.

Her lips pursed as she folded her arms over her small frame. "I want to postpone it until next week."

"No," he insisted. "You're going. Don't worry about the gala. I have years and years of bourbons coming out. I'll save you a bottle from the first batch."

"I hope to be out before you launch in the fall." She laughed, then patted his cheek. "I just wanted to be by your side for your big night."

Sam took her shoulders and pulled her into a hug. "I know you did and that's all that matters. But, for me, I need my mother to get well and heal."

Her arms came around his waist as she laid her head against his chest. "I knew you'd say that," she murmured.

Sam eased back and glanced down. "Then why are we having this conversation?"

"I was hoping you'd convince the facility to let me come in on Saturday morning instead."

One day. She was asking for only one day because she wanted to show her support for him.

"Please."

Sam kissed her forehead and nodded. "I'll call them today."

For what he'd paid and the strings he'd pulled to get her into the place, he had no doubt they'd accommodate her arriving later.

"I have to tell you that there may be an issue with

Rusty," he told her, but cut her off when she opened her mouth. "It's nothing I can't handle. I'm just giving you a heads-up. This is all business. He has no clue I'm his son and I'd like to keep it that way for as long as possible."

Nick had opted to tell the old bastard, but Sam wanted to keep that truth bottled up until this ordeal with the liquor licenses was settled. He wanted the local liquor industry to be opened up, where Rusty wasn't the sole provider to the resorts and restaurants in this grow-ing area. Once Rusty had lost some of his momentum and clout, Sam wouldn't mind telling him the truth at all. There would be no grand father/son bonding time, he was sure, which was just fine with him, but he did wonder how the old man would react.

Thankfully, by that time his mother would be in her facility and away from Rusty's influence. Sam didn't want that man anywhere near the people he cared about…hence having Maty move in with him.

"Don't mess with him any more than you have to," she told him. "I mean it, Sam. He's evil."

"He is," Sam agreed. "But I'm smarter and I have more power. I'm not afraid of him."

"I just don't want to worry about you while I'm gone."

Sam stepped back and smiled. "Then don't. I prom-ise to visit and call and check on you often. You'll know exactly what's going on."

Her eyes welled with tears and he swiped the mois-ture from her dark skin. "I'm so sorry I'm doing this to you," she said. "You have so much to worry about without always rushing to help me."

"I have nothing else to do if you're not well," he countered. "So, are you ready for the gala? You have the dress and shoes? I have a stylist coming to do your hair and makeup."

Good thing he had a handy assistant who could make all of this happen for his mother and Maty. He just wanted the two women in his life to have a perfect night and he didn't want either of them to worry about a thing.

She laughed. "I can do my own hair and makeup."

"Maybe I want to pamper you." His cell vibrated in his pocket, but he ignored it. "Just plan on being available from about ten that morning until I send a car to pick you up."

She smiled and reached up to pat the side of his face. "I'm really proud of you. I just want you to always know that. I don't know what would happen to me if it weren't for you."

Sam tamped down his emotions. He needed to be strong for her. She'd cared for him so long and now it was his turn to make sure she found a way back to taking care of herself.

"I know you struggle with this addiction, but we're going to make it better."

He pulled her into an embrace once more, hoping to prove to her how much he loved her, to reassure her he would always be here no matter what.

Rusty wouldn't get near her or anyone else Sam cared for. He would do anything to stop that man from any more destruction.

Fourteen

Maty stared at her reflection in the floor-length mirror. She turned side to side and wondered if she'd made a mistake. Maybe she should've gone with the red dress instead. Something that made a statement instead of being boring and predictable.

"You're not going anywhere in that."

Maty glanced over her shoulder in the mirror and saw Sam standing a few feet behind her. He wore a white button-up shirt with the top two buttons undone, a black jacket and black dress pants. He'd even groomed his hair for the occasion, but that jaw scruff was still prominent and so damn sexy. A little rough and a little class all rolled into one mouth-watering package.

He was all hers...at least for now.

But it was that dark, heavy gaze that raked over her twice that confirmed she had indeed chosen the perfect dress.

Her stomach knotted with arousal and anticipation for the night to come. She had no idea what to expect, but she knew there would be something phenomenal.

"Damn." Sam took a step toward her. "Remind me to give my assistant a raise and that stylist an extra tip. I really should keep you home all to myself."

"You can't miss your own gala," she told him.

He curled his fingers around her biceps and pulled her back against his chest. Their stares met in the mirror. Feeling his warmth combined with those eyes that continually captivated her had her wanting to ditch the very public event, too.

"Maybe we could be extremely late," he suggested, grazing his lips along the sensitive spot between her neck and her shoulder.

His hands slid around her waist and covered her abdomen. Maty tipped her head to the side and laced her fingers through his.

"I think we should just go now before we get to a point we can't leave," she suggested. "Think of it as foreplay and when we come back tonight…maybe I'll let you see what I'm not wearing beneath this dress."

Sam groaned and spun her around. Maty yelped as she caught herself and grabbed hold of his shoulders. His mouth came within a breath of hers.

"Don't tease me," he growled. "I didn't know I'd come in and see you looking like sex wrapped in silk."

Maty loved knowing she could affect him so strongly. Whatever was developing between them was more intense than she'd ever expected. When she'd been forced to come back to Green Valley, she'd truly had no idea what to expect with Sam. She wasn't sorry she came back; she just didn't like the circumstances regarding her return.

But she couldn't be sorry about any of it now. Even though she hated Rusty for putting her in an impossible situation, this path had led her back into Sam's arms. She wondered if she would stay there.

Maty toyed with the top button of his dress shirt. "Maybe if you're good, I'll let you unwrap me later."

He started to lean in, but she skirted around him. As much as she wanted his mouth and hands on her, she couldn't let that get started. Once he touched her in any sort of intimate way, she knew this dress would be off and her hair would be a disaster.

"I'm all set to go," she told him, swiping her delicate gold clutch from the vanity.

Sam crossed to her and slid his hand over the curve of her hip and leaned in. "There's no one else I'd want by my side tonight. This means more than anything."

His words sank in as he escorted her out with his hand on the small of her back. She'd expected him to say something else sexual or maybe even trail those lips along the side of her neck to drive her wild.

But he'd been sincere with his words, giving her a glimpse of that heart of his. Maybe there was a future for them. Maybe she could stay here and build her new life. She wasn't that far from Virginia.

Is that what she wanted to do? Did she want to start this whole new chapter of her life back where she'd begun? Was she ready to risk her heart, her future, on one man in the hopes that he could love her back?

Love her back.

Maty stopped in the foyer as the realization slammed into her.

"You okay?" Sam asked as he glanced to her.

She wanted to tell him, to be completely open and honest with her feelings. This sudden burst of happiness consumed her, but now was not the time. He had the most important night of his career just ahead and she wanted him to be solely focused on the dream he'd worked so hard for.

What if he didn't feel the same as she did? Then she'd put those words out there and the evening would turn awkward and uncomfortable.

Maty smiled and turned to face him. She framed his face and briefly touched her lips to his.

"I'm great," she told him. "But when we get back, I have something to tell you."

His eyes widened. "Are you pregnant?"

Maty laughed. "No, but good to know that would freak you out."

He blinked and shook his head. "I actually want a family someday, I just... Damn it, you threw me there. Do you want to tell me what's on your mind now?"

Maty reached for his hand and laced their fingers together. "When we get back."

"Is that before or after I unwrap you?" he asked with a sultry grin.

"Depends on if you can wait that long to unwrap me," she replied with a wink. "Now let's get to your gala. You can't keep your guests waiting."

Samples of Hawkins ten-year bourbon flowed amongst the guests. The very first barrel ever used sat on display in the middle of the main lobby area. A framed letter sat atop the barrel explaining Sam's journey to this moment.

He glanced around at the mingling guests and couldn't help the swell of pride that overcame him. This was what he'd been waiting for his whole life. That sense of accomplishment, that sense of worth.

But something was missing. He'd thought this night would bring a feeling of wholeness that he'd been lacking, but there was still a void he couldn't put his finger on.

He caught his mother's gaze from across the room where she had been chatting with a restaurateur from Miami. She looked positively beautiful in her simple blue gown. When she smiled at him, he knew they were going to be alright, *she* was going to be alright.

"Mr. Hawkins."

Sam turned toward the boisterous tone and smiled as the governor approached with his hand extended.

"Great turnout," Governor Pate said, pumping Sam's hand. "Great bourbon, too."

"Glad you're enjoying yourself, Governor."

"I'd like to purchase a barrel for my inauguration," he went on.

"Expecting another win?" Sam asked with a grin.

"I didn't go into this expecting to lose." He laughed. "I'll have my assistant get in touch with yours next week. This is by far the best bourbon I've ever had."

Sam nodded. "I'll be sure to let my assistant know to expect a call."

His eyes roamed over the governor's shoulder and landed on Maty. Her back was to him—her back with that damn low-cut dress that exposed too much skin. Where black fabric did cover her, the satin hugged every damn curve.

Sam returned his attention to his guest. "If you'll excuse me," he said.

The governor turned and zeroed in on Maty. "Of course. You're a lucky man."

Sam smiled and nodded in agreement as he stepped away.

This was it. This was what had been missing in his life. Maty Taylor. Had she always been the one for him? Obviously so, but it had taken years apart and her stepping back at the most vulnerable time for both of them. Maybe that's the only way they could heal and grow together once again? Maybe this was the moment in time when they were supposed to be together and sixteen years ago had just been all wrong.

Everything was right now.

As he walked to her, he spotted Nick and Silvia across the room. Nick's arm slid around his wife's waist and he pulled her to his side in that protective way Sam totally understood.

He hadn't had a chance to speak to his brother, yet… Sam loved thinking of Nick in that way. To Sam's knowledge, Nick hadn't heard a word about the private council meeting that supposedly took place this afternoon. Sam couldn't worry about that right now, but he would be looking into it as soon as this gala was over… and after he delivered on his promise to Maty of their own private celebration.

While he couldn't wait to get back home with her, he also knew she had something she wanted to tell him. That split second when a baby popped into his mind had scared him, but after a moment he sort of liked the idea of her carrying his baby. There would be nobody else in the world he'd want to have a family with.

But he had to tell her the truth. All of it. About Rusty, about Nick. Would Lockwood being Sam's father be a complete turnoff for her? Would she not want to associate with Sam after what Rusty had done to her? Would she feel threatened because the man had attempted to ruin her career and her life?

The fear was extremely real.

Sam was approached multiple times before he could make it across the room to Maty. By the time he'd extracted himself from all of the congrats and handshakes, Maty was gone.

He turned again and found her up on the second floor where the wraparound balcony overlooked the main area. She was standing next to his mother and Maty's hand was on his mom's arm as the two smiled at each other.

Sam's heart swelled and filled with such emotions, he couldn't even describe the collision of them all. His past stood right in front of him…his future, too.

Moving to the one set of steps that led to the second floor, Sam nodded in greeting to several guests as he passed through. He couldn't wait until he unveiled the bottle design in the next hour. Anxiety bubbled within because he had no idea if Maty would remember or if she'd even care that he'd taken her drawing from when they'd dated.

He hoped she remembered. He hoped this was just another puzzle piece in merging their lives back together.

"Sam."

He turned just as he'd gotten to the bottom of the steps. Nick and Silvia approached him and Sam moved over to clear the path for other guests mingling.

"Sorry I haven't been around to see you guys, yet," Sam stated. "I appreciate you all being here."

"We wouldn't be anywhere else," Nick told him as held up his tumbler. "This stuff is amazing, man. Seriously. I can't wait to have it in my resort."

Sam stilled. "What?"

Nick smiled, but Silvia chimed in. "We wanted to tell you in person that the council has overturned the law and Rusty is no longer top dog."

As if Sam's night could get any better. He glanced to Nick.

"Are you positive?" he asked.

Nick nodded. "I got a call from my source just before coming here."

Elated and more than intrigued, Sam crossed his arms and shifted so his back was to the crowd, to give them a little privacy.

"I have to know, who is this source?" he murmured.

"Councilman Perry's son." Nick chuckled. "I buddied up with him a few weeks ago when I learned he had moved back to the area. I offered him the position of resort manager and a lot of perks. Though John will make an excellent manager, his first job was getting in the room with his dad. I had the right person in our corner who helped make our case."

Sam couldn't believe it. He honestly could not believe what was happening. All of his dreams, new ones and old ones, were coming together to make a path for his future.

"Does Rusty know?" Sam asked.

Nick shrugged and finished his tumbler of bourbon before handing it off to a member of the waitstaff.

"That I'm not sure of," he replied. "If he doesn't now,

it won't be long before he does. So we both need to be aware that he will likely retaliate in some way."

"Hopefully he's too busy fighting his other battle with the rumor of him skimming from the charity he endorses."

But knowing Rusty, he wouldn't just go away quietly. Hell, he wouldn't go away with blaring horns and whistles. Someone like Lockwood would never admit defeat.

"Maybe if he finds out he's my father, too, then he'll realize—"

Nick's eyes widened and Silvia's gaze darted over Sam's shoulder. He turned to see his mother and Maty standing just behind them. He'd been so consumed with his own thoughts, he hadn't even heard them approach.

"Rusty is your father?" Maty whispered as if she couldn't bear to say the words.

He shifted fully to face her. "Maty, I—"

She held up her hands. "No. Just answer my question."

Sam swallowed and glanced to his mother who stared back at him with such sadness and sorrow. He hated that he'd kept this from Maty. He should've told her when he learned the truth about her situation, but at that point he honestly hadn't known if he could trust her.

"He is," Sam confirmed. "And Nick is my half brother."

Maty's wide eyes never moved from him. The noise around them continued as if his entire world hadn't just blown up in his face.

"Let's go into my office and talk."

Sam started to reach for her, but she gathered her dress in one hand and held on to her clutch with the other. She stepped up to him and her eyes narrowed.

"I won't cause a scene here," she muttered between gritted teeth. "But we have nothing to discuss, so I'm leaving."

He'd almost rather she throw a fit, scream at him or cause that scene. The low, quiet tone laced with hurt and regret gutted him.

"Don't go," he pleaded. "Just…stay. I don't have any right to ask, but I'm asking anyway."

She tipped her chin and glared. Oh, now she was pissed combined with the hurt, and that combination was never good.

"I'll find my own ride," she replied before she skirted around him.

Sam turned to see her stride gracefully through the crowd, even pausing to smile at the guests. She wasn't causing a scene. The random onlooker would never know the turmoil that had just surfaced.

Even though he'd lied and hurt her, she still put his needs first, which spoke volumes about this woman he'd fallen in love with. Damn it. He loved her with his entire heart and she was walking out…and he didn't believe she was just leaving the distillery. She was leaving him. Again.

"Go after her."

Sam glanced over his shoulder. "It won't matter, Mom. She's too upset."

"I didn't know," Nick stated. "I'm sorry, man. I didn't even think."

Sam sighed and turned back to his brother. "I'm the one who said something and I'm the one who should've told her to begin with. But the timing was never good and then I just… Damn it."

"Why don't you go to your office and take a minute?" his mom suggested. "We can cover for you and say you're with a potential client."

Sam shook his head. "No. I'm going through with this night. I won't let Rusty take everything from me."

Of course he'd love to blame all of this on Rusty, but everything that had happened in the last five minutes was all on Sam.

Despair like he'd never known before settled deep. What was supposed to be the best night of his life had suddenly turned into the absolute worst, and all of this could have been avoided if he'd only been honest. If he'd only realized sooner that Maty wasn't the enemy.

She was his everything.

Fifteen

She was a damn fool.

Maty stared at her meager bag and refused to let the tears flow. Her life had been reduced to one bag and a heartbreak she didn't know if she'd ever overcome.

She did know one thing—Rusty and Sam deserved each other.

After calling for a driver to come pick her up, she'd come straight to Sam's house to gather her things. There was no use in staying here. She'd just have to get a hotel for the night and head back to Virginia in the morning. She was simply too exhausted to think about driving tonight.

She glanced down to her gown and laughed at the absurdity. She needed to get out of this dress and leave it behind, but she hadn't even given her wardrobe a thought. When she'd come back, her only concern had been to get her things and get out. But she couldn't exactly leave in a dress that didn't belong to her.

Maty pulled in a shaky breath and reached up to slide the thick straps down her shoulders. With the drape front and back, the dress was easy to slip out of.

"Leave it."

Startled, Maty spun around, holding the top against her chest as she pulled the straps back up and met Sam's intense stare.

"What are you doing here?" she asked.

He filled the entire doorway, hands shoved in his pockets, as he continued to hold her gaze.

"You're in my house."

If she wasn't taking off the dress, she could at least take off the jewelry. Maty slid her finger over the clasp of the gold bracelet and unlatched it.

"You left your own gala," she said, stating the obvious.

He lifted a shoulder and stepped into the room. "I stayed long enough to unveil the new bottle. There are enough people there to cover for me should I be needed now. Some things are more important."

He'd left the gala.

The night he'd been planning for months, years. He'd left to come find her.

He hadn't chased her years ago, but he did now.

"I'm getting my stuff and I'll be gone," she informed him. Even though part of her thrilled to the idea that he'd come for her, that gesture didn't excuse the fact that he'd deceived her.

"Do you want to hear my side?" he asked. "You above all people know there are two sides to every story."

Maty took out one earring, then the other. She took off all the jewelry and placed each piece back in the appropriate velvet pouches. She attempted a few calming breaths before turning back around.

"You admitted to Rusty being your father," she reminded him. "That's pretty damning evidence that you were playing me, unless you tell me that Nick told you only moments before I overheard you."

The muscle in his jaw clenched and Maty's heart cracked a little more. She chewed the inside of her cheek, willing the pain to hold off until she could be alone and have herself a glass of wine and a good cry.

Until then, she would shore up every ounce of strength and get through this…just like she had every other soul-crushing blow life had thrown at her.

"I only learned of Rusty being my father a few weeks ago," he told her. "That first time you called, I was in the middle of opening a letter, but your call distracted me."

Maty nodded. As much as she wanted out of here, she deserved an explanation.

"I ended up opening it a little later in the day. Apparently, it had come in the mail while I'd been out of town," he went on. "I discovered that it was Nick's mother who sent the letter. She passed away, but not before having three letters sent out to Rusty's sons."

Maty went to the edge of the bed and wrapped her hand around the post. "Three letters? Nick, you, and who is the third brother?"

Sam shook his head. "We have no idea. Nobody has come forward. Either they don't know, they don't believe the letter from a stranger or they don't care that Rusty Lockwood is their father."

She still couldn't process all of this. The man she'd

once loved was the son of the man who'd blackmailed her in a vile, evil way. Is that the type of man Sam had turned into? How could she trust anything he said?

"What did Rusty say when you told him?" she asked.

"I haven't told him," Sam stated. "Nick met with him last month and Rusty knows that connection, but he doesn't know about me."

"Are you afraid to tell him?"

Sam stared at her a moment before raking a hand over his stubbled jaw. "I'm not afraid of him, but I don't want to open that door just yet. As long as I have this secret to myself, then I still have a hold over him."

Maty could understand that. She also figured telling Rusty wouldn't change a thing. The man had no heart and he likely wouldn't care about children. Whatever Sam decided to do had to work for him…because she was no longer in the equation.

"You have to live with your own decisions," she told him. "Every choice has a consequence, some good and some bad."

"Are you referring to Lockwood or yourself?" he asked.

Maty swallowed. "Both."

"I never intended to hurt you."

"But you did."

Hadn't she warned herself this could happen? Hadn't she felt that sinking gut sensation the moment she saw him face-to-face again? How could she love someone and hate them at the same time?

Because she didn't hate Sam. She hated his actions and the heartache, but she could never hate him.

"When you first came to me, you were working for my enemy," he explained. "I had no idea the woman you'd become. For all I knew, you wanted to work for him. I couldn't trust you with the truth."

Well, that declaration hurt, but he had a point. They didn't know how the other had turned out. Sixteen years was a long chunk of time for personalities and morals to change.

"So once you got me in your bed and then moved into your house, were you still unable to trust me with the truth?"

Sam took a step forward. She didn't stop him. Maty kept her eyes locked on his, refusing to back down or show that she couldn't handle this situation even though she felt ready to crumble.

"I was going to tell you the truth, Maty." He stopped right in front of her and stared down with those dark, mesmerizing eyes. "I want to build something with you and I wanted to wait until this gala was over, until I saw what was going on with Rusty, to tell you everything."

"That's what I would say, too, if I'd been caught."

"It's the truth," he insisted.

Maty gave his defense some consideration. Even if that had been his plan, the fact of the matter was he hadn't trusted her enough, or their relationship enough, to tell her the truth. After all Rusty had done to her, hadn't she deserved to know what she was dealing with? From the moment Sam realized she was a nonthreat, he should have revealed the truth.

"It may be the truth," she amended. "But that doesn't make your silence all this time any less painful. You had to have known how much this would hurt."

Sam swiped a hand along his jaw, and she heard the coarse hair bristle against his palm. "I thought any time I told you that it would look bad, that you'd be hurt. I wanted to get to know the real you again, to make sure I could trust you. And then, things escalated and I was so focused on you and my mother…"

His voice broke on that last word and a piece of Maty's heart broke right along with it. No matter what his intentions were, he still had to own up to his actions.

She came to her feet, but he didn't step back. Her chest brushed against his and she had to steel herself against all of those instant emotions and needs. Now was not the time for sex. Intimacy wouldn't solve her problems.

"I need to get out of this dress," she told him. "And I need to leave."

He stared at her another minute and she wished he'd move because she couldn't stand this close and remember the promises they'd made to each other for tonight.

A bubble of emotion welled up in her throat. She was supposed to be professing her love to him, letting him know she wanted to try this again. Instead, they were standing here utterly broken and holding on to very little hope.

"You can keep the dress," he told her, his tone husky.

"No, I can't."

He nodded and took a step back. "Then change and come to my den. Please."

She didn't answer right away, in fact it was on the tip of her tongue to tell him no, but in the end she nodded her agreement.

Sam turned and left her alone in his bedroom. Maty blew out a breath she didn't even know she'd been holding. She quickly slid out of the dress, wishing this evening could've ended on a different note.

She laid the dress out on the bed and stepped back.

She eased out of one heel and then the other, and laid those at the foot of the bed near the dress. She pulled out a pair of jean shorts and a tank from her bag and slid into those.

After gathering everything together, she headed out of the master suite and went down to the den. Her heart beat heavy in her chest, nerves curled through her. She had no idea what to expect or what he wanted to tell her. All she knew was she needed some space. She needed to clear her thoughts and really evaluate what she wanted to do with her life.

She'd been thrust into this situation with Sam in such a pressurized manner, and then she'd fallen into a heated fling. Now she needed to take a giant step back and sort out each of her thoughts.

Pulling in a shaky breath, Maty stepped around the corner and into the den. Only the soft glow of an accent lamp on the desk lit the room. Sam stood at the window, staring out into the dark night. Maty took one step into the room, but remained at a good distance.

"The letter is on the desk if you want to read it," he said, without turning to face her.

Maty considered her options, but was intrigued and still stunned by this entire ordeal so she crossed the office, sat her belongings down and picked up the paper.

She scanned the words at first, trying to take in all of it at once, but then she went back through it slowly. The worry and concern came through so clear from the woman who wanted her only son to know the truth and for Sam to help Nick through this difficult time. Maty had never met Nick's mother, but from this letter Maty could tell the woman had been brave.

"I can't imagine what she went through keeping that

secret all this time." Maty placed the letter back on the desk. "Are you ever going to tell Rusty?"

Sam glanced over his shoulder, his eyes raked over her and she couldn't suppress the shiver. He looked at her with hunger whether she wore a ten-thousand-dollar gown or a pair of cut-off shorts.

"Probably not," Sam replied. "He deserves nothing from me, certainly not the truth. If he wanted to know about his child, he would've helped my mother instead of buying her off."

Maty glanced around the den, unsure of what to do next. While he battled his demons with Rusty and his mother, Maty wondered where she would have even fallen in the lineup of the chaos in his life. Maybe that's another reason why he hadn't told her. Maybe there was too much going on.

Well, she had enough turmoil in her life as well. She couldn't just give him a pass right now, not when her own emotions were so jumbled up and all over the place.

"Before we left earlier, you said there was something you wanted to tell me."

Maty turned her attention to him. "What?"

Sam started toward her, his eyes fixed on her. "When we were ready to walk out the door for the gala," he reminded her. "You stopped and said you'd talk to me later. Do you remember what you wanted to say?"

She remembered. Nothing had changed, yet everything had.

Her feelings hadn't just vanished. She couldn't turn off the emotions or ignore the pull. She could, however, guard her heart from here on out.

"I was going to tell you that I love you," she replied with a tip of her chin. "I was foolish enough to think maybe we were starting over, that we were a team—I believe that's the word you used."

He took another step and started to reach for her. "Maty—"

"No." She held up her hands and moved back. "That's what I was thinking and now you know. I need to get out of here. It's late and I'm exhausted."

"Where will you go?" he asked. "Just stay. Stay in another room and I promise not to bother you. Hell, I'll leave. I need to know you're safe."

Maty shook her head. "Don't be absurd. You're not leaving your own house. I'm a big girl, Sam. I'll be fine. I'm not your concern anymore."

Something shifted in his gaze, something that she couldn't quite pinpoint, but she knew Sam enough to know that he battled so much within himself.

Maybe they both needed time to think, to heal.

"You weren't just my concern," he countered. "You were my life. Then, now. I want to see where this goes. I don't deserve to ask for a second chance, but… I'm asking anyway."

Maty wished life was so easy that a few simple words could wash away all the hurt and build a bridge to start new on the other side of pain.

"We rushed into all of this," she told him. "And it was fun. It was great. I actually felt like you might be falling for me."

"I was. I am." He raked a hand over his hair, making it stand on end. "Damn it, Maty. Take the master bedroom. Lock the door. I promise I won't bother you and we can talk in the morning. Just don't leave when you're this upset and it's late. You have nowhere else to go."

He made a valid point. She had nowhere to go and very little money right now.

"I'll take a guest room," she told him. "I can't guarantee anything come morning, but I'm tired and you're right that I have no place else."

That hurt to say, hurt even more to live. She'd never been so vulnerable in all her life, but she still had common sense.

"I'll get your stuff moved," he told her.

"I can get it," she replied. "I just… I need some space."

The muscle in his jaw clenched as he nodded. His dark eyes never wavered from hers. Maty wanted him to wrap those strong arms around her and tell her that everything was fine, that all of this was a big misunderstanding, that Rusty wasn't his father and he hadn't lied.

Since there was nothing left to say for now, Maty turned, grabbed her things and decided to claim the farthest room away from Sam's.

"I love you, too."

The soft words were delivered in such a heartfelt, genuine tone, Maty stilled, but she didn't turn around. She didn't want to look in his eyes right now. Maybe that made her a coward, but she mentally and emotionally couldn't handle it right now.

"I hope you mean that," she murmured, then walked out with her broken heart and unshed tears.

Sixteen

The morning light slid through the sheers over the balcony doors and Maty rolled over to grab her phone. She'd gotten little sleep and was no less confused and hurt this morning than she'd been last night.

Sam had kept his promise and left her alone. She tapped on her screen and saw where he'd texted her.

I'm at the distillery so take all the time and space you need. I meant what I said last night.

He loved her.

Part of her fully believed he did, but the other part, the part that was in pain, wondered how he could keep something so monumental from her if he had such strong feelings.

Maty sat up in bed, but didn't reply. She did notice that he sent that text at about four in the morning, so clearly he hadn't slept well, either. A guilty conscience would do that to a person.

She shoved her hair from her face and opened a social media app. Maybe snooping into other people's lives would help her forget hers for a moment.

The first thing she spotted was a shared link to an interview with Sam about the opening of his distillery. And damn if she didn't click on it to read more about the man she couldn't ignore.

She scrolled through, reading the answers to how he'd gotten his start, how he bought the building for the distillery and turned it into Hawkins. She scrolled on down and saw an image of the two of them. A candid shot with his hand on the small of her back, she was laughing at something someone said off camera, and Sam had his eyes firmly fixed on her. She zoomed in and stared at his face. There was an expression in his eyes that she hadn't seen before…or maybe she'd just never taken the time to really notice.

He looked at her as if she were his whole world. That gala had been bustling with so many important people, billionaires from all over, from all fields, and in the still shot of this moment Sam didn't appear to care about any of that.

Maty's throat clogged with emotion as she continued scrolling. She got to the question about the bottle design and how he came up with that. Beneath the question was a photo of the bottle.

She stared at it, wondering herself how he'd come up with it. The bottle with its square edges, tall and thin base with an etched glass neck and a gold top. A bold *H* dominated the front of the glass bottle.

Maty continued down to read his answer and she gasped.

When I was first dreaming of all of this, someone very special to me drew this bottle. She was just playing around, but it has stuck with me all these years. I knew if I ever reached this point, there was no other design I would want.

She quickly scrolled back to the bottle image again.

Memories came flooding back. She remembered the day she'd doodled this bottle. They had been eating pizza and drinking a beer that he had brewed. It was awful, the pizza and the beer, but they'd laughed and dreamed and she'd scribbled out a design.

And he'd kept it alive all these years.

The cracks and bruises on her heart started to mend. Her vision started to blur as tears formed. She dropped her phone into her lap and finally let the tears flow. They flowed for the loss of her parents, the irreversible paralysis to her brother, the blackmail from Rusty and the betrayal from Sam.

So many blows in such a short time. She had to heal from the inside out and really evaluate what she wanted for her future. She needed a vision, something to hold on to and give her the hope she'd been missing for so long.

Sam was that hope.

Even when she'd pushed him away last night, he'd opened his heart and revealed his true feelings…and she fully believed he loved her. The look on his face in that picture, the fact that he'd held on to that drawing from sixteen years ago, and how he'd protected her from Rusty and cared for her brother. He continually showed her over and over his true feelings.

He might have made a mistake, but perhaps she had too when she left all those years ago. Maybe she should've believed they could have it all, careers and love.

So why couldn't they have it all now? There was nothing stopping them.

Maty swiped the dampness from her face and tossed the covers aside. She wanted to get to the distillery right now, but first she had to at least shower and not show up looking like a haggard insomniac. She was about to reclaim her future…she had to look her best for the man she loved.

"You okay, man?"

Sam blinked and shook his head as he turned his attention from the empty bourbon bottles to Nick.

"Yeah," Sam lied. "Just didn't get much sleep last night."

A complete understatement. He'd lain awake all night hoping to hear Maty outside his door, praying she'd come to talk to him and give them another chance. He'd screwed up in not telling her the truth about Rusty. He should've known he could trust her, that she had never had a vindictive bone in her body.

"We can do this another day," Nick told him.

Silvia reached out and patted Sam's arm. "It's okay to take some time off."

Sam shook his head. "No. I'd rather work, and there's nothing else I'd rather do than get my brother and his wife all set up with their first order for their resort."

They'd decided yesterday to meet this morning and Sam hadn't wanted to cancel or postpone. No matter what was going on in his personal life, he had a distillery to run and this order was too important for Nick and Silvia.

The clicking of heels pulled his attention toward the lobby. Maty strode through the open area, heading straight toward where they stood gathered around a tasting table. She looked too damn good with her long hair down and wavy, skinny jeans, black heels and a simple black tank. Those glossy red lips hit him with a punch of lust.

He glanced to Silvia and Nick who were both smiling like they knew something he didn't.

"Excuse me," he muttered as he stepped away from the table.

Sam crossed the distance to stand before Maty and she offered a smile that had all the nerves in his belly easing.

"Just to be clear, you were a jerk for not telling me the truth."

Sam bit the inside of his cheek to keep from laughing, but he nodded his agreement. "I was."

"But I can see your side of things and I don't believe you were purposely being sneaky."

This was all so different from their conversation last night. He'd thought for sure the more she thought about what he'd done, the angrier she'd be.

"What made you see my side?" he asked.

She glanced over his shoulder and Sam turned to see their audience smiling like idiots. He laughed.

"Ignore them," he told her.

"We can go," Silvia suggested.

"No, we can't," Nick added. "I want to make sure he doesn't screw this up again."

Sam couldn't help but laugh a second time.

Maty stepped around him and walked to the tasting table. He watched as she picked up one of the empty bottles and held it out.

"This," she explained. "Why didn't you tell me you used my design?"

Sam shoved his hands in his pockets and shifted his stance. While he'd rather not have Nick and Silvia watching everything, he also wasn't letting this moment go. Maty had come to him and he had to believe that meant she wanted to give him another chance.

"I wanted to surprise you last night when I revealed it to everyone," he explained. "I wasn't sure if you'd remember, but I just thought the gala was the perfect place to show you I used your design…and to tell you that I love you."

"We really should leave them alone," Silvia whispered.

Nick took her hand. "We'll be right over there," he said, pointing toward the lobby.

Sam waited until they walked away and turned back to Maty. "I do love you," he reiterated because he couldn't tell her enough. "I wanted last night to be perfect and special for both of us. I want you on this journey with me because you've been there from the beginning."

Maty's eyes welled with tears as she bit her bottom lip. Sam couldn't take this distance for another minute. He reached for her at the same time she reached for him. He grabbed hold of her hands and pulled them to his chest.

"Tell me that we can try this again," he implored. "Tell me that I didn't screw up to the point you want nothing to do with me."

Maty leaned forward and touched her forehead to his chest. "I want everything to do with you. Everything," she murmured. "I know why you did what you did and I know you love me. I'm just scared, Sam. Scared of a future with my career, my brother, you."

He eased back and tipped her chin up so he could see her eyes. "You're the strongest woman I know. You have nothing to be scared of on your own, but with me at your side, we'll slay everything in our path."

"You sound so certain that everything will work out."

A tear slipped down her cheek and he swiped it away with the pad of his thumb. He never wanted to see her cry, never wanted her to feel any pain.

"I am."

"What about Rusty?" she asked. "He'll try to destroy both of us."

Sam smiled and framed her face. "Listen to me—Lockwood is a nonissue. He's not a problem for me and he sure as hell won't be a problem for you. Nick told me this morning that Rusty was arrested last night for his connection to stealing from Milestones. I'm sure he'll be out soon thanks to his other lawyers and he'll fight the charges as best he can, but he's too busy now to be a problem for us."

Maty closed her eyes and pulled in a shaky breath. Sam took the opportunity to feather his lips across hers and a relief swept through him when she wrapped her arms around his neck and opened to him.

Sam settled his hands on her waist and held her close, never wanting to let her go. She threaded her fingers through his hair and eased back just enough to look up at him.

"I guess this means I'm staying in Green Valley," she said with a smile.

"Forever," he told her.

"Excuse me."

Sliding his arm around her waist, Sam turned to the lobby. Nick and Silvia were staring at a stranger who had just come in. The man was tall, with wide shoulders, jet-black hair. He screamed money in a groomed and polished sort of way.

"I'm sorry to just drop in," the man stated. "I know you're not open to the public today, but I was hoping I would catch someone. I'm looking for Sam Hawkins or Nick Campbell."

Nick's gaze jerked over to Sam. Maty tensed at Sam's side.

He curled his fingers around her hip, offering silent assurance. "I'm Sam Hawkins."

"And I'm Nick. What's this about?"

But Sam knew. He looked in the man's eyes and knew before the words came out of his mouth.

"My name is Reese Conrad and I know this is going to sound crazy," the man said as he pulled a piece of paper from his back pocket. "But I got this letter in the mail."

Maty gasped and Sam released her as he took a step forward toward Nick. Nick's eyes remained on the stranger and the letter…no doubt the one from his mother.

"I think you two are my brothers."

They'd finally found the third sibling. A total stranger, but Sam had heard the name Reese Conrad. He was part of the Conrad family who owned elite, upscale restaurants all along the East Coast.

But who was this stranger, really? Reading about someone, seeing their name and face in a magazine or online didn't give much insight into their integrity. Only the positives were highlighted. So how would Reese Conrad change the course of events with Rusty?

Sam felt Maty's delicate hand on his back and he knew no matter what came in this next chapter, he could do anything with her at his side.

Whoever this stranger and half brother was, he would certainly change the dynamics of the relationship with everyone involved. Maty hoped for Sam and Nick's sake, that Reese was nothing like their monstrous father.

* * * *

COMING SOON!

We really hope you enjoyed reading this book.
If you're looking for more romance, be sure to
head to the shops when new books are
available on

Thursday 14th May

MILLS & BOON

LET'S TALK
Romance

For exclusive extracts, competitions
and special offers, find us online:

- **f** facebook.com/millsandboon
- 🐦 @MillsandBoon
- 📷 @MillsandBoonUK

Get in touch on 01413 063232

For all the latest titles coming soon, visit
millsandboon.co.uk/nextmonth

MILLS & BOON

THE HEART OF ROMANCE

A ROMANCE FOR EVERY KIND OF READER

MODERN

Prepare to be swept off your feet by sophisticated, sexy and seductive heroes, in some of the world's most glamourous and romantic locations, where power and passion collide.
8 stories per month.

HISTORICAL

Escape with historical heroes from time gone by. Whether your passion is for wicked Regency Rakes, muscled Vikings or rugged Highlanders, awaken the romance of the past.
6 stories per month.

MEDICAL

Set your pulse racing with dedicated, delectable doctors in the high-pressure world of medicine, where emotions run high and passion, comfort and love are the best medicine.
6 stories per month.

True Love

Celebrate true love with tender stories of heartfelt romance, from the rush of falling in love to the joy a new baby can bring, and a focus on the emotional heart of a relationship.
8 stories per month.

Desire

Indulge in secrets and scandal, intense drama and plenty of sizzling hot action with powerful and passionate heroes who have it all: wealth, status, good looks…everything but the right woman.
6 stories per month.

HEROES

Experience all the excitement of a gripping thriller, with an intense romance at its heart. Resourceful, true-to-life women and strong, fearless men face danger and desire - a killer combination!
8 stories per month.

DARE

Sensual love stories featuring smart, sassy heroines you'd want as a best friend, and compelling intense heroes who are worthy of them.
4 stories per month.

To see which titles are coming soon, please visit

millsandboon.co.uk/nextmonth

MILLS & BOON

MODERN

Power and Passion

Prepare to be swept off your feet by sophisticated, sexy and seductive heroes, in some of the world's most glamourous and romantic locations, where power and passion collide.